2006

To Pattie,

Hope you enjoy.

Robert

THE ANGELIC PROPHECY

THE ANGELIC PROPHECY

Robert L. Hecker

A Mundania Press Production

Mundania Press LLC
6470A Glenway Avenue, #109
Cincinnati, Ohio 45211-5222

To order additional copies of this book, contact:
books@mundania.com
www.mundania.com

Cover layout by Stacey L. King
Book Design and Production by Daniel J. Reitz, Sr.
Marketing and Promotion by Bob Sanders
Edited by Jennifer Scholz

Trade Paperback ISBN-10: 1-59426-256-X
Trade Paperback ISBN-13: 978-1-59426-256-2

eBook ISBN-10: 1-59426-257-8
eBook ISBN-13: 978-1-59426-257-9

First Edition • November 2005

Library of Congress Catalog Card Number 2005934682

Production by Mundania Press LLC
Printed in the United States of America

10 9 8 7 6 5 4 3 2 1

Chapter 1

Ambassador Anthony Stonz knew it wasn't the storm that had yanked him awake.

Prophetically, the storm that lashed Washington, D.C. with hurricane wind and driving rain had seemed to come out of nowhere. The low-flying squall, sweeping up from the Gulf of Mexico, had battered itself to near-death on the spine of the Appalachians. Then, inexplicably, the storm's tendrils had managed to pull themselves together like spilled mercury, allowing it to vent its fury on the nation's capital. When Stonz awoke at 2:00 A.M., the storm's voice of thunder was threatening every building in Washington with hurricane-force wind and thick chains of lightening that even the heavy rain could not conceal.

Instinct told Stonz that the storm was merely a *causa proxima*, and the real reason for his apprehension was something else, something far more ominous. Although the sensation of alarm was so vague as to be undefined, he had learned long ago not to discount these warnings, especially when he had been experiencing a niggling malaise for several weeks. Something was amiss and it would be well that he discover what it was before, like the storm, it grew into the apocalyptic Armageddon.

But where to start?

He switched on the bedside lamp and got out of bed. As he put on his slippers, a random thought made him smile. Why did he need slippers? The wall-to-wall carpet in the luxurious town house was thick enough to protect his feet even if it had covered a sheet of ice. The answer came to him when he walked to the sliding-glass door that opened onto a second-floor balcony and stood looking at the pouring rain and the wind-tossed branches of the big cypress trees that lined the street below. It was too early in the fall for the leaves to fall, and although they had changed color, they clung to the whipping branches with the desperation of life.

Stonz could sympathize with the leaves; if they lost their grip, they were dead. Could his dysphoria be caused by a sense that something, somewhere was threatening his grip?

He had to get out into the storm, to feel its fury, to allow it to tell him its portentous message. He unfastened the security bolt on the door and slid it back. Instantly the wind whipped into the room, sending the brocade ceiling-to-floor drapes flapping. He left the door open as he stepped outside.

He moved to the front of the balcony, letting the mist-laden wind lash his exposed skin like the stinging tentacles of a jellyfish. He gazed into the darkness of the lowering clouds, but there were no answers in their black eternity.

He knew that the ugly portention was not caused by anything earthly. He had firm control of all his programs and all were going well. No. Instinct told him that this—this adumbration—had its roots in prophesy. But which one? The only thing of which he could be certain was that the event was going to be bad and would take all his abilities to forestall. There was one other thing of which he could be certain: He would defeat this intrusion as he had all the others, and he would survive as he always survived.

And yet, there was something about this apprehension that was—

"Anthony?"

He did not turn. Had a similar premonition awakened Selene? Not likely. Although she had a remarkable prescience that often bordered on the divine, she had not experienced the disturbing forebodings that seemed to be plaguing his life lately. More likely, she had heard him open the sliding-glass door or had been awakened by a burst of cold wind that had penetrated the space below the door that separated their apartments.

"You're going to catch pneumonia out there."

He turned and saw that she had captured the flapping drapes with her arms. The study of mythology had always fascinated him, and seeing her standing with the wind molding her satin nightgown to her perfect body and tossing her cloud of black hair, staring at him with eyes as dark and turbulent as the storm clouds, took his breath away.

Still, her remark almost made him smile. She knew he never got sick, but to please her, he came back into the apartment and closed the door. Experiencing the storm had been unproductive anyway. The moment of concentration had given him no clue about the cause of his mounting concern.

"Look at you." Selene felt the side of his pajama shirt. "You're all wet. What on earth were you doing out there?"

"Thinking." He went into the bathroom stripping off his damp pajamas as he did so. She followed him, and unfolding a bath towel embroidered with his initials, began to dry him. There was no sexuality in the procedure. She knew that while he admired her beauty, he had no interest in physical sex. He was only fifty-five and consciences exercise and genetics had given him a strong muscular body. But his mind controlled his body with an iron discipline. To him, his body was a necessary vehicle he would gladly have abandoned if he could somehow do his work with mentality alone. Although he took great pleasure in Selene's incredibly beauty, it was as an artist would admire a remarkable painting, certainly not something that he could allow to interfere with his agenda.

Her beauty also had a practical side. Coupled with a sensual innocence, her exotic beauty gave her an allure that was devastating to men and was one of the primary reasons he had sought her in the first place. Men who probably would not give him the time of day were glad to take a lunch if they knew he would bring his personal secretary.

"What is it?" she asked. "Is something wrong?"

"I'm not sure. Probably not. More likely it's just the storm."

She was silent as she blotted his thick, graying hair. She, of course, knew he was lying. She always knew. But she also knew that if he thought she could be of help, he would have told her.

"I know," she said. "It woke me too. At least, I think it was the storm."

There was an implied question in her statement. She was telling him that she had sensed his fear, for that, he admitted, was what it really was—fear. But fear of what? Splinters of thought seemed to swirl through his brain as though driven by a tornado, and he couldn't seen to hold any one of them long enough to form a concrete hypothesis. He felt as though, like Sisyphus, his mind was struggling to roll a boulder up a mountain. But just as he reached the top, the boulder escaped his grasp and he was forced to start again.

With Selene's soft breath on his shoulder, it occurred to him that perhaps she could help. Articulating his thoughts would demand that he bring out details that subconsciously he might be subverting. He had used the technique before, but never with Selene. But she was the only one he could trust with this problem. "Something is going on," he said. "I can feel it."

When he paused, she immediately began probing as though she knew what was expected of her. "Is it imminent?"

"No. It's inchoate. But...ominous."

"Here. In Washington?"

He hesitated, letting the ghosts form into thoughts. "I don't think so. Not here. Not yet."

"Not yet? But in the future?"

"It threatens everything. But it's out of reach."

"Then, if it isn't imminent, perhaps you should let it make its appearance."

He made a low growl as he captured one of the swirling thoughts. Whatever it was, having it come to him was one of the things he feared.

At the sound, Selene looked up. "You have faced such problems many times. You'll know what to do when the time comes."

He smiled, and the concern in her eyes cleared. "You're right. Let it grow. When it takes on substance—if, indeed, it does—then I'll know."

"But not too much," she admonished gently. "Don't let it get out of hand."

Her words struck him with a sudden chill. There it was: the thing he had been avoiding. The sheer magnitude of the threat. It was coming, and this time, it would take all his talent, all his energy to prevent the destruction of all he believed.

With the force of will that was his trademark, he banished the thought. Selene was right. Let the danger gather, take form. When it became tangible, he would deal with it as he had always dealt with trouble: eradicate it.

"Go back to bed," he told her. "There's nothing to fear."

She smiled and said, "I know."

Stonz watched her walk back to her apartment. It was there in the set of her shoulders, the strides of her long legs, the tenseness in her arms. She knew.

Chapter 2

The worry was small but insistent, like drops of water forming a stalagmite. Except that forming a stalagmite took eons while the ennui in Michael Modesto's mind seemed to be growing at an alarming rate. Was something wrong with him, or was he simply growing old? He had a reputation as a party animal, a reputation that had been earned in countless hotel rooms and bars. He had not set out to acquire the reputation. It was genuine. He loved the companionship, the noise, the women, even the drinking, although he had never needed alcohol to hit a party zone, and he was smart enough to stay away from drugs.

But during the last year the pleasure had begun to fade. He still enjoyed being on stage with his band. He still reveled in the adulation of fans crowding the bandstand. But when somebody threw a pre-gig party like this one, he found it increasingly difficult to get into the mood. It all seemed so false.

As he became more and more jaded, he developed a real talent for hiding his boredom. His laughter, while it did not come as often, did not give a hint of insincerity. His movements, when he chose to move, were with the cat-like languor that was almost a trademark. And listening to his humor-laced conversation, no one could possibly have a clue that he was playing a role, a role that lately he found increasingly hard to sustain.

Leaning against a wall with a drink in one hand and a cigarette in the other, he found himself looking past some girl who was talking to him in a piping little-girl voice that belied her adult body in hip-hugging tight pants and a belly-revealing t-shirt.

A year ago he would have been coming on to the girl. By this time he would have been looking for a place where they could be alone long enough for a white-hot jump session. But now he was too occupied with introspection to work up even a fake passion. It had taken awhile to identify the worry, but when he had finally zeroed in on the problem, it had shaken him. His real fear was that the ennui might not stem from a declining interest in partying, but, rather, that the root cause might be a declining interest in the whole band scene, in the music itself.

If that were true, then he was in big trouble. Unlike sex, he could not fake the music. The emotion had to be there. When passion died, so did the music. A lot of bands had been able to fake it for a time, but eventually their fans sensed the emptiness and went somewhere else.

Was this happening to him?

Someone had put on a CD of their Bikini album and the heavy beat of "Nuclear Heat" shook the walls. It was his least favorite song on the album. Even so, its driving beat that should be shivering through his gut, instead, did nothing for him except jar his sinuses.

Maybe at 25, he really was getting too old for metal music. Lately he'd even begun to think that some old Sinatra ballads sounded cool.

He wished he could find a place to sit down. He'd hurt his knees playing high school football, and they tended to lock up if he stood in one place too long. But every chair, every couch, everything flat, supported one or more people. They were all young, all held drinks, and all were laughing. But were they really having fun? Every one of them was here because they wanted something: a story, a picture, sex, money, or a chance to rub shoulders with fame. Staring at the homogenous mix of men and women—some of the guys wearing fashionable suits, some in expensive grunge de jur, and the girls who, like the girl in front of him, all seemed to have dyed hair, naked navels and rictus smiles under hard eyes—he suddenly had an overwhelming urge for fresh air.

He handed his drink to the girl. "Here, doll. Keep this warm."

She stopped chirping in the middle of a sentence, her eyes blinking at the realization that she was about to lose her only shot at the great Michael Modesto. As he shouldered his way through the crowd, he heard her calling, "I'll wait for you, Michael. Right here. I'll wait."

He had to ask a couple of people to give him a little room before he was able to step out onto the small balcony. When he closed the sliding glass door behind him, he realized why nobody else was on the balcony. It was stuck precariously on the side of the building high above the hotel entrance, also the air was hot and humid. The humidity came as a surprise. Southern California was desert country; it wasn't supposed to be humid, especially at night. And it wasn't supposed to rain until late December or January. Apparently, the gathering storm, instead of sliding down from Alaska, had charged north from a hurricane off Mexico, bringing with it tropical heat and a welcome promise of rain.

He dropped his cigarette and crushed it under his western boot. The moisture-laden air felt good. It reminded him of home. In eastern Texas at this time of the year, the humidity would be giving way to cooler fall weather and fallen leaves would begin to carpet lawns and forest paths.

The twenty-seventh floor was high for L.A. so he had a nice view of the city's ocean of lights that stretched miles to the far darkness that was the Pacific Ocean.

A quick flash of distant lightning startled him. He couldn't remember ever seeing lightning in L.A. He waited for the thunder that followed lightning, but instead of the magnificent clap he always heard in Texas, there was nothing but a growling rumble. That was California. It not only never rained, its attempt at thunder was as feeble as a minor chord in chamber music.

But the humidity was cloying, and he was reaching for the sliding glass when in the room he saw that everyone had frozen in a tableau with their heads turned toward the hall door where his manager, Benny Bond, was shouting something as he tried to force a girl out the open door. Probably a party crasher. She sure didn't look like she belonged with this crowd. For one thing she wore no makeup that he could see. Not that she needed any. Only someone with classic features could wear her thick, blonde hair pulled severely back and braided in a long queue so that it focused all attention on her face and eyes, eyes that just had to be blue. Also, in her white knee-length dress, she looked more like a nun than a groupie.

She was tall, with good shoulders. And while she was not struggling, she was not moving either, which tended to make Benny very unhappy. His fat neck bulged over his collar as he put more effort into his task, but the girl simply braced her feet and peered over Benny's head as though searching for someone in the crowd. Benny was on dangerous ground. She was probably looking for a wayward boyfriend or husband who would not appreciate the put-down. If the boyfriend didn't deck him, the girl might. Either way, it was Benny's problem.

Creed Jazak, the band's drummer, laughed and yelled something at Benny that Michael couldn't hear over the heavy pounding of the CD music. But Benny must have heard Creed because his chubby face reddened. He braced his feet and yanked at the girl's arm so hard she stumbled back, hitting her shoulder on the edge of the open door, and she grimaced with pain.

Stifling a thought that screamed at him that if he interfered he could make it worse, Michael slid back the glass door and shoved his way through the crowd toward Benny and the girl. The girl saw the movement and her gaze locked on him like radar on a moving target. She took a step toward him, and Benny hauled her back. Michael was close enough now to hear her say, "I only want to talk to him a minute."

"No way!" Benny almost screamed. "Michael doesn't see anybody I don't set up."

Michael stopped. Oh, shit. She was after him. No wonder Benny was hanging onto her like a leech. He knew bad news when he saw it.

"But, I just—"

Benny cut her off. "You want his body, get in line." He yanked her toward the door. "Creed, help me get her butt outta here."

Lyle Derick, the bass guitarist, laughed. "Blow in her ear, Benny. She'll follow you anywhere."

Creed took hold of the girl's other arm. "Come on, baby. You're not Michael's type."

The girl was not putting up a real fight, as though she was more embarrassed by all the attention than she was angry, and Benny and Creed got her turned toward the door. "I don't care about his type," she said. Her voice was taut but under control. As they shoved her out the door, she turned her head to look back at Michael. "Mister Modesto!" she called. "I only want a minute!"

The group stalled as Benny's rotund body was stymied by the narrow doorway. Aaron Dulac, the band's keyboardist, pushed someone aside and moved to help. "Here. Let me give you a hand."

Aaron reached around the girl with one hand and his fist closed over one of her breasts while his other hand clutched at her buttocks.

The girl made a sound like a spitting cat. Yanking her right arm free of Benny's grasp, she pivoted sideways and smacked Aaron on the jaw with her fist so hard his head snapped back. At the same time the music ended with a crashing chord.

In the abrupt silence Aaron's voice was loud as he yelped with pain and anger, "Hey! Not the mouth, damn it."

Lyle Derick barked a laugh. "What the shit difference does it make? Nobody's gonna kiss you."

"Screw you, asshole," Aaron gritted. He reached for the girl. "You bitch! I'm gonna—"

Michael lunged forward and grabbed Aaron's arm. "Hold it, Aaron. What the hell is going on?"

"That stupid broad tried to split my lip."

"He grabbed me!"

Benny regained his grip on her arm. "Damn it! Get the shit outta here."

With Creed's help he resumed shoving the girl through the doorway. She looked back at Michael, her eyes pleading, "I just want a second."

"Yeah, Mike," Lyle Derick said with a dirty laugh. "She wants to talk. She don't want your miserable body."

"I told you," Benny shouted. "Nobody talks unless I—"

It was something in the girl's eyes, something between defiance and pleading, that made Michael blurt, "Okay, okay. Cool it. Let her go."

Creed let go of the girl's arm and his lips curled. "Big mistake, Mike. She's strong as a Black Widow."

Benny kept his grip on the girl's other arm. "No way, Michael. She's gotta be after money."

"Is that right?" Michael asked. "You after money?"

She shook her head. "No."

"You a lawyer?"

"No. I'm an R.N."

Surprise brought Michael's chin up. What the shit would a registered nurse want with him? "Okay. You've got one minute."

He turned and began edging through the crowd toward the bedroom, sensing that the girl had broken free from Benny and was close behind him. Most of the people were watching the girl, their voices muted as they whispered behind knowing smiles.

She saw the direction Michael was heading and said, "Not there. I won't go in there."

Michael stopped and half turned. He didn't know whether to be amused or angry. "It's the only room were we can be alone. I promise I won't jump you."

Her lips twisted, but not in a smile. Her glance was almost frantic as she searched for an alternate meeting place. "The balcony. There's nobody there."

"That's because it's a starting to rain."

"I'll only be a minute."

"Bull shit, Michael," Benny yelped. "All you need is to catch cold."

"Yeah, Mike," Aaron Dulac said. "Want a blanket?"

Michael had been on the verge of calling off the conference, but the note of derision in Aaron's voice made him change his mind. "Fuck you, asshole," he snarled.

In quick strides he went to the sliding door and yanked it open. Creed's voice followed him out the door, "She said she only wanted a minute, Mike, but even you aren't that fast."

He choked back a suitable reply. The girl didn't look like someone who would find amusement in smartass dialogue. There was no sign of a smile as she walked past him into the humid night air. In a way he was glad she had chosen the balcony. With no chance of fooling around, he was already beginning to regret his impulsive decision, and the sooner he could get rid of her the better.

Lightning flashed again, nearer this time, the air cooled by a fine mist of rain. That was another reason he was glad they were on the balcony. She might be a Viking but she probably wouldn't want to stay out long in the rain.

At the railing she turned to face him. The one thing in her favor was that she was damn fine looking. Tall. Almost as tall as his own 6'1", she wore white, laced, walking-shoes with flat heels. Her features were Nordic, high cheekbones and wide-set eyes. He couldn't tell their color in the dim light, but they looked pale, probably light blue or gray. She had an athlete's body. Wide shoulders. Narrow waist. Good hips and a nice ass. Not much in the way of boobs. And she was damned strong. Benny and Creed had been having a tough time getting her out the door.

She wore a light sweater over the white dress. Then he realized it wasn't a dress exactly; it was a uniform. A nurse's uniform. So she hadn't been lying, unless she was playing dress-up to get to him. A nurse, for God's sake. One thing was certain: if she was after an autograph or something, she sure as hell was original.

Still, she might be some kind of a nut so he stayed just inside the door, his arms folded across his chest, poised to move quickly if she made a grab for him.

"Okay," he said. "What the hell is going on?"

"It's about children. I—"

Michael's palms came out in an abrupt gesture. "Whoa! I don't know you. I never jumped you."

She took a step toward him. "No, no. I don't mean it that way..."

He reached for the door. "I've got no kids. Don't want any. Get the shit outta here!"

She grabbed his arm and he was astonished at her strength. "No. You don't understand. It's not for me. It's a charity. For children. Babies! Crack babies!"

Michael let go of the door handle. On the other side of the glass he caught a glimpse of Benny hurrying toward them. "I don't do charities," he snapped. He pulled the door open and raised his voice. "Benny."

The girl saw Benny moving toward them and spoke rapidly. "I know you don't. You're famous for being selfish. You don't care about anybody but yourself."

Michael's stifled a quick exasperation. "That's right. You do your thing; I'll do mine."

"Yes, I know. I've heard your so-called music."

"What's wrong with my music?"

"That would take too long. And I've only got a minute."

"Wrong. You had a minute. Time's up."

"No it isn't. I've got twenty seconds."

"You're not wearing a watch."

"Okay. Thirty seconds."

He stared at her for an instant, unable to believe that humor—even desperate humor—could lurk behind such an anguished expression. He laughed and slid the door shut in Benny's face. "Okay. Tell me why I should give up my time and money for some crack-head's kid that some bitch was stupid enough to have in the first place."

"Because it wasn't the baby's fault. And somebody's got to take care of it."

"Yeah, well, not me."

"Of course, not you. I don't give a damn about you. Or your music."

He took a step back, startled by the realization that she meant it, and almost laughed again, but her expression brought him up short. "So you don't want me and you don't want my music; what is it you want?"

"Your money."

He studied her face, her serious face with eyes that dared him to attempt ridicule. So he kept the disgust out of his voice as he answered, "You said it wasn't about money."

"I lied."

He suppressed a desire to slap the self-righteous look off her face. "All right, bitch. You know so much about me, you know I don't give away money."

Her brows pulled together in consternation as though he were a school kid who wasn't paying attention. "I know you're not going to write a check. That's too direct. Money right out of your pocket. And it'd probably give your manager a heart attack. So okay. No money. Just a little of your time."

"Time? That's more precious than money."

She glanced through the window at the party guests standing with drinks in their hands and shallow smiles on their faces and her expression of contempt brought a hollow feeling of recognition to Michael's chest. This party, this whole gig, his music that had a life span of about three months, this was the reason for his weariness. His life was sloughing away in miniscule grains of wasted time like a sand dune in the wind.

His voice was maddeningly defensive as he continued, "So what is it you want?"

"No money. A concert. A benefit concert. You wouldn't even feel it."

He shook his head. "Forget it. I've been down that road. No benefits. We're booked solid."

She stared at him, her lips tight with what he thought was consternation. "All right. Just let me talk to you. A couple of hours." She glanced at the people in the room again. "If you can spare a couple of hours."

At her words, a disgust born of experience with other women kicked in. How often had he heard those words before? She was just like the other groupies who wanted to get him alone for a sweat session.

But her expression and the insolence in her voice made him realize instantly that he was wrong; she had absolutely no interest in his body, probably had no interest in him at all. The realization that here was a beautiful woman who was not dying to go to bed with him came as something of a shock, and for some unidentified reason that he found disturbing, he wanted to make a good impression, so he said, "Okay, I'll give you a half-hour. But I'm telling you right now, it won't do any good. Call Benny tomorrow. He'll set it up."

"No. I mean now. Tonight."

He jerked his head back and stared at her. A crazy. He should have known. "Forget it." He reached for the sliding glass door.

She put her hand on his arm. "Wait. The hospital. Come with me to the hospital. See for yourself. It won't even take an hour."

Her move had brought her close in front of him so he could almost feel the anxiety that was reflected in her voice. How long had it been since he'd felt that much passion about something—or someone? Being with her, being close to anyone with her heated commitment, might help him revive his own waning passions, and it would sure as hell be more exciting than anything he would find at some party.

"Okay. If you'll promise not to break my arm."

She gave a small sigh and some of the fire drained from her eyes. She looked down at her hand on his arm as though noticing it for the first time. "Oh. Sorry."

When she took her hand from his arm, he felt a sudden loss, as through he had been absorbing some form of strength from her grip. He pulled the door open, but hesitated before stepping aside for her. "No strings. I don't promise a thing."

"Right. No strings."

She went past him into the room, heading for the door. As he followed, he noticed everyone in the room looking at them. Creed said something to Aaron and they laughed. Aaron caught his eye and gave him a thumbs-up. They were all thinking the same thing: he was on his way for a wild ride in the hay. How could they think otherwise? It was always like that when somebody left a party with a girl, even one as wholesome looking as this one. Sometimes the prissy ones were the hottest. They probably figured that under that starched white dress was a body that probably couldn't wait to release all its pent up inhibitions.

He took hold of the girl's arm and shoved roughly through the crowd, anxious to get away from the knowing looks and snide remarks. He would tell by the girl's tight lips and lack of complaints about his manhandling her out of the room that she was also aware of the looks and whispered remarks.

At the door Benny winked as he pulled the door open for them. "Don't forget. We've got a stage rehearsal tomorrow at three."

"Yeah, yeah," he said. "I got it."

Inside the elevator, he poised his hand over the buttons, "You got a car?"

"Yes. Valet parking."

He pushed the button for the hotel lobby and the elevator started down. The awkward silence gave him time to think and he thrust his hands into his pockets. In truth, he had no desire to see a bunch of sick kids. Seeing anyone in a hospital gave him a helpless feeling and babies would be worse. But if he didn't go, it might also mean he would never see her again. Looking at her, he decided, was worth the price.

"Where is this hospital? I don't want to be all night."

"Not far. I'll have you back to your party in an hour."

The way she'd twisted the word 'party' made him stiffen in quick resentment. Who was she to condemn his life style? Or anyone's for that matter? One reason he'd left Texas in the first place was to get away from judgmental people like her. So why was he here?

"What's you name?"

"Mary. Mary Schaeffer."

"Mary? Mary Anne, I bet."

"What's wrong with that?"

"Nothing. It's probably fake anyway."

"Fake? Why should it be?"

"If you're abducting me, I doubt you'd tell me your real name."

She was silent for a moment. "How much ransom do you think I could get for you?"

He glanced at her. She wasn't smiling. "More people would pay you to keep me than would to get me back."

"Are you that hard to get along with?"

"I guess you don't read the trade papers. I'm supposed to be a prima donna."

"Are you?"

He grinned. "Yeah. I guess I am."

Walking through the hotel lobby he let her get a little in front of him. He liked the way she walked, with her back straight, her head up, putting one foot straight in front of the other like a model, causing her hips to move in a provocative rhythm. After looking at so many girls wearing low-cut, hip-hugging jeans, it came as an amusing surprise to him that he should find a body in a nurse's dress to be so sexy. Maybe it was the contrast. Whatever it was, he wouldn't mind a little more of it.

Her car, when the valet attendant brought it around, proved to be an old Honda with an injured front fender and a layer of dust. She looked it with a rueful smile. "I haven't had time to get it washed."

"It'll fit right in with my mood." He meant it to sound humorous, but the phrase came out sounding exactly like he felt.

If she caught the innuendo, she gave no hint. she opened her purse, but he dug a crumpled twenty-dollar bill from his pocket and handed it to the attendant who gave him a two-finger salute and a "Thanks, Mr. Modesto." He held the door and Mary slipped in behind the wheel.

The passenger door groaned when Michael pulled it open, and he saw her wince. As he gingerly settled into the seat, he noticed that the inside of the car was immaculate. Apparently, she made sure her white uniform would remain pristine.

Instead of starting the engine, she said, "Would you mind fastening your seat belt?"

He gave her his version of a macho smile. "I don't like seat belts."

"My insurance company does. Do me the favor?"

He considered getting out. Here it was. His excuse to run. He reached for the door handle. If she said one word, he would bolt. But she remained grimly silent, staring straight ahead making no move to start the engine.

Abruptly, it struck him as funny. How many women would have talked to Michael Modesto like that? He laughed and snapped the belt in place. "You're right. You look like a maniac driver to me."

She started the car. "That'll be the day."

Traffic was light and she drove fast but cautiously. Actually, he was grateful for her cautious driving. Most women he rode with seemed to feel they had to prove their daring, and he usually spent the entire drive trying to look cool but with his toes clinched like talons.

He leaned his head back against the headrest and closed his eyes. She was silent, and the silence sounded good. The only sounds were the quiet purr of the engine, the murmur of the wheels on the rain-slick road, and the whisper of the wipers. He would not have believed he could endure riding in a car without the radio shattering the environment, but strangely, he enjoyed the silence. He wondered if he turned on her radio what kind of music he would hear. She probably had all the buttons set on symphony or 'oldie' channels.

Through cracked eyelids, he studied her. She drove leaning forward slightly, her entire attention centered on the road. He would bet that if she spoke she would not take her eyes off the road.

To test his theory he said, "Where you from?"

"Here. I live in Glendale."

He had been right. Her eyes had not wavered a fraction of an inch. Somehow, the fact was comforting as though it also implied that she would be just as straight forward about telling the truth. There could be no subterfuge in such intensity.

How different she was from the other women in his life. None of them would have been able to remain silent for more than thirty seconds.

"Tell me about this charity." He shifted a little in the seat so he could watch her as she talked.

"It's not very big really. It's kind of just getting started so nobody knows much about it. But they will. We've got plans for a national campaign."

"For crack babies."

"Not just them. For all at-risk babies."

"Like AIDs. Fetal alcohol syndrome."

She turned her head to stare at him for about half a second, then jerked her gaze back to the road. "What do you know about FAS?"

A picture of a little boy flashed through his mind, and he turned away from watching her. It wasn't a pretty picture. He and the boy's father, Jeff Berg, had been high school friends. Jeff played drums, and it had been Jeff who first got him interested in music. When he could play a couple of cords on the guitar without sounding like a cat sliding off a tin roof, they'd kicked around the idea of starting their own band. The plan had fallen apart when Jeff got his girl friend knocked up. The idea of a band had really fallen apart when Jeff married her and went to work in her father's plumbing business. They still might have been able to work out the band idea except that the girl proved to be a secret alcoholic who drank like a fish all during her pregnancy. By the time Jeff and her family found out about it, it was too late for the baby, and it was born with severe mental and physical abnormalities. Taking care of the poor little devil took all of Jeff's energy, nailing him to a cross he would never escape.

He'd still hung out with Jeff as much as possible until the baby was about two years old. Then watching the little kid's struggles began to get to him. He finally had to get away to keep his compassion from taking over his life. That had been five years ago. Now he was on his way to get involved with the same kind of pain. Watching one little kid fight a losing battle with life had been bad enough, now this girl was going to force him into having his heart torn out by God only knew how many more? He sure as hell didn't want to find out. He considered telling the girl to stop the car. Walking away would be the smart thing to do.

And the easiest.

But he'd come too far to back out. He could always do it later. There was no way he could get involved with abused kids without screwing up his life and all he'd worked for. A little contribution, maybe a benefit. That was it. The trick was not letting the kids get to him.

By the time she drove the car into the large parking lot of a sprawling hospital complex, he felt that he had his head in control, and he was able to take in the surroundings. Discreetly hidden lights illuminated five-storied, sand-colored buildings that were set amid a variety of trees and bushes and green grass so that the hospital looked as though it had been dropped into the middle of a park. A sign with bronze letters on the front of the nearest building indicated that this was Hollycrest Hospital. There was no wind, and the misty rain sifting silently through the strategically placed lighting gave the setting the eerie ambience of an abandoned world.

After parking in an area reserved for hospital personnel, she walked toward the entrance with the same concentration she had used in driving, long strides, back straight, head up, eyes straight ahead. Michael was surprised that she made no attempt to shield her head from the misty rain. Most women would have died before allowing a drop to touch their hair.

The hospital's lobby was paved with terrazzo, and with their wet, slippery shoes, they slowed their pace, the sound of his boot heels echoing from a high ceiling. Mary waved at two elderly ladies behind the reception desk without stopping and they smiled and nodded.

At a bank of elevators, she pushed the 'up' button, and while they waited, she said, "You never did tell me how much you know about fetal alcohol syndrome."

"Not that much, really. I have a friend who has a FAS little boy."

"Oh." She didn't say "I'm sorry" like most people. Maybe when you're around something so traumatic for a long time, you get used to it.

The elevator, typically, was large enough to transport hospital gurneys. She pushed the button for the fifth floor, then stood silently facing the closed door until he asked, "How long have you been a nurse?"

"Four...No, five years now."

"Always in pediatrics?"

"No. I started out in surgery. But I didn't care for it."

"Couldn't stand the blood and guts?"

"It wasn't that." She turned her head to look at him and the low overhead lights gave a flaxen sheen to her hair. "It was..." She hesitated as though sorting through memories that she did not enjoy. "I didn't like to see the...the fear."

"Not the pain and suffering?"

"When you choose to be a nurse you expect that. But they don't train you for the patient's fear. I couldn't handle it."

"Well, I suppose most people are afraid of dying."

"I suppose so. But it's buried in your mind. Most times you don't even think about it. But the operating room...well, it's a powerful reminder." She turned her head to stare at the closed elevator door. "Some people have a lot of trouble with that."

He moved up a step so he could study her profile. "But kids don't?"

She smiled a little. "No. Not the babies."

The door sighed open, and she led the way down a wide corridor paved with polished asphalt tile. A plaque on the wall indicated this was the pediatrics section. As proof, the walls were decorated with framed pictures, crayon-drawn by children, probably patients since many were of children in hospital beds. To Michael's surprise, without exception the children in the pictures looked happy. Even those with full-body casts or with their limbs supported by enough ropes so that they looked as though they were caught in a giant spider web, were smiling. He wondered whether the wide smiles were due to artistic license or whether all kids were hard-wired optimists. Probably the latter. These kids were too young to have acquired much wisdom about life's miseries; they would learn soon enough.

At a central nurse's station, Michael waited while Mary told one of the nurses on duty they were going to the incubation ward. The nurse nodded as she shot a puzzled look at Michael as though he looked familiar but she couldn't place him.

In a small dressing room, Mary unwrapped two hospital gowns and handed one to Michael. "Put this on over your clothes."

He slipped on the gown and Mary tied it shut in the back. She gave him a hat like a shower cap and he pulled it on at a rakish angle. Mary grimaced and pulled it down, tucking his hair inside.

"You've got no respect for style," he said.

'You've got no respect for germs," she replied. "Wash your hands."

Feeling like a surgeon with his freshly washed hands held gingerly in front of him, Michael followed Mary down the hall. She used her hip to push open one side of double doors that had small, glass windows and held the door open so Michael could enter. Although the room was fairly large, it was so chock-a-block with incubators and other machinery that it seemed small. Each incubator was festooned with tubes and cables leading to electronic monitoring equipment. Infants occupying the incubators were wired like aliens under study. Some were asleep. A few feebly moved their arms or legs like skewered insects. Others had their eyes open but lay inert as though they recognized there was no hope of escape.

There were no unoccupied incubators.

Mary said "Hello, Stell" to a black nurse who was bent over an open incubator changing the diaper of a baby that was so emaciated that it could only mew in protest.

Stell glanced over her shoulder, and her smile would have lighted a good-sized city. "Hi, Mary." When she noticed Michael, she stopped smiling and her eyes widened. "My God! You did it."

Mary acknowledged her triumph with a nod. "Stell, this is Michael Modesto. Mr. Modesto, Nurse Stella Bingham."

Michael nodded. "Hi."

Stella said, "Glad to see you. Excuse me. I've got a very impatient young man here."

"Yeah, sure," Michael said. "Need any help? I washed my hands."

The smile came back, wider than before. "Like you'd know how to change a diaper."

Michael thought of the many times he'd taken over for an exhausted Jeff and his return smile was rueful. "Sure. We were so poor I had to change my own."

"I'll bet." Her eyebrows lifted in a roguish tilt. "If you need any help now, let me know."

Michael grinned. "I'll do that."

One of the other babies interrupted with a cry of distress. Mary opened the incubator and used a clean cloth to gently wipe a film of sweat from the writhing tiny body.

"It looks like it's in pain."

"She is. Withdrawal can be very painful."

She had emphasized the 'she' to remind him, no doubt, that the children where not 'its', they were persons. It would be better to make a mistake about gender than to imply they were not little souls.

But she was sure as hell right about the kid being in pain. Witnessing a couple of his friends writhing in the agony of withdrawal when he was a dumbassed teenager had gone a long way toward keeping him from being sucked into the hell of drug addiction. Still, he knew that he might have given in to temptation if he'd become hooked on some girl who had goaded him into proving his cool. Thank God he had gone for girls who thought music was cooler than dope.

But this poor little kid. Dope withdrawal almost killed idiots who were adults. How bad must it be for a baby who looked like a sneeze would kill it?

Michael watched silently for a moment. The baby's face was pinched with pain; its skinny arms and legs convulsed and its tiny hands clenched into helpless fists. Perspiration oozed over its clammy skin as fast as Mary could wipe it away

"Can't you give her something?"

"We have. But she can't tolerate too much medication."

"Will she die?"

"Maybe not. Babies—most babies—are fighters. Even preemies like these are amazingly tough."

Michael turned away. He didn't want to watch such a one-sided fight any longer.

"The kid's mother. Has she seen this?"

Mary nodded. "It tears her up. But she won't stop."

"She's done this before?"

"This is her third."

"But not her last."

"When you pay for crack with your body, you don't think of the consequences."

"Consequences for who? It's the kid who suffers. Not a damn thing's gonna happen to her."

"It takes its toll. She has her own pain. That's why she takes drugs in the first place."

"Bull. Everybody's got pain. She picked the easy way of dealing with it."

"You think her life is easy?"

"Hell, yes. As long as her body holds out and she can find people like you to take care of her 'consequences,' she hasn't got a care in the world.

She started to reply, then hesitated. "Assuming you're right, it's not the baby's fault. She needs someone to hold her." She picked the baby up and held it toward Michael. "Here."

Michael backed a step. "Not me. I'm not her mother. Or her father."

"Babies don't care who holds them. That's why we have surrogates. Go on. Take her."

Michael's arms were frozen at his sides. He didn't want to touch the baby. He didn't want this thing to become personal. It was easy to refuse a charity if you were a dispassionate, anonymous donor. But the minute you allowed yourself to empathize with the victim, they had you.

But Mary was giving him no choice. She was practically pushing the baby against him. Cursing silently for allowing himself to be manipulated, he took the baby in his arms. He couldn't believe the baby's weight. Her tiny body had all the substance of a fragile bird, and for a moment he was terrified at the thought of dropping her. Cradling her in the crook of his left arm, he moved his right hand to supported her head. At his touch, she stopped trembling, and her tiny eyes opened, cleared, focused on his face. Her eyes. He couldn't tear his gaze from her eyes. They seemed to grow larger, darker, sucking him into their depths like dark whirlpools. And as he sank deeper and deeper, the sounds in the room, the people, objects, everything disappeared, sucked into the expanding pools. A sudden shock of agony like a strike of lightning shook him. The pain spread, increasing, agony that radiated through his body, spewing from his brain like a river of molten lava, burning away his fingers, his hands, his feet, every organ, every emotion. Spasm after spasm racked him, coursing from his body, consuming his body until there was nothing left except the deep, dark pool.

He was lying on something cold. A floor. His legs were drawn up in a fetal position, his hands clenched beside his face. Other hands were shaking him and someone was calling, "Michael! Michael!"

He opened his eyes. Mary. She was kneeling beside him, her hands on his shoulders, her face drawn in a knot of worry.

Memory rushed back and he gasped, "The baby! Where's the baby?"

Mary's eyes closed for a second, and she let her breath out. "Oh, Michael. We were so scared."

He pushed to a sitting position, surprised at the effort it took. The woman, Stella, was kneeling beside Mary, looking at him with the skeptical gaze of a professional nurse.

"Don't get up," she said. "Left me check your blood pressure."

She got up and went to bring a portable blood pressure apparatus.

With relief, Michael felt his strength returning. He started to get up, and Mary pressed him back. "You shouldn't move."

"I'm all right." He pushed to his feet, swayed, but recovered quickly. "The baby?"

Mary indicated the incubator. "She's fine."

The baby was lying quietly. Her eyes were closed but not clinched with pain. Michael looked closer, then turned his head to look at Mary in puzzled surprise. "She isn't shaking."

"She's sleeping. For the first time in days."

Stella unfastened Michael's hospital gown so she could push up his shirtsleeve and clamp the blood pressure cuff on his bicep. As she pumped the cuff tight with air, Michael rubbed his face with his free hand, half expecting to find that his skin was burned away. "What happened? I remember holding the baby..."

"You kind of...fainted. I caught the baby. By the time I got it back in the incubator you were...well,...having a seizure."

Michael remembered the terrible pain and his brain seemed to compress. "A seizure? Oh, God."

Stella asked, "Have you ever had any problems with epilepsy?"

Michael felt the pressure on his head increase. "Epilepsy. God no."

The cuff on Michael's arm had expended its pressure and Stella checked his blood pressure. "One-twenty-two over seventy. Good."

"I'm surprised it's not through the roof," Michael said. "I've never had anything like that happen before."

Stella removed the cuff. "Let me see your eyes." Michael stood patiently as she looked at each of his eyes. "They look okay, but I suggest you see your doctor."

"I haven't been to a doctor in years."

"Maybe you'd better start."

She put her fingers on his wrist and looked at her watch as she checked his pulse rate. In a few seconds she looked up. "Sixty three. No fibrillation."

"Sixty-three. I'm usually about fifty."

"You've had a seizure. You're lucky it's not zero."

Michael's reply was interrupted by a faint squall from the baby. Her eyes were open, but she was no longer sweating nor trembling. Mary had been bending over the incubator. "Can you believe it. I think she's hungry."

Stella went to her side. "I think you're right. That's a first."

"I don't think she even has a fever."

Stella turned away. "I'll check."

Mary straightened and looked at Michael who was staring at the baby. "I don't understand this," she said. "A few minutes ago she was burning up. In terrible pain. Now..." She turned back to look at the baby. "She looks normal. Healthy. Well, she's still a preemie. Underweight. But...well...I just don't understand it."

Michael's mouth was dry, his brain spinning. He tried to remember the sequence of events: Mary had handed him the baby, he had taken her in his arms, he had looked into her eyes and...the pain had hit him, overwhelming pain, wiping out all consciousness. Now...

He stared at the baby. She was pumping her arms and legs, gurgling, her mouth agape, her eyes clear. A miracle. He had been part of what could only be a miracle. What the hell was going on?

He yanked the hospital cap off. "I've seen enough." He pushed the door open and walked out.

He heard Mary say, "Stell, can you hold on a little longer?" and Stella reply, "Sure. Go get him."

Mary caught up with him at the elevator where he jabbed the 'down' button as he stripped off the hospital gown.

"I'm sorry," she said, pulling off her own hospital gown. "I don't know what happened back there, but...well, I shouldn't have made you hold the baby."

Michael shook his head slowly. "I fainted. Jesus. I never did that before."

"I guess you've just got too much empathy."

"Yeah, something like that."

The elevator doors slid open, and they stepped inside. Michael pushed the button for the lobby.

He took a position facing the door with his back stiff and his feet apart, prepared to ward off any attempt she might make to take advantage of his vulnerability. But instead of making a pitch for her charity, she said, "I owe you a cup of coffee. There's a restaurant here in the hospital."

"You don't owe me a thing."

"All right. I'd still like to buy you a cup of coffee."

He turned his head toward her. She stood awkwardly holding both their hospital gowns bundled in her arms. When she had pulled her cap off it had messed her hair so that it framed her face with stray strands. Her cheeks were pale, her eyes wide with apprehension. She had the pathetic look of a wallflower at a high school prom hoping that someone would ask her to dance and afraid of what would happen if they did. He couldn't keep his lips from twisting in a smile as he said, "Make that a drink and I'll do it."

Her hesitation was scarcely noticeable. "All right. A drink for you, coffee for me."

"Okay."

Michael wasn't sure whether he'd won a point or not. He'd just blown one more chance to walk away with no obligations, no commitments. He'd done his duty. He'd gone to the hospital. Shit. He'd even held one of the kids. His fainting gave him a good excuse to bug out. Now he was putting his head back in the lion's mouth. This wasn't like him. But then, nothing he'd done tonight was like him. But it still wasn't too late to back out. A stiff drink would help him get back on track.

Chapter 3

Before they left the hospital, Michael waited while Mary dropped off the hospital gowns and caps.

Outside, the skies had cleared and a few stars fought the city lights. Crossing the parking lot, they walked around oily puddles of water that were spangled with shifting rainbows from the few perimeter lights. Far in the distance the departing storm marked its passage with diminishing lightning flashes and the faint rumble of thunder.

Maybe the thunder was why he didn't hear the men until it was too late.

Mary was inserting her key in her car's door lock when a voice behind them said, "Hey, bitch. Nice wheels."

Michael froze, cursing himself for forgetting to check around them as they'd moved across the dark lot. He was standing so close to Mary that he felt her start with surprise. The sound of her keys striking the asphalt was loud in the stunning silence.

Without moving his body, Michael slowly turned his head. There were two of them approaching nonchalantly, one black and one white or Latino. Early twenties, dressed the same: long white T-shirts under warm-up jackets and black pants so baggy and long that their white basketball shoes stepped on the frayed cuffs. Their hands were in their pockets, but Michael had no doubt that they clutched knives or guns.

They stopped a few feet away and surveyed Mary and Michael, evaluating the danger. The way they stood and the way their eyes flicked from Michael and Mary to the interior of the car, the surrounding cars and the deserted parking lot told him they were not amateurs.

The black man jerked his chin up while keeping his hands in his pockets. "You. Shit head. Gimme the money."

There was no nervous tremor in the voice, no time wasted asking questions, no stupid chitchat. Everybody knew what was going down. Just play your role and nobody gets hurt.

Mary stood perfectly still, her eyes wide with apprehension.

Moving carefully, Michael fished his wallet from his hip pocket and held it out. The man took a couple of steps forward and grabbed it. The Latino moved a little to the side so he could watch Michael and the few parked cars at the same time. Only a distant lightning flash followed by a sullen rumble of thunder made him shift his gaze.

There was close to a hundred-fifty dollars in the wallet and the man counted it swiftly. He extracted Michael's Visa and American Express credit cards, then deliberately dropped the wallet in a puddle of water. The arrogant gesture jerked Michael a step forward, and as though by magic, a switch-blade knife snicked open in the man's left hand and a nickel-plated revolver appeared in the hand of the Latino. When Michael stopped and took a deep breath, the weapons vanished back into the voluminous pockets.

The man stuffed the money in his pocket and held out his hand toward Mary. "Gimme."

She handed over her purse and watched silently as the man dumped its contents on the trunk of the car. She was beginning to tremble, but Michael judged that by the way her eyes had narrowed and her lips thinned, the trembling was due more to suppressed rage than to fright, and he put his hand on her arm. Her eyes slid to look at him, and he shook his head a fraction of an inch.

The man found Mary's small money purse and took out the bills. There were only two: a twenty and a one. "Shit," he snapped. He turned red-veined eyes toward Mary. "Where's the cards?"

"I don't use credit cards" Her voice was firm, steady.

An erratic breeze had sprung up, and when the man repeated "Shit," and in a sudden angry gesture, swept the contents of the purse to the ground, the articles bounced and scattered like wind-driven leaves.

Latino pointed at the fallen car keys. "Gimme the keys."

Michael picked up the keys and tossed them to the man who snatched them out of the air. The man backed a few steps and motioned toward the front of the car. "Get your asses over there."

Michael kept his hand on Mary's arm as they moved to stand near the car. The man jerked his head at his partner. "Come on. Let's go."

The Latino reached for the door on the driver's side and the black man started to go around the car toward the passenger's side. Suddenly he stopped and turned toward Michael. "Hey," he snarled. "You got a phone?"

Michael shook his head. "No."

The man stared at him, his eyes measuring Michael's six foot frame. If he planned on searching Michael, he changed his mind. "Yeah, you better not be lying."

"Hey, Dog," the Latino said. "What about the bitch?"

The man called Dog had been about to get in the car. He turned to look at Mary and he smiled, a wide, mean smile that matched the greed in his eyes. "Yeah, okay. Git in the car, bitch."

Mary's only move was to cross her arms over her chest in a protective gesture.

Dog said, "Shit," and moved toward her.

Michael gritted his teeth, more in disgust than rage. He had thought the men were professionals who would avoid a fight if at all possible. But they were behaving like a couple of teenagers, and he was going to have to do something they might all regret. He only hoped they really were as unprofessional as they were acting. He stepped in front of Mary. "You got the money and the car. That's it."

"Yeah, right," Dog said and his knife flicked open. He moved toward Michael, the knife held low, the blade weaving. The Latino started forward, his gun in his hand.

Looking into Dog's face, shadowed and made menacing by the dim light, Michael could see the man's future as clearly as if it were written on his forehead: Violence. Prison. Violence. Prison. Like Poe's pendulum blade, swinging back and forth in a lowering arc until the vision ended in a crimson splash.

There was no appealing to such a man.

Michael held up his hands, palms out submissively. "All right. Take it easy." He crouched a little, turning slightly so he could watch the second man.

Dog sneered, and as Michael feinted with his left hand, his knife came up, flicking toward the offered arm. Michael jerked his arm back and with his right hand swatted Dog's arm aside. In the same move he rammed the stiffened fingers of his other hand into Dog's throat.

Dog staggered back, his mouth wide, gasping for breath.

The Latino had come up behind Dog. He raised his gun and Michael shoved Dog hard against him. The man stumbled, and the second it took him to push Dog aside was enough for Michael to launch a kick to the man's arm and the gun spun from his numb fingers.

Instead of reaching for the gun, the man lunged at Michael who sidestepped and kicked the side of the man's knee. The man staggered and made a gasping groan that was cut off when Michael chopped down hard on the back of his neck.

Michael scooped up the man's revolver and turned to look for Dog. Too late. Dog was behind Mary, his left hand forcing up her chin, his right holding the knife's blade against her throat.

Michael took a step toward them, bringing up the gun. "Let her go."

"No way, man." Dog's voice was a harsh whisper. "Drop the gun 'r I cut her."

"You do and you're dead."

"Yeah? Which means the most, Dude? Savin' her 'r killin' me?"

The question stopped Michael with its simple logic. If he put the gun down the man would kill him, take the car and Mary and probably kill her after they finished with her.

He could, of course, shoot first and take a chance that the man's reflexes would not be fast enough to kill her as he fell.

He wanted to do it. There was no one around to see that he would be sacrificing her life for his own. But even as the thought flashed through his mind, he knew he could not. At some point in his life, a stupid, noble ethic had been driven into he conscious with such force that it transcended logic, making it impossible for him to sacrifice someone else's life for his own.

So what could he do? The man's eyes were focused on the gun, his own hands trembling as he stared, waiting for the least twitch of Michael's finger on the trigger. The gun. It was simultaneously the problem and the solution. He could not put it down and he couldn't keep it. If only there was a half way...

He almost jerked the gun as a thought struck him. In a Pavlovian response, the man's knife drew a trickle of blood from Mary's white throat and she moaned.

"Easy, man, easy," Michael said. "Look, I'm taking the bullets out."

Michael swung the cylinder out from the revolver and punched all six of the bullets into his other hand. He kept one and dropped the others to the ground where they bounced and rolled like deadly rain drops. Dog's eyes widened and for an instant Michael thought he was going to charge. "Hold it," he quickly said. "Look."

He held up the one bullet, then quickly loaded it into the gun's cylinder and snapped it shut, the metallic sound loud in the light.

"Okay. I've got one bullet in here." He stepped closer and twirled the cylinder, then aimed the gun between Dog's staring eyes. "You've got a five to one chance the gun won't fire. Let her go or we'll find out how lucky you are."

Sweat coursed down Dog's cheeks and dripped off his chin. His hand holding the knife trembled. "Shit." Dog's voice was little more than a whisper, his eyes staring. But he made no move to lower the knife.

Michael pulled the trigger. There was a click and Dog's eyes squeezed shut for an instant. The knife started to move and for a second Michael feared he had made a mistake.

When Dog realized that the gun had not fired he let his breath out. "You do that again an' I'll cut the bitch."

Michael pulled the trigger again.

Click!

Dog flinched and said, "Shit. I'll do it! I'll do it!"

Click!

Dog's face was a river of sweat, his hand trembling so badly that Michael could see he was clinging to an edge of control as fine as the edge of the knife.

"You're odds are down to two to one," he said. "Ready?"

"Shit," Dog snarled. He dropped the knife and pushed Mary away. He stood staring at Michael. "You crazy, man. You high as a kite."

Michael motioned with the gun. "Move away."

Dog moved to the side and Michael kicked the knife away. Mary had stumbled to her knees and he used his free hand to help her to her feet. "You all right?"

She felt the trickle of blood at her throat with trembling fingers. But her voice was strong and clear when she said, "I think so."

Michael turned to the Latino who was still sprawled on the cement, holding his injured knee. "The keys."

The man fished the car keys from his pocket and threw them at Michael's feet. Michael picked them up and handed them to Mary. "Get in the car. Start the eng—"

"Look out!"

He heard Mary's cry, and he started to turn as something hit him a jarring blow in the kidneys. Pain shot through him as sharp and fast as thought: Dog!

The gun fell from his numbed hand and he heard it strike the ground. He struggled to turn, to meet the attack he knew was coming. Blam! Pain blasted through his head as a fist clubbed him in the temple, and he was dimly aware that he had fallen, his face smashing into unyielding pavement.

He tried to move, to roll away, but it took all his will power to force his eyes to remain open, all the time wondering why he was not being kicked senseless. He saw the reason when he blinked to focus his eyes. Mary was swinging her fists at Dog, but he grabbed her and dragged her back toward the car.

Dog pushed her hard against the side of the car, then grabbed the gun from the ground. He picked up some of the bullets and shoved them into the gun's chamber, all the time muttering, "Kill em' I'm gonna smoke that mother."

The Latino was on his feet. Limping to the fallen knife, he picked it up. "Let me do it, Dog."

"Shit, no. I—"

Ziiissstt! Lightning chained down in a blinding flash, smashing into a huge tree. Smoke and fire exploded as the tree split as though struck by Thor's mighty hammer.

Booommmm!

The terrible power of a mighty thunder clap drove Michael to his knees, where he crouched, his ears ringing.

Dog and the Latino cowered, their hands over their ears. Above them, a sliver of moon had joined the stars in a velvet sky.

Ziisstt! Another chain of lightning smashed into the earth followed by a cannon roar of thunder.

"Holy shit!" Dog yelped. He straightened and brought the gun up, pointing it at Michael. Michael tensed. Caught in the open, he had nowhere to hide. Dog's lips curled showing clinched teeth.

"Jesus, Dog!" the Latino gasped. He grabbed Dog's arm and pointed at a glowing luminescence that had appeared in the darkness near the edge of the parking area. "What the shit is that?"

Dog turned his head to stare, the gun forgotten, his mouth gapping.

The glow pulsed, expanding, growing in brilliance as it appeared to lower, to move, rolling toward them in a giant ball of fire. Closer. Closer. Growing in brilliance, flames and sparks spinning off like wavering jets of white-hot gas.

Michael struggled to his feet, looking for Mary. She stood staring, mesmerized by the brilliant, blazing light. Michael grabbed her arm and pulled her toward the car. "Come on. In the car. Quick!"

The movement caught Dog's attention and his head swung toward them. "Hold it!" In one swift motion he swung the gun up and Michael braced for the shock of the bullet. He couldn't miss. Not at this distance. Click!

Impossible. Michael has seen him reload the gun.

"Shit!" Dog snarled. His finger tightened on the trigger.

A scream. From the Latino! His hands came up, his shoulders hunched, as a jet of brilliant flame from the ball of fire leaped toward them like a fiery laser beam.

Dog fled, the gun clattering on the ground, the Latino at his heels in a limping run. Michael's hand was on the door of the car, knowing even as he tried to wrench it open that it was too late.

Michael threw his arms across his face as the huge ball of light smashed into the ground and—vanished! One instant it was the blinding brilliance of a thousand suns, the next instant it was gone.

Why wasn't he dead? Incinerated by the lightning—if that's what it was. There was no sign of the luminescence, no lightning, no thunder.

Mary stared at the place where the fiery ball had vanished. "What...What was that?"

"I don't know. Ball lightning, I guess. I heard it could make a ball like that." He looked toward Dog and the other man who were running blindly, their feet splashing in the rain puddles.

She looked up at the clear sky. "But where did it come from?"

"Well, it sure as hell was here. Look." He pointed to a puddle of molten metal that sprawled on the asphalt.

"What is it?"

"The gun. Melted."

"It looks..." Mary stopped and looked closer at the molten metal. It had solidified in a twisted shape, following depressions in the paving. "It looks like a cross."

Michael glanced at the shape. "It's just a puddle." He picked up his wallet, the car keys and Mary's purse and she helped him gather its scattered contents. When he handed the purse to her he looked at her white face. "Let's get out of here. I'll drive. I know a little bar."

"Do you know a coffee shop?"

"Yeah, but..." He was going to say that she looked as though she could use a drink; he knew he sure as hell could. But he also realized that she would not take a drink. She might be suffering from the shock of almost being killed, but she would rather face a nightmare of shattered nerves than wrestle with some kind of moral guilt.

They were out in the street and she was staring straight ahead before she whispered, "They were going to kill us."

He knew she was right, but there was no point in adding fuel to her fear, so he said, "Maybe not. Most carjackers aren't into murder. Too many problems."

But he could see she didn't believe him. "If it hadn't been for that—that lightning...Why didn't it burn us?"

"Luck. Nobody knows much about why ball lightning goes where it does."

"Those men..." She put her hands over her face, then turned to face him. "Are you all right?"

His side ached where he had been hit. He gingerly touched his cheek. It had been scraped raw when his face had been driven against the rough asphalt. Damn! He was going to look like hell. But the scrape didn't feel too bad. The pain had virtually disappeared. Maybe a little makeup would hide it well enough for tomorrow's gig.

"I suspect I'll live."

Inside a coffee shop, he gingerly eased into a booth facing her. It was his first chance to really stare at her and he realized that with a little makeup, she would be a beauty. Great skin. Wide-set eyes above the kind of high cheekbones that models loved. And her eyes were the clear blue that would leap out of a photograph. Her lips—when they weren't pressed tight in anger or disgust—were seductively full and soft. Nice teeth, white and even, probably the work of a good orthodontist when she was young. But her hair...natural blonde—ash blonde. So clean it glistened. It was difficult to tell much about her figure. Probably had great legs if she ever showed more than from the knees down.

"We should call the police," she said, her voice just above a whisper.

Michael considered the idea, then shook his head. "They're long gone. We'd just get bogged down in paperwork."

"Well, we'd better get you back in the hospital anyway."

Michael was inclined to agree. He'd been so interested in looking at her that he'd forgotten his injuries. His face felt almost normal, but if his spleen or kidneys were injured, he might have internal bleeding. God. He could die.

The shock brought him up straight and he pressed his hand

against his back where the man had hammered him. Strange. A few minutes ago he could hardly stand. Now the pain was gone. There was no tenderness beneath his probing fingers, no twinges.

He looked at Mary. "You're a nurse. If I had internal bleeding, wouldn't I have some pain?"

"Of course. Probably excruciating."

"But there's...nothing. I guess I'm okay."

She pointed to his shirt front. "No. That's blood."

"From my cheek. I hit pretty hard."

She leaned closer to study his face. "I don't see anything."

He touched his cheek again. What the hell?! It was smooth, painless. "I swear it was scraped all to hell."

She shook her head. "I don't even see a bruise."

"So where did the blood come from?"

"You must have hit your nose. That would cause a lot of pain."

Michel felt his nose. It seemed all right. But there was blood on his shirt. "Well, it's stopped bleeding, so I guess it's okay."

"Are you sure you're all right. I thought he'd killed you."

Michael did not answer. He couldn't answer. When the man had hit him, the pain had driven him to the ground. He was sure that the blow had ruptured his kidneys. And he'd though he might have a concussion from hitting his head on the pavement. But now... There was no pain. In fact, he had never felt better. It had to be the euphoria of being alive. Tomorrow, when the pain returned, as he was certain it would, he would go for a checkup.

But there was something else...

"What happened at the hospital? With the baby?"

Mary stared at her cup of coffee. "I don't know. It never happened before that I know of."

"Yeah. I guess I was in the right place at the right time."

She lifted her head to look at him. "The right time? What does that mean?"

"Well, the kid was coming out of it. Cold turkey. I just happened to be holding her when it happened."

She shook her head. "It doesn't happen like that. Suddenly, I mean. Not like that."

"So what did happen?"

"I have no idea; maybe she just wore herself out and went to sleep."

Michael took a sip of his coffee. It was possible. Besides, what other explanation could there be? "I suppose so. It just seemed...well, odd. You ever heard of that before?"

"No, but we don't know that much about crack babies. They're all different. Some don't..." She paused and shook her head. "Some don't make it."

"So, I guess we should be grateful for small favors."

When Mary lifted her coffee, she had to hold the cup with both hands to stop its trembling.

"I'm taking you home," he said. "You should get some rest."

"But..." She put the cup back in its saucer. "We should talk about the benefit."

"That can wait."

She slowly shook her head. "You won't see me again."

"Sure I will. After this gig, we're leaving on a short tour, only a couple of months. I'll look you up as soon as we get back." She gazed at him, skepticism in her eyes. He made a cross over his heart. "Cross my heart and hope to di..." He stopped. He was not superstitious, but there was also no point in tempting fate. "Well, cross my heart anyway."

She sighed, giving in to an emotional release of tension as though she had been functioning on nerve alone, and Michael could see that the release left her drained of energy. She pushed her coffee cup aside. "I guess I'll have to trust you. I'll give you my number."

She tried to find a pen in her purse, clawing through the contents in mounting frustration. When she was unable to find the pen, she pushed the bag aside. "Oh, those damn people. They've ruined everything."

It distressed Michael to see a woman cry. It was one of the few things that made him feel completely helpless. He reached across the table and took hold of her hands with both of his. "Look. Don't sweat it. I'll...I'll think about that benefit. I can't promise anything but...I'll think about it."

She looked up, her eyes shining. "Are you sure?"

"Yeah." He pulled a paper napkin from its holder and handed it to her. "Here. I'll drive you home."

She dabbed at her eyes with the napkin. "But how will you get back?"

"I'll take a cab."

"You don't have to do that. I can drive. I'll drop you off first."

Her hands had steadied and her voice was strong, so he nodded. "Okay." He slide out of the booth. "I'll get a pencil from the waitress."

The few seconds it took him to borrow the pencil gave Michael time to think, and all the time Mary was writing her phone number, he though what he fool he was for promising he'd see her again. Her fresh beauty, her earnest innocence, her tears, were dangerous. He'd already made a promise that was going to be difficult to keep. He knew nothing about her or her charity. But, as he'd promised, he would think about it.

Looking at her tear stained face, he almost laughed. How was he ever going to stop thinking about it...or her.

Chapter 4

The General Assembly Hall in the United Nations' New York headquarters can be intimidating to a speaker. Not only is the room huge, seating more than two thousand delegates, alternates and staff members, but in addition, there are always hundreds of visitors and reporters from around the world. And interpreters watch and listen from special rooms constructed high up in the walls like glassed-in opera boxes. Below the interpreters' boxes, similar rooms are used by television crews recording every move, every sound of the speaker and the governing members on the dais.

The room, however, did not intimidate Anthony Stonz. Quite the opposite; he reveled in the sea of faces, the eyes locked on his presence at the lectern, the sound of his amplified voice reverberating from the curved walls of the great hall.

Seated at the United States' delegation table listening to Anthony's mellifluent voice rising and falling, smoothly transitioning from cajolery, to pathos, to anger, as he worked his audience with the skill of an accomplished actor, Selene felt her heart pounding. Her emotion, however, was not due to Anthony's inspiring words, rather, her heart struggled to contain her pride. How could Anthony stand so calmly before these hundreds of people, people from every nation on earth, people who clung to his words because as the U.N. Ambassador Extraordinary and Plenipotentiary of the most powerful nation on earth, the portent of his words could have stunning impact on their lives.

Even his looks were commanding. Standing more than six feet in height, his full head of silver hair, lean nose, and piercing eyes were analogous of his nations' bald eagle symbol. And his resonant voice held such warmth and compassion that it could bring tears to the most hardened of hearts. When it rang like a carillon, as it did now, it bored into your mind with such compelling force one wanted to leap from the trenches and rush into the cannon's mouth.

"—My friends," he was saying, "we are at war. War against the tyranny of poverty. War against evil. War against illiteracy. And war against war itself. The world is filled with ambitious barbarians, people who seek power at the expense of others. Such evil must be stopped!

And when it is stopped, when tyranny is brought to an end, there will be a day when the lion will indeed lie down with the lamb, because the lion will no longer be hungry nor the lamb weak. I see a day when the God of the Jews, of the Christians, of the Muslims, the Buddhists, the Hindus, the Shintoists, of every sect and religion will be the God of peace. But there can never be peace in the world until we are united in a commitment to peace. Let us unite, unite in peace—forever!"

At his final word, most of the representatives surged to their feet, applauding furiously. A few, primarily from Mid-Eastern countries, remained seated, their hands still, their faces sullen.

Selene saw Anthony focus on her, and she stopped applauding for a second to raise a fist in tribute. He replied with a smile before he turned to make his way from the dais, shaking hands with the U.N. Secretary and other members. Watching him, she realized that she was surely looking at the next President of the United States. She was probably the only person in the world who knew that the presidency had long been his secret goal, but until today, she had considered it more of a dream than a solid possibility.

She had to smile at her stupidity. Anthony always succeeded in his pursuits. In all the years she had known him, he had never failed to influence people and events in ways that produced the results he wanted. Some called him cold and manipulative, but she knew better; he simply had a view of the world, a goal for mankind that demanded ruthless dedication.

Whatever his goal, he never failed, moving from one difficult rung of the political ladder to the next with a sure—some said merciless—precision, with never a doubt about the goal or the outcome.

Until last night. What had happened last night?

When the meeting adjourned and she made her way out of the hall, people hurried to shake her hand. She knew some of the men were attracted by her beauty, hoping to become better acquainted. Most, however, were sycophants who knew that she was secretary to one of the most powerful men on earth. She smiled graciously at each one, but her mind was on last night. She had never seen Anthony so restless, so... she didn't like to use the word 'worried,' but for once, he seemed concerned about the future.

But there was no chance to talk with Anthony until they were seated in the big limousine and on their way to another of the endless receptions. When he noticed the direction they were heading, Anthony Stonz leaned forward and said to the driver, "Mosic, take us back to the apartment."

Mosic nodded and turned at the next corner.

Selene looked at Stonz. "We're not going to the reception?"

"No. We have work to do."

A note in his voice made Selene put her hand on his arm. "Oh? I thought it went well."

"I'm not talking about today. Something's wrong."

"Wrong? What?"

"I'm not sure, but... last night, something happened."

The cold menace in his voice made Selene shiver. What could possible cause Anthony to be so worried? The set in his face awakened a memory, and her fingers gripped his arm. Her voice was a whisper of alarm, "The Messiah?"

Stonz's face twisted into a grimace. "I don't know. Perhaps a true prophet. Either way, we've got to stop him."

"How? Is it possible?"

"I think we have a little time." He was thinking aloud and Selene sat quietly. "Right now, the transformation is too nascent to even trace."

A sliver of hope gripped Selene. "Maybe it's just a...an anomaly. There have been false prophets before."

"Perhaps. We can only wait. If it doesn't manifest itself again, we'll know it was a false alarm."

"And if it does?"

Stonz did not answer, but the look in his eyes made Selene move to the other side of the seat, her brows furrowed with worry. There had always been rumors, fatidic predictions about the new Messiah. Claimants had sprung up like weeds in the fourteenth, fifteenth and sixteen centuries; men like Shabbetai Tzevi, Jacob Frank and Joseph della Reyna had been hailed as the new Savior. But they had always proved to be mere mortals.

Even if Anthony had sensed the imminence of a new Messiah, it probably wasn't true. The very fact that the perception was so nebulous meant it had to be false. The power of a true Messiah, however inchoate, would shake the world like a bomb, wouldn't it?

She glanced at him. He had leaned his head back against the seat. His eyes were closed, his face smooth, placid. She relaxed and leaned her own head back. Even if the premeditation proved to be true, Anthony would know what to do. They were too close to success now to allow anything—or anyone—to interfere.

The limousine sped through the dark streets as though on a mission for the apocalypse.

Chapter 5

It had been embarrassing. The band had played so many one-night gigs in so many clubs that when Michael made his usual greeting to the audience he had forgotten where they were. After a brief hesitation, which he had covered so quickly that no one noticed, he launched into his standard glib mantra about the great town, the great club and, especially, the great fans. Then the band had begun the hit song from their album and nobody remembered anything except the driving beat. As he gyrated through his routine, banging his guitar while growling the lyrics, Michael thought what a waste of time it had been for him to agonize for hours writing the song's words. Nobody could understand a word anyway, not with Creed flailing away at the drums, Aaron pounding the keyboard like a maniac, and Lyle, Moss and himself killing their guitars and wailing and screaming like a trio of chainsaws with the sound cranked up to a decibel level guaranteed to flatten auditory hair cells like the shock wave of a meteor strike.

He also struggled with the thought that maybe it hadn't been the confusion of too many clubs in too many towns that had caused him to lose track of where they were. Maybe it was because thoughts of that nurse back in L.A. kept intruding at the damndest times. Any time his concentration flagged, images of her face leaped in to fill the gap. He'd thought he could exorcise her from his mind, but her name—and her face—were imbedded in his brain like fishhooks.

Sitting in the cramped dressing room during a break, he came to the conclusion that the only way to purge her from his mind was to bring the memory into the open. But how did he do that?

A benefit was out of the question; the guys would never go for it. If he gave money to her charity, he could wash his hands of the whole deal. Or he could just tell her to get lost, and that would also end it. That sounded like the best plan. But he couldn't do it on the phone. To make it really go away, he'd have to tell her to her face. And that would be tough.

The door opened and Benny walked in rubbing his hands. "I got it," he said. "It took some arm twisting, but I got it."

It took Michael a second to shift his concentration. "What's that?"

Benny raised his eyebrows, surprised that Michael should have to ask. "City Walk. In L.A. The Amphitheater."

Michael still hadn't shaken off all thoughts of what he had to do, and he replied with an unenthusiastic, "Oh. Good."

Benny held out his hands, palms up. "Oh, good? Don't fall all over yourself. I knock myself out and all you got to say is 'Oh, good'?"

Michael stood up and clapped Benny on the shoulder. "Sorry, Benny. I was a million miles away. You did a hell of a job. I know it's a tough gig."

Benny studied Michael. His mood had switch from elation to worry. "You sick or something? My God, you're not getting sick. Not now."

Michael gave him a reassuring smile. "No, I'm not sick. Just...thinking."

"Thinking!" Benny slapped his forehead. "Jesus. You aren't supposed to think. That's my job. I think, you play. Comprende?"

Michael glanced at his watch, then reached for the door knob. "Yeah, right, Benny. You think. I play. And everybody's happy."

He was going out the door when Benny asked, "About what? You haven't got a problem with the band, have you?"

Michael stopped, wondering how much he should tell Benny. Well, he would find out sooner or later anyway—if he decided to go through with the contribution. "A charity," he told Benny. "For a hospital. I was thinking about the band playing a benefit."

Benny stared at him as though Michael had just asked him to commit murder. "A benefit? Are you outta your mind? I'm busting my butt trying to save money and you want to give it away. Jesus. Get real."

"Yeah," Michael said. "That's what I thought you'd say."

As Michael went out he heard Benny mutter, "Thinking. Christ. That's all I need."

Michael grinned and headed for the stage. Benny was right. He had been a lot happier before he'd started thinking about Mary Schaeffer and her charity. He was candid enough to admit that the reason he wanted to see her had nothing to do with the charity. And the only way to keep the fascination from driving him crazy was to face it, to use his will power to get her out of his system.

But by the time they arrived in L.A. his resolve had weakened considerably. Instead of getting Mary out of his head, he wanted to see her more than ever. The desire was so compelling that it was beginning to scare him. It was all mixed up in his head like a maelstrom. But one thing was clear: Seeing her was a chance he had to take.

On Sunday, the first day in L.A. his calendar was clear, he awakened at nine o'clock, practically the crack of dawn, and lay in bed fighting thoughts about how he could postpone—or better yet, cancel—the confrontation. She would probably be working. No, it was Sunday and she was probably off work. Still, someone had to look after the hospital patients even on Sunday. Maybe he should wait until—

In a fit of disgust, he almost leaped out of bed. Come on, stupid. Get it over with!

Locating the phone number she had given him, he punched in the numbers, thinking he would ask her to join him for breakfast, although for her it might be time for lunch.

He allowed the phone to ring four times before he gave up with a sense of relief. He had tried. Now he could forget her.

He was still in his pajamas so he crawled back in bed. But he couldn't sleep. Her face kept popping into his mind, taunting him. Pulling the pillow over his head only brought her image into sharper focus.

This time when he crawled out of bed it was with a sigh of resignation. He was a fish on a hook and the only way to shake free was to cut the line.

His hotel room had a dedicated phone line for an internet hookup, and using his laptop computer, he was able to make a reverse look-up on her phone number and get her address.

But all the time he was getting dressed and driving the rental car through the quiet Sunday morning streets, the same litany of excuses tried to force him to turn the car around.

The doubts were so compelling that when he pulled to a stop in front of her apartment building on a street lined with untrimmed date palms and jacaranda trees, he did not immediately get out of the car. He sat for a moment, wondering why he was so loath to face her. It wasn't the charity. If she were a man, he could deal with it in about two seconds. No, it was her; he was delaying because he dreaded the look on her face when he told her there would be no benefit. But at least, it would be over. And that, too, bothered him. Why was that? He'd never had this reluctance in breaking up with any other girl? But with other girls there had been no concern about their reaction.

This time some idiotic part of him hoped that she would say the benefit did not matter; she wanted to see him again.

The thought caused a snorting laugh. Fat chance. Without the benefit, he was nothing to her.

He strode to the apartment's security door where he found the name 'M. Schaeffer' listed next to a call box. He punched in the code listed for her apartment, and while the phone rang again and again, he held fast to his resolve by telling himself that he had come this far he might just as well get the anticipated rejection over with.

After several rings with no answer, he breathed a sign of relief. He had tried. Now he would be free.

He started to leave, then stopped as a name on the list of apartment occupants caught his eye. Manager.

Cursing himself for doing so, he punched in the manager's code.

While the phone buzzed, he wondered what aberration in his upbringing had given him such a stupid code of honor. All the people he could think of, bar none, would have ignored any thought of an obligation to the girl. They would have slept soundly with no tormenting thoughts of crack babies and homeless children.

After the buzzer rang three times, he was about to turn away when a man's voice on the intercom said, "Manager."

Now there was no turning back.

Michael tried to keep a tone of defeat out of his voice as he said, "Sorry to disturb you, but I have an appointment with Mary Schaeffer, but she doesn't answer. Do you know if she's okay?"

There was brief pause. "It's Sunday. You know what time it is?"

"I know. I'm a little early."

"I said it's Sunday."

"I know that. I'm sorry to—"

"She's in church." The man's voice implied that he would like to have added, 'you idiot.' Instead, he simply broke the connection.

Michael's anger at the man's bad manners overcame his judgment and he redialed the man's code. When the man snapped, "I said—"

Michael quickly interrupted. "I know. Church. Which one?"

"Community Church. On Sycamore."

Michael managed to get out a "Thank you—" before the connection was broken with a sound that told Michael not to call again.

"Creep," Michael muttered. But now there could be no more excuses. If the man had only said he had no idea about Mary's whereabouts, he could have walked away with a clear conscience.

'He drove the short distance to Sycamore Street after looking up its location on a map he found in the car's glove compartment.

It had once been a lovely, cement paved street, lined with the beautiful trees that had given the street is name. But the pavement was now pocked with potholes, and tree roots had turned the sidewalks into uneven blocks like tectonic plates. The small homes set back from the sidewalk showed their age with peeling paint, lost patches of stucco, and lawns and flower beds that had given up expecting water.

The church was a small, New England-style, wood-frame building that looked as though it had been built at the same time as the surrounding homes and was equally shabby with a scruffy lawn, weathered paint and a couple of small holes in the stained glass rose window at the base of the belfry. Several beautiful Sycamore trees helped give the building a peaceful, friendly look. A low sign near the sidewalk indicated it was The Community Church of Jesus Christ, Reverend John Gregory, and that everyone was welcome. He took that as a good sign

The weed-speckled parking area at the side of the church was almost empty, and he saw Mary's Honda parked precisely between faded parking space lines. When he pulled in beside her car and shut off the engine, he could hear voices inside the church singing "Abide With Me." The chorus sounded decidedly thin.

After climbing a short flight of concrete steps, flanked by a narrow wheelchair ramp that led to ornate double front doors with one side open, Michael walked into a small foyer. From the foyer, three doors—two on the sides and one in the middle—opened directly into the church hall. Pews were on both sides of a narrow center aisle that led to a low dais with a lectern at front center. Benches for a nonexistent choir were against the wall on both sides of the alter area. Light from a second stained glass rose window high in the alter area and from small stained glass side windows bathed the room with multicolor. A large crucifix of Christ occupied most of the back wall under the rose window. On the left side of the dais, a small woman with her mouth clenched in grim concentration worked hard at an electric organ.

A collection basket on a stand near the door contained four crumpled bills: three ones and a five.

Michael hadn't expected to be going to church and he hoped that his jeans, mock turtleneck shirt, leather jacket and cowboy boots wouldn't get him kicked out. But looking at the congregation, he could see that his casual dress was not going to be a problem. There were only fifteen or twenty people in attendance, mostly elderly. Only a few men wore shirts with neckties. Many did not wear jackets. At the moment everyone was standing, singing timidly from song books that looked as care-worn as the hands holding them.

A slender man wearing a black suit stood on one side of the dais holding a Bible and singing with a tenor voice. He had thinning brown hair and a close-cropped beard. As he sang, he often reached up to adjust wire-rimmed glasses.

Mary stood in the front of the congregation, leading the song in a pleasant, clear voice. She wore a pleated, gray skirt, a velvet blouse in a different shade of gray, and a dark blue jacket.

She noticed Michael standing in the center doorway, and for an instant, her clear voice froze in the middle of a note and her eyes widened. She quickly picked up the cadence, but several members of the audience turned to see what had caught her attention.

She continued to sing as she watched him move to an empty pew near the rear of the room. He looked for a hymnal, but the rack fastened to the back of the pew in front of him was empty. He hadn't sung 'Abide With Me' since he was a kid, but to his surprise, the words came back, and he began singing quietly, finding a strange pleasure in the beautiful melody, something he rarely experienced in belting out a song with his band.

After the song ended with a ragged fading away of voices and organ music, Mary sat down in a front pew, and the man who Michael took to be Reverend Gregory, went behind the lectern. He cleared his throat, ran his fingers through his hair and adjusted his glasses. He smiled as though the congregation should be assured that he was friendly.

"Thank you, brothers and sisters. That was wonderful. Please be seated."

His voice was gentle, soothing, like a warm summer rain. Michael knew immediately why the church looked as though it hovered on the edge of bankruptcy. The man might be filled with religious passion, but he showed none of the drive, the passion necessary to operate a business, even the business of a small church. Not that a dynamic personality was necessary; there were many heads of companies who appeared to be equally kind and gentle. But such people had a core of steel that gave their enterprise a strong inner structure. Even Christ, gentle as he was, had been able to unleash the passion needed to drive the money changers out of his temple.

The Reverend cleared his throat again, apologetically. "Now, Mary Schaeffer has a message for you."

He moved aside and Mary took his place behind the lectern. Before she spoke she gripped the edges of the lectern so hard that her knuckles were white.

"Thank you, Reverend Gregory." She looks directly at the audience, her eyes level, sincere. "I guess you all know I'm a nurse at the hospital. I work in the orthopedic ward. Mostly with preemies—uh, premature birth babies—and other infants. Every day I see babies born to mothers on drugs, or alcohol. These babies are suffering. They desperately need help."

Her zeal had overcome her nerves, and she spoke with increasing assurance. "I'm working with a foundation designed to help these babies. But it's just getting started and we need funds; we need volunteers. We can't do it alone. Would any of you like to help?"

She paused, searching the audience for a response. But there was no response. Some people shifted uneasily, others could not look at her, but no one raised their voice or hand. From his place at the back of the room Michael suppressed a smile. They might feel sorry for the kids, but nobody wanted to give their hard earned money or their time to help out a bunch of drug addicts. He couldn't say he blamed them.

Mary bit her lower lip, then pressed on, but the little hope she'd had in her voice was gone. "It won't take much of your time. I promise."

She gazed at the audience with a hopeful little smile. Slowly the smile faded. "Well," she murmured. "Thank you." She stepped back and looked at the Reverend. "Reverend Gregory."

On the way to her place in the front pew, she put her hand to her eyes, her head sagging. Reverend Gregory slowly stood up and moved to the lectern. "Uh, well," he began. "Thank you, Mary. I'm sure we would all like to help if we could."

Michael had never seen such defeatism. Mary looked as though she was crying. The reverend's shoulders were slumped as though he were carrying an invisible world of trouble. Even the members of the congregation sat with their heads down, staring at their hands. He felt a surge of disgust that was so powerful it pulled him to his feet.

"Wait a minute," he said.

In the quiet room his voice echoed like a cannon shot. Heads jerked around as though pulled by a single string and eyes squinted at him in startled wonder.

The reverend stiffened and his head snapped up so fast he had to clutch his glasses. "Uh, sir. Are you volunteering?"

Michael edged out of the pew. "Volunteering? No, sir. No, sireee." He walked down the aisle and heads with mouths open and eyes wide swiveled to follow.

"I've got too much sense to volunteer. I'm with these good people. We've got too much sense to get mixed up in a wild scheme to save a bunch of babies." He was at the front of the room now, and he turned to look at the audience. From her place in the front pew Mary stared at him incredulously.

"Why should we?" His voice was quiet, but it cut like an edge of broken glass. "Their mothers are nothing but a bunch of drug addicts. Alcoholics." He pointed to Mary. "This lady said so herself. She admitted it. And we're good Christians. There are good kids out there, good kids who also need help, kids with good mothers and fathers. We're not going to waste our Christian charity on a bunch of druggies. You know how these things work. They start small. Right now she just wants a little of your time. Maybe send out a few fliers. Answer a few letters. So she gets you hooked."

Mary had half risen from her seat, her face white and her fists clenched. For a moment Michael though she was going to attack him, and he turned his back to walk up the aisle, speaking as he moved. "Then what? The next thing you know she'll want you to go to the hospital. She'll want you to look at those dirty kids. You'll see those incubators. You'll see those oxygen tubes in their noses. You'll see them struggle to breath. You'll see them threshing their arms and legs, fighting the pain of withdrawal. And that's what she wants. Oh, yes. She'll have you pick one up. Hold it, for God's sake. Hold a stinking drug addicts baby in your own arms like it was yours. Can you imagine?!"

He'd reached the end of the room, with every head turned to stare. He picked up the collection basket and started back down the aisle and the eyes followed, locked on his every move.

"And the next thing she'll want you to talk to their mothers! Drug addicts! Alcoholics! Then what? I'll tell you what!" He waved the collection basket. "Money! M.O.N.E.Y! She'll start to ask for money. Money for illegitimate babies. Of course, they may die without it. But what the hell."

Mary had moved to stand at the end of the aisle, waiting for him, her lips compressed in a thin line of rage.

He stopped in the middle of the aisle and his voice rose. "Their mothers are drug addicts! Why shouldn't they suffer?! That's the price for consorting with the devil. We won't let her drag us into that camp."

He paused, and his voice changed. He was into it now. It was as though he was on stage, giving voice to a new song, using his tone, his body, his emotion to pull the audience into his passion. He'd given them the verse; it was time for the chorus.

"Yes, siree. It starts little. Helping babies. Helping children. A little time. A little money." He whirled and flung his arms up. "And the first thing you know you've riled up the devil's camp! And the devil jumps up and says 'Don't help those babies. I forbid it! I got hold'a their mothers and I'm gonna get them!' And I don't know about you, but I'm scared to death of the devil. I'm sure not going to get him mad by loving those helpless babies. Yes, that's right: If we help those babies we'll be offending the devil, an none of us have got the guts to do that, have we? Christian mercy? What is that compared to fear of Old Scratch. I tell you, I'm afraid—I'm scared to death of that old devil."

He whirled and pointed at one of the men and held out the collection basket. "How about you? Are you afraid? Are you afraid to help those babies?!"

The man jerked his head back, his mouth slack. Then his jaw snapped shut. "No devil's gonna tell me what to do. I'll help." He pulled out a worn wallet and took out a five dollar bill, hesitated, then pulled out another, dropping both bills in the basket.

Michael cried, "Bless you, brother," and held out the collection basket toward a woman. "And you, Ma'am. Are you afraid of the devil?"

"No, sir," she snapped. "I'll help."

Michael walked down the aisle holding the basket out to different people and each one volunteered to help. When he came to the front of the room Mary moved aside for him. He handed her the basket, now almost filled with bills, and faced the congregation. "Good. The Christian spirit can lick the devil every time. We've got the devil by the nose, let's keep him that way with 'Lead Kindly Light.'"

He began singing the old gospel hymn, and with his urging, the people joined in. Still singing, he walked up the aisle and out the door.

In the parking lot he lit a cigarette and sat on the trunk of the rental car. He choked back a soft laugh. Why the hell had he done that? Looking back he realized it had really pissed him off when he'd seen Mary start to cry. He either had to turn and walk away or he had to do something about it. In this instance, doing something had been easy. As a kid he's seen fire-and-brimstone ministers work an audience, so he knew the routine. Once he got into it, he'd dredged up just the right emotional display necessary to sell the spiel and the audience had followed him like he was a Pied Piper. Now they were singing their heads off, probably feeling like they had one foot in heaven.

He was not surprised when a few minutes after the singing stopped, he saw the church doors opened and Mary come out. She stood for a moment at the top of the steps looking for him, and when she saw him, she moved briskly down the steps and walked toward the parking lot. The anger had left her face, but it was difficult to read the emotion that had taken its place. If he had to make a call, it would be consternation.

She started talking even before she reached him. "What happened in there? Why did you do that?"

Michael tossed away his cigarette. "Somebody had to. You bombed."

A hint of red appeared in her cheeks. "But suppose they believed you? 'The devil's camp,' for heaven's sake."

He grinned, knowing that it would irritate her. "It worked, didn't it?"

"Well, yes, but..." She looked more closely at him, and when she saw that he was smiling, she shook her head. "Oh, well. I guess I should thank you."

"My pleasure."

But..." She pushed at stray tendrils of her hair. "what are you doing here? You were supposed to call."

He shrugged. "Couldn't. I lost your number."

"So how did you find me?"

"The internet. They listed about a hundred Mary Schaeffers. I've been to see them all. You were the last one."

She rolled her eyes up, but she was smiling. "Don't you ever tell the truth?"

"Not if it'll get me in trouble."

"Lying could get you in more trouble."

He slid off the trunk of the car. "Join me for lunch. I'll tell you the truth."

"I'm not sure I want to hear it."

"You're right. I'll lie. It'll be a better story."

Her laughter had the same clear, innocence as her singing voice, and it made Michael wonder if she ever got mad enough to yell, mad enough to lash out in an emotional outburst. Probably not. He couldn't visualize her ever expressing any emotion by yelling. He had an aunt like that: she suppressed her anger, withdrew, only showing her rage through her rigid posture and an expression so stern it was more devastating than a tantrum. She had scared the hell out of him.

Chapter 6

The restaurant/bar was small, tucked between two shops on a street dappled with sunlight filtered through the leaves of old maple trees. Since it was Sunday morning there were few customers, which suited Michael just fine.

They sat in a booth upholstered with red Naugahyde. Although they sat side by side, to Michael's amusement Mary had made sure there was plenty of space between them. Light from a small sconce on the wall behind them reflected highlights from her hair, and Michael studied her from beneath his lashes as he toyed with his scotch and water. She stared at her coffee that she had leavened with a large dollop of milk, not cream.

Michael usually gulped down his first drink of the day, but for reasons he chose not to analyze, after one swallow he allowed the glass to sit in front of him untouched. For the first time in years he felt out of focus, disoriented. He hated the feeling of not being in total control of his life, his actions. It was one reason he'd never become involved with drugs or alcohol. His iron resolve was usually mistaken for aloofness, and in college had earned him the sobriquet of 'Mr. Cool,' a name he secretly enjoyed.

"You didn't have much of a crowd today."

"The usual. Most of our regulars."

"You mean that's it?"

She tried to smile. "Pretty much."

"And the collection—is that money for your charity?"

"After we pay the cost of running the church."

"You don't need a benefit; you need a miracle."

"Not a miracle." She straightened and her voice grew stronger. "Research. We just don't know enough about the effects of drugs on children. Your benefit would really help."

"Oh, yeah...about the benefit..." He hesitated. What he was about to say would put out the fire in her eyes, and he hated to see that happen. "The reason I came to the church..."

She leaned forward staring at him, her face set for bad news. He looked away. He had been trying to convince himself that his only reason for finding her was to talk about the benefit. But the truth was that the benefit was only an excuse; he had looked her up because he wanted to see her again.

But he couldn't tell her that. "The benefit..." He cleared his throat. "There might be, uh, problems."

"Problems?" She stared at him, expecting the worst.

"It's Benny and the guys. We've never done benefits. We don't do benefits."

"I see." Her voice said that she was not surprised.

"We'll make a contribution. A couple'a thousand. But we're pretty well booked up..."

Her voice was bitter when she said, "But you have time for parties."

Resentment made it easier for him to push aside his feelings of guilt and he gave it full rein. "What the hell do you know about it? What we do is damned hard work. It's murder on the nerves. We need to kick back when it's over."

"Harder than the nerves of those babies!"

"Well, they're not my babies!"

"Are you sure?"

The sneer in her voice startled him. It seemed so out of character with the warmth that had been such a part of her, and he stared at her, his face hard, fighting to control his fury. She realized what she had said and her eyes widened as though she couldn't believe the words had come out of her mouth. She took a deep breath. "I'm sorry. I didn't mean that, but...it isn't for me. You know that."

He picked up his drink and downed the remainder. The cold liquid helped take some of the fire out of his head. Time to change the subject. "Why me? Why'd you pick me for this charity gig?"

She seemed equally glad to talk about something else. "Well, you're famous. Your name would help a lot."

"There are a lot of famous people. More than I am."

"Most of them already have a favorite charity."

He wiped his hand across his mouth. "Yeah, well...more of them don't."

"I know. It seems like today helping children is not as popular as it is to get involved in politics."

"Politics is easier—and cheaper. Hugging Arafat or Castro gets you more publicity than donating to a charity."

"I know. Helping babies is not as exciting as making war."

Her tone of defeat grated on his nerves worse than if she had screamed and pounded the table. In an oblique way, she had to be referring to him. What did she expect? It wasn't his fault that those babies were crack-heads.

A picture flashed through his mind of dozens of premature babies writhing in agony as they struggled to breathe without the aid of incubators or respiratory machines and he shivered.

Mary was dabbing at her eyes with her napkin, and he caught himself about to make an impulsive promise. How many times had he suffered for having a quick tongue and an empty mind? A few tears and he was on the verge of blurting out something stupid. The more he thought about this girl and her charity, the more problems he could see.

Mary looked at him, her eyes showing resignation. "I'm sorry. I shouldn't push my problems off onto others."

He made a small gesture. "That's what charities do."

"I know, but...When you came to the church...I thought...well...how did you know the words?"

"What words?"

"To the songs. I heard you singing."

"I used to sing in a church choir."

"Oh? When?"

"I was young. Impressionable."

"It must have been strong. You remembered all the words."

He had to agree with her. When he had walked into her church and heard the singing, it had rolled back the years in a way he could not believe. The hours he had sat in church with his mother, the words of the minister, the words of the songs, must have had a tremendous impact on him. When he had made the pitch for money, it had been so easy to slip into the cadence of the fire-and-brimstone ministers he'd heard. The problem was that the words of those ministers had given him a conscious that now tore at his resolve.

He became aware that she was sliding out of the booth. "I think I should be getting back."

"Wait." He didn't want this time with her to end, and he searched for something that would keep her from leaving. "There is another way to look at it."

She stopped. "What's that?"

"Uh, publicity. We could use the publicity." He almost smiled, amazed that the thought had popped into his head, knowing that it was something he could sell to Benny and the guys. "I think Benny'd go for that. Hell, we might get more out of it than you will."

"If you do, think what you'd get out of a series of benefits."

He grinned at her. "You're dangerous. What is that, reverse psychology?"

She smiled. "No way. I doubt that it'd work anyway. I know you studied psychology at the University of Texas."

"I majored in music. But don't let it get out. It'll ruin my career."

Her mood changed abruptly, and she leaned forward. "When? I'd like to start as soon as we can."

"Well,...I'll have to check with Benny. We've got commitments."

"Those babies can't wait."

He shook his head. "They'll have to. We've got to set this thing up. Right now I don't know a damn thing about your church or the charity. Benny won't like that." He wanted to add that he didn't know anything about her either, but that could come later. It was enough to know that he would be seeing her again. And if this charity worked out, he would be seeing her a lot.

"The business end is already in place," she explained. "Reverend Gregory runs it. Except for the benefit itself, you don't have to be involved."

"Benny'll still want to check it out."

"I'll get the papers together."

"Yeah, okay." He hoped her paper work would survive scrutiny. It was going to be hard enough to sell Benny on the idea without any business problems. "But don't forget: we're only here a month."

She caught one corner of her lower lip between her teeth. "Maybe in the meantime you could speak again...at the church."

"Oh, no." The words erupted from him without thought. He stared at her, then shook his head. "It was fun, but that's it."

She cocked her head, studying him. "You were really good, you know. I'll bet you could fill the church."

"No, way. I'm no preacher."

"You could have fooled me. I thought you were wonderful."

He hadn't felt the kind of pleasure her words gave him in a long time. It was like the time he'd played for an audience the first song he'd ever written, and they screamed their approval. The wonder of it had blown him away, not because they liked his music, but because they understood what he was trying to say. Apparently, Mary hadn't merely heard the words; she understood the meaning behind the words. Even though he had chosen them simply to invoke a response, they still had come from his head. And, let's face it, they had worked—he had been pretty damn good.

But do it again...?

He had to look away from her face. She had a way of looking directly at him with wide, questioning eyes that got under his skin, eyes that could cause him to make promises he couldn't keep. And, for some reason, he didn't want to lie to her. That alone was disquieting. He lied to girls all the time; it was part of the game. But he knew that whether he lied or told the truth his chances of getting this one in bed were nil.

He sighed and wrote the number of his cell phone on a napkin "Give me a call when the papers are ready."

When she took the napkin, she put her hand over his. "Thanks. God will bless you. I know."

He didn't dare look at her eyes. Those eyes had gotten him in enough trouble already. But the worst part was that he didn't mind. He even felt pretty good about it himself. For now. The problems would come when he told Benny.

Anthony Stonz always wrote his speeches in long hand, using a legal notepad and a pencil, then dictated the results to Selene. When people heard his speeches, with words and brilliant ideas flowing from his lips so effortlessly, they assumed they were as easy to write as they were to speak. If they only knew. He sometimes spent hours agonizing over a single paragraph or phrase.

But now he was having trouble concentrating. When he slapped the pencil down on the notepad, Selene looked away from her computer's monitor, her brows drawn in worry. She said nothing. She knew what was bothering him.

Stonz pushed back from his desk and stood up. He selected a Cohiba cigar from its humidor and began the process of lighting it. The meticulous process, Selene knew, always calmed his nerves.

Using a cigar cutter that had been a present to him from the president, he carefully cut off the precise amount that would leave an opening appropriate for the cigar's size. Then, using only his index finger and thumb, he held the cigar in his mouth while he lit a wooden match which he allowed to burn for a few seconds away from the cigar so that its fumes would not contaminate the cigar's flavor.

When the match was burning properly, he carefully positioned its flame one centimeter from the cut end of the cigar. With the precision of a watchmaker, he applied the tip of the flame to the cigar's outer wrapping of thin cedar leaf while puffing slowly and rhythmically until the burn was set and the draw to his satisfaction. A satisfying expulsion of a cloud of smoke signaled the end of the procedure.

Taking the cigar from his mouth, he contemplated the burning end as though it were the lodestone of an oracle. "He's in California," he said. "Los Angeles."

They were in the study of his New York apartment. It was a large room with a fireplace where gas-fed flames licked at ceramic logs. Except for the fireplace, the two side walls were floor-to-ceiling with bookshelves. The books, except for dictionaries, thesauruses and volumes of encyclopedias, consisted primarily of law books and tomes on religion. All showed signs of usage over a long period of time. Several editions of the Bible appeared to be especially worn. There were no books of fiction.

Two leather covered armchairs and a huge leather covered couch did not seem out of place in the room. The parquet floor of maple and oak was partially covered by a large, antique Persian Isfahan carpet.

At the far end of the room, a massive desk of dark oak was situated in front of a bay window that provided a view of Central Park.

Selene's desk was smaller, functional. She watched Stonz as he began an agitated pacing, trailing cigar smoke. "Do you know who he is?" she asked.

"His name is Michael." He stopped and made a tight smile. "Why am I not surprised."

Selene realized he had referred to the archangel Michael. "Did you expect it to be someone called Bob or Pete?"

He chuckled and when he resumed pacing, his steps were slower, studied. "The name has no significance. The only thing that matters is that he has been chosen."

Selene took her fingers from the computer's keyboard. They were trembling. "Is it too late? Can...can you stop him?"

"Perhaps. He hasn't begun yet."

"Does he know?"

"I don't think so, which makes him vulnerable. I might be able to arrange...something."

"I hope so. You're so close."

"I know." Stonz stopped in front of the fireplace and spread his hands to soak up the warmth. "Read me back that last part."

Selene was momentarily taken aback by his sangfroid. Their whole world might be falling around them like the temple of Dagon, but Stonz did not appear to be concerned. She shook her head in admiration before she turned back to the computer. When she put her fingers back on the keyboard, they had stopped trembling. Anthony would know what to do. He always knew what to do.

Chapter 7

Michael held a glass of bourbon in one hand and gently beat on the edge of the bar with his other hand. The hours since he had left Mary had given him plenty of time to think. It had been stupid to promise a benefit performance. It wasn't just a matter of the time it would take; the logistics alone would put a hell of a strain on Benny and the guys in the band. Her promise that Reverend Gregory would handle everything meant little. There would be travel arrangements, hotel accommodations, tax ramifications and problems in dealing with all the other charities that, thus far, he had been able to keep at bay.

In frustrating indecision, he had made a quick choice between going out for a drink or calling one of the many chicks who had given him their numbers during one of their L.A. gigs. Somehow the thought of losing himself in the hot body of a willing stranger did not seem as appealing as it usually did.

It was just one more thing he knew wasn't like him at all. He pounded his hand once more on the bar, harder this time. "Damn!" The bartender paused in rinsing glasses in the bar's sink to look up at him. He had the look and the moves of someone who'd been at his job a long time and had heard a lot of stories

"That bad?"

"It's getting there."

"Job or woman?"

Michael put his untouched drink on the bar. "I guess you could say both."

Since it was Sunday evening the bar was almost deserted. There was a piano in one corner surrounded by chairs to make a piano bar, but no one was playing and the seats were empty. Above the bar a TV was tuned to a baseball game with the sound turned down as though neither the bartender nor the few people in the room had any interest in the game.

The bartender shook his head. "You do got problems."

"Yeah," Michael agreed. He shoved back off the bar stool. "But I know what to do about one of them."

"Which one?"

"The woman."

Behind him he heard the bartender laugh. "You picked the hard one."

Michael shook his head and waved his hand. The man was probably right.

He had parked near a street light and he used its light to look up Mary's phone number. He took his cell phone from the glove compartment, but before he dialed, he checked the time. Eight-fifteen. She should still be up. Although she might be at her church if they had evening services.

The phone rang three times before she answered. After her 'hello' he said, "Hi. It's me."

"Me?"

"Michael." She did not answer immediately and he added, "Michael Modesto."

"I know."

She was silent waiting for him to speak, as though expecting bad news.

In a way, she was right because he planned to tell her that she was out of his life, the whole gig was out of his life. The smart thing would be to tell her now when he didn't have to look into her hypnotic eyes.

But he didn't want to end it that way. "I need to see you."

"Now? Tonight?"

"Yeah? Can I come over?"

Again she paused as though she read something in his voice she didn't want to hear. "It's pretty late. I don't think that would be a good idea."

He smiled to himself. That was the understatement of the year. Seeing her might be the most stupid thing he had ever done in his life. But not seeing her could drive him mad. The only solution was to tell her how she was driving him crazy, and after she laughed her head off she would send him on his way and he could get on with his life. "You may be right," he said. "But... well, after I left you, I got to thinking. I need your"—he searched for the word—"advice."

There was life in her voice now. "All right. I live..."

"I know where," he interrupted. Then, before she could change her mind, he added, "I'll be there in fifteen minutes."

All the time he was driving to her apartment building he kept telling himself that it wasn't too late to turn around, to get his life back. Except he wasn't sure that he could go back to his old life. Events of the last few weeks had changed him until he didn't know who he was or what he wanted.

So he had to see her. Only she could close the door that seemed to be drawing him into some dark chamber.

He had his explanation all laid out by the time he arrived at the apartment building and punched her code in the intercom. When she answered, she gave him the number of her apartment on the tenth floor and buzzed the door open. He couldn't tell from the tone of her voice whether she was happy or angry.

Walking toward the elevator, Michael noticed that the apartment building had the comfortable feeling of long-time tenants, probably mostly senior citizens. He punched the button for the elevator.

In New York, Selene had turned back the carpet in Anthony's study to reveal a large pentagram meticulously painted on the parquet floor. All lights had been turned off, and the only illumination came from candles on the floor around the pentagram. The room was strangely silent as though all sounds of the outside world had been sealed away.

Selene knelt in the center of the pentagram, using both hands to hold a thick red candle that, as it burned, gave off the aroma of myrrh. Her only garment was a voluminous, white, silk gown that highlighted her bronze skin. She had removed the pins from her hair, and it hung below her shoulders like a skein of black water.

She was not looking at the candle in her hands. Her gaze was fixed upon Anthony Stonz as he stood before her, his eyes closed and his hands clasped in front of his chest. His face was composed, but his lips moved in a whispered incantation. Over his suit he wore a long, black cloak lined with scarlet cloth that glistened in the candlelight. Only the working of his tightly clinched hands betrayed the strain of his concentration.

Kneeling with the folds of her silken gown swirled across the pentagram, Selene struggled to hold the heavy candle steady. It was hot in the room, and she could feel perspiration building on her neck beneath her hair. She was supposed to concentrate on someone named Michael, to lock his image in her mind so that Anthony could work his spell. But the strain of holding the heavy candle was building, and it was becoming increasingly difficult to hold her concentration. Pain shot up one arm and she winced. Instantly, Anthony's eyes popped open, staring at her, their pupils dilated, and she responded by locking out the pain in her arms. Anthony's eyes closed, and he resumed his subliminal incantation.

The elevator doors slide open and Michael's hearing was assaulted with a type of music he had managed to avoid for years. He recognized it immediately: Montovani, a hundred or more violins sawing away at 'A Walk In The Black Forest' like a group of demented Gypsies.

Elevator music. He put his hands over his ears and backed a step. The stairs. He should take the stairs. Hiking up ten floors would be a chore, but it was preferable to enduring even thirty seconds of the cloying music.

He started to turn toward a nearby door bearing a sign that indicated it would open to stairs, and sudden panic seized him. He couldn't turn, couldn't move. It was as though his body had frozen. At the same time he felt an overpowering urge to move forward. He took a step, surprised to find that he could move toward the elevator. Another step. His feet seeming to have a will of their own. He reached the edge of the open elevator door just as the music swelled to a joyous climax as though each of the hundred violinists considered himself a Paganini incarnate.

To Michael the sickening sweetness of the sound was like fingernails being dragged across a blackboard, and he yanked open the door to the stair well and pounded up the stairs two at a time.

Anthony Stonz dropped his hands to his sides and said aloud, "Shades of hell!" The words startled Selene, and she almost dropped the heavy candle. She seldom heard such disgust in Anthony's voice. And there was something else, something she had never heard. Could it be defeat? That was impossible. Anthony Stonz never failed. And yet... something new had been there.

Anthony stepped forward and held out his hand to her. "Relax. Our time will come."

Selene blew out the candle, and with a sigh, set it on the floor. She took Anthony's hand and he helped her to her feet. Her legs felt stiff and cramped, and she took care to stay clear of the other candles as she stepped out of the circle.

She was about to pinch out their flames when Anthony stopped her. "No. The time will be soon. For now, rest."

She was glad she did not have to extinguish the candles. Lighting each one was a complex ritual, one that she enjoyed, but also one that was physically and mentally demanding. It had been a long time since she had been called upon for a theurgy, and she had allowed both her mental and physical capabilities to become weak.

She went to the big couch and stretched out, one arm across her eyes. Assisting Anthony, concentrating with such intensity, was terribly tiring. It had to be even more tiring for him. She wondered how long before they would begin again. It couldn't be too long; the candles on the floor would not burn forever.

At Michael's soft knock, Mary opened her apartment door and smiled. "Michael. Come in." She wore the same clothes she had been wearing at the church except that she had changed her shoes for a pair of oxfords with low heels.

Michael stepped inside and stopped, stunned. The layout of her apartment was pretty much as Michael had expected. The hall door opened into a living room with wall-to-wall carpeting in a soft beige color. A closed door on the right probably lead to a bedroom and bath. A small kitchen on the left could be seen through a large serving opening. A miniature fireplace had been sandwiched into a corner. A sliding glass door opened to a small balcony with a wrought-iron railing painted white. A barbecue grill with three spindly legs was on one side of the balcony near two white-plastic chairs.

What amazed Michael was the way she had transfigured the apartment with an elegant Louis XV Rocaille motif that seemed singularly out of place in a Los Angeles apartment. The oblong, mahogany table and chairs of the six place dining set had graceful, intricately carved, Louis XV-style legs. The bottoms and backs of the chairs were upholstered in rich Tudor style tapestry. In the center of the highly-polished table a French Faience vase held red and yellow roses that filled the room with a faint scent. A handsome sideboard displayed delicate, translucent ceramic porcelain china and fine crystal glassware. An ornate writing desk, with gleaming brass handles and drawer knobs, was highlighted with exquisite gold leaf marquetry. The arm chairs and the couch were upholstered with rich tapestry that matched the dining chairs. A low cocktail table in front of the fireplace held a sparkling silver tea set.

The walls displayed a panoply of prints, serigraphs and paintings that ranged from somber portraits to colorful still lifes and landscapes in elaborate, multi-tiered frames highlighted in gold tones that matched the Rococo furnishings.

In one corner a grandfather clock swung its long pendulum with stately insouciance.

Mary closed the door. "I must say, this is a surprise."

"Yeah, I know." He stood looking around the room. "Nice place."

"I like nice things. And they don't cost that much more."

"I'll bet."

"No, really." She helped him shrug out of his jacket. "Sit down. Would you like something to drink?"

Michael had been about to ask for a beer, but it would be like drinking beer in church. "Uh, no, thank you. Maybe some coffee if you've got some made."

She hung his jacket in a closet beside the front door. "I have if you don't mind instant."

"No, no. That's okay."

She closed the closet door and went into the kitchen area. Michael was not sure the delicate-looking chairs would support him without collapsing. Moving cautiously, he made his way to the sofa and sat down gingerly. Seeing him perched on the edge of the couch, Mary said, "Don't worry. It's stronger than it looks."

"Yeah, okay." He slid back on the tapestry, but still did not trust the couch's spindly legs enough to relax.

"What's the matter?" she said. "Was the party boring."

"What party?"

"You left in such a hurry this morning I thought you had something on your mind."

"Well, it wasn't a party." She did not answer and he heard the rattle of crockery. She had to be burning with curiosity about why he had called but was allowing him to take his time about explaining. "I, uh, called because...I've got to talk to you."

"Oh?" She came back into the room carrying a tray with a large ceramic coffee pot, two coffee cups, a sugar bowl, a milk pitcher and white cloth napkins with crocheted pink borders. She placed one of the napkins on the polished inlaid wood of the table before setting down the tray. "Have you changed your mind?"

"Changed my mind?"

"About the benefit."

"Oh. No, that's no problem."

"I'm glad to hear that." Instead of leaning over the low table to pour the coffee, she pulled up a chair and sat down. The pot had to be heavy, but she held it easily, tendrils of steam from its spout rising around her face.

"It's about what happened in the parking lot—and the baby."

"Cream and sugar?"

"Black. A little sugar."

She ladled half a teaspoon of sugar into one of the cups, stirred and handed it to Michael. He took it carefully. Spilling coffee on the spotless carpet would be a sacrilege.

"What about them?" she asked.

"I can't believe they really happened. I get the feeling they were all in my mind. Maybe I'm losing it."

He'd kept his voice casual, a half smile hiding his concern, but he could tell by the way she looked at him that she was not fooled. She had caught the underlying tension.

"I saw them, too," she said. "I think God is trying to tell you something."

"Yeah, like I'm the next pope. I haven't been in a church since I was a kid."

"But you did get a foundation. And when religion sinks in, it stays. It's in the roots, a solid core of decency, whether we like it or not."

"Well, He made a mistake this time." In a sudden burst of angry resentment, he turned his face upward and said, "Hey, God. Whatever it is you want, forget it. You got the wrong sinner."

Mary gasped. "Don't say that."

Michael turned to face her. The dam had burst and his face was set in lines of frustrated anger. "Look. I don't know what the hell is going on. I don't want any of it. Including the babies or the damn benefit."

She froze, her chin lifted in surprise. "I see."

Michael hated himself for the hurt in her eyes. But the fear was out of control, and he could not stop himself from adding, "None of this happened 'til you showed up. So just butt the hell out of my life."

Mary stood up. "I had nothing to do with it."

Michael went to the closet and took out his jacket. "Well, somebody did. And it sure as shit wasn't God."

He pulled on his jacket and reached for the door. Mary hurried toward him. "Michael, this has got to have some meaning. You can't turn your back."

"The hell I can't." He opened the door, then paused. "I'll make a contribution to your fund. But that's it. Just get out of my life."

He left the door open, striding down the hall toward the elevator. Mary stepped into the hall and started after him. "Michael. Let's talk about this. Please, Michael."

Michael jabbed the elevator button. The hell with the elevator music. He'd be damned it he was going to walk down ten flights of stairs.

"I don't care about the contribution." Mary had almost reached him when the elevator door slide open, and ignoring the saccharin music, he quickly stepped inside. There was an elderly man and woman in the elevator, and they moved aside to make room for him. He reached for the lobby button but saw that it was already illuminated. He turned to face the door and caught a glimpse of Mary's stricken face as the door slid shut. It was an image that he knew would haunt his dreams for a long, long time.

In his study, Anthony Stonz shook Selene awake. Stonz had been pacing, but she had drifted into an uncomfortable sleep.

She was awake instantly and stood to take the red candle that Anthony had already relit.

"Hurry," he said. "We don't have much time."

The candles that surrounded the pentagram were still burning and Selene estimated that she had only slept a few minutes. She quickly took her place inside the pentagram holding the heavy red candle in front of her. Anthony was already in his place, chanting, his voice a whisper, his eyes closed, his nostrils pinched with concentration.

The elevator had just started down when there was the sound of a thud as though something had bumped against the low ceiling, and the elevator shook and abruptly stopped. The elderly woman gasped and reached for the man's hand. "What was that?"

"It's all right. It's all right," the man murmured, but he stared at the ceiling, his face white.

Michael, too, stared at the partitioned ceiling. But he could see nothing unusual. He reached for the illuminated lobby button and was about to push it when the elevator shuddered and its floor abruptly dropped from beneath them. The woman screamed, a single piercing note that incredibly continued as the elevator plunged down, down the shaft in total free fall.

Michael fought against panic. He battered at the stop button, but it had no effect. He realized that he had only seconds to live—unless he did something. What? What? Lie down! Spread the force of impact! It was the only hope! "Down!" he yelled. He flopped down on his back. "Lie down."

If they heard him, the man and woman paid no attention. They clutched each other, the woman's scream climbing as the elevator gathered speed in a careening plunge.

Michael reached to pull them down, then realized it would make no difference. At the rate they were falling, it wouldn't matter. Nothing would matter. He found that he was muttering a prayer, which struck him as odd since he had just rejected God. The thought raced through his mind that everyone, when they knew they were going to die, instinctively reached out for something, anything that would protect them against the impending unknown. He...

Bam!

The explosive sound blasted his mind as a giant force slammed his body. A brilliant burst of light split his head before the light exploded into blackness.

Swarms of fireflies spangling the darkness. Spinning, swirling, advancing, retreating. How odd that they should slowly converge into a pinpoint of incredibly bright light like the tip of a welding torch. The light grew, became golden, moved toward him. He lifted his hand to shield his eyes, but the light was so bright his hand had no effect. He tried to shut his eyes, but for some reason they refused to close.

Even as he feared for his sight, the light softened, elongated, coalesced into the form of a human hand, a golden, glowing hand. The hand pointed, moved, writing in pulsing, glittering letters of gold. And the letters formed words: "I AM THE WORD AND YOU ARE MY MESSENGER." The words became fire, suspended in the darkness, burning into his mind.

Michael tried to speak, to question the words, to ask their meaning. But no sound came, and the words, the hand, disintegrated in a pyrotechnic burst of cascading golden light, and the light was swallowed by a profound blackness, leaving Michael with a bewildered sense of loss.

It was sound that pierced the horrifying darkness. To Michael's surprise he was able to blink.

He immediately closed his eyes against gritty dust. Dust? He knew it was dust because he could smell it. Dust that sucked into his lungs, making him cough.

Dust? Where did it come from? And why was he lying on his back listening to thumping sounds coming from somewhere above him. And voices. The voices of people, excited people.

He lifted his head. He was lying flat on something hard, his side jammed against some kind of crumpled wall. He sat up and felt debris of wood—or was it metal—fall off his body.

Oh, shit. The elevator. He must be dead.

He lay quietly thinking about his life. Was it true that he would now have to pay for his sins? If so, which sins were the worst? It did not seem reasonable that the small transgressions he had done when he was a kid would have much weight in the final judgment. The worst he could remember was stealing another kid's bicycle—which he had sneaked back to the kid the next day when his conscious kicked in. He had never cheated anyone, nor beaten up on anyone who didn't deserve it. There were the women, of course, but all his relationships had been mutual so, in his view, they shouldn't count against him. What about the ambivalent feelings he had for his father, hating him for leaving, and loving him for the good years before he had left?

On the other hand, he could not remember doing anything noble that would earn him a seat next to God. He was just an ordinary guy who tried to slide through life with as few problems as possible, hurting nobody deliberately and trying not to be hurt.

Well, maybe he would not make it to Paradise, but it didn't seem to him that he should be condemned to hell either.

And what about the hand and the golden words? They could not have been born of earth. He had to be in heaven.

So why was it so dark?

He coughed and spit out dust. Wait a minute... You don't cough if you're dead. You don't smell dust. You don't hear somebody pounding on the closed elevator door a few feet above you. And you don't hear the excited voices of people working on the door.

But if you're alive, you would feel pain. After falling ten floors, you would be writhing with the pain of broken bones and ruptured organs. Except there was no pain. He felt the same as when he had stepped into the elevator.

Oh God! Those people. The elderly man and woman. They had to be here.

He struggled to his feet and more debris tumbled to the buckled and twisted floor. It was too dark to see, but by feeling he determined that the roof of the elevator had collapsed, tilting away so that it hadn't crashed down on him. A tangle of elevator cable lay on top of the fallen roof. Talk about luck. The cable had to weigh hundreds of pounds.

The man and women had been standing on that side. They had to be dead. His suspicions where confirmed when he tried to move some of the twisted metal and wood and stepped in sticky fluid. He recognized it instantly. Blood.

Above him, the blade of a fire axe had been wedged between the double elevator doors and they were forced open a crack. "Give me a hand," someone said, and immediately people got a grip on the doors and they were slowly pulled apart. "Careful," someone called, and Michael recognized the voice of the manager. "It'll be at the bottom."

Through the swirling, light-spangled dust, Michael stared at the wreckage. He had been right about the collapsed roof. The horrible impact had twisted and tilted it so that its full force had smashed into the other side of the elevator. The side where he had lain was virtually untouched, even the floor—twisted and splintered everywhere else—was intact. Blood spilled from under the wreckage and through rents in the floor.

"I see it," a woman cried. "Oh, Lord. The roof's caved in."

As though to echo her thoughts, someone else said, "Oh, Jesus. They've got to be dead." Michael coughed, and the voice changed. "Wait. Wait. Something's alive."

The woman cried, "Michael! Oh, my God, Michael."

Mary! "Mary. I'm okay. I'm okay."

The manager, leaning through the open door, was almost pushed over the edge as the crowd behind him surged forward. He caught the edge of the door and shouted, "Back! All of you. Get back. Harry, let's have some help here!"

A security guard pushed to the front of the group, and at his urging the crowd reluctantly backed a few feet.

"Michael." Mary's voice was scarcely more than a whisper. "Are you all right?"

Michael lifted both arms. "I think so."

Holding fast to the edge of the door jamb with one hand, the manager reached down as far as he could. "Here. Can you reach my hand."

Michael gingerly stepped over the wreckage and, reaching as high as possible, gripped the man's hand.

"Got him," the manager said. "Somebody give me a hand."

A tall man knelt beside the manager and extended his hand. There. Michael grasped it, and with others helping, he was pulled up and over the edge where he sprawled on the floor.

He scrambled to his feet, saying, "Thanks. Thanks a lot." He took a step toward the open elevator door. "There were two others in there."

The first man turned to the security guard who was trying to hold back the crowd. "Harry. Find a ladder or something."

The crowd had virtually surrounded Michael, but Mary clawed her way to him. She threw her arms around him, hugging him with a fierce possessiveness. "Oh, my God," she cried. "I thought you were dead."

"So did I." Michael glanced toward the open elevator doors and said to the manager, "Those other two people. They're dead. I'm pretty sure."

The manager stared at Michael as though seeing him clearly for the first time. He pointed at Michael's shoes. "That's blood? You're hurt."

"No. It's from"—he motioned toward the open elevator doors—"them."

"Jesus," the other man said. "You don't even have a scratch."

Michael took his arms from around Mary and looked at his hands, turning them over to look at their backs. "You're right. Not even a scratch."

The manager shook his head. "That's impossible."

"I know," Michael agreed. "I know."

Mary brushed dust from Michael's shoulders. "You look terrible. Come on. I'll brush you off."

To relieve her anxiety, he said lightly, "The old brush off all ready?"

When she answered, he could tell by her tone that she was not fooled. "All ready? I've known you two months. That's a record for me."

In Mary's kitchen, he stood quietly while she used a brush on his clothing. To him, her gentle brushing, her soft breath and the faint odor of perfume was extremely erotic, and to break the spell, he took the brush from her to flick the dust from his pants legs.

The spell was further ruptured when she said, "I still don't understand how you could go through that without getting hurt. I mean, badly hurt."

"Me either, unless..." He stopped, wondering whether she would think he was crazy if he told her about the golden words.

"Unless what?"

He couldn't stop himself. He had to find out if what he had experienced was real. "When you were helping them open the doors, did you see anything, uh, unusual."

"How do you mean 'unusual'?"

"Sort of like a...a light."

"You mean inside the elevator?"

"Yeah?"

"No, it was—" She pulled her chin back to stare at him. "A light? Like we saw at the hospital?"

"Kind of like that, yeah."

"Oh, Michael." She sank down on a kitchen chair, never taking her eyes from his face. "You saw that same light. And you weren't hurt."

"It wasn't exactly the same. This was..." Now she was really going to think he was crazy. "It changed into a hand and, uh,"—he shook his head—"it wrote words."

She stood up slowly, her hands gripping the edge of the table.

"Words? What did they say?"

"They said...you're not going to believe this."

"Michael!"

"Okay. They said 'I am the word and you are'—and this is the incredible part—'you are my messenger.'"

"You are my messenger?"

"Yeah. Whatever that means."

She came to stand in front of him, her eyes huge. "Don't you see. That's why you weren't hurt. You're His messenger."

Michael shook his head. "Oh no. Not me. Big mistake."

"If it was a mistake, you'd be dead."

"I'll probably keel over the minute he realizes."

"Don't joke, Michael." She moved away, brushing back her hair. "That's all it said? There was no message?"

"Of course not. I think it was all in my head, sort of like a concussion."

"Then explain the baby, what happened in the parking lot. It has to be more than a...a hallucination."

Michael put the brush on the table. "It doesn't matter. I'm no messenger. Not even of God. Especially of God. No, thank you."

She looked at him with her mouth open. "But you have to."

He headed for the door. "No, I don't. This is a free country. And right now the only message I want to hear is 'This one is on the house.'"

Anthony Stonz took the candle from Selene, helping her to her feet. She swayed, drained of energy. "Is it all right?" she asked. "Did we do it?"

Stonz's lips tightened, his eyes half closed as though to conceal the thoughts behind them. "No," he said softly. "We failed."

Selene brushed her mane of hair away from her face. "Failed? I don't understand."

"He's being protected. We'll have to find another way." He turned and slowly walked toward his desk, his head bowed, his shoulder slumped. "Another way," he repeated.

Selene stood, unable to move. She had never seen Anthony fail, not in anything. A chill made her shiver. How was it possible? And what did he have in mind for this person who could not be killed? If not death, what?

Chapter 8

During the last two nights of the gig in Los Angeles Michael performed as though in a daze. His miraculous escape from death in the elevator accident—an accident that no one could explain—had been covered in all the newspapers and the band had played to packed houses. Habit carried him through the performances. Fortunately, the band had played the same material for so long and in so many venues that Michael could perform the routines automatically.

But there was no fire, no drive, in his performance. The audience could not tell that anything had changed, but the guys in the band could.

At the end of the gig, they were in the dressing room removing stage makeup and changing clothes when Creed Jazak come over to Michael's table. Creed shook a cigarette from a pack and offered the pack to Michael. "Hey, man," he said. "How's it going?"

Michael shook his head at the offered pack. "No thanks, Creed. I've given 'em up."

Creed glanced at the other guys and pulled his lips down in an expression of disbelief. "Maybe that explains it."

Michael looked up at Creed's reflection in the big mirror in front of him. "You got a problem with that?"

Creed lifted his hands. "Shit no, man. I just wanted to make sure you're not hurtin' somewhere."

"Hurtin'? You think I'm hurtin'?"

The other guys had turned to listen. "Yeah, well, you've been playin' like a fuckin' zombie. We figured you got to be hurtin'...maybe from that accident."

Michael controlled a rising irritation. Creed was right. He knew he'd been playing like his head was in another state. And, in truth, it was. When firemen had removed the mangled bodies of the elderly couple from the wreckage of the elevator, and a subsequent medical examination proved he hadn't been harmed, he'd been in shock. Actually, it was more denial than shock. Because he knew why he hadn't been killed. It had to be connected with that writing he'd seen, something about the 'Word' and him being a messenger of God. It had to mean that, somehow, his life was protected. Shit. He could probably jump off the Eiffel tower and not even break a bone.

But it wasn't just the feeling of immortality that had his brain all screwed up. It was the idea that maybe he actually had been chosen. But why? And what the shit was 'the message'? He felt as though the Sword of Damocles was dangling over his head, and when it fell, his life would no longer be his own, that everything he liked to do, everything he wanted to do, would all be skewered like dreams on a spit. And all because a stupid mistake had been made, and there wasn't a damn thing he could do about it.

How could he concentrate on the music when some outside force was, one by one, ripping away the strings that tied him to his past and his future, then used the strings to drag him to...to what? To some unknown fate? But one he was certain he would not like.

Well, he did not plan to go willingly into someone else's nightmare. It was his life and all the mystic signs, all the phantasmagoric proclamations of God-only-knew-who, were not going to force him to do anything.

"Sorry about that," he said to Creed. He turned in his chair to face Lyle, Aaron and Moss. "I know I've been playing like shit. I guess I was more shook up than I thought. But we're not due in Phoenix 'til next week. I'll have it together by then."

"Yeah, well," Aaron said. "Maybe we c'n find you another elevator. We could use the publicity."

They laughed and turned away, the rift healed. Creed started to move away, then paused. "You comin' to the party?"

Michael nodded. "Hell, yes, man. You know me. When I start missing parties, you'll know I'm dead."

Creed slapped him on the shoulder and moved away. Michael went back to taking off his makeup, but he did not like the image he saw in the mirror. He had lied to Creed. He would go to the party; he had to go to make everybody think he was back to normal, but he would not enjoy it.

The realization brought a surge of anger. That was being taken from him, too. But not if he could help it. They might be able to force a change in his style, but whoever they were, they couldn't keep him from enjoying his life.

He was wrong about the enjoyment. The party was so typical it was boring, like a song that had been rehearsed so much it had lost all its spontaneity, all its fun. As he had done on stage, he moved through the party like an automaton, laughing at the raunchy jokes, drinking more than he should, smiling at the groupies while trying to guess which one would be easiest to get rid of if he took her to bed.

He was talking to an exotic brunette with incredibly red lips and white teeth when he found himself comparing her to Mary. Mary's lips were not as full, but they had a sweet, fresh look. This girl's lips were so artificial they looked as though she had bought them from the same people who had done her dead-black hair. And Mary's eyes did not have the wise look of a hooker. And Mary certainly would find something to talk about beyond the way the Rolling Stones were sounding more like Arrowsmith every day, and how could U2 win so many awards when they hadn't had an original song in five years. Just for the hell of it he asked her whether she thought tax money should be used to provide hospital care for at-risk babies of illegal immigrants. After a painful thought process, she decided that rich people got all the breaks, except, of course, for band guys and movie stars who deserved every cent they could get.

It was then that Michael realized that his ennui was not because of the manifestations. He could ignore them. His problem was Mary Schaeffer.

He escaped to the balcony and closed the sliding glass door behind him. It didn't help any that this was the same balcony where he'd stood with Mary when they had met. She was the problem. She was what was screwing up his head.

But the most frightening thought was that he had ceased resisting; he actually enjoyed thinking about her. And that was the most frightening realization of all. From time to time, there had been other women who had occupied his mind, but they had always involved sex, and simply finding another girl who was even better in bed had wiped them from his memory.

But how could he get out from under the spell of this one when sex was no part of it.

He smiled ruefully. What a crock. Sex was a big part of everything.

Looking at the lights of the city, he wondered how much loving was going on behind all those windows. How many of it was pure animal lust—at least for one of those involved—and how much of it was real love, two people drawn to each other's arms by the power of love.

It would have to be like that for Mary.

And for him...

He wanted her more than he had wanted any woman. But was it because of lust or love?

He drained the last of his drink. That was a puzzle he would never solve. The price would be too high. Because it would have to be total commitment. Mary would never give in to lust. For her, sex would have to be part of a package, a package of love—love and respect—all tied up with a neat marriage vow complete with a ring and a promise of 'until death do we part.'

Would that be so bad? Was he ready for marriage, for kids?

All he knew was that life had ceased to be fun when he wasn't with her, and the only way to cure that kind of a fever was either to give in to it, to help it run its course, or to cut the cord, cold turkey, stop seeing her and allow time to do its work.

The thing to do was to throw himself into his work, to shake off the lethargy and regain that lost joy in music that could eclipse the pain of not seeing her.

He heard the door behind him slide open, but he did not turn. He was in no mood to make contact with anyone at the moment so when he heard a girl's voice say, "Michael?" he grimaced with irritation. He turned meaning to tell whomever it was to bug off. Then his mouth came open in a tide of pleasure, and he gasped, "Mary."

He had just about convinced himself that she was just another girl, a brief heartbeat in the scope of his life that would soon fade into a mystic memory. Now, one look at her and all his resolve vanished. The sensation was a mixture of joy at seeing her and dismay because this renewal was like a drink to an alcoholic, sending him into a spiral of drunken misery.

She had stopped just inside the door as though unsure of the reception she would receive, but when he was silent, she moved toward him. "I hope I'm not intruding."

Michael shook his head. She had been intruding ever since he had met her. "It's okay. I'm just surprised to see you."

She made a small grimace of deprecation. "I'm surprised to be here. I, uh, wasn't going to see you any more."

He did not answer, allowing the silence to express his disapproval. She nodded, scarcely moving her head, and turned toward the door.

Michael reached to stop her, her name on his lips, but he clamped his jaw shut and let his hand drop. He turned away, waiting for the sound of the door.

But it was her voice he heard. "Look. I'm sorry, but you can't just ignore this."

He did not turn. "Yes, I can."

"If you really are a messenger, it won't stop."

Disappointment made him grip the railing. He'd thought she was talking about their relationship, that her feelings for him were growing too strong to ignore. What a fool he was. Her only thoughts of him concerned the manifestations. He turned to face her, and disgust at his mistake made him growl, "It'll stop when you get out of my life."

Even in the dim light from the glow of city lights, he could see her face grow pale. But her eyes remained steady, staring at him as though she could convince him by their power. "I'll be glad to get out of your life as soon as I'm convinced I've...made a mistake."

"Well, be convinced. Do I look like a messenger of God? For Christ's sake, I've got a rock band. I've got rings in my ears. Tattoos. I drink, for Christ's sake. Does that sound like a God damned messenger of God? 'cause if it does, you're in the wrong religion."

"You're alive. That's proof enough."

"It proves I'm a lucky son-of-a-bitch."

"And the light? The baby?"

"For Christ's sake, we've been over that. It was just a stupid coincidence." He turned his back again so she could not see how desperately he was trying to convince himself while trying to convince her.

"All right," she said after a pause. "Do one thing for me. If I'm wrong I'll be out of your life."

"I already told you, we'll make a contribution."

"Not that." She hesitated. "I want you to speak again, at the church."

"The church?" He turned his head toward her. "Why?"

"When you spoke there, it was like...well, like you belonged. I think you felt it too."

He had felt it. Standing in front of the congregation, speaking from his heart, had felt more natural than standing in front of a mob of teenagers with obscenities rolling off his tongue like they were a part of him, accentuated with gestures he wouldn't want his mother to see. But he couldn't admit that to Mary. He could not even admit it to himself. "It was a show," he said. "Just another show. Without the bad words."

"Then do it again."

He turned to face her. "Again? No way."

"Why not? It'll prove it one way or the other."

Her words brought a chill of fear. He did not want it proved. He wanted to hold onto the wide, easy road of rejection. He did not want to be forced along some unknown path he would never choose for himself. "No," he gritted. "I don't need that."

"Yes, you do. I know it'd haunt me forever...not knowing what could have been. You'll never get over it. Never."

He sighed. At the moment he would give almost anything to be convinced she was wrong. Except that she was not. He was already haunted by doubt. Perhaps returning to the church would put the whole thing in the realm of just other bad dream.

"All right. When?"

"Tomorrow's Sunday. Why not tomorrow?"

"Tomorrow?" So soon? He needed time to think, time to marshal his forces of logic. But still... Why not get it over with? Nothing would happen. Nothing could happen. And the sooner he proved it the sooner he could get on with his life. He licked his dry lips. "I, uh, I wouldn't know what to say."

"If you are a messenger, it'll come to you."

"And if I'm not?"

"Then you'll just make a fool of yourself."

The image of him standing in front of a laughing congregation almost made him sick. But if he did come off looking like a complete idiot, it would be the sign he was looking for, the sign that he was just who he thought he was, a kid from Texas who made a damn good living fooling the teenagers into thinking he was some sort of musical guru. "Tomorrow," he said. "You're right. Tomorrow will be the end of it."

"Or the beginning."

"The end," he said, his voice flat and hard. "Believe me, it'll be the end."

Chapter 9

It had never seemed right to Michael that a Sunday morning should be cold and overcast. Sunday was God's day, a day of sunlight and warmth. It was not supposed to be a day that looked as though it might rain at any moment.

But perhaps God had presented him with a day that matched his mood. All during the drive to Mary's church he had struggled to find a theme—he refused to use the term 'message'—for his coming sermon. Writing a speech should be like writing a song: you thought of a theme, then built the lyrics and the music to support it. The difference was that a song usually just popped into his head. But nothing had popped into his mind for the speech.

Maybe he was trying too hard. All he had to do was wait until something came to him.

Except he didn't have time to wait. He had maybe an hour before he'd be standing in front of a bunch of people without a damn thing to say.

He had dressed for the role. His insecurity had dictated a dark suit, a black shirt, and a conservative dark tie with enough red in it so he wouldn't look like a wise guy from some mob. He had pulled his long hair back and fastened it into a pony tail that made him feel like an idiot but which, he had to admit, made him look pretty damn cool.

But the clothes failed to lure some reluctant Melpomene to help his dried-up creativity. He was still pondering when he pulled into the church parking lot. There were few cars in the lot. He wondered if it was because he was early or because hardly anyone was going to show up. He smiled as the thought crossed his mind that maybe they had heard he was going to speak and had decided to stay home and watch some real preacher on TV.

He parked next to Mary's car and sat for a moment with the car's engine running trying to convince himself that he should just drive away and get on with his life. That's what his father would have done. How many times had he heard his father say, "Just go with the flow. Life has got enough problems without making your own."

But that philosophy had made his father a loser, a man with no future beyond the day. Of course, Rusty Modesto never considered himself a loser. He was just an average, hardworking, beer-loving hard-hatter who stayed out of trouble by going with the flow. To him life was a matter of luck, and he was unlucky. And when you got fed up, you went looking for a rainbow in a bottle. Luck. Life was all a matter of luck.

But experience had taught Michael rarely to accept anything at face value, especially the axioms of his father. Observation had convinced him that his father was as wrong about luck as he had been about so many other things. You made your own luck, and today he was doing a damn poor job. Instead of moving ahead, he was digging himself into a hole that threatened to turn into a grave. The smart thing to do was to stop digging. But there was one thing his father had said that rang true: To stay out of trouble, go with the flow. So he was going with the flow. He just hoped the flow was going in the right direction.

A tapping sound on the window yanked him out of his thoughts. Mary. She was leaning over smiling at him through the side window.

He turned off the car's engine, and she stepped back so he could open the door and climb out.

"Hi," she said. "I'm glad you got here early. We can go over a few things."

Looking at her he experienced a koan like a dash of crystal clear water. She was the reason he had come here today. It wasn't to find out about miracles. It wasn't to search for some secret truth that could save his soul. And it sure as hell wasn't to find out if he really was a messenger of God.

He stared at her for a moment, allowing the wonder to sink in. She wore a navy blue suit with a double-breasted jacket over a pale blue blouse that highlighted the blue in her eyes. A skirt matching the jacket reached to her knees. She had piled her hair high and secured it with French braids. Her only jewelry items were small earrings encrusted with sparkling, diamond-like cubic zirconium.

"Go over a few things," he repeated. "Yeah, fine."

As they walked to the church she moved aside a little so she could look at him. "You look great," she said. "I like the suit. And the tie."

She did not mention his hair, but he decided it was because she had too much class to gush.

"I wore it so you wouldn't have to buy one for the funeral."

Her steps faltered. "What funeral?"

"Mine, when I fall on my sword."

She laughed. "You'll do fine. It's just another stage."

"Not the same thing. I know what I'm doing in front of the band. Now..." He shook his head. "I have no idea what I'm going to say."

"Oh. Well, just talk about how hard it is to be a Christian. They always love that one."

"Yeah, I can talk from experience."

He had answered lightly, but the more he thought about it the more he realized that she might have given him the theme he had been looking for. And given a subject, he had been known to discourse at length as though he knew what he was talking about. He was feeling a lot better when they entered the church.

Michael noted with satisfaction that there were only three or four early arrivals sitting quietly near the back studying what he assumed were Bibles. If no one else showed up, he wouldn't have to look into an ocean of bored faces. Reverend Gregory had been checking to see that music books were in the racks in the back of the pews, and he hurried to meet them holding his hand out to Michael. "Mister Modesto. I'm so delighted you could be here."

"Yeah, I'm glad I could make it," Michael said, but under his breath he added, "Oh, yeah I am."

Gregory continued with his instructions as they followed Mary down the aisle. "Mrs. Gardner always plays an intro; then I give an opening prayer. After that Mary leads the congregation in a hymn. Then comes the sacrament. I'll say a few words and we'll sing again, then I'll introduce you."

"Okay," Michael agreed. "Sounds like a plan. But be ready to jump in if I bomb."

Reverend Gregory smiled and patted him on the shoulder. "I'm sure you'll do just fine. Now, if you'll excuse me..." Without waiting for an answer he returned to checking the hymnals.

Mary indicated the first row of pews. "You can sit here. I'm going to go out front."

"Yeah, okay." Michael sat down, and reached into the breast pocket of his suit. "Damn. Forgot my pen. Do you have one I could borrow?"

"Yes. In my purse. Be right back."

She hurried up the aisle. Michael had to get a firm grip on his resolve to keep from turning his head to watch her walk away. She was one of the few women he could remember who looked almost as good from the back as she did from the front—almost.

He had remembered to bring the small notebook he usually carried to jot down ideas for songs, and when Mary returned with the pen, he was leafing through it, stopping from time to time to check something he'd written long ago.

"Here you are."

Damn. He'd forgotten to watch her come back down the aisle. That had to say something for his dedication.

"Thanks," he said, taking the pen. It was a fine Cross ball point. "I won't steal it. Not in church."

"I hope not," she said. "It was a gift."

"Oh? A boy friend?" The pen was expensive. Not something that would be given by a casual acquaintance. He had spoken casually, but he waited tensely for her answer.

"No. My parents."

He smiled. He was really glad to hear that. Maybe she didn't have a hot and heavy boy friend.

"If you need me," she added moving away, "I'll be out front."

"Okay. Oh, may I borrow your Bible?

"Of course. It's there on the bench."

For the next several minutes, he concentrated on making notes, trying to memorize the good ones, even though he couldn't remember ever seeing a reverend or a minister looking at notes when he spoke. Maybe it was considered gauche. He certainly didn't want to be the one to challenge established protocol. Just get up, throw out a few biblical quotations and sit down. He would have proven to Mary—and himself—that he was no messenger of God or anyone else.

As he made his notes, he heard behind him the rustle and low voices of people sliding into the pews. Mrs. Garner, after a few tentative notes, began playing random but appropriately ethereal chords. When Reverend Gregory walked down the aisle and took his place at the lectern, Michael glanced behind him. The room was half full, about what it had been when he'd been here the last time. No one sat in the front pews. There seemed to be a tacit rule that they were reserved for speakers. And every eye behind him seemed to be focused on the back of his head, giving him a mounting sense of vulnerability.

Gregory cleared his throat loudly to stop conversation. When the rustling and muted conversations died, he intoned a short prayer. During the prayer Michael sat with his head lowered but with his eyes open, staring at the worn wood of the floor. Listening to the prayer gave him a feeling of deja vu. How often when his mother was alive had he sat on the hard bench of a church pew and listened to the voice of a reverend droning out a prayer?

After signing off with "In the name of Jesus Christ, Amen," the reverend sat down and Mary come down the aisle, carrying a song book. She stopped in front of the dais and asked everyone to stand. When everyone had dutifully obeyed, she nodded to Mrs. Gardner who began a plodding rendition of 'Lead Kindly Light.' Mary had a pleasant voice, but it was small and she had to strain to be heard. But with help from a couple of strong voices in the congregation, the group was dragged through the song like heavily laden barges being pulled by tugboats.

When Mrs. Gardner brought the song to a crashing close, Mary shut her song book with a smile and sat down beside Michael, sitting bolt upright with her legs tucked back under the seat.

After sacrament was served by two young deacons, Reverend Gregory again took his place behind the lectern. In a low, monotonous tone be began speaking about why there was so much evil in the world, punctuating his speech with memorized passages from the Bible.

The reverend finished speaking amid total silence. He cleared his throat and went to sit down. Michael wanted to look around to see if the silence was caused by awe or because everyone had fallen asleep.

In Michael's opinion it had not been a bad sermon, but the Reverend's delivery was so dry and uninspired that he sounded insincere. And Michael knew that when you're alone in front of a crowd, the worst thing you could do was to sound insincere. The old saying that 'you had to believe before you could make others believe' was wrong; you only had to make others think you believed.

That was what he had to do when it was his turn to speak: he had to sell sincerity.

Mary stood up and motioned for the audience to stand and they struggled to their feet, song books in hand. She told them the page for 'Abide With Me' and Michael winced. He was hoping they would launch into something a little more rousing.

When the song finally trailed off in ragged harmony, Mary closed her hymnal and paused before she said, "We have a visitor today: Michael Modesto. Those of you who were here a few weeks ago might remember that Michael spoke to us. He was very, uh, moving. And he has agreed to speak again today. Michael."

She smiled at Michael and went to sit down.

He stood up and turned to face the congregation. "Thank you, Miss Schaeffer." He looked at Gregory. "Reverend, may I borrow your Bible?"

Gregory blinked and slowly handed him the Bible. Holding the Bible over his head with one hand, Michael walked to a place in front of the lectern. He had a momentary panic when he heard his own footsteps. Lord, it was quiet. When he and his band came out on stage, kids were screaming and yelling so loud the sound hid any mistakes. But here...Well, what the hell. If they didn't like him that was their problem. They would never see him again anyway.

He squared his shoulders and turned, scowling, ignoring individual faces, forcing himself to see the congregation as a single, impersonal unit. Abruptly, he brought the Bible down, slapping it into his other palm with a sound like a cannon shot. At the same time he shouted, "Judgment day!" and heads snapped back as though he had slapped them.

In a calmer voice he went on, "Yeah, it's coming. Judgment day. But you'd better not wait to clean up your act. Today, all you hear is that you shouldn't be judgmental. Judge not lest you be judged. I say that's bull. You are going to be judged! Reverend Gregory said it: the devil is loose and if you don't judge yourself, he'll do it for you. There is such a thing as right and wrong, good and evil. You've got to make a choice—a judgment. Ever hear of a prophet named Mani or Manichaeus? Lived in the third century. Pagans believed everything in the world—good or bad—came from a single God. There were minor

Gods, but one supreme source. But the prophet Manichaeus got it right. He said there were two forces: God and Satan, good and evil. It's that simple. If you don't teach your kids to know the difference—if you don't teach yourself to know the difference—God help us. You've got to be judgmental."

He bound to the dais and stood behind the lectern. "Judge yourself!" He slapped his hand on the Bible with a resounding whack that brought gasps from the audience. "How do you do that? How do you program yourself to do what is right? You do it like you would any other project. Program your mind. Give yourself a mind-set to do what is right."

He went on speaking off the top of his head, calling up every cliché that he could remember, "What you think is what you get," and "Act like the person you want to be," and the favorite of Coach Vince Lombardi: "You can't win unless you prepare to win."

From somewhere in the past, a passage from the Bible leaped into his mind and he found himself saying, "And I saw the dead, small and great, stand before God: and a book was opened which is the book of life: and the dead were judged according to their works." He knew he had misquoted, but it didn't matter.

He left the dais and strode up the aisle, talking as he moved, "You hear that? You will stand before God and you will be judged! Judgmental! What will be written in your book of life? Good or evil! Who controls your life? God or Satan? Because the devil is here. No, you can't see him. He's like the wind. You can only see evidence that he's here. He'll never stand up in front of you and tempt you by saying, 'Forget the word of God. Forget everlasting salvation. Come with me. I'll give you rewards right here on earth.' Oh, no. He's too smart for that. So what does he do?"

Deliberately, he dropped his voice to a wheedling whisper. "He starts with little temptations. He knows you won't steal a dollar, so he gives you the chance to steal a dime. He knows you won't hate Jesus Christ, so he gives you the chance to hate your neighbor." His voice grew stronger as he began building toward his climax. "He knows you won't condemn what you *know* is good, so what does he do? He calls good evil and evil good!"

Watching the faces of his audience, Michael almost laughed at their intense, unblinking concentration. Damn. He was good.

He quickly moved to the front of the group and made a dramatic spin as he shook the Bible at the audience and his voice thundered, "But beware! The Prophet Isaiah tells us: 'Woe unto thee that call evil good and good evil, that put darkness for light and light for darkness, that put bitter for sweet and sweet for bitter.'"

He stepped up onto the dais and leaned over the lectern, staring into the rapt faces. "In your heart you know, you know what is good and what is evil. Who is going to rule your heart?—God or the devil?"

Then he made the mistake of wondering what the hell he was talking about and he went dry. His mind searched for words, a quotations, something to fill the dreaded silence, and came up empty.

He looked at the audience and his gaze centered on Mary. She was sitting on the forward edge of the seat, her hands clasped together in front of her chest, her eyes so wide they looked frightened. Seeing her, his sense of panic vanished. He smiled at her and said the words that he remembered almost all the reverends he had ever known had used to end their sermons: "Thus sayeth the Lord. Amen."

The congregation was silent, only their eyes moved as he stepped down from the low stage and went back to his seat beside Mary. He had no benchmark to determine whether their breathless silence was good or bad. One did not applaud in church. And you sure as hell didn't whistle and scream like a demented teenager. So how did you know if you were good or terrible?

He leaned over and whispered to Mary, "How'd I do?"

Her eyebrows pulled down in studied concentration. She turned her head and started to say something, then stopped. Instead, she whispered, "We need to talk."

Michael slumped on the bench. Her noncommittal words had to mean that he had bombed. Well, what had she expected? He was no preacher. Maybe bombing out was the best thing he could have done. She sure as hell would never ask him again, and he could get back to his hedonistic life.

Reverend Gregory moved to the front of the room, and he nodded toward Michael and smiled. "Thank you, Brother Michael. You've given us a lot to think about."

The thought that popped into Michael's mind was: Brother Michael? Oh, shit!

"Now," Reverend Gregory said. "Sister Mary will lead us in a closing number."

Mary stood up and moved to the front of the room. "We will close with—" She stopped and looked down at her empty hands, her mouth forming a small circle of surprise. "Oh," she said. "I forgot my book."

She blinked and looked up at the audience as though surprised to find she was standing before them. She took two swift strides to the front pew where she'd been sitting and picked up her song book. "Well." She laughed with the real pleasure that Michael liked to hear. "I've never done that before. I believe we'll close with..." She thumbed through the book to a page marked with a bit of paper."...page one twenty- seven, 'I Have A Message.' "

Michael jerked his head up, wondering why she had chosen that particular song. Was she mocking him? Well, hell. He never claimed to be a Billy Graham. It had been her idea for him to speak.

But watching her as she sang, her face flushed in earnest rapture, her eyes bright and guileless, he realized that she could never have such malicious thoughts. If the song were meant to send him a message, it had to have been chosen by a hand other than hers.

The thought made him shiver, and he picked up his hymnal, concentrating on the music so he could ignore the nagging suspicion that he should have said more. Much more. But the words had eluded him. They seemed to be lurking somewhere in his mind, indefinite, elusive, shadows just out of reach. Could it be "The Message"? The more he thought about it, the more his irritation turned to a slow anger. Was he to be tormented by this damned "Message" for the rest of his life? Was he supposed to just keep talking until he accidentally hit upon the truth like a bunch of monkeys pounding away at typewriters until they produced 'Hamlet'?

Actually, there was no reason for him to dwell upon it. This was his last speech. He had taken a shot at the silk and produced dross. If there was some great "Message," someone else would have the honor of delivering it.

With the realization, he felt a tremendous sense of relief. It was over. He could go home with a clear conscious.

As the congregation poured their hearts into the song, Reverend Gregory passed a wicker donation basket among the sparse group, starting at the rear and working his way toward the front. He did not extend the basket toward Michael sitting alone on the front pew, and Michael assumed it was because he was a guest, which was too bad because he knew that the church had to be struggling and he would have chipped in at least a hundred.

When the song ended Reverend Gregory handed the basket to Mary, then intoned a brief closing prayer. As soon as they had murmured "Amen" the members began edging out of the pews and walking up the aisle. Reverend Gregory hurried to take up a post outside the door where he shook hands with everyone and invited them to return next week.

Michael was in no rush to leave. He wanted to get away as quickly as possible, but Mary had said they had to talk. He hoped she meant to tell him his services were no longer required.

She moved toward Michael, holding out the basket. He assumed it was a hint for his missing contribution, and he reached for his wallet. His hand stopped when she said, "Look, Michael. This has to be twice as much as we ever got before."

It didn't look like much to Michael. The small basket was less than half full and most of the worn and crumpled bills he could see were ones with only one fiver. The entire contribution probably would not add up to fifty dollars. He reached for his wallet again. "He forgot me," he said. "I want to be saved too."

She gave him a sharp look of disapproval, as though to admonish him for joking about something so serious. "You don't pay to be saved. Besides, you were the guest speaker. That's contribution enough."

"Maybe." He extracted a hundred dollar bill from his wallet and tossed it in the basket. "But I like to hedge my bets."

She started to reach for the bill, then hesitated. "Well, we certainly could use the mo—the contribution."

"Call it a farewell gift."

"All right, but..." She looked up at him, her eyes wide. "Farewell? You're not coming back?"

He smiled and shook his head. "It's like bungee jumping. You do it once to prove to yourself you've got the guts. But twice only proves you're stupid. In my case, I've done both."

"But everybody liked you." She held up the basket as evidence. "They never gave this much before."

If this was more than they usually took in, it meant that they probably only picked up ten or twenty dollars each Sunday. Hardly enough to keep paint on the building. But that was their problem.

"Yeah, well...It was fun but not that much fun. Besides," He grinned. "I don't have anything more to say."

"I don't believe that. You must have a million things you could say."

"Right now, I can only think of one: what about lunch?"

Taken by surprise, her eyebrows lifted. "Lunch? Oh. Well, I usually have lunch with John."

He looked toward the door where the Reverend was shaking hands with a woman in a wheelchair. He was not pleased by the idea of having the Reverend along, but he could hardly refuse to ask him. "Bring him along," he said, keeping his face impassive so she could not see his disappointment.

Mary smiled and began walking toward the door. "Good. I'll ask him." Michael fell in beside her as she added, "Maybe he can talk you into coming back."

Michael was silent. The only person who could possible bring him back was her. And going to church was not his idea of a date. In a way, he was not clear about what a date with Mary should be. Where did you take such a girl? What did you talk about when the entire date was not designed to get her into bed as soon as possible. He would have to give that some thought.

Reverend Gregory was helping an elderly women down the wheelchair ramp next to the front steps when one wheel went off the ramp. Reverend Gregory fought to pull the wheelchair upright, but the combination of the woman's weight and the misaligned wheels was too much for him and the chair teetered on the edge of disaster.

Mary hurried to help, but Michael was quicker. He leaped forward and grabbed the wheel on the down side and muscled the wheelchair back upright. He steadied the wheelchair and the two men eased the chair down the last step.

Only when the wheelchair was on the level concrete walkway, did the woman release her death grip on the armrests. She was breathing hard and put one hand to her face before she looked up at Michael and reached out her hand. "Thank you, young man."

"You're welco..." Michael did not finish the sentence. Her hand closed around his and...Pain! Michael grunted in shock as pain slammed into the base of his spine as though he had been struck by a powerful electric current. He stood, frozen, unable to move, his eyes bulging. Pain! Pain gripped his back. Pain so intense he couldn't breath, couldn't think. Then his legs collapsed and he fell to the concrete. He was aware that his eyes were open, staring into bright sunlight, but the pain would not let him blink, would not allow him to move as wave after wave of agonizing pain radiated from his spine.

Darkness began to close in. Blessed darkness that eased the pain, sucking him into an oblivion that took away all feeling, leaving only the memory of the elderly woman staring at him.

And the darkness grew dense, and like a malignant pool, began to envelop him. Frantically he struggled, but it was a struggle against a drowning horror. He couldn't breath. He couldn't move.

Then, just as the suffocating darkness poured into his brain, it wavered, retreating before a glimmer of light.

He struggled, tried to shout, tried to reach the blessed light. And the light grew brighter, overpowering the darkness. Brighter. Brighter. Driving away the horror. And the pain. The darkness! The darkness was the pain. And the light was forcing it away, driving it into eternity. Bright light. Flooding into a blinding brilliance filled with such an overwhelming sense of love and compassion he wanted to remain in its joy forever.

A voice. From far away. Calling his name. And the light dimmed, faded. He reached for it. Struggling for words, for some way to hold it.

"Michael. Michael." It was Mary. Calling his name. Driving away the blessed light.

He wanted to tell her not to call him, not to drive away the paradise.

Feeling returned. But no pain. The light had cleansed his body with a consuming fire, a fire that burnished his senses into incredible sensitivity. He had to get up, to move, to prove that he was not paralyzed by the attack. Because it had to have been an attack. Someone must have struck him from behind. He probably had a fractured skull. That would explain his feeling of paralysis.

Almost frantically, he struggled to rise, pushing himself up with his arms. But his legs would not respond and he stared at them in amazement. They felt weak, detached.

"Michael!" Mary knelt beside him. "What happened?"

"Somebody hit me," he gritted. He grabbed the railing beside the steps and tried to pull himself to his feet. "I—"

Mary and Reverend Gregory helped him stand. At first he had to support himself by holding to the railing of the ramp, but his legs were growing stronger by the second.

He saw the woman who had been in the wheelchair standing next to him, holding on to the railing with both hands, her mouth open in incredulous wonder. Only her eyes moved as she looked down at the wheelchair that had fallen on its side.

Reverend Gregory stared at her, as though his mind was unable to comprehend what his sight was projecting. "My God." His voice was a whisper, afraid to break the spell that was holding the woman erect.

Mary looked from the woman to Michael. "It happened again. Just like with the baby."

Michael shook his head. "No. I don't want that."

Strength had returned to Michael's legs, and he righted the woman's wheelchair and pushed it toward her. "Here, lady. Here."

She reached out toward the familiar chair, with one hand. She took a tentative step, her lips pressed tight against anticipated pain. She paused, steadied herself. She released her grip on the banister and took two more steps. Her taut lips relaxed into a smile, and she looked at Michael. "Thank you," she said. "Thank you."

Michael reached up and, locking his fingers behind his head, walked away. "I don't want this," he said. "I—don't—want—this."

The woman wavered and took a step toward the banister. "I guess I'm a little weak."

Reverend Gregory quickly grasped her arm. "Mary," he said. "The wheelchair."

Mary reached for the wheelchair, but the woman shook her head. "No. The steps. I'll sit on the steps." She looked at the wheelchair. "I'll never sit in that again."

Michael kept on walking. The woman was right; she would never have to sit in the wheelchair again. And all because she had taken his hand. Maybe what had been happening to him was not some morbid illusion. Maybe he really had been chosen to be some sort of messenger of God.

He wiped a hand across his face. Messenger of God? He did not want that! He might have been dissatisfied with his life, dissatisfied with where it was headed, but it was better than this! If he was a messenger, what the hell was the message? Healing people? And half killing himself in the process? That was no blessing; that was a curse.

He would reject it. He would not be forced into a life he did not want. Even God would not do that to him. Would he?

He had reached his car in the church parking lot and he got in and drove away, away from the church, away from Mary, away from God.

Chapter 10

In Washington, D.C., Anthony Stonz, his coat collar turned up and his Homburg pulled down to protect against the cold, walked slowly along a street fronted with sagging industrial buildings. His hands were clasped behind him, his head bent in thought. He neither saw nor heard the occasional car that sped past. If he were concerned that he had strayed into a neighborhood where the only people who prowled the darkening streets were predatory animals looking for prey, he gave no indication. His mind was occupied with the conundrum of a man he had yet to deal with but who might be beyond his capabilities. He had learned the man's name from a brief article in a Los Angeles newspaper about a man who had miraculously survived an elevator crash that had killed two other people. "Michael Modesto," he murmured. "Michael. Prescient?" He shook his head. "No. Improbable. And yet..."

It was the 'and yet' that was causing him to lose sleep. Events of the past few weeks were understandably vague, but from what he had been able to ascertain, this Michael Modesto had experienced an authentic theophany. Was he the long awaited Chosen One? Or was he simply a prophet, a messenger?

It was all so vague that searching for the truth was like peering through shifting fog with only brief glimpses of an apocalypse. "Aye. There's the rub," he muttered. Apocalypse or apocryphal? Had Modesto's escape from the elevator crash been due to divine intervention or pure luck? He had to find some way to be sure.

His steps quickened as the glimmer of an idea began forming.

"Hey, man."

The lazy insouciance of the voice hid its menace so that Anthony was not immediately alarmed. He looked up, his steps slowing when he saw the figure of a large man blocking the sidewalk ahead of him. The man was dressed against the cold with a bulky jacket and a watchman's knit hat pulled so low it almost covered his small, mean eyes.

Anthony changed direction to walk around the man, but the man took a step to the side to block his path, forcing Anthony to stop and face the man or to shove past him, a move that did not carry a lot of wisdom.

The man held out one of his hands. "Give it up, man." His voice still had the lazy tone of someone who did not expect an argument, the tone of experience and infinite confidence.

At first Anthony considered complying. He carried considerable money in his wallet, but it certainly would not hurt him financially to part with it. If it had not been for the sense of frustration that had permeated his thinking for the past several days, he probably would have done so. He was actually reaching for his wallet when an uncharacteristic flush of anger took over his thinking. He lifted his head to stare into the man's eyes.

"I don't think so," he said.

The man's scowl abruptly changed to a look of alarm and his eyes, locked on Anthony's stare, grew round, bulging. To Anthony's surprise the man was able to get the gun out of his pocket. Then the hand began to tremble and the gun slipped from his fingers. For an instant Anthony was afraid the jar of the gun hitting the pavement might make it fire and he winced. He was not worried about being shot, but the sound could have unwanted consequences, primarily a loss of time should the police arrive and began asking questions.

But the gun did not fire and Anthony shifted his attention back to the man whose body had become as ridged as an ice carving. "Go to the police station," Anthony told him. "Confess your sins." Anthony almost smiled. He liked his choice of words so much he said it again. "Confess your sins. And," he added, "sin no more. Go."

Anthony stepped aside and the man stepped past him and began to walk away. "Wait," Anthony said, and the man stopped without turning. "Don't forget your gun."

The man returned and scooped up the gun. He dropped it in his pocket, turned and walked away.

Anthony clasped his hands behind his back, bent his head and resumed his walk. "Now," he whispered. "Where was I?" Michael Modesto. He had to find a way to learn the truth about the man. He could not confront the man directly; if Modesto really had been chosen, he would have to lay the groundwork carefully. He needed someone... He smiled as the solution came to him. Selene. Oh, yes. Selene was the answer.

Anthony was almost smiling when he straightened and quickened his pace. Tomorrow, he thought, may not be such a bad day after all.

Chapter 11

For three days Michael refused to speak to Mary or Reverend Gregory. They called the hotel several times, and at one time Mary had come to the hotel and knocked on his door. He had called security, and they escorted her away with the admonition not to come back.

They were a difficult three days. There had been one band rehearsal that had gone badly because Michael was unable to concentrate on the music. And he had not been able to explain why. When Creed had made a joke about Michael acting like he was in love, he had sized on the excuse, reasoning that if Creed were right, as soon as they were on the road again, away from the girl, he would be okay.

The guys had been both amused that the great Don Juan of heavy metal had been bitten by the love bug and disgusted because his infatuation might end up costing them money.

But they were not suffering nearly as much as he was. He was torn between a burning anger at the way his life had been disrupted without his consent, and a mounting sense of wonder that God had chosen him.

There was another feeling that smothered all his other emotions and would not allow him to sleep, to rest: Why him? Even if there was a message—a message that God evidently would reveal to him when he was ready to do so—why had he been chosen to be His messenger? If there ever was someone who was unworthy, it was he.

Hour after hour he walked lonely streets, lay awake at night, reviewing his life, searching for clues that should have warned him about what was coming. But his life had been ordinary, like that of most any child growing in a small Texas town. His mother had died of cancer when he was fifteen, but except for the overwhelming loneliness and a sense that somehow he might be responsible, his life had not changed so much. That was until his father had begun drinking. The loss of his wife had seemed to loose demons inside Russell Modesto who took an increasingly powerful hold on his life, demons that he had learned to escape by drinking. And as the demons grew stronger, he had to drink more to hold them at bay. He managed to do so for five years. Then the liquor had helped him make the final escape, and he had died in an alley with a half empty bottle in his hand.

But by that time, Michael had been taking care of himself for several years. His father and mother had purchased a small house before she died so he did have a roof over his head, and he had survived by a series of after school jobs ranging from flipping hamburgers to construction carpenter.

He wasn't sure why, but he had always realized that the way out of poverty was through education, and he had never allowed anything to interfere with his studies. Fortunately, he loved to read, and that, coupled with a compelling sense of curiosity, had helped him endure the hard work of putting himself through the University of Texas.

Looking back, Michael could see nothing in his life that could offer a clue as to why he should be chosen.

Could it have been his music?

Music has always been a part of his life. His mother had played the piano and the times he sat beside her on the piano bench as she played Mozart and Beethoven, formed some of his most vivid memories. His father, although he had no great love for music, was a natural musician. He could pick up most any musical instrument and in a short while be playing familiar songs. But the only instrument he really cared about playing was the harmonica. Michael could remember summer evenings when his father would sit on the front porch and play like a Gypsy, and the neighbors would gather to listen. When they had found his body in the alley he'd had the half empty bottle of cheap wine in one hand and his old harmonica in the other.

Nothing. There wasn't a thing in his past that could have led him to this place.

The miracles were even more disturbing. If there hadn't been witnesses, it would be easy to believe that it was all a series of mental aberrations. Mary had been there when they had been accosted by the men in the parking lot. She had seen the light and the avatar. She had also been there when he had healed the baby. And Reverend Gregory and several other people has witnessed the healing of the woman in the wheelchair.

Suppose he was schizophrenic. Mental aberrations would seen perfectly real, logical. Perhaps all these things were figments of his mind—including Mary and the Reverend.

Impossible. The guys in the band had all seen her, talked with her. And the hospital with the babies was certainly real. Wasn't it?

The one truth was that he could not concentrate on his music until he had exorcised the demons—if they were demons—from his brain. Perhaps all the 'miracles' were simply random natural acts that had somehow occurred in a sequence that implied authenticity.

He needed proof. And the gateway to that proof was Mary and her church.

He called Benny on his cell phone and said he had to talk to him.

Benny hesitated before answering, and Michael wondered if he might be with a girl. But Benny must have sensed the urgency in his voice because he did not argue. He told Michael to come to his hotel room.

When Michael entered the hotel elevator, he steeled himself for trouble. Ever since the crash he had to force himself to enter an elevator. But he was dammed if he was going to allow one accident to control his life. It would take time, but he would work his way through this fear just like he would conquer the other. Besides, what were the odds that the same thing could happen twice.

As soon as Michael stepped out of the elevator, Benny came out of his hotel room as though he had been waiting with the door open. He was wearing a suit and necktie and Michael wondered if he had cut short a dinner to meet him.

"Christ," Benny said as he hurried to meet Michael. "What the hell's wrong? Couldn't it wait?"

"I guess it could, but I thought you'd like to know as soon as possible."

"Know what?" They entered Benny's suite and Benny closed the door. "What have you been doing? You look like shit."

Michael couldn't look at Benny. He crossed to the windows and looked out over the lights of the city. "I haven't been sleeping much."

Michael heard the clink of glass as Benny poured himself a Scotch over ice and added water. "Too damn much partying. You've got to cut down before you kill yourself. You want a drink?"

"It's not partying. No thanks."

"No? Yeah, well, okay. So what is it? Money? You want more money?"

"No. It isn't money."

"So what is it? Something's sure as shit bothering you. You've been playing like you've got your head up your ass."

Michael pushed his hand through his hair and turned. "Benny, do you believe in miracles?"

"It's a broad. I knew it. You met some stupid broad and she's making you nuts.

"No. Well, yes, in a way."

Benny took a swallow of his drink, his hand shaking. "Christ. That's no miracle. That's biology. You think you're in love and your whole life turns to shit."

"But that isn't why I wanted to see you."

"What the shit else is there?"

Michael licked his lips. This was going to be difficult, especially since he was so unsure that what he was about to do was the right thing. "I'm quitting. Quitting the band. At least, for a while."

Benny's hand holding the glass paused in midair. Behind his glasses, his eyes narrowed. He lifted the glass and emptied it in one swallow. "So," he said. "It is money."

"No, Benny. It's about...Benny, I'm either going crazy or I had a vision."

Benny crossed to a sideboard and poured himself another glass of Scotch. This time he did not add water before he took a long drink. "Probably crazy," he said. "You think you're in love and your brain turns to mush."

"I'm not kidding, Benny. I saw the hand of God."

"That's nothing. I've seen elephants."

"This was a vision."

Benny ginned at him over his glass. "Like that poem: Abbu Ben Adam?"

"Something like that. He told me I'm a messenger."

Benny studied Michael, his eyes shrewd. "So you're a little crazy. A rock group? It'll help."

Michael began walking around the room, unable to remain still. "I had the vision. In the elevator."

"The elevator? Yeah, you told us about that. You were lucky."

Michael shook his head. "Ten floors. Not even a scratch. Nobody's that lucky."

"So it was a miracle. That's no reason to quit the band."

"Last Sunday I went to Mary's church—"

"Mary! That broad? That explains it."

A surge of fury shook Michael. "God damn it. Cut out the bullshit! I'm telling you something here!"

Benny slowly put his glass on the sideboard. He moved to stand directly in front of Michael. "Okay," he said softly. "So tell me."

Michael put his hand over his face for a moment, waiting for the heat to abate. He looked up at Benny. "When I left the church I helped a woman in a wheelchair. I touched her. All I did was touch her. And I...I fainted, I guess. But she walked away." He grabbed Benny's arms. "Benny, she walked away."

Benny stared at him. "Yeah. That sounds like a miracle."

Michael released Benny's arms and moved back. "You don't believe me."

Benny lifted his hand. "You believe it. That's what's important. But it's got nothing to do with the band."

Michael shook his head. "Maybe not. But I've got to find out."

"Find out what?"

"If I really am a messenger."

"Yeah. How? Another elevator?"

"By being a messenger. Which means I can't travel with the band."

Benny studied Michael, searching for some sign of humor. "This is some big joke, isn't it?"

Michael shook his head. "No joke. I'm working with the church."

"For how long?"

Michael hesitated. "As long as it takes."

"But it's just on Sundays. Right?"

"For now."

Benny's eyes were skeptical, his brow furrowed. "Then you could do gigs during the week."

Michael couldn't look at Benny. His next words would not only betray Benny, but they would betray all the guys in the band. One more reason to resent this rock that God had put on his shoulders. "I told you. I'm out of it."

Benny face pulled into a puzzled frown. "For God's sake, Mike. You guys are right on the edge."

Michael shrugged. "Things change."

Benny put a palm to his forehead and turned away. "This is crazy." He swung back to look at Michael. "What about your friends? You going to take them down with you?"

"They'll do all right without me."

"Like hell. You're the engine. Without you they're just a bunch of stiffs."

Michael bit his lip. He didn't like to be reminded that he was letting down the other guys. "Well, I can't help that."

"Shit, yes, you can. Give up this cockamamie horse shit. Get back to what you do."

"I can't."

Benny waved his hand, brushing aside the words. "None of this shtick happened 'til that nurse showed up." He shook his finger at Michael. "Wake up, kid. She's using you."

Michael fought back a burst of anger. "Look, Benny, I didn't ask for this. I'd give it up in a God damned second if I could. But I can't. Damn it. I can't. I'm stuck. I can't quit. Not until I find out what the shit I'm supposed to do! Until then..." He walked to the door, and pulled it open. "Until then, this is my life."

Benny's mouth had come open and, now, he closed it slowly. "Okay, kid," he said softly. "It's your life, I guess. If there's anything I can do..."

Michael shook his head, unwilling to speak, afraid he might turn back.

Benny shrugged. "Yeah. Well, you know where to make that call."

Michael went out and pulled the door shut, the click of the latch loud in the silence. He stood with his hand on the knob, trying to analyze what had just occurred. He had lost one of his best friends, a friend who would probably never see him again.

Chapter 12

Mary had been more than a little surprised when Michael telephoned and asked if he could see her. She hesitated before answering and he interpreted her hesitation as an indication that she really did not want to see him. Then she explained she had to be on duty at the hospital in less than an hour. He could stop by, but he could not stay long.

She broke the connection, and Michael stood staring at the phone in his hand. It was the first time he could remember that a girl had hung up on him, and he couldn't decide whether to be amused or angry. He glanced at the clock. Ten o'clock. He hoped she wasn't making up an excuse.

Actually, he decided, it was best that he did not spend too much time with her. Being near her had become increasingly disturbing. He often found himself thinking about her throughout the day. And at night the preoccupation not only made it hard to get to sleep, but she had taken over his dreams.

He was profoundly ambivalent about the intrusion. He enjoyed thinking about her. He enjoyed the day dreams as much as he did those at night. But the pleasure was pierced by a shard of panic, a sense that he was sinking deeper and deeper into a relationship that would end a phase of his life he was not ready to end.

But it was strictly a one way street. Mary might have taken over his dreams, but he definitely was not part of hers. She had been cordial to him, even friendly, but she definitely was not overwhelmed by his charm.

Of course, he had the excuse that all his time spent with her had been centered on her charity work or her church. Or, he remembered, about the strange things that had been happening to him. But one thing was definite: none of it had been romantic.

If their concentration on business had not allowed him to unleashed his full panoply of charm, she certainly had not given him any indication she wanted it any other way.

Maybe that was the secret of her allure: indifference. She had displayed little interest in him as a person and absolutely none as a potential lover. What had started out as a relief that she was so atypical had, somehow, turned into an irritation. He had thought he was too mature to succumb to the old game of wanting what he couldn't have, but his glands were proving him wrong.

Except there was no 'game.' She was not playing hard to get; she simply was not interested. The thing to do was to confront the problem. End the relationship before it got out of hand. Then he could concentrate on what was happening to his mind.

By driving like a fool, it only took him twenty minutes to reach Mary's apartment. He punched in her code, and she rang the door open for him. In the building's foyer the elevator's door was open and barricaded with white plastic sawhorses. Workmen's electrical cables snaked in from outside the building and angled down into the dark, yawning pit.

Michael hurried past, not wanting to be reminded of the accident. He climbed the stairs two at a time and was panting when he tapped on Mary's door.

She was wearing her white uniform and white shoes. Her hair was swept back and caught up in a high pony tail. She wore no makeup or jewelry and had the clean fresh scent of soap and water.

She smiled when she noticed Michael fighting for breath. "I thought you were in good shape."

"I thought so, too. Next time I won't run."

She closed the door. "You ran up the stairs? All the way?"

"Yeah. If I did that every day I'd really get in shape." He grinned at her. "How about it? Every day all right with you."

"Sure," she said with an equal smile. "And when you get here you can run right back down."

Michael grunted with feigned disgust. "Kill joy."

Mary moved to the small kitchen area. "I'll make some tea. That'll help."

"Couldn't hurt." He went to watch her deftly pour boiling water over tea bags that she had already placed in cups.

She made no mention of his refusing to see her when she had stopped by. Instead, without looking up from her task, she asked, "Why did you want to see me? I hope nothing's wrong."

"No, no." When she carried the tray to the coffee table, he followed and gingerly sat on the antique-looking couch. She sat beside him and handed him a cup of tea. Sitting so close to her, Michael was glad his hands were occupied in holding the cup. He guessed that serving the tea was no social inspiration. She probably had worked out the defensive maneuver a long time ago.

She half turned to face him, waiting for him to speak, her eyes disconcertingly direct and calm.

Michael did not hurry. He was undecided whether to start with some inane remark or to get to the point. The decision was taken out of his hands when he saw her glance at her wrist watch. He cleared his throat before he said, "I talked to Benny."

"Benny?"

"The band manager. I told him I was quitting the band."

She had just taken a sip of tea, and she lowered the cup slowly. "Why?"

He made a small shrug. "These 'things' that have been happening. I thought I'd better look into them."

"Then you really believe you're a messenger."

"I have no idea. But I've got to find out. I just can't believe it could be me."

She gently put her cup back on the tray. "Why is that so impossible?"

"Maybe it wouldn't be if I were more religious. But even when I was a kid and went to church, I was always Pharisaic."

She lifted an eyebrow. "Pharisaic?"

"Observing the form but not the spirit."

She nodded. "A lot of people do that."

"But they don't fall ten floors in an elevator and come out without a scratch."

"Maybe some do. We can't possibly know about every miracle."

"I hope you're right. But what about those other things? They can't all be coincidence."

She sat very still for a moment, her head lowered. Then she raised her head and looked at him. "I don't think they were."

Michael put down his cup and stood up, moving as he spoke. "If they weren't, then they must have been miracles." He stopped as a thought stabbed. "The elevator." He turned to face her. "If it really was a miracle, then maybe it wasn't an accident." Mary did not answer, but her brows drew down in disbelief. "And if it wasn't an accident, who caused it to happen?"

Mary put both hands against her cheeks. "I can't believe God would kill two people."

"I can't either. But if it wasn't God...if it wasn't some kind of test...Well, it had to either be a real accident, or..." He stopped and bit down on his lip, shaken by a bizarre thought.

Mary turned her head to look at him, her eyes huge. She had to have been thinking the same thing because she said, "Something—or someone made it happen."

The idea gripped Michael and he walked to the window, taking time to let the thought stop spinning in his mind. Could the accident have been planned? Michael shook his head. "Nobody knew I was going to be in that elevator. It had to be coincidence."

"And if it wasn't?"

He hesitated, struggling to put the idea into some kind of recognizable perspective. But that brought him back to his original question: Why? And why him? His past had no more influences that could have led him to be a messenger of the devil than it did to be a messenger of God. "I've got to find out." He turned from the window. "The point is: how?"

"You could just wait for another...miracle."

"That might take weeks, months." His lips twisted in a rueful smile. "I guess I could jump off a building and see if I lived."

She winced and stood up. "There has to be a better way."

"I hope so."

"I was thinking...If God really does want you as a messenger,"—she spoke slowly, thinking through her words—"maybe we should give him a chance."

"A chance? How do you mean?"

"You could become a reverend—like Gregory."

"A reverend?" He stared at her as though his eyes could discern her true intentions. Satisfied that she was not joking, he said, "You can't just say you want to be a reverend."

"Why not? You don't need a license."

"I know, but...you've got to be...well...ordained."

"No, you don't. Anybody can start a church."

"But they should have some sort of credentials. A degree in theology. Something."

"Why? How many priests have degrees? How many ministers or reverends? How many evangelists?"

"And some of them are charlatans."

"Having a degree doesn't guarantee you're honest.

"But you don't want to make a fool of yourself either."

She almost smiled. "Haven't you noticed: Charlatans never make fools of themselves."

She got up and carried the tray into the kitchen.

Michael went to stare out the window. If he really was a messenger, why not become a reverend? It would give credence to his sermons. It also meant the end of his career in music. It meant giving up all he had worked for through so many years, exchanging it for a calling he was not even sure existed. But he could think of no other way.

He walked into the kitchen. "Maybe you're right. I either have a message or I'm going crazy. I guess I've got to give God a chance."

She was washing the cups at the sink, moving mechanically as though considering the implications of what Michael had told her. "Where will you preach?"

He did not answer immediately, allowing her to think she had opened a new door. "That is a problem. I suppose I could rent some place..." He let his voice trail off, waiting for her to pick up the cue.

"The church," she said, just as he had hoped. "You could be like a permanent guest speaker. You wouldn't even have to be a minister."

"You don't think Gregory would mind?"

"I don't think so. Everybody liked you."

Watching Mary's movements, so precise and automatic as though she never left dirty dishes in the sink, he had a strange desire to put his arms around her and tell her she was the main reason why he wanted to be part of her church. He might be able to rationalize the visitation and the miracles, but he could not deny his attraction toward Mary. Was it simply infatuation or was he really in love? Spending time with her would bring proof one way or the other.

He was about to take two huge steps in his life and needed proof before he made either of them permanent.

"When can I start?"

"There's not much point in waiting." She went to the small closet near the door and took out a sweater. "Why not this Sunday?"

He helped her put on the sweater. "Good. The sooner the better."

She opened the door and took keys from her purse as they moved into the hall. "What will you talk about?"

He hesitated. The times he'd spoken before, he'd pretty much winged it. But if he was really serious, he had better start thinking of something to say. On the other hand, if he was a conduit for God's message, he didn't want to block its path with prattle. "You said it before: If I really am his messenger, God will tell me what to say. I think I'll leave it up to him."

"That makes sense." She locked the door and started toward the stairs.

They had only taken a few steps when Michael stopped. "Oh, shit. What about the benefit?"

"What about it?"

"I quit the band."

She stood looking at him, biting her lip. Then she shook her head ruefully. "I'm sure God will provide."

"I sure wish to Christ I knew what he had in mind."

"We'll know when it's time."

Walking beside her Michael wished he had her faith. It would make everything so simple: just trust in God. Well, God had provided one thing: He had allowed him to meet Mary. He wondered whether she felt the same joy at being close to him as he felt being near her. Probably not.

When they reached her car in the apartment's subterranean garage, he waited while she fished her keys from her purse and unlocked and opened the car door. Before she got in, she turned to face him, her face only inches from his. He stared at her lips, fighting a powerful urge to kiss her.

She sensed his temptation and smiled. "No," she whispered. "Remember. You're a messenger of God."

He blinked, the spell broken. "It's okay," he said. "I'm allowed to kiss angels."

"In that case..." To his surprise she quickly brushed her lips across his, then ducked into her car. He was still standing, mesmerized with pleasure as she drove away. It was only when he was heading back to his own car and his heart had settled into at least a semblance of its usual rhythm, that he was able to turn his thought to the enormity of what he had done. Sunday. If he really did go to the church on Sunday, he would have taken another giant step along a road that had no end, at least no end that he could see.

But he did have three days to think about it. Three days that could change his life.

Chapter 13

The next three days both dragged and sped by. One thought occupied Michael's waking hours: If he were a messenger of God, what was the message? What was he supposed to say?

He purchased a Bible_and poured over it, searching for revelation. But while its pages offered an overwhelming surfeit of wisdom, they provided no eurekan flash of inspiration.

He wondered whether the ancient prophets had experienced the same uncertainties, the same doubts. How easy it must have been for the disciples of Christ. They had sat by his side, talked with him, touched him. If they were confused, if there was something they did not understand, they had only to ask. Then they could carry his messages to the world with the certainty of divine ordination.

All he had was a vision and strange 'happenings' that had no rational explanation.

Men who truly believed they were God's messengers had come and gone for hundreds of years. Their messages were as numerous and varied as were their gods. It mattered not whether the message was brief and clear, such as the Ten Commandments, or long and convoluted such as God's instructions to Adam and Eve, each was certain his view was correct.

Curiously, God rarely seemed to make a personal appearance, and none at all since the very earliest millennium. He always conveyed his messages through angels or prophets. The exception was when he spoke through his son, Jesus Christ, and mankind had been agonizing over the words of Christ for two thousand years.

By Friday evening Michael's head throbbed with a combination of confusion and depression. Sunday, the time for his next sermon, marched toward him with the frightening inevitability of a Roman legion. He had tried calming his nerves by playing music, but the only music he really enjoyed was the kind of hard rock he played with his band, and its driving beat was hardly conducive to meditation. It was much more satisfying to take his guitar from its case and work on a new song even though he probably would never get the chance to play it.

He resisted asking for help from Reverend Gregory or Mary. If the Reverend knew the message, he would have given it long ago. And Mary...

There was an even better reason why he resisted calling Mary. Somehow she had settled into the back of his mind, slipping into his thoughts at the oddest times, interrupting his studies like a Siren with a call so lovely, so compelling that it was easy to abandon his frustrating studies for warm musings about her face, her voice, her smile, her every move and gesture.

And that was all in his mind; he could never concentrate on his search if she were beside him in reality? The fear that he would make a total fool of himself by coming on to her was even greater than his fear of disintegrating in front of the church congregation.

But by Saturday evening he was desperate. He still had no message, not the glimmer of an idea. Dialing her number, he rationalized by telling himself that his need for her ecclesiastical help was so great that it would overcome any emotional attraction.

It was after midnight when Mary finally answered her phone. "Yes," she said cautiously.

"It's me. Mike."

"Oh, Michael." Her voice echoed the relief of the single woman answering her phone late at night and finding the caller was someone she knew. Then a new note of anxiety crept in. "Are you all right?"

"Yeah, but...No, I'm not. This thing is driving me crazy."

There was a pause as though she was preparing herself for bad news. "What thing is that? You are coming to the church tomorrow?"

"I don't know. What's the point? I haven't been able to come up with a thing. I haven't got a clue."

There was another pause before she put on a new tone, the tone she probably used for talking to confused children, "Don't worry about it. You can speak of just about anything. I'm sure they'll love it."

"That's not the point. I'm supposed to have a some kind of stupid message. I've got nothing."

The helpless anger in his voice brought another pause before she said, "Oh. Well then, why don't you let God decide."

Michael's snort of derision as much as said that God hadn't been of much help. "And how do I do that? Throw myself in front of a train and wait for another miracle?"

"No. Just say whatever comes into your mind. If you really are his messenger, it'll be the right thing."

It was Michael's turn to pause. How could he make her understand that he didn't want to do that. It had been all right to wing it when he had been screwing around, but now it was no longer a game. He had chosen a path that led to a new future, an unknown future that was going to require a new level of dedication, a real search for truth. It was terrifying to think he might stand in front people who expected some great revelation and have nothing to say. Or come out with something so inane, so stupid that they would laugh him off the stage.

Suddenly, an even more terrifying thought struck him, and he said, "Suppose I say the wrong thing? And they believe me?"

"The wrong thing? What do you mean?"

"I'm not a real preacher. I know that. Who am I to tell anybody how to live their life?"

"How many ministers do you know who are trained psychologists?"

"How does Gregory live with it? What he says can effect their lives in ways he'll never know."

"He does it because he believes what he tells them. It's part of him."

A deep sense of despair almost overwhelmed him. "Maybe that's the problem. I don't believe. Not really."

"You will. It'll come to you. I know it will."

"Yeah, maybe. But the people won't know that. In the meantime, I might ruin somebody's life"

"I'm sure God won't let that happen."

"Oh. I wish I had your faith."

She was silent for a moment, then said, "Prayer. You will find the answer in your own heart."

Her answer struck Michael speechless. In all his searching for truth, he had never thought of prayer. He almost laughed at his stupidity. But he also realized why it had not occurred to him: he didn't believe in prayer. He was so used to depending upon his own capabilities, his own brain, that the idea of asking for help was anathema.

But beneath all his success there had always lurked a certain anomie, a feeling that he was undeserving, the unlucky victim of some divine joke and that eventually it would all come crashing down.

Well, that day had come, but not in a way that he would have suspected in a million years.

"Okay," he said. "I guess you're right. What have I got to lose?"

She sighed as though she had been holding her breath. "I'm sure you'll find the faith you're looking for. Just give God a chance."

"Yeah, right."

She waited for him to continue, but he was lost in the wonder of this new direction his life had taken, and she said, "We'll see you in the morning?"

"Yeah, okay," he heard himself say. "I'll be there."

He hung up the phone. Prayer? How did one go about it? It seemed to be a requirement that one kneel and fold one's hands together.

He had called Mary from his bedroom phone so it seemed natural that he kneel beside the bed. The light? Should it be on or off? He decided it made no difference, so he left it on.

Feeling more angry than penitent, he clasped his hands and rested them on the edge of the bed. Yeah. That felt natural. Now if he could only keep the way he really felt out of his voice...

He closed his eyes, bowed his head and searched for the proper salutation. He decided to take a simple, direct approach. "All right, God," he began. "I give up. You've got me on my knees. And I admit it. I need help. You said I was to be a messenger. Your messenger. But you forgot to give me the fu—the message. So I'm asking for it now."

He paused, waiting, hoping for a koan of wisdom. When there was none, he added, "Please, God. I'm asking for your help. Show me the way. If you really want me to be your messenger, show me the way, God."

He waited, listening. There was no sound, no light, no heavenly host.

He took a deep breath. "All right, God. I guess I didn't really expect anything."

Bracing himself on a book lying on the nightstand next to his bed, he heaved to his feet. When he took his hand away, the book fell to the floor with a thud. He picked it up. It was the Bible he'd been reading before he called Mary.

"Okay God," he said aloud. "I'll assume you've given me a sign. Although I have no idea what you're trying to tell me. Something about your book, I guess. Okay, okay. Tomorrow at the church, I'll leave it up to you."

Preparing for bed, he wondered why there had been no direct answer to his prayer. Nothing but an ambiguous sign. Books fall. It did not mean they had been pushed by the hand of God. Which meant he was no closer to the truth than he had been before praying.

In bed, waiting for sleep, he tried to think of a time he had been more disappointed. No, not just disappointed. Disappointed and frustrated. His one consolation was that he could always quit. Thank God he had not burned any bridges behind him. If God ignored him tomorrow as he had tonight, he would hand in his resignation and go back to his band. Making music was something he could do without feeling like a straw caught in a whirlwind. Tomorrow was the day. The ball was in God's court.

At Dulles Airport outside Washington, D.C. it was after three o'clock in the morning. When Anthony Stonz tried to move through the security check point with Selene, there has been a minor confrontation. The female security person said that guests were not allowed to accompany ticketed passengers to the boarding area. She had been adamant in her refusal, and it had been necessary to prove his identity before she waved them through.

Arriving at the boarding gate he said to Selene, "When you get there—" Suddenly, he caught his breath and hunched his shoulders, reaching inside his Armani topcoat to rub his chest over his heart.

Selene put her hand on his shoulder. "Anthony! What is it?"

"A prayer." His voice changed from a distressed whisper to a tone of satirical humor. "He's asking for God's help."

"And this time?"

Anthony's voice had regained its strength. "Like the others."

Selene let her breath out in a soft sigh. "Then it's all right."

He nodded. "For now."

Anthony glancedaround as he adjusted his clothing. Once again this man Modesto had surprised him. But he was sure there would be many more surprises before the situation was resolved. The one consolation was that the man was undoubtedly suffering more than was he. It had to be wrenchingly fearsome to suddenly find yourself in a role of such responsibility, a role that you were ill equipped to play. Could this Modesto possibly sustain such a momentous role? It was possible that the very heavy burden would break him without any outside intervention. History was replete with the graves of men—and women—who had broken under the weight of such heavy responsibility.

But all of them—with one or two exceptions—had been impostors. A few had actually believed they were the new Messiah, the chosen one. In the end, they, too, had imploded, some taking their followers with them.

Still, he could not take the chance that this Michael Modesto would succumb to the pressure, especially when the signs were so strong that, while he might not be the actual Messiah, he could well be some sort of an angelic prophet. Either way, he was a menace that had to be stopped.

"Do not contact this man directly," he instructed Selene. "Let him make the introduction."

"How should I do that?"

Anthony Stonz thought a moment, allowing the images to form. "There's a church. There are services tomorrow morning. Go there."

"A church?" For a second Selene's luminous dark eyes clouded with worry. "I'm not comfortable in churches."

"You'll get used to it. Volunteer. The objective is to get close to this Michael Modesto."

Selene's lips lifted in a tiny smile. "How close?"

Anthony's voice sharpened. "Be circumspect. If he has a message, I want to know what it is. All of it. I want nothing to obscure the pronouncement." Then his own lips twisted. "Not yet."

Chapter 14

At nine thirty Sunday morning, Michael drove into the church parking lot. He stared in astonishment. The lot was almost half full, and he hit the steering wheel with the palm of his hand in disgust. He had hoped to arrive early enough to avoid encountering anyone until he could escape into the church. The last thing he wanted was people asking him questions about what had happened last Sunday.

He sat in his car until it appeared that the last of the arrivals had entered the church, and he heard organ music. He was so bent upon avoiding encounters that he almost forgot his Bible, which would be a disaster since he had no idea what he was going to say. He was still searching his mind as he hurried to the church.

He had assumed that shifting responsibility to God would ease his mind. Instead, he was plagued with the thought that either God had deserted him or had already sent him the "message" and he had either ignored it or failed to understand. Either way he was going to get up in front of a bunch of strangers and make a complete fool of himself. He contented himself with the thought that they were, after all, strangers, people he would never see again.

He climbed the concrete entrance steps with his head down, and almost ran into someone standing in the church doorway. He said, "Excuse me" and started to go around when he looked up into one of the most exotic faces he had ever seen. She had olive skin, so rich and pure it looked artificial. The eyes she turned on him were set above high cheekbones and were almond shaped, very dark, with thick black lashes, probably due to some oriental blood in her background. Her lips were unusually full, lush, glistening in the sunlight. Her hair was pulled back severely from her smooth forehead, held in place by tortoise shell combs on each side of her head, with the back looped back upon itself until it fell in a long ponytail almost to her waist.

Her height and slender form as well as the way she wore a matching suit jacket and skirt reminded him of a *haute couture* model. The dark blue color of the suit material was relieved by tiny pinstripes and a snowy white blouse. The hem of the skirt ended demurely just above her knees. Her shoes had three inch heels, but their black color and plain style told him that their owner was chic but practical. She carried a small purse, beaded in black with white stripes to match the pattern of her suit.

She stepped back with a smile. "Sorry." In that one word there was the hint of an accent.

Michael returned the smile and was about to edge past when she said, "Excuse me, please. But...are you with the church?"

He nodded. "I suppose so. At least today." He noticed the way she clutched her purse in a grip so hard it appeared that she would crush its fragile beauty. "May I help you?"

"Yes. Uh, could you tell me...where do I stand?"

"Stand?" He wondered what sort of church she had been attending. He glanced toward a group of people who were hurrying from the parking lot. "Come. I'll show you."

Her smile was quick and nervous. "Thank you."

Michael took hold of her elbow to lead her into the church. She took one step and stopped abruptly, her dark eyes peering into the church foyer as though expecting an attack.

"It's okay," Michael assured her. "Just like all the other churches."

She attempted a smile, and her tongue touched her lips as delicately as a bee touching a flower. She took another step, and to Michael's surprise, she took a deep breath of relief. What on earth, he wondered, had she expected. She probably had not been inside a church for a long time and expected God to punish her in some way.

"Good," he said. "I think you'll like it here."

She did not hesitate as she allowed him to lead her down the aisle. People already seated turned their heads to stare as they passed. Michael could not blame them. The girl was so strikingly beautiful she would turn heads in a monastery.

He ushered her to one of the pews near the front of the room. "Here. This is a good place."

She moved in but did not immediately sit down. "I'm not sure...uh, could you, perhaps, tell me what I must do?"

"Well, you don't have to do anything really. Just stand up when everyone else does, and sit down when they do. If you want to join in the singing,"—he took a hymnal from its rack and handed it to her—"here's a hymnal."

She started to reach her hand out, then paused, staring down at the small book. "It's not a Bible?"

"No. It's a song book."

"Oh." She took the book gingerly like she expected it to be burning hot. When it proved to be benign, she looked up at Michael with a smile of triumph. "Thank you."

Mary had been talking to Reverend Gregory near the organ. Seeing Michael and the girl, they walked toward them. "Hello," Mary said. "I was beginning to worry." She wore a print dress that made Michael think of summer and a smile that made him think of spring.

"Hello." Reverend Gregory echoed. "I'm glad you could make it."

Mary looked toward the girl, her eyebrows raised expectantly and with an expression in her eyes that Michael hoped was jealousy.

"Oh, Mary," he said. "We have a new parishioner. This is..." He looked at the girl.

"Selene." She smiled and held her hand out to Mary.

Mary took her hand and returned the smile. "Welcome. I'm Mary Schaeffer. And this is Reverend Gregory."

Gregory shook her hand. "Welcome. If you have any questions, don't hesitate."

"Thank you, Reverend." She turned her eyes toward Michael. "And you are..."

"Michael," Mary said quickly. "Michael Modesto."

Selene's smile froze for an instant. A flash of panic glazed her eyes and was quickly gone. "Oh, you're Michael."

"You've heard of him?" Reverend Gregory asked.

She gave a condescending nod. "Yes. You might say he's the reason I'm here."

Reverend Gregory looked at the people crowding the aisle. "It looks like you're not the only one. Excuse me."

He left them, hurrying toward the church entrance where people were beginning to bunch up.

Mary smiled at Selene, "I hope you enjoy the service. Michael, may I see you a minute?"

She turned to move away and the move bumped Michael's arm. The Bible dropped from his hand to the pew bench next to Selene. Instinctively, she reached for it. Suddenly, she yanked her hand back and her head jerked up, her face drained of color.

Michael picked up the Bible. "Sorry." The thought that crossed his mind was that the girl suffered some sort of psychosis. Fear of books, perhaps. She had experienced some difficulty in picking up the hymnal. It seemed totally incongruous that anyone of such physical perfection should have mental problems. But the human brain had it's own agenda. He could certainly attest to that.

He nodded to Selene. "If you'll excuse me. We'll be starting in a few minutes."

"Of course." She had recovered her composure and sat down next to the middle aisle with her hands folded in her lap, her purse and the hymnal close by her side.

As Michael walked away, he noticed that no one attempted to edge past her to reach the empty section of the pew. He smiled when he saw several people walk around and came in from the other side. Apparently, it would have been like forcing one's way past a princess.

As he took his place in the front pew, Michael was astonished to see that every pew was filled. So maybe he hadn't bombed last time.

There was another big difference. Usually before the service started, people quietly conversed with family members and friends. Not today. Today almost everyone was silent, staring at him. He did not mind the staring; it was the silence that was disconcerting. It was as though they expected him to have a halo around his head. His smile felt stiff even to him, and he tried to hide his sense of hypocrisy by murmuring greetings to those near him without having the least idea of what he was saying.

At a signal from Mary, Mrs. Gardner ended her playing by plumping her hands down on the keyboard and the organ emitted a loud wail of protest. Reverend Gregory hurried down the center aisle to forestall a repeat of the warning chord.

Gregory rushed through his standard welcome and benediction, showing that he, too, was not used to staring into so many expectant faces. When Mary led the congregation in "I Am A Servant of the Lord," it seemed to Michael that the entire congregation was trying to race through the old hymn like it was hip-hop.

Listening to the singing, Michael wondered why those with the worst voices were always the loudest. Except there was one voice, one voice that soared with the clear brilliance of an angelic host. Michael turned his head to find its source.

It was Selene. She stood with her shoulders back, her head high, inches taller than the women near her. She held the hymn book high enough so that she did not have to glance down to read the words and her voice soared with the shear joy of singing. Those near her, though they continued to sing, glanced at her from the corners of their eyes, wondering, no doubt, if she were some incognito celebrity

Michael was beginning to wonder himself. A voice like that would be hard to keep hidden from talent scouts. But he could not recall seeing pictures of her in the trades. Maybe she was in opera or only sang in church choirs. Somehow, he doubted that, since she had been unfamiliar with the hymnal, although she was singing as though she knew the song. Perhaps she was an accomplished musician who could sight read the piano score. He only hoped she continued to attend services. That voice would bring more money to the donation basket than he could on his best day.

As the sacrament was served, the congregation participated with palpable impatience. If they possessed so little reverence, Michael wondered why they had come. Apparently, they expected him to imbue them with piety through some sort of verbal osmosis.

The thought only added to his apprehension. With every passing second, panic welled higher inside him. He was almost time for him to speak and he still felt no inspiration, no sense of direction.

After the sacrament and another song that may have seemed interminable to the audience, but which, to Michael, seemed to end far too soon, Reverend Gregory took his usual place at the lectern.

Michael assumed that he would have a few minutes of respite while Gregory gave his sermon, but to his dismay, Gregory said, "First, I would like to thank all of you for being here this wonderful morning. And I know you didn't come here to listen to me, so here he is, Michael Modesto."

Michael tried to stand. But he found he could not. He thought that his legs had gone to sleep because they seemed leaden, unwilling to move. Mary put her hand on his arm. "Michael, what's the matter?"

He cleared his throat. "Nothing." Clutching the Bible, he forced himself to his feet. During the few short steps to the dais, he clearly heard a rustle of whispers from the congregation as people speculated about who he was and what he would say. He caught the word 'miracle' and shook his head in disbelief. If he really could perform miracles he would certainly not be here. The thought made him smile and with the smile, came a realization that if the guys in his band could see him now they would be on the floor howling with laughter. Because it was a joke. He was about as qualified to be a preacher as he was to be a plumber.

But these people didn't know that. They were here because they wanted to believe. They wanted a performance, and like any actor, it was his duty to give it to them. All he needed was a good script.

But the pages of his script were blank.

Or were they? In his hand he held the greatest script ever written. All he had to do was find the right place.

No. That was wrong. All he had to do was allow God to show him the right place.

When he stepped onto the low dais next to the lectern, he turned and stared at the congregation, silently. His gaze found the girl, Selene. She sat with her back ridged, looking at him with such unblinking intensity that for a moment he shivered. He forced his gaze away, scanning the earnest faces, staring until the last of the murmurs trailed into an expectant silence.

"Thank you."

His voice was low, warm, friendly, just the way it should be at the beginning of a gospel song. He turned his head to look at Reverend Gregory who had taken a seat on the side of the stage near the organist.

"Thank you, Reverend Gregory for inviting me back." He turned back to the audience. "I know that many of you—I should say all of you—are wondering what a rock musician is doing standing up here. Frankly, I'm kind of wondering myself."

There were a few nervous titters until Mary turned her head to glare at the perpetrators.

"In fact," Michael continued, "I even wondered what I was going to talk about. As you might have guessed, I'm not an ordained minister and this is a little out of my field. In fact, you could say I was terrified."

This time the titters were fewer and quickly stifled.

"Until a short time ago, I had no idea what I was going to say. Then I decided to leave it up to God."

He held the Bible upside down so that its pages fanned out. "So God, what have you got in mind?" He quickly turned the Bible, leaving the pages open, and slapped it down on the lectern so hard and unexpectedly that heads snapped back in surprise.

In dead quietness, Michael moved behind the lectern and looked down at the open pages. "Now this is interesting. You'd think it would have opened somewhere in the middle. That would accord the laws of probability. But no. God makes his own laws. It fell open here, way over in the Book of Luke. Chapters nine and ten. Okay. Now what? There are a lot of words on those two pages. Which words does God have in mind for us today? All right. We'll let him decide."

Michael, with the all the reverence of a snake oil salesman, closed his eyes and held his right hand high over the pages. He could almost feel his audience lean forward as he let his hand fall, pointing with his finger. He opened his eyes. He gave the audience a fateful stare, allowing them to savor the suspense before he looked down at the page.

"Ha!" he said. "If you think God wasn't guiding my hand, listen to this." He picked the book up and read: "Whosoever shall receive this child in my name receiveth me; and whosoever shall receive me receiveth him that sent me: for he that is least among you all, the same shall be great." He paused in a calculated emphasis and looking up at the audience. The complete silence, the expressions of such total attention stunned him. This was no game. Not for them. To them, the words he was saying so blithely were lifelines of hope. The words held meanings in their lives that he could not comprehend. He had no right to play the Pharisee.

When he looked back at the page, he had to blink to refocus his eyes. His voice was quieter when he finally located the text. "And John answered and said, Master, we saw one casting out devils in thy name, and we forbad him, because he followeth not with us. And Jesus said unto him, Forbid him not; for he that is not against us is for us."

And as he read, the words seemed to enlarge and to burn, burn as though they were branded into the page with a finger of fire.

He closed the book. He did not need it any more; the words were seared into his mind as clearly as they had been branded into the page.

"You hear that?" His voice sounded strange to him, disembodied, heavy, dredged from somewhere deep inside. "'Forbid him not; for he that is not against us is for us.' Jesus didn't ask to see the credentials of the man who was casting out the devil. And if you believe in Jesus Christ then you also believe in the devil. Jesus did, and he may be in heaven, waiting for the time of The Return, but the devil—the devil is right here on earth. And until he does return, Christ is going to need all the help he can get. Evil is here, I tell you. The devil is here. No, you can't see him. You can't hear him. You can't feel him."

As he spoke, conjuring words and phrases, he began to feel like an automaton, as though he were outside himself, watching a performance. Fascinated by words that seemed to come from nowhere, he left the lectern and strode down the aisle, talking as he moved.

"But beware! Beware!" He lifted the Bible above his head. "The Prophet Isaiah tells us, 'Woe unto thee that call evil good and good evil, that put darkness for light and light for darkness, that put bitter for sweet and sweet for bitter.

"In your heart you know. You know what is good and what is evil. Who are you going to let rule your heart?—God? Or the devil?"

Standing in the center of the congregation, he was struck by the concentration reflected in the faces. Unbelievably, they were hanging on his every word, and he experienced a familiar thrill. He had them now!

In total silence, he moved back behind the lectern where he opened the Bible again and read, "And I saw an angel come down from heaven, having the key of the bottomless pit and a great chain in his hand." Michael made his voice stronger, firm. "And he laid hold on the dragon, that old serpent, which is the devil, and Satan, and bound him a thousand years."

He paused dramatically, allowing the words to sink in. This was it. This was how the message would come. All he had to do was open his mind and God would provide the message.

"A thousand years."

Lowering his voice to a conspiratorial whisper, he allowed words to pour from his mind, words about the fulfillment of the prophesy and how it was up to them to do their own fighting with the devil until the time of the thousand years...when he should deceive the nations no more.

He stopped, took a deep breath, suddenly conscious that he was just mouthing words. He felt there was something he was leaving out, something important.

But nothing came to him. Nothing.

A pulse began to throb painfully in his temple and he pressed his hand to his forehead. He had failed. The peculiar sensation of opening his mind, to being a conduit, had yielded no great truth, no apocalyptic 'message.' It was over and he was done.

He held up the Bible. "Thus sayeth the Lord. Amen!"

No one moved nor spoke as he stepped from the platform and returned to his seat. Mary shifted to give him room to sit down, her eyes wide and a little frightened.

Michael tightened his lips. He had done his best. If it had fallen short of her expectations, too bad.

"Thank you, Michael." It was Reverend Gregory. He had moved behind the lectern and was looking down at Michael. "I think I'm speaking for all of us when I ask you to speak to us again next week."

From the congregation came murmured sounds of "Amen" and "Yes, yes."

Michael's throat tightened. Apparently, a few in the congregation had believed him. But did he want to go through that again? Did he want to spend hours trying to discern the true message? The answer was an emphatic 'no,' and he sat silently.

Taking Michael's silence for accent, Reverend Gregory said, "Wonderful."

Michael shook his head, but Gregory had already shifted his gaze to Mary. "Now, Mary, would you lead us in the closing hymn?"

Mary got up and turned to face the room. She cleared her throat before she said, "I think 'The Bible Tells Me So' would be most appropriate. Page twenty-three."

With Mary leading, the congregation launched the song on a spirited journey to God's ear while Reverend Gregory supervised passing of the donation basket. Michael did not have a song book and he tried to remember the words of the old song, but except for a word here and there, it had vanished from his memory.

Near the end of the song, the voice of Selene soared with such purity that one by one the remainder of the congregation fell silent, standing with their lips parted, their eyes fixed as though the sound had metamorphosed into a vision.

When the song ended, Selene's voice seemed to linger with such mesmerizing power it was several seconds before anyway was able to emerge from the hypnosis.

Later, after Reverend Gregory's closing prayer, several people came to the front of the room to tell him, "Oh, you were so wonderful," and "We'll be here next week," and "I'll bring my son and daughter. They haven't been to church in Lord knows when. But I'm sure they'll want to hear you."

Michael smiled and murmured that he would certainly try to appear, God willing. But he was speaking a lie. It was easy to make such a promise now amid the adulation, but away from the influence of the church and with a week to think about it, a week that probably would be filled with nightmares, he was sure he would change his mind.

He started up the aisle to look for Mary, but was stopped by Reverend Gregory. "Look," Gregory said. "I can't believe it." He held the donation basket so Michael could see that it was filled to the top. While most of the bills were of small denominations, several were twenties. "I'll have to get another basket." Gregory's voice reflected disbelief. "Can you believe it? Another basket." A new thought jerked his head up. "You really are coming back next week, aren't you?"

Michael looked away. He did not want to make a promise he might not keep. "I suppose so. Unless things change."

"Things?" Alarm tinged the Reverend's voice. He glanced at the money in the collection basket. "What things?"

Michael did not understand the compulsion that had brought him to the church; how could he explain it to someone else? Today he'd felt as though he was close to the truth. But next week? Would God speak through him next week? He had to find out, so said, "I mean, if it's God's will."

"Oh. Yes, of course." The Reverend shifted the basket so he could secure the bills inside with the palm of one hand. "Have you seen Mary? I've got to show this to her." Without waiting for an answer Reverend Gregory hurried away.

Michael had no desire to face anyone, and there surely would be people waiting outside to talk to him. He heard Mary's voice and saw her standing in the aisle talking to the beautiful girl with the magnificent voice. What was her name? Oh, yes: Selene.

Moving to join them he heard Mary say, "I've been wanting to start a church choir. You have such a fabulous voice. Would you be interested?"

Selene stood between the pews near the aisle, her head turned, her eyes searching the room as though she expected to see someone she knew. At the question, her eyes focused on Mary. "What? Oh, a choir. I don't really know."

"You are coming back, I hope."

"I'm not sure about that either. I'm, uh, sort of a visitor." Her eyes shifted to again search the room. When she saw Michael approaching, she smiled.

Mary turned her head to see what had caught the woman's attention. "Oh, Michael. You know Miss, uh, Selene. Did you hear her voice?"

"Couldn't help it," Michael said. "You were terrific."

"Thank you. I enjoy singing."

"If I had a voice like yours, I'd never stop."

"You have a good voice. I heard you singing."

"Thanks," he said, "but I wouldn't call that singing."

"Don't be so modest. I thought you were great."

Michael felt an unexpected pleasure. He could not be sure whether she was simply flattering him or if she really meant it. It did not really matter. Here was one of the most beautiful women he had ever seen smiling at him and telling him she thought he was great. "Well, thanks." He stood grinning at her like a fool.

Mary said, "I asked her to sing in a choir."

"That's a great idea." Michael tore his gaze away from Selene. "We've got a choir?"

"No, but...I want to start one."

"Great idea." He looked at Selene. "You will, won't you?"

"I'm not sure. Are you going to stay here? With the church, I mean?"

Michael hesitated. He seemed to be living from week to week, unable to break away and unwilling to stay. Would he be here next week? Or next month? In the end, it depended upon God's will. He lifted his hands. "Who knows? It looks like it."

Mary put her hand on his arm. "Oh, but you've got to. Everyone wants to hear you."

"That's right," Selene added. "If you'll be here, I'll be here."

"Well, then I guess I'll be here."

"Fine." She stepped into the aisle. "I'll see you next week."

"Oh," Mary said. "Wait." She picked a hymnal from the rack and handed it to Selene. "Take this with you. You might like to look at some of the songs."

It seemed to Michael that Selene took the hymnal reluctantly, and he wondered whether her aversion to the Bible had anything to do with it. "All right," she said. "I'll see you next week."

Michael watched her with an uneasy feeling. Standing near her, it was impossible to escape her aura. But as she moved away it was almost like being released from a trance. Still, he hoped she really would return.

"Beautiful, isn't she?"

He turned to face Mary. "Who?"

She smiled. "Don't give me that. I'll bet she'll bring as many of these people back next week as you will."

"Well, a lot more men, that's for sure."

"Including you?"

He cocked his head. "Do I detect a note of jealousy?"

"You sure do. Any woman who wouldn't be jealous of her would have to be out of her mind."

He put his lips close to her ear, as much to drink in the scent of her hair as to achieve privacy. "We can talk about it over dinner."

"Dinner? Don't you mean lunch?"

"Both."

"Impossible. I'm supposed to work tonight."

"No dinner, no speech next week. You want to disappoint these people?"

She turned her head and looked at him out of the side of her eyes, but she was smiling. "That isn't fair."

"You know the saying: everything's fair in love and war."

"But this is neither one."

"I wouldn't be so sure." Michael had chuckled as he replied, but the humor was designed to hide the truth, the truth that he wanted to be with her.

He never discovered what her answer would have been. They had been slowly moving up the deserted aisle and had reached the foyer when a women who had been talking to Reverend Gregory just outside the door rushed into the church. Michael recognized her; she was the elderly woman from last week, the one who had been in the wheelchair.

"Oh, Mr.—Modesto," she gushed. "I'm glad I caught you." She grabbed Michael's arm in a grip so strong he winced. "You've got to help me."

Michael stared at her, torn between the wonder that she had been able to move so fast, and a fear that he might have done something that could result in a messy law suit. "Well, now—"

He was interrupted by the woman calling, "Nancy, he's here." At the same time she attempted to draw Michael toward the church entrance where Reverend Gregory was talking to a young woman who carried a blanket-wrapped baby in her arms.

The young woman started toward Michael, holding the baby before her like an offering. Outside the open door, on the walk leading to the sidewalk, Michael saw that Selene had turned to watch.

The young woman had large dark eyes, high Slavic cheekbones, and a mass of dark hair that she had attempted to control by pulling it back into a chignon. At one time she had been very pretty, even beautiful, but now her face was twisted into a tragic expression of pain and...something else. Michael recognized what it was with a sinking feeling: Her eyes, her trembling lips radiated a desperate hope. Her steps as she approached, were stumbling, her legs weak with fatigue.

The woman almost fell, and Mary moved to steady her, saying, "Are you all right?"

The woman shoved the baby toward Michael. "My baby. Please."

Michael turned his head. His brief glimpse of the baby's pale face and sunken cheeks told him that if it wasn't already dead it might soon be. This could be far worse than what he'd experienced with the baby at the hospital. "Oh, God," he muttered. He could not, he would not go through the debilitating pain again.

He stepped back, searching for a way to leave, but unless he wrenched the elderly woman's grip from his arm, he was trapped.

Reverend Gregory came toward them. "Michael, the baby's dying. She's been to clinics. They've done what they can. Perhaps a blessing..."

Dying? Oh, God, no. Michael had to force his voice past the constriction of fear in his throat. "No. I can't."

"Michael," Mary said. "You've got to try." Her puzzled look told Michael that she had no idea what the price would be.

The older woman said, "You can. You cured me."

Reverend Gregory nodded. "Yes, yes. Michael, you've got to help if you can."

If you can? The words charged Michael with hope. Perhaps it had all been an illusion, some sort of psychosomatic wish fulfillment. The elderly woman might have been confined to the wheelchair because of some imagined disability. He could have been the worst kind of charlatan, but the woman's hope had been so strong that it had effected a cure, just as a hypnotist could make some people forget their deformities or phobias, at least for a time. All he had done was take away her psychosis and she had walked.

But psychological or not, he had absorbed her anguish, and it had almost killed him. And this was no psychosomatic illness. This baby was near death. How bad would a transmigration be? He desperately did not want to find out.

He backed away, shaking his head. "No, no. I wasn't me. It was God. Ask Him. Ask Him."

"We have asked," the elderly woman said. "He led us to you."

"Michael," Mary pleaded. "You've got to. Please."

Then Michael made the mistake of looking into the eyes of the baby's mother. It was like looking into a Torquemadan dungeon, and pain lanced through him of such intensity that his legs almost buckled. And he knew that whatever he suffered, it could never match the young mother's agony.

He straightened, took a deep breath. "All right. I'll try. But just because it happened before...well, don't expect miracles."

"I know. I know," the elderly woman said. "But you can. You can."

She held the baby out to Michael. He was about to take it in his arms when a dark premonition made him stop. If it did happen, if it was like before, the pain might make him black out. He shook his head. "You hold her."

The woman looked at him as though suspecting a trick, and she continued to hold the baby out toward him.

Mary said, "He doesn't have to hold her. He only has to touch her."

The woman's face cleared. "Oh."

She stood close in front of Michael, cradling the baby in the crook of one arm as she uncovered the baby's head.

Michael looked down at the baby. It was so still, so helpless. There was no sign of breath. The swaddling blanket had parted enough so that he could see it's tiny hands, and as he watched they slowly opened and the tiny arms moved as though reaching toward him. Even then, he might have been able to turn away, but the baby's eyes opened and he was lost.

Michael watched, fascinated, as his own hands moved, reached toward the baby, and he knew it would be like putting his hands in fire. They almost touched the baby's head and he steeled himself, his teeth clenched, his eyes slitted against the expected pain.

They touched. And it struck! Pain! Terrible pain! Worse than fire! The gates of hell swung wide, and he tumbled into a caldron of all the agony of the world. He wanted to scream, to cry out 'stop! stop!' but his teeth ground together with such force that he could only groan.

Then a point of darkness appeared inside the fire, growing into a horror of impending doom as he was drawn toward it. But he welcomed the doom. End the agony! He plunged into the darkness!

Oblivion. He had no feeling, no sensations, only his mind lived, imprisoned in an infinity of blackness. A blackness of fear. This was death. A world of eternal fear, a fear that shredded all mortal rationality. Soul shattering, eternal damnation fear, unrelenting fear that would sear his brain forever, for eternity, relentless fear in a darkness so dense, so overwhelming he was drowning in darkness.

Light!

Hope exploded.

Out of the vast depths of liquid darkness, a pinprick of light. He fought the fear, willing himself to move, to seek the light.

Hopeless. He had no strength to move, no sensations beyond the fear. But the light, somehow, grew brighter, larger, moving toward him, and he fought to rip a prayer out of the dark caldron of horror.

The light responded, grew larger, brighter, cleaved through the darkness with a sword of fire held by a figure of light. The sword swung in a fiery arc, rending the darkness, destroying the fear, driving it into the vastness with rays of hope. And the figure of light looked at Michael with a gaze of such humility and compassion that Michael wanted to flow into its world. He reached with his hand, reached to touch the figure that he knew was eternal life, and the figure lifted the mighty sword and placed the handle in the hand of Michael.

The figure began to recede and Michael tried desperately to call, tried to tell the figure not to leave him, not to let the awful fear return. But he had the sword, the sword of fire, and when the fear surged back, he swung the blade and was no longer afraid. Holding the fiery blade before him, clutching the handle with both hands, he strode into the darkness.

Chapter 15

Although it had been a favorite retreat for Washington bureaucrats for years, Burning Tree golf course was made famous by President Dwight Eisenhower in the 1950s. Even so, its reputation as a place where national and international deals were made had been largely kept secret. So no one paid attention as the foursome of Ambassador Anthony Stonz, Senator George Bailey, Democrat of Georgia, Secretary of State Mitchell Carruthers, and lobbyist Amid Haraut, worked their way around the course.

They were heading for the club house while totaling their scores when Senator Bailey grunted with satisfaction. "You're a hell of a partner, Anthony. Every time I play with you I cut ten strokes off my game."

Anthony Stonz shook his head ruefully. "I don't see how, Senator. I can't break eighty to save my soul."

Secretary Carruthers snorted. "But you always win."

"That's right," Amid Haraut agreed. "You're a clutch player: just enough to win."

Stonz smiled to himself. He was naturally athletic, and it had not taken too many years of practice to give him a game good enough to get him invited to play with the most influential of the empire makers. He could easily have beaten most of the men with whom he chose to play, and although he hated to lose, he had also realized that it did not pay to be the best player when the real game involved a deal.

Today, however, it was important that his partner win, but not by such a big score that it soured the day for Carruthers and Haraut. "Luck of the Irish," he said.

The group had reached the golfer's entrance to the club house, and Senator Bailey jerked his head toward the bar. "Going to join us for a shooter?"

Stonz considered the offer. He usually did not drink alcohol, but the chance to gain influence with these three men was too great an opportunity to pass up. He smiled, on the verge of accepting the invitation when the cell phone he carried on his belt vibrated gently.

"Excuse me," he said. He knew who the call was from. He flipped the phone open. "Hello." He looked up at the men. "My secretary. I've got to take this."

"Selene," Senator Bailey's lips lifted in a salacious grin. "You really are a lucky bastard."

Anthony grinned back. "Don't I know it."

Amid Haraut said. "Give her my love."

"And mine," Secretary Carruthers chimed in.

"The fellows send their love," Stonz said into the phone. "Hold on a minute." He lowered the phone to his side. The three golfers had begun walking toward the clubhouse, and he said, "Oh, Senator, can you give me a minute tomorrow?"

Senator Bailey called back over his shoulder, "Any time, Anthony."

Secretary Carruthers stopped and looked back. "When do we get a chance to get our money back?"

Stonz had started to bring the phone back to his ear, and he laughed. "Any time you'd like, Mitch."

"Saturday then."

Stonz made a swift calculation. Would he be here next Saturday? It would depend upon this call from Selene. He had known the call would be coming when a short time ago he had felt such a chill of dread that his heart had fibrillated, and he had almost fallen. Another miracle by Michael Modesto. Senator Bailey had reached to steady him, asking if he was all right, and he had recovered quickly enough to pass it off as a mere stumble.

He knew then he would have to go to California, but first he had work to do in Washington. "Saturday it is. That good for you Senator? Amid?"

They both waved agreement and went into the clubhouse.

Stonz lifted the phone. "Selene. What happened?"

"Another miracle. A baby. It was almost dead."

"And he brought it back to life. What was his reaction?"

"He acted like he was going to die himself. Then he fainted."

Stonz knew then that the problem was not as critical as he had thought. This Michael Modesto would not be anxious to perform miracles if they came with so much pain. "Stay with him. I want to know everything he does."

"I'll try. A girl named Mary asked me to join the church choir."

"Mary? That would be the nurse. Do it."

There was a short pause before Selene said, "Anthony, I'm not really comfortable in church. If I—"

"Just do it!" he snapped. He immediately softened his voice. "Selene, you'll get used to it."

"All right," she said. "If you say so."

"I'll have to go out there soon. Until then, I need you to watch him. Understand?"

"Yes." Her voice was the familiar whisper that always happened when he was forced to exert his authority. But the important thing was that she would do what she was told. She did not really have a choice.

Chapter 16

Michael gradually become aware that he was lying on his back with his eyes closed. He felt dizzy, disoriented. His head throbbed and his body was too painful to move. And overlaying the pain was a patina of dread. Something horrible had happened . What was it?

Then he remembered and his dread deepened. The baby. Death. He had almost died. Almost? His throat was dry and his chest was crushed by a heavy pressure. A heart attack. Had his heart stopped beating? Did that mean the baby was dead? Maybe they were both dead.

But if he were dead, how could he hear voices?

He willed his eyelids to open and winced as light stabbed into his pupils. When he managed to focus his eyes, the first thing he saw was the baby's mother, tears on her cheeks. Crying? He felt a chill of horror. The baby! It must be dead!

Then he heard the baby squeal, and he realized that the woman's tears were tears of joy. Immediately, the pain in his chest lessened as his own heart resumed a steady beat.

But the pounding headache reminded him that it was an experience he never wanted to repeat, although the woman's rapture almost made the pain worthwhile. Almost.

He took a rain check with Mary on both lunch and dinner.

By the next day his body pain had vanished, but the headache continued to pound. After a time he began to think that if God wanted to punish him for something, no punishment could be worse than he was already enduring. Actually, he was not certain whether the lingering headache stemmed from the physical toll of the healing or because his brain was in so much turmoil. It was not only the enormity of the task ahead of him that burned through his mind, it was also fear that all the miracles, all the visitations were schizophrenic aberrations, and he was making a monumental fool of himself. And overriding all his worried musing was the thought that if the visitations were real and not simply the result of some delusional psychosis, was he worthy of the task?

Suppose he actually had been chosen to be a messenger of God;

what was the message? It was the foul miasma of uncertainty that was driving him crazy. Not the visitations. Not the miracles. The personage had given no hint of what he was supposed to say, no clue about what he was supposed to do.

Had ancient prophets suffered the same uncertainty, the debilitating doubts? Would the apostles had been so fervent if they had not known Christ personally? Would they have believed Christ was the son of God if he had not been able to perform miracles? Without his miracles, Christ would probably have been considered just another evangelist.

And what of his own miracles? Coincidences? Or proof that he really was God's messenger?

But overriding all was the fear that he would not recognize the real message if he did stumble upon it. People had been pouring out so called "messages from God" for generations. Obviously, they hadn't hit upon the 'right' one, or he wouldn't have been recruited now. What could he possible say that hadn't already been said thousands of times? There was no point in him reinventing the wheel.

Damn!

He knew so little about religion, about God, so few of His words and His commandments. Why couldn't he have paid more attention when he was a kid in church? Outside of a vague memory of a few biblical quotations, he had no knowledge of prophets and messages already given, subjects already covered.

One of the biggest mysteries to Michael was his inability to quit, to simply walk away. The way things were going, there would be no peace of mind for him until he retreated to his old decadence. So why didn't he?

It wasn't a subconscious fear of God's wrath nor his innate hatred of failure that kept him from giving up. In truth, it was something much more tangible, but equally incomprehensible: Mary.

It seemed that each time he saw her he was dragged deeper into an irreversible obsession over which he was losing all control. Being a supposed messenger of God was confusing and abhorrent, but there was no confusion in his feelings about Mary. The trouble was that the two were inexorably bound together. If he abandoned his quest for the message, he would lose Mary. Even if, somehow, he could possibly give up Mary, would it end the quest? He did not think so. He would have to continue his search and trust that God would give him some guidance.

Once he decided that he had no option except to see the mission through to its end—whatever and whenever it was—Michael began his metamorphose by moving out of the hotel into a rented apartment in Toluca Lake, an up-scale bedroom community in the San Fernando Valley not far from Glendale. At the public library, he checked out an armload of books and carted them back to his apartment.

He began with a study of world religions. He expected his studies would be limited to Buddhism, Christianity, Judaism and Islam and was taken aback by the sheer numbers of their branches. The tree of Christianity alone had dozens of branches: Catholicism, Zoroastrims, Anglican, Protestants, and those branched into Moravians, Greek Orthodox, Russian Orthodox, Methodist, Episcopal, Presbyterian, Mormon, Quaker, Baptist, Unitarian, Congregationalist and dozens of splinter groups and churches. After encountering Brahmanism, Taoism, Confucianism, Shintoism, Hinduism, and even mysticism, deism, nihilism, theism and hundreds of gods and goddesses ranging from Shiva to Zeus, he realized that he would never be able to analyze the depths of these religions. Still, maybe he didn't have to. Instead of studying the religions themselves, he could concentrate on the great prophets, the philosophers—those who had been seekers of truth. If they hadn't actually hit upon the great 'truth,' they surely would have winnowed out the chaff and, perhaps, had come up with rational insights.

So, he poured over the works of Socrates, Plato, Aristotle, Dewey, Spinoza, Descarte, Kierkegaard, Kant, Berkeley, Nietzsche, James, Locke, and St. Thomas Aquinas.

He couldn't study them in depth; that would take a lifetime and his time was short.

It was while despairing over the likes of Anthropomorphism, Epiphenomenalism, Solipsism and Pragmatism, that it gradually dawned upon him that he was doing it all wrong. He did not have to conduct a substantive analysis; he would never in God's green earth find time to cover the pontificating of every philosopher or prophet or professed Messiah. What he really had to find was a way out for himself.

This responsibility, this horror that had been thrust upon him, was it unique? If not, how had previous 'messengers of God' found mental if not physical sanctuary?

He searched without direction, without guidance, with only one goal: to put meaning to his strange experience. Had others been able to heal the sick? Had others experienced the horrific consequences? Was the power to heal intrinsic with being a messenger, or was it unrelated?

He discovered that through the ages many men from many nations had thought they were either the Messiah, the Mahdi, the Krishna or 'The Heavenly King.' There was Simon Bar Kokba during the reign of the Emperor Hadrian, there was a man who called himself Moses in the fifth century, and there was Serene of Syria, David Alroy of the Middle East, Muhammad Ahmad of Sudan, Mirza Ghulam Ahmad of India, Solomon Molcho of Asia and Europe, James Naylor, the English Quaker, Daniel Philipovitch and, some thought, Rasputin of Russia as well as William Riker and Father Devine, among others, of the

United States. All had considered themselves to be divine, messengers of God. Had they all been wrong?

There were no answers. Even if one of the ancients had solved the enigma, he had left no clue, no theorem that would provide proof of his emancipation.

Time after time he followed a thread that held out hope of leading to proof that their words actually were the words of God. But each time the lead gradually diminished into nothing. He came to feel that he was a traveler on a road with immeasurable branches, all narrowing into paths, and the paths narrowed into trails, trails that gradually vanished in thickets of suppositions, superstitions and rationalizations. The one axiom he was able to glean was that 'truth' was directly proportional to 'faith.' Without faith, no proof was sufficient, and with faith, no proof was necessary.

And his own divine message? After a week he had no more idea what it was than when he had begun his quest. There had been no epiphany, no blinding vision, nothing but the memory of being handed a fiery sword, an image that only added to his confusion.

The only thing he knew for certain was that even if one of the ancients had solved the enigma, he had left no clue, no theorem that would provide proof of emancipation.

There was one possibility that he had to force himself to reject over and over. He was going mad! It was all a grotesque hallucination. Except that babies had been cured. The woman in the wheelchair had walked. He had survived the elevator crash.

Unless they, too, were all figments of a mad mind. And Mary? The Reverend Gregory? Were they all chimeras?

But there was too much evidence that they were not. If Mary were a figment of his imagination, so were Benny and Aaron and Creed and all the other people who had seen and talked with her.

By Friday his head was reeling with rejected ideas. Despite his determination to keep Mary at arm's length, he called her, reaching her at the hospital. As he knew she would, she agreed to help him research a topic for the Sunday's sermon. She would meet him that evening after work. Her only hesitation had been when he suggested she come to his apartment since that was where he had his research material.

When she walked in he helped her with her coat and hung it in the closet. Glancing at the apartment, she shook her head. "We'll have to do something about this."

Michael was a little miffed. He had paid extra for a furnished apartment, and while the furnishings were not exactly French Provincial, they were modern and comfortable. But then, what did he know. All he looked for in furnishings was a place to sit and a place to sleep. If he woke up and his back wasn't sore, it was good enough.

Mary still wore her white nurse's uniform and the starched material made a slight rustling sound as she went to a table near a sliding glass door that opened to a small garden area. She looked at the scattered books and papers with a smile. "You have been busy."

"Not really. I just brought these in to impress you."

"Well, you've certainly succeeded."

She picked up some of the books and pamphlets and looked at their titles. "Spinosa, St. Aquinius, Socrates. Even the Bible. If they haven't been any help, what can I possibly do?"

Michael stared at her lips and stifled a suggestive reply. "You've had a lot more experience with this than I have. I was hoping you could give me a idea for Sunday."

"You did very well last week. Why don't you do the same thing? Let the Bible guide you."

He picked up the Bible, weighing it in his palm. "I got lucky. It just happened to open at a place I was familiar with. But I can't depend on that. I don't know it that well."

"Well, why not pick a place in advance, something you do know?"

"Yeah, I could do that. But..." He put down the Bible and moved to the center of room, his back toward her, searching for a way to explain his dilemma. "I want to find the real message."

"The message? Whatever you say will be a message of some kind."

"Of some kind, yes." He turned to face her. He clenched his fist. "But I've got to find 'the' message. The one he told me to give."

"He? The angel?"

"That's right. It was right there, words of fire. But for some reason, he didn't tell me what to say." He sat down in a chair, running his fingers through his hair. "It's driving me crazy."

"It doesn't have to be that way." She quickly crossed the room and pulled up a chair so she could sit facing him. "He will tell you when the time is right."

"But that could take weeks, months." He looked at her, his forehead lined with worry. "Maybe never."

"That may be." She paused, and glanced at the books on the table. "But does it really matter? You'll be giving other messages."

"That's what I've been telling myself. But what if they're the wrong messages. What if I'm leading people down the wrong path?"

"If you are a messenger of God, that can't happen."

"Yeah, if."

"You've had proof of that: the woman in the wheelchair, the babies. They weren't figments of your imagination."

"I hope to hell not."

"So, if you continue to follow your conscience, one of them may be right."

He looked up with a twisted smile. "Like rolling dice. If I roll them long enough eventually I'm bound to make my point."

"And when you do, you'll know. I know you will."

"Unless I seven out."

"That won't happen. I know it won't. And someday—"

"Someday!" He stood up abruptly and slapped his palm on the table causing Mary to flinch. "I want it to end! This isn't my life. For God's sake, I'm a musician, not a damned preacher! I want to get back to the thing I know, the people I know."

He should not have said that. He knew it the moment the words left his mouth. Mary straightened in the chair and stared at him, hurt rimming her eyes. "I see," was all she said.

He took a step toward her. "I didn't mean it like it sounded. You're the one good thing that's come out of this. I want you in my life." He did not know why, but he stopped short before adding "forever." He rationalized by telling himself that he didn't want to frighten her away by coming on too strong.

Mary studied him silently and he forced a smile and waved his hand. "I'll be all right. This is just all so damned new."

"You're really scared, aren't you."

Michael froze, his face half turned away. "Scared? Me?"

She indicated the litter of books and papers. "All this. You don't want to—as you call it—'wing it' because you're afraid you'll say the wrong thing? I don't think so. Failure.." She moved to stand in front of him. "That's it, isn't it? You're afraid you'll make a fool of yourself."

"It won't be the first time."

"Don't you see? There can't be any failure. Not with the word of God."

"And just what is that fu..." He stopped before he used the expletive. "What is His 'word'?"

"It will come. Give it time."

Michael turned away, his shoulders slumping. She was telling him the same things he'd been telling himself for a week. God might not give him 'the message'; but He would never allow him to commit blasphemy either. Would He?

She went to him and took hold of his arms. "Michael, it's not up to you. You know that."

Her face so close to his forced a sharp breath past his suddenly dry lips. "I don't know that." His reply was unnecessarily peevish and he pulled away from her grip so he would not have to look at her face.

She put her hand on his forearm. "It was an angel. An angel of God."

Michael shook his head. "I thought angels were supposed to help. I feel like hell." He turned his head and looked at her, his brows furrowed. "What if Benny was right. I am being used."

She took her hand from his arm, "We wouldn't do that."

"I don't mean you. But what if that...that personage wasn't from God?"

Mary's head snapped around. "What?"

"Well, suppose he's not an angel. How the hell would I know?"

"Yes." She stood for a minute, her head down. "I suppose Lucifer could do all those things." Her head came up, her eyes clear. "But if you're a foil of Lucifer, he wouldn't try to kill you."

"Kill me?"

"The elevator. If you are the messenger, he'd try to stop you."

Michael took a deep breath. "Oh, shit. Just what I need."

"He might try again. Michael, you've got to be careful."

"Not if I quit."

She shook her head. "I doubt that he'd believe you."

A new tingle of fear caused Michael to close his eyes. "As long as I'm the messenger, he can't touch me. But if I quit—if I'm allowed to quit—he'll probably kill me."

Mary did not answer, but her silence told him that she agreed.

Suddenly, the entire conversation seemed so bizarre that Michael could not suppress a choking laugh. "This is crazy." He went to look out at the garden. "What the hell ever happened to free choice? Everybody's telling me what to do." He snorted with disgust. "Even God."

"My God, Michael. It's the greatest calling anyone could ever hope for."

"Calling!" He turned to face her. "For what? Messenger! I don't know any message! Shit, I'm just a stupid rock jock. I don't even know what the hell I'm doing. Why pick me? I don't want the job!"

"You can't refuse. You just can't."

Her words added fuel to a knot of anger that had been building in Michael's chest. He had always resisted when pushed. His father had called him a rebel, and his mother had learned to couch her orders in the form of suggestions. Now it was an angel—or a demon. "You always have choices," he said. "Benny's right. This isn't for me. Get somebody else for your sermons."

Mary's eyes grew large, unblinking. "You can't mean it."

"The hell I can't. I quit."

There. He'd said it, even though he half expected a fiery sword to strike him down.

Mary did not immediately answer. Her face had the stricken look of being unable to fully comprehend. "But don't you realize what it means? You've been chosen!"

"But I don't want to play."

"How can you refuse the word of God?"

"Easy. Let him get some other sucker."

Mary took a step toward him, her hands out. "You can save lives. You'd give that up?"

"That's something I'll never do again. No way."

"But... why?"

Why? How could he possibly explain? "Honey, you don't know.

You can't possibly know."

"I know that you have performed miracles. How much more can you do?"

"I didn't ask to be God. If he wants miracles, he can make them himself. He doesn't need me."

He went to the door and opened it. "I'm sorry this didn't work out. I'll see what I can do for your charity, but it'll have to be my way. "

Mary walked to the door, moving as though she were suddenly weary. Before she stepped into the hallway, she turned her head to look at Michael.

"It isn't up to you, you know. I've seen what you can do. You can't turn your back on that. You just can't."

"The hell I can't. On Sunday, don't wait for me."

As she stepped into the hall, he saw tears mist her eyes and they moved him more than any command. It was only the memory of the horror he'd felt when he touched the dying baby that allowed him to close the door. There would be no more miracles. not on this Sunday, not on any Sunday.

Chapter 17

Michael closed his eyes, unable to look at the emptiness of his room. It wasn't his fault. He had given God his chance and God had abandoned him. But it wasn't God he was going to miss, it was Mary. And he couldn't have one without the other.

He glanced at his watch. Ten o'clock. Not too late to call Benny and give him the news. He dialed Benny's cell phone, but the line was busy. Well, it would be best if he went to see Benny anyway. He'd go tomorrow.

Except there would be no sleep for him until he had the situation settled. It would be like closing the door on the nightmare of the last few weeks, the dawn of a new day.

Driving through the dark streets, he couldn't keep his attention on his driving. In a sense he felt a profound relief that it was over, that the huge responsibility was at an end, but at the same time, he felt an emptiness, an almost painful sense of loss.

But there was also an insistent sense of guilt. Maybe Mary was right and it was his lack of faith that was holding back the word of God.

Whatever the reason, he was damned glad it was ...

Abruptly, the engine sputtered, jerking his mind back to his driving. He worked the gas petal, but the engine continued to sputter. Gas? No. The tank was half full. He pulled to the curb where the engine gave a last gasp and died.

Thank God he kept his phone in the glove compartment. He started to use the auto dial to call his auto club when he stopped. How could he give them directions? He had no idea where he was. His mind had been so preoccupied he had paid little attention to his driving.

He peered out the windshield looking for a sign or a familiar building, something that would help him get oriented.

The widely spaced street lights illuminated a collection of shabby shops and industrial buildings. The area was a model of urban blight. In addition to garish signs, many in Spanish, that proclaimed each building's occupant, graffiti decorated every flat surface on every wall and building.

All the shops were closed, their entrances secured with chained bars and metal grills.

There was one small stucco building in the middle of the block that caught his eye. On the front of the steeply slanted A-frame roof was a large white-painted cross. A glass-protected sign on the wall near the doors proclaimed the building was home to "The Holy Church of God." A short flight of broad steps led to an open door. Dim light from inside spilled onto the steps.

To Michael, the church seemed oddly out of place. This did not appear to be a neighborhood anyone would chose for a session of quiet introspection.

Taking the phone with him, he got out of the car and walked to the nearest corner, keeping a wary eye out for anyone approaching. But there was no one. Except for the whisper of far off traffic, there was no sound, no movement.

At the corner, he located the street sign and gave its name and the block number to the auto club's operator. He grimaced in helpless anger when she said it would be at least a half hour before the tow truck could arrive. One more indication that it had been a bad day.

Walking back to the car, he couldn't stop looking toward the small church. It was as though the open door beckoned him to enter, to go through into the light.

He jerked his eyes away and rubbed his hand across his face, breaking the hypnotic connection. Now he could think. What was so tantalizing about the church? Nothing. Except for the short time in Mary's church, he'd had no compulsion to enter a place of worship. Why should he? Religion had nothing he wanted, especially now when he had just broken the bonds of responsibility.

And yet, he could not shake off the feeling that if he did not investigate, the compulsion would bother him for God-only-knew how long, like an unidentified melody running through his brain.

With a growl of exasperation, he put his telephone in the car's glove compartment, locked the door and strode to the church, all the time telling himself he was a fool. If he went barging into the church, people inside would either throw him out or call the cops.

He paused just inside the door waiting for his eyes to adjust to the gloom, half expecting some force to yank him inside. But there was only silence, deathly silence. It was simply a small community church, much like Mary's, with two rows of polished wood pews, a small dais with a pulpit, and a large, gold-leafed crucifix on the rear wall. There was a single open door at the left of the dais leading to the church office. Dim light from several small, suspended chandeliers, scarcely penetrated the gloom.

The room was deserted. But it didn't matter. Somehow, he didn't think it was a person that had drawn him to the church.

He shivered. What he was feeling was not wonder; it was fear, not fear for his life, but fear for the direction of his life. And with the fear was a familiar anger, anger that something, or someone, was trying to control his very existence.

But it was his life. The hell with them.

He started to leave, to walk away, staring out into the night. Was he being manipulated, or was it all in his mind? He had to find out.

Muttering "Stupid, stupid," he turned and walked down the aisle toward the pulpit, his steps on the worn wooden floor sounding loud in the silent room.

He stopped in front of the dais. Steeling himself for a bad reaction, he deliberately looked up at the face of Christ on the crucifix. The artists who had created the image had given the eyes the standard expressing of sad contemplation, but they were lifeless, blank. It was just a statute, plaster or wood, the kind he'd seen so many times it no longer had meaning.

The sense of relief was so strong he shook his head in wonder.

Then—a sound.

He'd been so sure he was alone in the church he was startled by a soft thumping sound. He jerked his head toward the source of the sound: the side room. The sound came again, and he let his held breath out with a sigh. Sweeping. Someone was sweeping the floor. Probably a janitor.

"Hello," he called. "Anybody here?"

The sound stopped, and an elderly black man came through the door carrying a push broom with bristles so worn they had a permanent backward curve. But the man wasn't a janitor. He wore a tired black suit with a snowy-white reverend's collar. His close clipped hair was haloed with silver.

He stopped when he saw Michael, and his eyes came alive as though he was surprised to see anyone in his church. "Yes?" he said. His voice was deep and soft but filled with the power of someone used to speaking from a pulpit.

Michael was at a loss for words. He had absolutely no idea what he could say that would explain his presence in the man's church. "Uh, excuse me," he said. "Are you the minister?" Stupid question; of course, he was.

The man smiled. "Reverend Paul." He held up the broom. "I'm also the janitor. It keeps me humble." He chuckled and glanced around the small church. "As though I needed the excuse."

Michael liked the man immediately. "I, uh, the door was open..." He stopped. There was no explanation for why he was here.

The reverend stared at him, his head cocked. "Everything okay?"

Michael nodded. "Yeah. My car broke down. I'm waiting for the auto club."

"You're welcome to wait in here."

Michael shook his head. The last thing he wanted was to push his luck by sitting in the church for twenty minutes. "Thanks, but I think I'll wait in the car."

"Okay. If they don't show up, I'll be here."

Michael said, "Thanks," and started up the aisle. Then he stopped and took a fold of bills from his pocket. He peeled off a five and offered it to the Reverend. "Thanks, again."

The reverend smiled and shook his head. "No need for that."

"Call it a contribution."

"Oh, that's different. There's a box by the door."

"Okay."

He began walking back up the aisle toward the open door, feeling the reverend's puzzled gaze on his back. He had only taken a few steps when he stopped, staring at the open front door, staring into the darkness beyond the door. Out there, in the night, was safety. Out there was his old life, a life in his own control. Why was the desire to escape into the darkness so strong? The church was supposed to be a haven, not the darkness outside. So why wasn't he bolting for the door?

He turned, astonished that he could bring himself to do so. "Excuse me," he heard himself ask, "do you have a minute?"

The reverend had been leaning on his broom, watching. Now he straightened and chuckled. "I think I can spare a few seconds." His eyes said he knew why Michael had stopped even before he said, "What can I do for you?"

"I'm not sure, but...I need to talk to...somebody."

"Somebody?" The reverend's eyes turned toward the crucifix behind the alter. "Are you sure it's me you want to talk to?"

The words "Yes. You." were wrenched from Michael. He did not want to get close to the figure on the cross; that was the door to confusion.

The reverend studied his face. He was no longer smiling. He motioned toward the front pew. "Unless you'd prefer my office."

"No, no. This'll be fine."

This time the reverend's smile and the accompanying chuckle had a studied tone, designed to put the man with the problem at ease. "I'm glad you said here. For some reason bill collectors prefer my office."

Michael sat on the front pew. The reverend leaned the broom against the back of a pew and sat down beside him, his gaze soft but inquisitive.

"Don't worry. I, uh,..." Michael paused. His lips were bone dry. This was stupid. What could he possibly say to this man? A confession? It would be like a shrift to a priest. There were things in his life that could bear confessing, but they had nothing to do with his uncertainty. If it hadn't been for the strange happenings with the baby and the elevator, he wouldn't even be here.

"It's like this, Reverend. A couple of funny things have happened to me. Maybe you can make some sense of it."

"What kind of things?"

"Well, I..." How could he explain without sounding like a lunatic? He couldn't look at the man as he said, "It started, I think, with a ball of light."

"A ball of light? Like a U.F.O.?"

"No. More like lightning. I was being mugged. It, uh, melted this guy's gun."

The reverend's eyes changed, became wary. He shifted uneasily and Michael realized how stupid he must sound. "Okay. Forget the light. It really started with the baby..."

The reverend's brows pinched down. "Something with a baby?"

"Yeah. It was sick. A crack baby. Then I touched it and I...I got this terrible pain. But the baby got better. Just like a woman in a wheelchair. But I swear I had nothing to do with it."

"A woman? In a wheelchair?"

"All I did was touch her, her hand. I...I had this awful feeling like it was my back. I guess I fainted. But she got better. She could walk."

"You think you healed them, the baby and the woman?"

"Well, yes. But I think that what happens is...I kind of take on what they have. I think they call it transmigration. I hate it."

"I imagine so." The reverend's voice was still warm and friendly, but it had taken on a new tone, putting a shield between them.

Michael twisted around to stare at the man. "What I want to know is: what would have happened if the baby had died? Would I have died, too?"

The reverend returned Michael's stare for a moment with the same beatific expression as the figure on the cross. "Have you talked to your own priest or reverend about this?"

Michael had the sinking feeling that the man had no idea what he was talking about. He shook his head. "No. I don't have one. Not really."

"I see. Have you tried prayer?"

"Well, prayer is kind of a one-way communication. I'd like some direct answers."

The reverend clasped his hands and his face relaxed as though Michael had lifted a load off his shoulders. "Direct answers. Yes. If your heart is in your prayer, you will receive your answers."

Defeat settled upon Michael like a familiar cloud. Here it was again, passing the buck to God. "Do you really believe that?"

The man avoided answering by getting to his feet. "The only one who can answer you is God,"—he indicated the figure on the crucifix—"or the son of God."

Michael rubbed at his eyes, feeling defeated. He wanted to get up and walk out of the church, to leave his doubts and anxieties behind like he would shed a hated coat. But maybe the man was right and the way to assuage his conscious was to go through the psychological anodyne of prayer. Maybe here, here in front of Jesus, a prayer might bring an answer.

"Maybe you're right."

"Do you want me to join you?"

"No. No thanks." The last thing Michael wanted was to have some stranger listening in when he laid bare his soul.

The man stood up as though to end the encounter. "He listens to me. I'm sure he'll listen to you." He picked up the broom and went into the side room. To Michael's relief, he closed the door after him.

Michael stood up and slowly walked to the dais. His legs did not want to move. He had to force one foot in front of the other, his mind twisting and turning like a snake in a trap, searching for escape, for something to say. Even so, he was not ready when he reached the edge of the dais. He started to kneel, then decided he would have a better chance of his words getting through if he moved closer to the crucifix. He stepped up on the low stage, and after looking around to make sure he was still alone, he knelt so close he was almost touching the feet of the figure on the cross.

He clasped his hands and bowed his head, searching his mind for long forgotten words.

"Holy Father." He smiled. He'd almost added, 'I have sinned,' like they did in the movies when they went to confession. Instead, he said, "Okay. I'll put it to you straight. I haven't been in church for years, except those times with Mary. The truth is I wouldn't be here now if these crazy things haven't been happening. But maybe they're not happening. Maybe I'm just...losing it. If I am. I guess it's my own damn fault." He lifted his head to look up at the face on the crucifix. "Sorry. Anyway...If I'm not losing it, what the hell is going on? I—"

He stopped, his mouth frozen in disbelief. A light. Beginning to outline the head of the figure on the crucifix. A light...like the one he'd seen in the parking lot and the elevator. He stared, mesmerized, as the light expanded, became brighter, so bright he had to shield his eyes. At the same time a soft wind tugged at his clothing, a warm wind, gentle as a caress.

Then the wind died and the light softened so that Michael was able to stare directly at it as it framed the face on the cross. The eyes in the face shifted, looked straight at him, and Michael folded his arms across his chest defensively.

The figure moved. It's arms came down and one hand pointed at the floor in front of Michael. Fire streamed from the finger tip and Michael smelled the acrid odor of burning wood. The finger moved, and as Michael stared in disbelief, words burned into the floor: 'BEHOLD! I AM THE SON OF GOD AND THOU ART MY FATHER'S MES-

SENGER.'

Smoke obscured the words, smoke that rose in a cloud, shrouding the figure, only the eyes glowed through like burning coals.

A familiar hand of gold appeared out of the smoke, and again flame blazed from the finger tip, spelling out the words 'BEWARE! BEWARE THE FALSE PROPHET! BEWARE THE ANTICHRIST! BEWARE!"

As Michael watched, his eyes wide and staring, acrid smoke rose from the burning wood, hiding the words. When the smoke cleared, the branded words had vanished.

Michael's stare lifted to the figure on the cross. The light still outlined the figure's head, but now the arms again where outstretched on the cross; the eyes, no longer glowing, stared down at him, and Michael felt such a sense of warmth and compassion that tears came to his eyes.

Then the light began to fade, to recede, like the fiery sky of a setting sun. Michael reached out, to stop it, to hold the strange euphoria that he never wanted to lose. "No," he called, his voice hoarse, pleading. "No, don't go."

But the light dimmed and was gone, leaving the figure nothing more than gold-painted plaster, it's sad eyes blank, staring at nothing.

"You all right? I thought I heard something."

The reverend stood near the open office door, still holding the broom as though only seconds had passed since he had left the room.

Michael tore his gaze from the crucifix. He took a deep breath and wiped at his face with a shaky palm. "You did." He gestured toward the wooden floor. "Look."

The reverend took a step forward. "What? I miss a place?"

Michael stared at the floor, the memory of smoke still strong in his nostrils, the words still burning in his brain. But the floor was clean, unmarked. He jerked his eyes back to the figure on the crucifix. Had he imagined the whole thing? He slowly shook his head. "I don't understand. He was here. I heard Him."

"Who?" The reverend glanced around the small church. Even in the dim light it was obvious that the church was vacant.

Michael's voice was just above a whisper. "Jesus."

The reverend gave him a hard look, the kind he would use to evaluate the words of a drunk—or someone insane. "Well," he said, his voice placating. "Why not? Did He say anything?"

Michael was reluctant to tell him; the man must already think he was crazy. But he needed this man, he needed his sanity verified. "He said that—I'm God's messenger."

The reverend did not laugh. He did not smile. Instead, he simply looked skeptical. "Uh huh. If you say so. What was the message?"

Michael straightened. He couldn't blame the man for thinking he was crazy. He almost believed it himself. He glanced down at the floor, searching for some form of vindication. But the worn wood was just as it had been when he came in, without a trace of singed wood or tendrils of smoke. "I don't know."

Relief flooded the man's face. He had probably expected a torrent of words, some glorious Manichean prophesy. "Then He must have been divine. Mortals always have some great message that's going to save the world."

Michael knew exactly how the man felt. He himself was beginning to think the entire thing had been a figment of his imagination. "Yeah. I think you're right." He had to get away, out into the real world where he belonged. "Well, thanks."

He was walking toward the door when the reverend called, "If you find out what the message is, let me know."

Michael waved affirmation without turning. It wasn't until he was climbing into the car that he realized he was holding his breath, and he slumped in the seat, breathing deeply. He'd been holding his breath because he'd been afraid that some apparition, some hallucination would appear before he could reach the safety of familiar surroundings.

Without thinking, he turned the ignition key and the car instantly started. He sat for a moment, listening to the engine. It ran smoothly, without a hint of sputtering. So, it had been a plan. He had been manipulated into entering the church.

He drove away, searching for a busy boulevard. For once he wanted heavy traffic. He wanted to be surrounded by reality, by people, by things, safe from phantoms and illusions. But had it really been an illusion? Mary had seen the ball of fire. And others had seen the miracles of the babies. This time, however, he had been alone.

There had to be a logical explanation. He remembered reading about people who unconsciously caused strange things to happen such as objects moving or even flying. At one time it was believed that such phenomena were caused by poltergeists, but investigators had discovered that they were actually a form of psychokinesis.

But in the church; Reverend Paul had heard nothing, seen nothing. Either the man was not meant to be a witness, or more likely, it had never happened. And yet, when this latest manifestation was added to the other 'miracles,' he had to believe it was real.

'You are my Father's messenger.' The words might have been only in his mind, but God had put them there just as he had put the fiery sword of responsibility in his hand.

'Beware the Antichrist.' What had he meant by that? Could it have anything to do with the elevator accident?

He hunched over the steering wheel and peered into the night. He would have to tell Mary. He might be a messenger without a message, but now there was no turning back.

Chapter 18

On Sunday morning Michael awakened with an increasingly familiar sense of impending doom. In a few brief hours he would be standing in front of people who expected him to bring them a divine message and he had no message. But his road had been carved in rock by the hand of Christ and refusing was no longer an option.

He needed help, and the only one who could even comprehend what he was going through was Mary, provided she would even speak to him.

He arrived at the church early hoping to be there when she arrived. But her car was already in the parking lot, and, strangely for this hour, were several other cars. Even more strange, from the church he heard the sound of singing. Was he late? Had they changed the time?

Depression was a heavy weight when he climbed the steps with all the enthusiasm of a man climbing the steps of a hangman's gallows.

Inside, he found several people already occupying the pews. Mrs. Gardner was playing the organ with more restraint than usual while Mary led a small choir made up of five men and women and the girl, Selene. Like Mrs. Gardner with the organ, Selene kept her voice sotto so she would not overpower the other singers. But when the music called for bravura, the soaring rhapsody of her voice raised the hair at the back of Michael's neck

The song ended with a rousing crescendo from Mrs. Gardner and Michael applauded as he moved down the aisle. "Bravo! Bravissimo!"

Mary took a step toward him, her expression inquisitive. "Well, hello."

Michael put on a smile. "I changed my mind."

She came toward him with both hands extended. She wore a clinging, pale blue, knit dress with long sleeves. "I'm glad. I was really worried."

He took hold of her hands, marveling that hands that looked so delicate could have such strength. "You might not be so glad. I still have no idea what I'm going to say."

"Do what you did last time. Let the Lord decide."

He released her hands. "It's gone beyond that." He glanced around the room. Everyone, even the members of the chorus, were staring at them. "Is there somewhere we can talk?"

She nodded toward the foyer. "I think John will let us use his office." She turned to the choir members. "I've got to talk to Michael for a moment. Why don't you practice number 124, "We All Have The Power." Selene, would you lead?"

Selene had not heard. Her eyes, locked on Michael, burned with such intensity that he almost expected to feel some sort of curse.

"Selene," Mary said again and Selene's eyes cooled, refocused on Mary.

"Yes?"

"Would you take over for a moment? Number 124."

"With pleasure." Her voice, with its hint of some unfathomable accent, was warm honey, and Michael again wondered why she was not famous. With that voice, those incredible eyes and her sultry beauty she could have been a movie star—or a voodoo priestess. He also wondered why she had chosen to be in this small church. She belonged in a cathedral or a palace.

He walked with Mary up the aisle and into the Reverend's office just off the vestibule where Reverend Gregory sat at a desk, using a magnifying class to study passages in the Bible. He looked up when Mary and Michael entered. "Michael. Mary said you weren't going to be here. Is something wrong?"

"No, no," Michael said hastily. "Mary's going to help me with my speech. We were just looking for a quiet place." He turned back toward the door. "We'll go outside."

"No. It's okay." Reverend Gregory pushed to his feet. "It's time for me to be out front." He paused at the door. "I'm glad you're here."

"Thanks," Michael answered.

The minute the door shut Mary said, "What is it? You said you were quitting."

"I changed my mind."

"Oh?"

"I should say I had it changed for me."

She regarded him silently, waiting for him to explain.

He searched for words that would not make it sound as though he was losing his mind. "You're not going to believe this."

He sank onto the room's single chair and put his face in his hands. When he looked up and saw the concern in Mary's expression, he realized that he did not have to worry about her reaction. She would believe his story because she wanted to believe. She wanted to believe almost as much as he wanted not to believe.

"Last night," he began, "after you left, I thought I'd better talk to

Benny. I was driving over to see him when...the car stalled."

Mary took a step toward him. "Stalled? Are you all right?"

"Yeah. It was on a side street. I was able to pull over."

Inside the church the chorus began to sing and the sound gave Michael a sense of unreality. He stood up. He need activity, something to keep reminding him that this alien world was now his world. There was little space in the cramped office, so he walked around behind the desk, feeling reality in its bulk. "It happened in front of a small church—kind of like this one—I have no idea where. Anyway, I went in and...well,... the damndest thing happened."

She stared at him, her eyes bright, her body ridged. "What? What happened?"

"There was this light. Like in the parking lot. Then...Jesus—the crucifix—came to life."

Mary sucked in her breath. "Did he speak? This time, did he speak?"

"Well, no, but...he wrote words...in the floor...with fire, if you can believe that."

"What did they say?"

He hesitated, feeling like an idiot. "They said: 'I am the Son of God.' And 'Thou are my Father's messenger.'"

"Is that all?"

He shook his head and slumped into Reverend Gregory's chair behind the desk.

Mary raised her hand in a gesture of impatience. "Michael, what else did he say?"

Michael stood up and put his hands flat on the top of the desk. The voices in the distant choir lifted as though to underscore his words. "He wrote...on the floor: 'Beware the false prophet! Beware the Antichrist!' Now, what the hell did he mean by that?"

Mary's face had lost it's color. "The Antichrist? Did he...did he say who?"

"No. After that he went away. I looked for the words...to make sure, but they were gone. All of it. The light, the smoke, the words. It was like they'd never been there." As he sank back onto Reverend Gregory's chair, the music of the choir ended, leaving him with an empty feeling of finality. "I'm not sure they ever were."

He leaned his head back against the high back of the chair. "Maybe it's all in my head. Maybe this whole thing—you, the church, the visions—they're all in my head."

"No!" The rejection exploded from her. "I saw the light. And you healed that woman and the babies.

He looked at her, blinking, almost expecting her to vanish. "How do I know any of this is real?" He got up and thumped the desk to confirm its reality. "This desk. This room. I might wake up in a minute and find out it's all a dream...a damned nightmare."

Mary came around the desk and put her hands on his shoulders. "If it's a dream...even a nightmare...then we're both having it. Because, I'm here. I'm here with you. And I'm real. You know I am."

"How do I know? I've had dreams about beautiful women before."

She looked into his eyes, her gaze level. "What would it take to make you know? What can I do to make you realize?"

Her lips were inches from his and Michael fought an urge to pull her closer, to taste the lush sweetness of her lips. His voice was harsh as he joked, "You could let me make love to you. That should prove it."

She stiffened and went still, her lips parted in startled disbelief. Then they came together in a firm line before she said, "All right. If that will make you believe."

Michael's throat was suddenly dry. She was offering herself to him, something he was almost sure she had never done with anyone. It would be so easy to put her to the test. Not here. This was not a good place for what he would like to do. Tonight, in her apartment, her bed. All he had to do was tell her to prove it. Her eyes told him she would.

He turned his head. He could not refuse her offer if he looked at her face. When he had himself under control, he gently pushed her back. "Thanks." He mustered up a grin. "That really would be a dream." He quickly moved to the door before he could change his mind. "This may not be reality, but I'll play it out...until I wake up."

He was reaching for the door knob when she said, "Then you'll speak today?"

"Look," he said. "I don't want any more...visitations. I'll keep on with the church. Maybe that'll keep Him quiet."

She looked at him and a strange darkness crossed her face. "That part about the Antichrist... Are you afraid?"

He stiffened, trying to conceal his surprise. He forced himself to relax. "Not the way you think. Not of getting hurt. I just don't want to make any mistakes." She started to say something and he raised his hand. "One thing: No more miracles. No healing. Okay?"

Her face softened and she nodded. "It's up to you, Michael."

When he stepped into the foyer, he was surprised to see that the church was now completely filled. Many crowded the small foyer and others stood outside on the steps and the walkway. Reverend Gregory stood just outside the doorway listening to voices raised in protest, and Michael heard him say he was sorry there was no more room inside, and the fire department would not allow standing in the aisles.

When the people noticed him, heads turned and voices died. Michael put on a smile, and as he passed Reverend Gregory, he hissed, "What is this? Who are all these people?"

"They've come to hear you. We've never had so many."

Could Gregory be right? Had all these people come expecting miracles? If so, they were in for a big, fat disappointment.

Chapter 19

Michael sat in the front pew with his eyes closed, his mind open, receptive, desperately searching for inspiration. As usual, he had no idea what he was going to say and time was growing short.

When there was no inspiration, he opened his eyes, focusing on the distant crucifix, silently praying that the figure would put words into his mind.

But instead of a heavenly message, his mind became aware of a subtle perfume. Selene sat beside him on his left, and he turned his head slightly to look at her. Her hands, locked together, rested on the hymnal in her lap. Her eyes were closed, her breathing ragged. Despite the perfume, she practically radiated fear.

"Relax," he whispered. "It isn't that bad."

She took a deep breath. "Is it that obvious?"

"You think you're nervous, I'm dying."

She turned her head. "You? But you're the messenger."

Michael's smile froze on his lips. He had to lick them before he could reply. "Who told you that?"

She stiffened and a flash of panic crossed her face. "I just...heard it...somewhere."

Michael put a hand over his eyes. Damn. No wonder so many people had shown up. What a bunch of hypocrites. Someone had started a stupid rumor and now they expected some earth shattering prophesy. Well, any prophesy he could come up with would be straight from Michael Modesto's imagination.

He turned to Selene with a forced smile. "Thanks. You just saved my life."

Her eyes widened. "Oh? How?"

"By giving me a topic for today. Prophesy."

She returned his smile, and Michael felt a warm sense of pleasure. "I can hardly wait," she said. "Your prophesies will be of interest to..." She paused and her smile vanished as though she had mentally bitten her tongue. "...to everyone."

But Michael scarcely noticed. His mind was already occupied with his subject. Prophecies. He would have to come up with something good but believable. He could lead into it with some quotes from the Bible. If there was one thing the Good Book had in abundance, it was prophecies.

Michael hardly looked up from his perusal of the Bible during the opening ceremony and the sacrament. The only time his concentration wavered was when the choir sang and the beauty of Selene's voice drew his attention like an angelic Lorelei.

His introduction by Reverend Gregory startled him and he had a flash of panic. He wasn't ready. He had scarcely read through Revelations, trying all the time to memorize key phrases that would give his words some semblance of authenticity. But time was running out.

During his introduction by Reverend Gregory, there was the sound of restless movement in the congregation, a few coughs, whispered conversations. All sounds died when Michael rose and moved to the front of the room, the Bible in his hand.

He turned and pointed at the audience. "Hypocrites! So many hypocrites. Where were you last Sunday? And the Sunday before that? What suddenly gave you the urge to come here today? A revelation? A visitation? A miracle? Ah, there we have it. A miracle. You didn't come to hear the word of God. You didn't come to accept the sacrament. You came because you heard there was someone here who could perform miracles. And that makes you hypocrites."

As he pronounced the words, Michael felt as though he were talking to himself. If anyone was a hypocrite, it was he. Would he be in church on a Sunday morning if he had not received a visitation? Had not witnessed miracles? He would more than likely be in bed nursing a headache from a long Saturday night party.

But apparently God did not care if he was a hypocrite. He had been told to deliver a message, and by God, he would deliver a message.

"But that's all right. There's an old saying: 'Stupidity might get you into trouble, but it's pride that keeps you there.' It's the same with hypocrisy. It got you here, now I hope its something more than looking for miracles that keeps you here. Because,"—he increased the volume of his voice—"there are no miracles!"

The audience gave a collective gasp and Michael smiled inwardly. He had been right. It was the miracles. Now he had to turn the negative into something positive.

He raised both arms in a gesture of power. "These are the latter days?" He flipped open the Bible to the place he had kept with his finger. "It says in Acts One, Verse seven, 'It is not for you to know the times or the seasons.' "

He continued speaking, searching for words that would sound the right note. "Matthew tells us the signs: wars and rumors of wars, nations will rise against nations and kingdoms against kingdoms. And there will be famines, pestilence and earthquakes." He crossed the platform and stood behind the lectern. He was keenly conscious of the sea of faces turned toward him, and it gave him a familiar thrill to know that they were mesmerized by his performance. "But when have we not had those? But who am I to prophesy that these are the latter days. There have been countless prophets who have predicted the apocalypse: Hippolytus of Rome, Montanus, Zoroaster, Nostradamus, William Miller."

He listened to himself, pleased that he was able to remember so many quotations, so many names. But he also listened uneasily. It did not seem that what he was saying was the message he was searching for.

"And I'll make you a promise. A prophesy. These are the last days before the mighty Armageddon. The last days before the Apocalypse. The day when only the righteous will survive. And I promise you that if you'll carry this spirit of brotherhood with you, if you will live your life with the feeling you have here today, you will be among the chosen. That is my prophesy and my promise and my miracle."

He paused for effect. He could say more. They were hanging on every word. They would listen and they would believe. The thought filled him with sudden fear. He had no right to play with their faith. He closed the Bible and said, "The grace of our Lord Jesus Christ be with you all. Amen.

He had taken a step toward his place beside Mary, when he suddenly jerked to a stop and almost shouted, "Beware! Beware the Antichrist."

He tensed, alarmed. What the hell was he saying?

"He will send false prophets. He, himself, will pretend to speak for God."

The shock of hearing the words was so shattering that, for an instant, his eyes lost their focus and his voice faltered. He shook his head and his eyes came into focus. His mind was so occupied with the strangeness of the situation, that he scarcely saw the faces before him. The few that he could bring into focus had such expressions of fear that he was struck dumb.

He could not leave them like this. He had to say something more. He reached into his memory and seized upon a phrase, "But we need not fear." He held up the Bible. "Because here is your salvation. 'If we endure, we shall also reign with Him; if we deny Him, He will also deny us.'" He pointed the Bible at the congregation like it was the hand of God. "The Lord knows those who are His. Amen."

He sat down between Mary and Selene in oppressive silence. He had bombed. He had been doing well until he got off on that tangent about an Antichrist. It has come to him out of the blue, blazed in his mind like a sudden stroke. Could it be the message? Somehow, he did not think so.

"You were wonderful," Mary whispered as she stood up. She turned to the audience. "Will you please stand and join the chorus. We will sing: 'Take My Hand, Precious Lord.'"

As two young deacons began passing collection baskets among the congregation, the members of the chorus got up and formed a line behind Mary. All except Selene. She sat as though frozen, her face pale, her eye glazed.

Mary took a step and put her hand on Selene's shoulder. "Selene. Are you all right?"

Selene turned her head and looked at Michael. "Why...why did you say that?"

"What? The Apocalypse?"

"The...other."

Michael immediately knew who she meant. "The Antichrist?" He shook his head. "I don't know. It just came to me." She remained seated, her body rigid. She looked so distressed that he smiled and added, "Don't worry. It isn't me."

Life came back into her eyes, and she drew in a breath. "I'm glad to know that."

She stood and took her place with the chorus. Her face was still pale, but when she sang her voice soared with its amazing glory. Michael listened, enraptured. He dreaded for the song to end, not only because he loved to hear Selene, but because when the song ended he would have to face those he knew would be waiting for another miracle.

After the song, the congregation remained standing while Reverend Gregory said the closing prayer. But instead of immediately heading for the door, most of the congregation remained in their places, staring at Michael.

He struggled to contain his dismay. So much for his really compelling lecture on hypocrisy. They weren't here out of a desire to reach out to God. They were here for a sideshow, and he was the clown. Well, not this time.

He turned to Mary. "What about lunch?" His voice was so harsh with disgust that it was impossible to conceal it.

She nodded, her eyes questioning. "Okay."

"I'll meet you at..." He was going to suggest they meet at his car, but he realized that the people outside would probably follow him to his car. "...at the restaurant. You know where it is?"

"Yes. I remember."

"Okay. See you there."

He stalked down the aisle, moving fast, not looking into the eyes of those he passed. Several people held out their hands to him, but he thrust his hands in his pockets so he would not touch any of them. There was no way of knowing whether a handshake could conceal some malady that would strike him like the hammer of Thor. He vowed that if he ever had a church of his own, it would have a door of escape in the apse.

He had to shoulder his way through the throng in the foyer, his hands in his pockets, hiding his anger and trepidation behind a smile and friendly nods. At the top of the steps, he stopped, dumbfounded. There were at least ten people in wheelchairs waiting on the cement walk, all looking at him with such hope and longing that his anger was replaced with an equally strong surge of despair.

In the street in front of the church, a white van with the letters KRLA defied a red-painted curb behind a fire hydrant. A man with a TV camera on his shoulder was photographing a woman with a microphone who was interviewing an elderly man in a wheelchair. Someone shouted, "There he is." She quickly turned to look, and the cameraman swung his camera toward the church.

Michael took the steps swiftly and walked on the grass beside the cement walk, on the opposite side from the TV reporter, moving as fast as possible, but not so fast that it looked like he was running. As he passed, each wheelchair, each person, swung toward him. He steeled himself to ignore the reaching hands the pleading eyes and despairing voices.

He had made it almost to the end of the line when a man in a wheelchair whipped it in front of him with remarkable agility, forcing Michael to either stop or fall over him. "Wait. Help me. Come on. Do it!" The man's voice was not pleading; it was a command more than a plea, a tone that insisted Michael had a duty to heal, and if he refused, he was a selfish son-of-a-bitch.

Michael stared at the man, gripped by something in his manner. The man was young, probably not more than 30. His clothes were old, worn, even his shoes were shabby with wear. His hair was disheveled, dirty, as though it hadn't been washed in weeks. His face was plump, his round cheeks covered with an unshaven dark stubble. Black, red-rimmed eyes under heavy, dark eyebrows, glared at Michael, demanding attention.

"Come on. Help me," he repeated in the same angry tone. "You can do it. I heard you can do it.".

A peculiar feeling swept over Michael. Somehow, he knew the man could walk if he really wanted to, and the thought filled him with rage, and he snarled, "Help yourself, you miserable bastard. There are people here who can't walk. But you...Get the hell out of that chair." He heard people gasp and grow silent.

Michael knew his rage was unjustified; a psychosomatic handicap was no less a handicap than a severed spine. But not now; not here, not in front of all the eyes and withered limbs. "There's nothing wrong with you," he repeated, his voice hard, cruel. "Get the hell up!"

The man's mouth came open and something like guilt darkened his eyes. His hands began to tremble and his feet jerked spastically. Then his fingers tightened on the arms of the wheelchair, and he began to push himself up. He paused, hanging, terror in his face.

"Up! Get up!" Michael started to hold out his hand, then, remembering, yanked it back. He wanted none of the man's helplessness, the man's bitter anger. "Up, damn you. Get up!"

The man struggled to his feet. He stood swaying, wonder in his open mouth.

"Now walk! Walk, damn you. Walk!"

The man's mouth came shut. He took a step. Someone at his side steadied him, and he took another step. Another. He turned toward Michael His mouth moved, gasped, but no words came out. He nodded and tears spilled down his cheeks.

Michael stepped back, his draining anger leaving him weak and disgusted. Suppose the man had not responded? He would have looked like—he would have been—an insensitive bastard. As it was, they thought it was another display of his power to heal.

People had begun to gather around him with more approaching, and Michael almost shoved them aside in his hurry to get away. The TV reporter and the cameraman had flanked the line of wheelchairs and were hurrying toward him

Michael had almost reached freedom when a woman shoved a girl against him. She couldn't have been more than ten, and he caught hold of her to prevent her falling. His hand touched her head and his own head snapped back as agony exploded in his ears. He gasped and jerked his hand back and ran, ran toward his car, stumbling across the grass, his hands pressed over his ears, pressing hard against the pain. Twice he bumped into trees but scarcely felt the impact.

At his car his fingers trembled so badly he almost dropped his keys before he got the door unlocked. As he raced out of the parking lot, he caught a glimpse of people outside the church staring after him. A small group was knotted around the young girl whose face wore an expression of bewildered surprise.

He couldn't hear! It suddenly dawned upon Michael that he hadn't heard the car door slam shut, hadn't heard the engine start. He couldn't hear the engine now! That's what was wrong with the girl. She was deaf. And now he was the one who couldn't hear.

But the pain was lessening. And as the pain vanished, his hearing slowly returned. "Oh, God. Thank you," he breathed, profoundly grateful that he would hear his voice.

By the time he parked at the restaurant, the pain was gone and his hearing was back to normal. He shut off the engine, but he did not get out immediately. He needed a minute to examine an idea that had crept into his mind, an idea that could be his salvation. The idea had grown out of the realization that this time it hadn't been too bad. The pain had been intense for a few minutes, but nothing like when he had healed the crack baby, and certainly, nothing like when he had brought the other baby back from near death. Perhaps that was his way out: heal the little things. Stay away from the paralyzed, the dying, the seriously deformed. And the blind. He did not think he could deal with being blind even for a short time.

But deafness, broken bones, bunions—he almost laughed—if the pain did not last much longer than it had with the deaf girl, he could endure.

And the man in the wheel chair? He had been able to stand. He had been able to walk. Had it been another miracle or had his cure been as much a matter of psychology as the cause of the malady?

It really didn't matter. The point was that he had not touched the man. And without being touched, there was no transference. So it appeared that if he only worked with psychosomatics and those with ailments of a type whose pain he could handle, he could keep his image as a miracle worker.

The next question was: Did he want it?

The answer was easy: No.

He barked a harsh laugh. What choice did he have? His fate was being directed by some force that was not going to let him go until he had fulfilled his destiny, whatever it was. For a time during his sermon, when he had experienced the disconcerting euphoria, he had hoped it was a sign, a sign that he was giving the required message and that his mission would be fulfilled.

He knew it was not true. He had been so carried away by his sermon that he had been lost in some ethereal world. But the words he had spouted had not been the 'message.' He was still trapped.

Chapter 20

'Michael wished he had suggested meeting at a bar instead of a restaurant so he could order a drink instead of coffee. He could use a cigarette and a stiff shot of scotch, more likely a double. But he might just as well get used to being a teetotaler. Priests, reverends and pastors might be able to imbibe, but an evangelist, out on the edge of glory, was expected to be a shining example not far removed from sainthood. Others could hide their peccadilloes, their all too human imperfections, but not him, not now.

He wondered whether the rigid expectations precluded sex. He rather doubted that they did. If God had wanted celibacy in his messenger he would have chosen a priest, or somebody too old to care. He certainly would not have chosen Michael Modesto, a man with a deserved reputation for being a lover. Once his band had begun to have some success, the girls, the groupies, had thrown themselves at him like rose petals strewn in the path of Roman heroes. A line from a poem popped into his head: 'It was roses, roses all the way, and after that—the dark.'

Well, he might not have descended into darkness, but there were certainly not going to be any rose petals ripe for plucking.

Mary for instance. She could never be a groupie. He almost wished she were because then there would be no danger of falling in love. He already looked forward to being with her, something that had never happened to him before with any woman. A bad sign; a very bad sign. He would have to be careful.

His thoughts were interrupted by her arrival. He was not surprised to see Reverend Gregory with her, but he was surprised to see Selene. The two women walked toward him in front of Gregory, and Michael was struck by the contrast. Mary was almost as tall as Selene and her figure did not give away many points.

But it was like looking at Spring and Fall. It was not just the skin or eye colors. It was Mary's openness, her smile, her friendliness. Selene, on the other hand, radiated sensuality, but unassailable sensuality, protected by a cool hauteur. If he were an artist he would characterize Mary as a brook running clear and sweet, while Selene was a deep, dark river with mysterious—and dangerous—under currents.

Other people in the restaurant paused in their conversations to stare at the two women, the silence spreading as though the two were stones dropped into a pool of sound.

The booth was semi-circular and he stood up to allow Mary and Selene to slide toward the middle. When they sat down conversation in the room began again.

"I hope we didn't keep you waiting long," Mary said. "It was hard getting away from church."

"Nobody wanted to leave," Reverend Gregory added. "They thought you might come back."

"Once a day is enough. Whose idea was it to invite the TV?"

"Not mine. And I'm sure you didn't Mary."

Mary shook her head. "They just showed up like all those people. I guess the word is getting around that you're speaking."

"I'm not that good, " Michael said. "I think it was to hear Selene."

Mary smiled at Selene. "He might be right. You have a marvelous voice. Where did you study?"

"I've never had formal training. But when I was a child, I used to sing in a choir."

"Oh," the Reverend said. "Where was that?"

Selene hesitated, and Michael thought she was not going to answer. She clasped her hands tightly before she said, "China."

Reverend Gregory's brows lifted. "China? They have choirs in China?"

"My parents were missionaries. Or rather, my father was a missionary. My mother—he met my mother in China. Mongolia, really. She helped him after they were married."

Michael studied her face. Eurasian. That explained her somewhat exotic beauty.

"What church?" Mary asked.

"Protestant. I'm not sure of the denomination. I was only ten when my parents died."

Mary put her hand on top of Selene's. "Oh, I'm sorry."

Selene said, "Thank you," and eased her hands from beneath Mary's in a gentle retreat.

But Gregory did not notice her withdrawal. "I take it your father's family brought you to the United States."

Selene shook her head. "I never saw any of them. I was adopted by a...a family. They were quite, um, influential."

Michael could tell she was not comfortable talking about herself, and he started to interrupt, but the arrival of a waitress made it unnecessary.

After they had given their luncheon orders, Reverend Gregory leaned toward Selene to continue the interrogation, but Mary said, "Those TV people, do you think they'll be back?"

Michael made a sound of disgust. "After today? If they caught what happened, we'll probably have every station in the country."

"You mean the miracles." Reverend Gregory struggled to contain his excitement. "I think they caught it when you made that man walk away from his wheelchair."

"That was no miracle. The guy was psychosomatic. He just believed in me more than he doubted himself."

"It doesn't matter, does it? It worked. And when you brought back that child's hearing, everyone was impressed." Reverend Gregory frowned. "I'm not sure the TV caught that. They were on the other side of the crowd."

Mary said, "I hope they did. It'll really help raise money for the children's fund."

"Speaking of money," Reverend Gregory said, "we had three times more than last time, and that was more than we ever had before."

"Next Sunday," Mary added "we should do even better."

"How can we?" the Reverend said. "The church was filled to capacity. We can't do better than that."

Selene had been listening quietly, her eyes fixed on the restaurant's distant front window as though the view of outside traffic was more interesting than the conversation. Now her eyes changed focus. "We need a larger church."

Reverend Gregory smiled and tapped the table with his finger. "Of course. With the money we took in today we could make a substantial down payment on a new building."

Mary shook her head. "It'll take more than that. You'd have to remodel, and that'll take a lot more money."

"A loan. I'm sure we could get a loan. Maybe I can find a building that's already a church. For enough money, they might sell."

"It wouldn't have to be an existing church. If we can find an auditorium or a theater, it wouldn't take much to convert it."

Selene had been studying Michael. "What do you think, Mr. Modesto? Do you want a larger church?"

Mary and Reverend Gregory turned their heads to stare at Michael who had remained silent, hiding his growing dismay. It was easy to read their thoughts: Why would he not want a bigger audience? It would mean more money for Mary's charity. They didn't have the ghost of idea about how the thought of dealing with larger crowds disturbed him. Because he realized it was not his speaking they came for, it was the healing miracles, and larger crowds meant more sick people. He could never deal with that.

"Well," he said. "We don't want this thing to get out of hand—"

"It wouldn't," the Reverend interjected. "Everything would be exactly the same. Just a little bigger."

Michael had the impression he was on the edge of a whirlpool, moving faster and faster, spinning inevitably toward a black hole that would suck him in. He put his hands flat on the table. "Look, I want to help the charity. That would be great. But I don't intend making this my life's work."

Reverend Gregory looked at him without understanding. "But...why not? You have a God-given ability to move people, to help people. You can't turn your back on that."

"I was doing the same thing with my music."

"It's not the same thing," Mary said. "This is the work of God."

"Then the money doesn't mean anything, does it?"

Mary's face reddened. "I didn't mean it like that?"

"Of course, not. It's not for the money. So we don't need a bigger church, do we?"

"But the money wouldn't be for us. It would be for the children, the babies."

"Trust in God. He'll look after them?"

"Maybe that's what he's doing."

Michael slumped back in his seat. If she was right, it was all on his shoulders. Instead of making him feel better, he felt infinitely worse.

Reverend Gregory cut into his thoughts: "We've got to be realistic. If we're going to continue, there are going to be more people, especially after that TV goes on the air. We can't make them all stand outside."

They were staring at him, waiting for an answer. But how could he explain why he feared expanding the church? He could hardly understand himself. "All right. But before you make too many plans, there's something you should know."

Reverend Gregory tensed, ready for bad news. Selene turned her head to look at him.

"Mary knows this: The only reason I'm doing this at all is because I..." What he was going to say sounded foolish in the harsh reality of the restaurant. But it had to be said if he was to avoid being sucked in deeper and deeper. He took a breath and continued. "I received a visitation. Some kind of an angel. I was told that I'm God's messenger."

Reverend Gregory stared at him, his mouth open. "A visitation? You saw an angel, like Moses?"

Selene leaned forward, he eyes boring into his. "The message. Did the angel tell you the message?"

Michael shook his head. "No. That's the trouble. I don't know what it is." Selene settled back, her face again inscrutable. "But," Michael continued, "I'll tell you this. After I find out what it is, after I finish with it—whatever it is—I'm finished. My job is done. When that happens you don't want some monster church on your hands."

Reverend Gregory rubbed his hand across his face. "I see. That accounts for the miracles. And you assume they will vanish as soon as you finish your, uh, mission?"

"I think they will, yes."

"But you have no idea when this could be."

"No, I don't. It could be next week. Or next month."

"Or next year."

"Or," Selene added, "never."

Michael slowly nodded. "That's a possibility."

A possibility, he might have added, that he had kept locked in the back of his mind. What if he never found the message? He would be doomed to the hell of avoiding the anguish in people for the rest of his life. All those eyes. All that misery, misery he could cure with a touch of his hand, if he was prepared to pay the price. It was a price he dreaded, a price that he would fight to avoid, even though the fight would harden his mind and corrode his soul, in the end damning him to a worse hell than any of theirs. That, he realized, was the black hole he desperately wanted to avoid.

"My guardian," Selene said, interrupting his thoughts. "I'm sure he could help find something suitable."

"Is he in real estate?" the reverend asked.

"Not exactly. But he has friends who are. Would you like me to ask him?"

Reverend Gregory's quick smile froze when Mary lifted her hand and glanced at Michael. "What do you think, Michael? Should we take the chance?"

Michael had heard their voices through a veil of denial. He held back a scream of protest. Gregory was right. He had a Hobson's choice between two equally horrific guilts. He could quit, turn his back on the message of God, or he could continue but turn his back on the pain of the sufferers. "Yeah," he said, knowing that whichever road he choose, it would be paved with agony. "Let's roll."

Two hours later Ambassador Anthony Stonz, stopped pacing the polished parquet floor of his den and reached for the phone, holding his hand poised over the receiver until after the first ring.

"Yes?" he said.

"He speaks very well," Selene told him. "You know what happened outside."

"He avoided the difficult ones. He did not want the pain."

"There was a child. He cured her hearing."

"I think that was an accidental encounter. Was that your impression?"

"Yes. He was trying to get to his car. The child's mother pushed her in front of him. He couldn't avoid her."

"And there was a television crew there."

"Yes. But I'm not sure they were able to see what happened with the child."

"No matter. The harm has been done. I should have seen that.

What about next week? Is he going to continue?"

Selene did not immediately answer as though his admission of making a mistake had stunned her. Then she said, "Yes. They're planning on finding a larger church. I, uh, I told them you might be able to help." Stonz did not answer immediately, and Selene added, "Shouldn't I have done that?"

"No, no." Anthony Stonz had not answered because her words had conjured up a sea of possibilities. Apparently Michael had no idea of the nature of the message nor, of more importance, when it would be revealed to him. But it could be tomorrow, or next week. So, he had to be stopped as soon as possible.

"I will be there on Wednesday. Make the arrangements."

He hung up and immediately began dialing another number. He had appointments to cancel, arrangements to make. This disruption could not have come at a worse time. There were important votes coming up at the U.N., important conferences.

But there was no sense in whining; when someone such as this Michael Modesto appeared, they had to be dealt with before they grew too strong to handle. But how? He could not stop him with any of the usual methods. He would have to find another way. And to do that, he should know more about the man, even though the learning would consume time, time that might be critical.

Anthony Stonz smiled to himself. This Michael person was human; he would have vulnerabilities. All he had to do was find them. Correction. He only had to find one.

His first call was to his travel agent.

Chapter 21

Reverend Gregory telephoned Michael on Friday. He had looked at several places that might be suitable for the new church but with little success. A few structures did fit their requirements, but were too expensive, and those that were within their budget were no better than the current church.

He ended up saying, "I'm afraid we'll have to make due with what we have until we build up our credit.

"I hope the weather stays good," Michael told him. "We're going to have a lot of people outside."

"Maybe we can rig up some loudspeakers. At least they could hear."

"Good idea. And you'd better get some more contribution baskets. We wouldn't want to leave them out."

After he hung up the phone, Michael returned to puzzling over his speech for the coming Sunday. He had again made a raid on the library, but the sheer volume of books, articles and pamphlets on religion had left his brain churning with indecision.

He believed in books. He had long ago come to the conclusion that no matter how esoteric or obscure the subject, someone, somewhere had written a book or article about it.

By Friday, with his head on the edge of exploding, he called Mary. "I need your help again. Can I come over?"

"I'm working the swing shift. Can we make it tomorrow?"

"Okay. Call me when you're ready."

He replaced the phone slowly puzzling over a twinge of disappointment. He knew the disappointment was not because he would not have Mary's help immediately, but because he had looked forward to sitting near her tonight in cozy darkness instead of tomorrow in harsh daylight. Why should that cause such a sense of disappointment? He had definitely decided to keep their relationship plutonic.

But maybe it was not dreaming of her that was causing him to lose sleep. Maybe it was because he had not been with any woman for weeks. In truth, he had not thought much about sex, which was another miracle. His brain, his psychic had been so occupied with the church and the illusive 'message' that it had pushed everything else aside. But his glands had their own agenda. They cared nothing for angels or messages. Besides, he rationalized, maybe he needed a break from his intense research. He'd heard the band was in town breaking in a new guitar player, playing at a club on the Sunset Strip.

He could tell something was wrong the minute he walked into the club. The guys were on a small stage pounding away at 'Bad Love,' and to most of the people in the club, the music probably sounded just like it did when he'd been with the band, but the new lead guitar wasn't cutting it. He was a tall kid, made taller by shoes with two inch thick soles, who wore his shirt open to show his skinny chest. He had memorized Michael's arrangement and some of his chops, but he didn't have the moves nor the little licks that fleshed out the arrangement.

Still, the kid was pretty good and given enough time would probably get into it.

Apparently the band's name could still bring them in because the place was crowded. The head waiter recognized Michael and without asking if he was alone, had a couple of bus boys bring in two chairs and a table with a top about the size of a Stetson hat. Michael had them set it up by the back wall where he hoped he wouldn't be noticed. It was a vain hope. He had hardly sat down before he noticed several people turn to look at him and point him out to their friends. So much for fame.

He ordered a bottle of Château Léoville Barton. Watching the waiter pour a glass of the wine, Michael had an uneasy feeling that he did not belong here. Not any more. His world now was filled with the sound of a church organ instead of a rock band. His world now was middle-aged people wearing jackets and neckties instead of kids in tee shirts and girls with bare midriffs. And his world now sure as hell did not include fifty dollar bottles of red Bordeaux.

But the girl who came to his table was straight out of his past. She had a mane of blond hair and was young enough so that her face still retained its youthful beauty. She wore the standard cutoff tee shirt showed her bellybutton above a pair of tight jeans. She had a cigarette in her hand, and her smile was purely angelic.

"Hi, Michael," she said. "Remember me?"

Michael did not remember her. But he remembered lots of 'hers' so he returned her smile. "Sure." He motioned her to sit down, and she settled onto the chair, moving carefully to prevent her jeans from slipping any lower while at the same time holding her shoulders back to display her breasts to advantage. It looked like a move she would have had to practice to make it work.

Michael raised his hand to a waiter as he said, "I have to confess, I can't remember your name. Suzie, isn't it?"

"Close. It Arabella."

"Blondes aren't named Arabella."

"Real blondes aren't."

The waiter brought a glass and Michel poured wine for the girl. He did not ask if she would prefer something else. He had already decided he didn't want to kill the bottle himself. Not like the old days when he would have killed it and probably another.

The 'old days.' He shook his head. That was only a couple of months ago.

"A penny for your thoughts," Arabella said.

Michael had seen Creed staring in his direction, and suddenly he did not want to talk to any of the guys. "I was thinking that this place is awfully crowded."

She answered as he knew she would. "We could go somewhere quieter."

"Yeah." He got up and dropped a $100 bill on the table thinking as he did so he would have to start watching his money. Being a preacher did not pay much.

The band was coming to the end of the song, and Michael practically shoved the girl ahead of him as they wiggled through the crowd. Several people reached for his hand and he ignored them. He could tell by the look on their faces that they thought he had turned into some kind of arrogant jerk, but actually he was afraid to touch them. Suppose one of them had some sort of ailment and he would inadvertently experience the person's pain. Damn. Why wasn't there some way he could turn the miracles off? He felt like King Midas, afraid to touch anyone for fear they would turn into gold. He excused his seeming arrogance with a lewd grin and a nod toward the girl, and they managed to make it out the door.

While he waited for valet parking to bring his car, the girl suddenly twined her arms around his neck. "I can hardly wait to see your place," she whispered.

At her touch, Michael cringed. If she noticed a look of apprehension on his face, she gave no indication. Nothing. No pain. No blackness. Either the girl was incredibly healthy or he had lost his powers. Either way, it was a huge relief. He pulled her close. "Did you bring your pajamas?"

"Do I need them?"

She turned her head in invitation, and he kissed her. Her lips were soft and her tongue delicate, but she tasted of stale tobacco. She wrapped one leg around his and pressed her hips hard against him in an age-old promise. A tingle of alarm shook Michael when the move failed to produce the expected reaction. Instead, the thought that crossed his mind was of Mary. Would she behave like this if he were to kiss her? His chuckle at the absurd thought broke the kiss, and Arabella tilted her head back to look at him from under lowered eyelids.

"What's so funny?"

"I am," he said. He put his hands on her buttocks and pulled her against him. She said, "Oooohhh," and wriggled her hips. Abruptly, Michael said, "Shit," and turned away from her.

She jerked her head back and stared at him. "What's the matter?"

"I just remembered. I left the gas on in my apartment."

"The gas?" Her puzzled look changed to alarm. "It could blow up."

"If it hasn't already." The parking attendant pulled up in his car, and Michael said to Arabella. "Wait here. I'll see if it's safe."

The attendant held the car's door open, and Michael handed him $5 and hurriedly slipped behind the wheel. In his last glimpse of Arabella she was standing at the curb with her hands limp at her sides, her expression one of disbelief. He wondered how long she would wait.

While driving back to his apartment, his humor turned to concern. He used to enjoy sitting in a club with a glass of wine, listening to a good band, smoozing with friends, coming on to a good-looking girl. But tonight it hadn't been fun. Shit was right. He hadn't even wanted to go to bed with Arabella, and she was a fine looking bitch. This messenger of God thing was really screwing up his life.

A new thought almost caused him to run a red light. Was it possible that his change was not due to some ghostly visitor. It had all begun when he met Mary. She had captured his attention before the first event. And she had begun to occupy more and more of his thoughts—and his dreams.

He sighed with disgust. The role of messenger might be over some day, but he was beginning to doubt that he would ever recover from Mary.

Chapter 22

The next day apprehension still clouded his mind. It had been Mary's idea to put aside the books and go for a walk in nearby Johnny Carson park. She had found that sometimes inspiration could not be forced, but it often came to her while walking, as though the physical activity released some enzyme in the brain.

Michael had never done much walking, and certainly not when seeking inspiration. Looking for some divine truth by strolling in the park was the last thing he would have tried.

Still, he had come to a dead-end with the books, and pillow pounding half the night had generated no ideas. He had hoped that talking with Mary would generate inspiration. But warm sunshine, trees ablaze with fall leaves, and air fragrant with the scent of flowers and newly mown lawn, were not conducive to intellectual pursuits. Tomorrow's problems with sermons and miracles had no room in a mind filled with the amazing pleasure of walking with Mary.

She had fastened her hair in a long ponytail that, as she walked, swung like a metronome, beating out the rhythm of his heart. The touch of her arm or the brush of her hip created bursts of pleasure.

If there had been no other assault on his senses, her presence alone would have made it impossible to concentrate on his sermon. Would any other woman have the same effect? After all, he had been attracted to Arabella last night—for a while. Perhaps this infatuation with Mary would vanish just as quickly when he knew her better. Was it Mark Twain who said, "Everyone has a dark side like the moon that they show to no one?" He wondered what Mary's dark side could be.

Actually, he really knew very little about her. He didn't even know her birthday or anything of her background. He broke the silence with, "You never did tell me where you're from."

She had been walking with her head down, pondering some thought. Now she lifted her chin. "Here. I mean, California. Long Beach."

"A native? I didn't think there were any."

"You're thinking about the past. It seemed like everybody was from out of state. But all those people had kids. My folks were from Wisconsin."

"Long Beach. I've never been there."

"When I was a kid it was a retirement community. But today it's a real city. One of the biggest shipping ports in the world."

"What made you decide to be a nurse?"

"I didn't want to be a secretary."

"There are other jobs."

"What made you decide to be a musician?"

"I take the point. It's not really a decision; it just kind of creeps up on you."

"My parents think I should have been an astronaut."

"An astronaut?"

"I think it's because my dad hoped I could get him a ride in a space shuttle."

Michael chuckled. "My dad wanted me to own a brewery. I think he wanted to be sure he'd always have enough beer."

They walked a moment in silence, caught up in memories.

"Were your folks religious?"

Her question seemed curious to Michael. She probably believed he had been chosen because he had a deeply religious background.

"Not really," he said. "That's what makes this whole thing so damned strange. My dad would hardly set foot in a church, except sometimes for Easter or Christmas.

"What about your mother?"

"Just the opposite. She was really into religion. But I kind of think a lot of it was so she could put up with my dad."

"Was he, uh, abusive?"

"No. He really loved her. He just couldn't handle alcohol. But he wasn't one of those belligerent drunks. He just got morose."

"But they stayed married."

"Yeah."

"Mine didn't. They divorced a couple of years ago."

"Oh. No telling how long my mom would have lasted if she hadn't died."

"Oh, I'm sorry."

"Yeah, me too." They walked a few steps in silence before he added, "Maybe it's just as well. Seeing me in front of my band would probably have killed her."

"She would be proud if she heard you in church."

Michael swallowed a sudden lump in his throat. Mary was right. His mother would have been thrilled to hear him speaking in church with people hanging on his words, believing every thing he said. Then he remembered why he was here with Mary. "Yeah. Until now."

"Well, if she were here, what would she like you to talk about?"

Her words triggered memories of his mother's voice. "Satan. She was hell on wheels about Satan. Blamed him for everything."

"Then that's your subject."

Michael shook his head. "Been there, done that. I need something fresh."

Mary thought a moment. "Last Sunday you said something about the Antichrist."

Michael stopped walking. The message. Could that be the message? The words of the angel were seared into his mind as they had been seared into the floor of the church: 'Beware the Antichrist.' "Of course," he said. "The Antichrist."

"Good. Nobody talks much about him. But I think everybody would like to know more."

Excitement churned through Michael. Concentrate on the Antichrist. That had to be the message. Why else would he have received the warning? If Mary was right—if he was right—this could all be over by Sunday. "Yeah." He glanced at his watch. "I'd better get started. I've got a lot to learn."

"We've got a lot to learn. I want to help you on this."

"Okay, okay." He glanced around. The sky was suddenly bluer, the air sweeter, the sun warmer. "I'm lost. Which way is the car?"

Mary took hold of his hand and pulled him toward a side path. "This way."

He did not let go of her hand all the way back to the car.

Back in his apartment, looking up passages in the Bible while Mary poured through his books, Michael's euphoria began to be replaced by doubt. The whole subject was overwhelming, vague and abstruse. There were hundreds, thousands, of words written about Satan, but very little about the Antichrist. All they had learned was that the Antichrist was thought to be male, like Satan. But he was a separate entity, under the control of Satan. Which left Michael with a new dilemma.

He dropped his pen on his note pad. "I don't understand. Why did Christ say to beware of the Antichrist and not beware of Satan himself?"

Mary had just snapped on a lamp and she turned to him, her lips pursed in thought. "It does seem odd."

"Maybe they really are one and the same."

Mary came over to peer at his notes. "Did you find much in those books?"

"Very little. It's almost like he's invisible."

"Hmmm. I wonder why?"

He leaned back and rubbed his eyes.

Mary asked, "Tired? Want to stop awhile?"

"No. Just my eyes. I'm not used to all this reading." He laughed. "Since I left the university, I don't think I've read a book a year."

"Here. This always helps me." She moved behind his chair and began massaging his temples. "Tilt your head back a little."

Michael's mouth parted in awe at the effect of her gentle touch.

He had been to masseurs in the past and their manipulations had always relieved his tensions. But he had never experienced such a sense of peace. Her touch laved him like warm honey.

He had an overwhelming desire to hold her, to touch her, to make her know that she was becoming part of his life.

He was reaching to touch her hands when she said, "I was thinking, maybe we don't have to understand. We don't have to understand how a bomb works to fear it. We only need to know that it exists, and if we're not vigilant, it can hurt us."

Michael straightened, his mind automatically sorting through the possibilities, "So you're saying that all we have to do is spread a warning, like a fire alarm."

"Right. Then the fire can be controlled before it hurts somebody."

"But how are we going to convince people that there really is a fire?"

She sighed. "I don't know. We can only try." She glanced at her watch. "I've got to be going. I have to get ready for work."

It took all of Michael's will power for him to stand, ending the bliss of her gentle touch. "Thanks for the help. I think I've learned enough to make it sound like I know what I'm talking about."

The weariness vanished from Mary's face. "Of course. If it is the message, God will surely put the words in your mouth.

"I hope to he—I hope you're right."

When they walked to the door, he was startled to notice that it was turning dark outside. "We forgot lunch. We'd better stop somewhere for dinner."

"We'll have to take a rain check. I'm already running late."

"But you can't work on an empty stomach."

She laughed with the soft chuckle that gave him so much pleasure, "I'll survive. I'll pick up a couple of power bars at the cafeteria."

"Oh, well." In a way he was relieved. He really wanted to get back to his books. "I'll walk you to your car."

"It's right out front. I'll be okay."

"You sure?"

"You're just looking for an excuse to procrastinate. Get back to work."

He had been lost in her eyes and her words brought him back to a reality of confusion. "Oh. Okay. I'll check them out."

"So, I'll see you at church."

"Right. See you at church."

The words seemed so incongruous to him that he almost laughed. Michael Modesto ending a date by saying he would see her in church. He was so amused by the thought that at first it failed to register when she turned back and quickly put her hands behind his head and pulled his lips down to hers. He was too stunned to react before she was gone. Only the sound of the door closing and the lingering memory of her soft lips gave evidence that she had been there.

He slowly went back to the table and opened the Bible. But he had no idea what he was reading. One moment he was riding the crest of a wave of elation, mesmerized by the wonder of her kiss, and the next moment he was drowning in a maelstrom of guilt and fear, fear about the coming sermon, guilt about his ambivalent feelings toward Mary. He longed to be near her, to hear her voice, to feel her touch, to breath the scent of her perfume. At the same time, he didn't want to be under her spell when he ended his quest.

He put down the Bible and stared at the scattered books and papers. He was tired of studying. He was like a student who had crammed so hard for a test that he could no longer sort out fact from fiction.

The thing to do was go out, have some dinner, clear his mind, then hit the books again.

He had put on a jacket and was opening the door when he heard the rustle of book pages behind him and he turned, startled. An errant draft was riffling the pages of the Bible. Strange. He didn't think he had left it open.

The riffling stopped, the pages settled slowly, lying still as death.

Michael slowly moved to the table, his legs as numb as his mind. Could this be a sign? Had the pages stopped at a significant passage?

He reached for the Bible.

What! He jerked his hand back as the pages again riffled, faster, faster, like leaves in a hurricane. Then, with a sharp thud, the book slammed shut!

No! Michael snatched it up. Where? Where had it stopped that first time? Why? Why had it slammed shut? Which was the message? Which was the sign?

Frantically, he thumbed through the pages, hoping that something would cause him to stop, praying that something would stay his hand.

Nothing.

Closing the Bible he put it back on the table. He stood staring at it a moment, praying that the miracle would happen again.

But it lay inertly. Wood pulp imprinted with ink. Nothing more.

He paused once more at his door, waiting for the sound of riffling pages. When there was no sound, he gently closed the door, feeling as though he was closing the door on some miracle that was forever lost.

On the red-eye flight from Washington D.C. to Los Angeles the Flight Attendant stopped next to the seat occupied by Ambassador Anthony Stonz. Everyone else in the first class section was either asleep or reading, but she noticed that Stonz was sitting tensely, his eyes open, staring at nothing. Leaning to bring her face close to his, she whispered, "Are you all right, sir?"

Anthony Stonz turned his head and the look in his eyes made the girl jerk her head back, her face white.

Then Stonz smiled at her, the same radiant smile that had won him friends throughout the world. "I'm fine, thank you."

She drew a quick breath before she returned his smile, her momentary alarm already forgotten.

"Perhaps you could bring me a small glass of Chablis," Stonz added, not because he wanted the wine but because he wanted to give the girl something to do, some familiar task to occupy her mind.

When she had moved away, Stonz leaned his head back against the cushion and closed his eyes. But there would be no sleep. He had to think about what he might find tomorrow when he went to the church and heard this man Michael Modesto. He must warn Selene not to acknowledge him. He would like to observe without being recognized. He smiled. For him, not being recognized should be easy.

Chapter 23

Sunday morning. Michael had not slept well, and he wondered why he should feel more apprehension about today than he had about last Sunday or the one before that.

Still, today was different. It was as though he had been performing in front of peasants, and today he would be performing before the king.

He tried to shake off the feeling as he finished dressing and ate a hasty breakfast of dry cereal because, as usual, he'd forgotten to buy milk. He could have stopped at a restaurant on his way to church, but he wanted to be early—very early.

He called Reverend Gregory and asked what time he usually unlocked the church. Gregory said that services stated at ten and he opened up at nine. Michael asked if he could possibly unlock at eight-thirty because he wanted to get there before any TV people showed up.

Gregory hesitated before he said yes. Michael figured it was because Gregory was thinking about publicity, and he knew the TV people would be upset if they did not see Michael.

But Gregory surprised him by saying, "I have to be there early anyway to let the work crews in. Don't pay any attention to them."

"Work crews. For what?"

"I'm having speakers and a closed circuit TV set up outside. For the people who can't get in."

"Yeah, well, I guess that's a good idea. But keep the reporters out. Okay?"

"Right. No reporters in the church."

"Okay. I'll see you at eight-thirty. Oh, tell Mary I'll be in the church office."

"Okay. I'll tell her. Uh, one thing: have you decided on a subject?"

It was Michael's turn to hesitate. "As of now it's..." He said the first thing that popped into his mind. "...the Antichrist."

He immediately wondered why he had not said the subject was Satan. During his research he had turned up so little on the Antichrist, he had considered abandoning the idea. It seemed that historians had been reluctant to discuss the subject—or were afraid to discuss it.

"The Antichrist?" Reverend Gregory said. "Are you sure?"

Was he sure? No. But lately he was not sure of anything. "You think I should change?"

"Oh, no, no. But...the Antichrist? I would think that something like, oh, the Sermon On The Mount might be more, uh, popular. More, you know, positive."

Michael was not surprised by Gregory's reaction. Gregory had his eye on the old collection plate. He could not really blame him; Gregory had undoubtedly struggled hand-to-mouth for years and now he saw a chance at some real money. But he sure as hell wasn't going to stand up in front of all those people and regurgitate some message that had already been done to death.

"I'll try to keep it positive," he told the Reverend. "See you at eight-thirty."

Before leaving for the church, he made a quick review of his notes and the books and papers. If he could find a starting point in the scriptures, he was sure he could wing it, especially since his audience probably didn't know any more about the subject than he did.

He found what he was looking for in 1 John Verse 2-18, and put a bookmark in the place. He would have time to memorize what John and the other prophets had to say while waiting for services to start.

He very nearly failed to get the opportunity to do any reading. Several vans were in the church parking lot and workmen lugged cables and boxes toward the church where they were setting up speakers and large TV monitors. Thick electrical cables snaked out of the church doorway to the boxes and monitors. Even thicker cables crossed the grass to TV vans parked at the curb. As Michael walked up the church steps, several of the workmen paused in their tasks to stare at him, and he hurried inside.

He stopped inside the door, staring. Under the direction of a woman with short blonde hair, wearing a dark, skirted suit over a white blouse, a crew of men were installing TV cameras mounted on pedestals in the rear of the church. Another man was checking a portable camera that was suspended from a harness he wore hanging from his shoulders. Reverend Gregory stood near the woman, with the helpless look of someone who had inadvertently opened Pandora's Box. The woman was a TV reporter who Michael had seen a couple of times, but he could not recall her name.

Michael had to fight back his anger to keep from turning and leaving. Gregory had said there would be no reporters inside the church. But judging from the stricken look on Gregory's face, he had lost control to the situation, which meant that he could either leave or go with the flow. Or he could make a scene and order them out.

But it would not be in the church's best interest to make enemies of the press. Then, too, the publicity would spread his message beyond the walls of the small church. It would also help bring in contributions.

There was another reason he did not protest that was closer to the truth: He was secretly pleased that he would be on camera. The program would probably be seen all over the country. This was the kind of power he had never been able to get as a rock star.

Still, he dreaded opening this door. It meant the closing of another door, making it more difficult to ever go back to his old life.

He was striding through the foyer toward the church office when the woman saw him and hurried to intercept. "Excuse me," she called. "Mr. Modesto, excuse me."

Michael had no desire to conduct an interview, not now. He wasn't ready, and for an instant, he considered bolting for the office door, but decided that he would probably have to face the woman sooner or later, so he turned and smiled. "Yes?"

"Mr. Modesto." She was taller than he had thought, close to six feet. She held out her hand. Her fingers were slender , the nails polished, but she had a powerful gripe, acquired, no doubt, from hours in a health club. Her teeth when she returned Michael's smile were the unnatural white of porcelain veneers. "I've been looking forward to meeting you."

"Thanks."

She sensed that he didn't know her name and a brief disappointment pulled her brows into a frown that just as quickly vanished. "I'm Naomi Morton. I'll be covering your sermon for 'Today's World.' You'll be our feature this evening."

"Oh?"

She expected him to be delighted, and at his chilly response she lost a little of her smile. "Uh, tell me. Exactly where will you be standing? I want to make sure we have our cameras where we can get the best coverage."

Michael gestured toward the front of the room. "There. In front of the dais. Oh, would you do me a favor and not put your cameras in the middle aisle? I like to move around."

Her exquisite lips pulled into a frown. "Move around. I see. That will make it, uh, difficult."

Michael's smile was beatific. "I'm sure you can handle it, Ms. Morton."

"Well, yes. My crew are all pros." She took a small note pad from her outside jacket pocket and a gold pen from her inside pocket. "Now then. Why did you make the transition from rock musician to evangelist?"

"I'm not an evangelist."

Michael moved to pass her but she sidestepped into his path. "What would you call yourself? You're not an ordained minister, are you?"

"I guess you could say I'm just a guest speaker, trying to spread the world of God." He again moved to pass her. "Now, if you'll excuse me."

"The word of God. That seems a little strange coming from the notorious Michael Modesto."

"The world is full of miracles."

Again he tried to step past her, but she was prepared for the move and again blocked his path. "Speaking of miracles... I would appreciate it if you'd perform them here, inside the church. It would be difficult to—"

"There will be no miracles." Michael shouldered past her. Before he entered the office, he saw her striding toward Reverend Gregory, her face set in angry consternation. Reverend Gregory picked up a hymnal and buried his face in its pages.

Inside the office, Michael closed the door and pushed the button in the knob to lock the door. He sat down at Reverend Gregory's desk and opened his Bible. But he did not read. His mind was locked on what the woman had said about making miracles. Was that what it was all about? With no 'miracles' would the TV people be here? Would the people themselves be here?

It shouldn't be like that. The desire to follow the teachings of Jesus Christ, to seek the truth of God, should be enough. But it wasn't enough; at least, it had not been enough when Reverend Gregory had been giving his sermons. He had been lucky to fill half the seats.

Without the miracles, would he do any better?

Many preachers had. Some had amassed fortunes, built huge cathedrals and attracted TV audiences in the millions. And all without miracles. Although, in truth, many did practice faith healing, which could be considered a miracle if it worked.

Could he build a following without the healings?

He snorted and opened the Bible. It did not really matter. His task was to deliver some 'message,' not to perform miracles. It made no difference whether he spoke to an audience of one or thousands. Once the message was delivered, he was off the hook.

Feeling somewhat better, he began studying the Bible, searching for additional references to the Antichrist.

As before, he had little success. There seemed to be few references to an Antichrist, although there were a number of references to a personage or power that would operate against Christ.

He glanced around the room, wondering whether there might be some nugget in one of Reverend Gregory's books that he could use. He started to get up than sank back He hadn't a clue about where to even begin searching and church was due to start in—he glanced at his watch—less than thirty minutes.

As though to underscore the rush of time, he heard the choir begin to practice, Selene's voice soaring above the others. Inspiration. That's what he needed.

After fifteen frustrating minutes of reading, he put down the Bible and began pacing the room, as usual, cursing himself for not paying more attention when he had been a regular church goer, trying to sift a sermon from his memory and the desultory references.

His concentration was interrupted by a soft rap on the door. It had to be the Reverend or Mary. The TV woman, Naomi, would not have knocked so softly.

It was Mary, wearing a pale blue knit dress with a close-fitting jacket and holding a small purse in her white-gloved hands, looking as fresh as a day after a spring rain. She had the kind of purity that made you want to drink it in with your eyes. But a purity that should not be touched, never touched, because touching might destroy the innocence.

She glanced at his open Bible on the desk and at his disheveled hair. "How are you doing?"

He lifted his upper lip in a show of disgust. "Terrible. You'd think the Bible would be littered with references to the Antichrist."

"Well, it's certainly apropos. I sometimes think that Satan is running the world."

"The Antichrist is not Satan. They're always referred to as separate entities."

"Are you sure? I thought it just another name, like Beelzebub, Lucifer, Belial, Old Scratch."

Michael's eyes widened. That was it: the nexus with the devil. That was the hook he had been searching for. He could talk for an hour about Satan with one hand tied behind his back. All he had to do was bring in the connection with the Antichrist.

Impulsively, he came around the desk and cradled her face in his hands. "Thank you. Thank you." He kissed her. Their lips scarcely touched for only an instant, but to Michael it was like a hot iron had been plunged into his brain. How could such incredible softness sear itself into his memory so deeply that he knew it could never be erased.

He stepped back quickly, and to hide his confusion, walked to the desk and picked up the Bible. When he turned back he had his face under control, but his heart continued to thud. The look on Mary's face did not help his control. She stood, not breathing, her body stiff, her hands clutching her purse. For an instant he thought she was furious, but her face remained tilted, her lips slightly parted, her eyes half closed, as though she, too, did not want to lose the memory.

"We'd better get started," he said.

Her eyes came into focus. "Oh," she said. She took a breath and turned toward the door. "Yes. We'd better get started."

They had only taken a step when she said, "Wait a minute." She opened her purse and took out a small comb. "You're hair looks like you just woke up."

He grinned at her. "I think I did."

Her face turned pink, and she refused to meet his eyes, but she was all business as she ran her comb through his hair. The last woman who had combed his hair was his mother, and he had been five or six years old. It had felt wonderful to feel his mother's gentle touch, but this was infinitely better.

She finished with a couple of pats. "There. The TV cameras will love you."

So that was it. She had not been so solicitous because she wanted an excuse to touch his hair; it was because she wanted him to make a good showing for the cameras.

It was probably for the best. When they left the office, he was able to keep his mind on his sermon.

Entering the foyer, he stopped in surprise. He had thought the church had been crowded last Sunday, but it was even more crowded today. In addition to the congregation squeezed into the pews, standing people jammed the foyer and spilled over into both side aisles. The two TV cameras in the back of the room had been raised so they had a view above the crowd while their operators stood on boxes. Michael could see that, beyond the open church doors, there were at least as many people standing outside as there were inside.

The first two rows of pews in the front had been roped off for the members of the choir, and as Mary and Michael sat down, the choir finished their practice and took their places while Mrs. Gardner segued smoothly into a threnody. Selene, despite wearing a high-necked, long-sleeved dress of dark purple, stood out like a dusky rose in a bouquet of daisies. Mary nodded to Selene and she came to sit beside her, moving with the gliding steps of a fashion model.

From his place on the other side of Mary, Michael leaned forward so he could ask Selene with a smile, "Are you ready to be a star?"

Selene shook her head. "I don't like all these cameras. They make me nervous."

"At least you've got help. I'll be up there all alone."

"You're used to it. I've seen those crowds at your concerts. By comparison, this is nothing."

"I had four other guys with me. And we knew what we were going to play."

Selene looked at him out of the side of her almond-shaped eyes, her pupils pools of darkness that obscured her soul. "And you don't know today?"

"The Antichrist." Mary volunteered. "He's going to speak about the Antichrist."

Michael had the strange sensation that the pupils of Selene's eyes dilated so that their pools became caverns, tunnels into fathomless depths. She closed her eyes before they could reveal their secrets.

When she opened them they were filled with amusement so that Michael realized that what he had seen had to have been an optical illusion or a trick of the lighting.

"The Antichrist," she said, smiling. "Does he really exist?"

"He?" Michael answered. "I thought it was a woman."

"Impossible," Mary added. "A woman couldn't be that devious."

"Oh? What about Delilah?"

"She was not the Antichrist."

"But she was devious."

"It wasn't her fault," Mary said with a smile. "She came from a bad home."

Their discussion halted as Reverend Gregory made his way to the pulpit. He nodded to Mrs. Gardner and she ended her introduction with a wailing chord.

In the street outside the church, a taxi double parked and Anthony Stonz got out. After paying the driver, he walked to a huge Sycamore tree where, clustered in its shade, a number of people were staring at two large television monitors that flanked the church steps. Large speakers near the TVs amplified Reverend Gregory's voice as he opened the services with a prayer. Stonz wore a dark suit, but he did not seem uncomfortable despite the heat. He stood easily, leaning his weight on his gold-headed cane, staring at a TV monitor without blinking. The only time his expression changed almost imperceptibly was when the choir sang and Selene's bell-like voice chilled the air like the waters of a cool brook.

When a young deacon passed among the crowd with a collection basket, Stonz's lips pursed in a half-smile as he extracted a $100 bill from his wallet and dropped it into the basket. Noting that the basket was almost full his smile broadened. It appeared that Michael Modesto was developing a following.

His chin lifted and his thin lips parted in anticipation when Reverend Gregory introduced Michael.

He was not the only one. Almost as one, the people outside the church sucked in their breathes and grew still. Even children who had been playing at the edge of the crowd moved to take hold of their parents' hands.

Anthony Stonz looked at the people's rapt expressions and his face hardened. He was glad he had not dismissed this latest prophetic threat. This one did not have the feeling of falsehood as had the others. He moved out into the hot sun, ignoring the heat so he could be closer to the speakers.

Inside the church Michael stood in front of the dais, his open

Bible in his hand. He stood silently for a moment, waiting for attention that was already palpable. Then he lifted the Bible. "Satan!" His voice stabbed the audience. Then it changed to the cutting edge of a sword. "Satan wants your soul. We are all, all coveted by Satan. And he will get his share. He always does. How does he do it when in our hearts we know what is good and what is evil? Why don't we just reject him? There has to be a reason. Why would anyone choose to do evil? There can only be one reason: they don't believe. They don't believe in Satan. They don't believe in the judgment of hell! Hell is not fashionable any more! I! Myself! Me! I am the only judge of my actions, so I can do anything I want. They even have a word for it: solipsism. I am the only reality. There is no heaven; there is no hell. Maybe they're right! If there is no God, there can be no Satan. The only way to be sure—the only way to be absolutely certain—is to die! So one fine day, you will know the truth. And if you're right and there is no God, then you got away with your evil. But if you're wrong—and you damn well are wrong—you and your evil are damned."

Michael moved into the center aisle, conscious that the TV cameras were tracking his every more, but no longer caring.

"Does Satan work alone? No, of course not. We know from the Bible that when Lucifer, the Prince of Light, was cast out of heaven he took with him all his followers. They're all here. Helping Satan. The demons: Asmodeus, Mahalath with her ten thousand demon attendants, Lilith, Mavet, Mammon. The list goes on and on. But there was one who was more faithful to Satan than all the others. One who hated the son of God and all he stood for, hated him with so much bitter venom that he was given the name of The Antichrist!"

As he talked, Michael had the sensation that his mind was racing ahead of his words, searching for facts, names, events that could be spewed forth in proper order and timing, information that had been packed into cubicles of his mind during hours of reading and a lifetime of listening. He was an actor who had memorized his lines so well, that he could ignore them, concentrating on their effect.

It was a strange sensation, but invigorating, too, because it left him free to move, to watch faces in the congregation, to be aware of the TV cameras, to hear his own words and to marvel at their impact. Was this him speaking with such strength and purpose? Was this him speaking with such a feeling of veracity?

"But is the Antichrist a man? Is he even human? History tells us that at one time or another the Antichrist was characterized as a city, a state, a nation, even a nationality. But they were wrong. All wrong. The Antichrist is human. He is a man. And he walks among us!"

He was now back at the front of the room, aware that Selene was staring at him with a look he thought could be of horror.

On the dais he posed in front of Christ on the cross, knowing that the juxtaposition would give depth and credence to his words.

"Can the Antichrist be conquered? No. Not by mere mortal. Because he is immortal. Reaching out for you. Subverting what you know is good. No, he will never be conquered. But he can be defeated. You defeat him every time you resist evil. You defeat him every time you obey the commandments of God." For emphasis he turned, and with a dramatic gesture, placed his hand on the chest of the figure on the cross. "You defeat him every time you hold to the teaching of Jesus Chri—."

A powerful bolt of energy surged up his arm, forcing his eyes to bulge, his body to jerk violently. The last thought that ran through his mind was that this had to be how it felt to be electrocuted. Crackling voltage, coursing through your body. Burning. Burning. Searing everything in its path until it reached your brain. Exploding in a fireball of blinding light and searing pain leaving...nothing.

Chapter 24

He knew he was in a hospital before he opened his eyes.

Was he dying?

He couldn't be dead or he wouldn't be in a hospital, and he wouldn't feel bandages on his hands, and the tight bandage on his chest would not be causing his ribs to hurt.

He opened his eyes.

He heard Mary's sudden gasp before his eyes focused on her face. She was seated in a chair near the room's single window and she quickly got up and came to stand beside him. Reverend Gregory was there too.

"Michael." Mary said. "We've been so worried."

"Why?" His voice came out as a whisper.

"You almost died." That was Reverend Gregory.

"Oh." He was not surprised at the news. When he had touched the figure of the crucifix, the shock and pain had been even worse than when he had touched the dying baby. He could easily have died.

He forced more strength into his voice. "The bandages. Why the bandages? Did I fall?"

"Yes," Mary said. "But...that isn't why."

The door opened part way and a nurse squeezed through. Michael saw several people behind her who tried to follow. She forced the door shut, but not before light from several cameras flashed.

"You're awake," the nurse said. "Good." Michael was wearing blue hospital pajamas, and she pulled the sleeve up so she could wrap a blood pressure cuff around his arm.

Michael suddenly realized that beneath the bed covers his feet were also bandaged. "What the hell happened? Why the bandages?"

"Stigmata," Reverend Gregory answered.

He knew about stigmata. It was when a person displayed the evidence of Christ's wounds on the cross. But psychiatrists did not believe their origin was supernatural. They were a demonstration that the mind was capable of unconscious control of the body.

He clenched his fingers and winced. "My God," he said. "I can't believe this."

"It happened," Reverend Gregory said. "We all saw it."

Michael became aware that it wasn't only his hands and feet that hurt. His chest hurt so much he could hardly breathe. "My side. I did fall."

"Part of the stigmata," Gregory explained. "There's never been anything like it."

Mary saw his puzzled expression and added, "The wound...in Jesus' side. You have that too."

"But those things are psychosomatic. You don't go to the hospital."

Mary shook his head. "Yours weren't. You almost bled to death. They had to give you a transfusion."

Reverend Gregory put his hand to his forehead. "My God. I can't believe this. The other things...the miracles. I thought there could be some logical explanation for them. Some coincidence. But this...this is real."

"Maybe not." It was the nurse. "The mind can do strange things."

"Have you ever seen anything like this?"

The nurse shook her head. "Not like this. But pretty close. I've seen people give themselves wounds you wouldn't believe."

"These aren't like that," Mary said. "These are real."

"Aren't they all."

"Well, I think it was a miracle," the reverend said. "It was on the news."

"Oh, God," Michael said, remembering. "What did happen? I remember touching the crucifix..."

"You kind of gasped, real loud. You stood there, with your hands out. Then blood came out of your hands. You collapsed. When we got to you, you had blood coming out of your side and from your shoes. It was real."

The nurse had finished taking his pulse and temperature. She stared at him, her brows lifted. "Well. It looks like you're going to be fine. Everything's normal."

Michael's hands had stopped hurting, and he worked his fingers to make sure. He held up his hand. "Take the bandage off."

The nurse's mouth came open. "I can't do that. The doctor—"

"Take them off!"

The nurse made no move, and Michael pulled himself to a sitting position and swung his legs over the side of the bed. There was no pain in his side. He held his hand out toward Mary. "Here, Mary. Take it off."

Mary glanced at the nurse. "He shouldn't be able to sit up. Not with that wound in his side."

"There is no wound," Michael said. "It's gone."

The nurse tightened her lips. "I'll call the doctor." She opened the door and slipped through, shutting it quickly.

Michael again held his hand out to Mary. "Go ahead. Take it off."

Mary hesitated, then unwound the bandage. When the last of the gauze dropped away, she stared at Michael's palm. "It's gone."

Reverend Gregory pressed his palms together. "Like it never happened. It has to be a sign."

Michael unwound the bandage from his other hand. "A sign of what? If God wants me to do something, why doesn't He come right out with it instead of all these damn signs?"

Reverend Gregory was aghast. "You shouldn't talk like that."

"Where are my clothes?"

"I don't know," Mary answered. "They were all...bloody."

Mary pulled open a small drawer in a cabinet next to the bed "Your wallet and money, they're here. And your watch."

Michael slipped his watch on. It was after two o'clock. He'd been unconscious for almost four hours. "Can you get rid of those reporters?"

"I doubt it," Reverend Gregory said. "Not after you were on the news."

"They're waiting for you," Mary said. "You'll have to say something."

Michael sighed in exasperation. He had no desire to speak to reporters. What could he say? He didn't know any more about what had happened than they did. But, sooner or later, it had to be done.

He stood up and pulled off his pajama top. He wobbled as his legs nearly buckled, and Mary reached a hand to steady him. "You shouldn't be out of bed. You lost a lot of blood."

"I'll be okay." But he did feel a little weak, and he sat down on the edge of the bed before he began taking the bandage from his waist. Mary moved to help him, and when they removed the last of the bandages, she peered at his side. "Not a trace. I can't believe it."

"Maybe it was all an illusion."

Reverend Gregory shook is head. "Impossible. The blood was real. They had to take your clothes away in a plastic bag."

"Speaking of clothes..." Michael reached over and took his keys from the drawer. "Reverend, would you go to my place and get me some clothes?"

"Yes. Of course. But, uh, what's your address."

"Oh, yeah. It's an apartment. On Riverside. Oh, damn. Forgot the number."

"Three-twenty-seven," Mary said. "It's right off Buena Vista."

As Gregory moved to the door, Michael could tell by the look on his face that he wondered how she knew where he lived. "It might be better if you get back in bed. I'll tell the reporters you're too weak to talk."

"Okay." He swung his legs up and lay back on the bed. "But I'm feeling okay now."

Before Gregory pulled the door shut, Michael could hear the reporters shouting questions.

"What happened after I, uh, fainted?"

"Well, as you can imagine, everybody was stunned. Then we all rushed to see if you were okay. There was a doctor in the audience and he was able to control the bleeding until the ambulance arrived."

"I've read about stigmata. It's all in the mind."

. "These were real. I saw them. You had a wound in your side exactly like someone had stabbed you with a spear."

"I guess I've got a good imagination."

She gently touched Michael's side. "It had to be a miracle."

Michael slumped back on the bed. "These damned miracles are going to be the death of me."

Mary studied him, her eyes puzzled. "I don't understand why you're unhappy. You've been chosen by God."

"Yeah, well, I've been chosen by somebody all right."

"Somebody? You don't think it was God?"

"You said it: If I was chosen by God, I should be happy."

"Satan? I don't believe it. He wouldn't appear as an angel. He wouldn't be ambiguous. You'd know what he wanted."

His smile was as tight and twisted as the feeling in his stomach. "It really doesn't make much difference, does it? Just so it gets results."

She froze. "Don't say that." Her voice was a whisper. "Don't ever say that."

"Yeah. I know. I guess I'm just a little..." He took a deep breath. "Mary, I just can't believe it. God would never chose somebody like me. Satan would. I can believe that. But God...? Why not choose the pope? The president? Somebody like that? But me? It just doesn't make sense."

"Not to you. It doesn't have to make sense to you."

"It sure as hell would help."

"Read your Bible. Nobody chosen by God ever ask for it. Look what happened to Job, Moses, Saint Peter. Terrible things. And we know they were chosen."

"But they all had one thing in common. Faith. No doubts. Me? I'm looking for the catch."

"Maybe that's because you won't give yourself to God. You're holding back, looking for that catch."

"There's got to be one in there somewhere."

"Let yourself go, Michael. Give yourself to God."

"I can't, Mary. Maybe I think too much. I've never been able to let myself go with anything." He tilted his head back and closed his eyes. "I guess that's why I never married. I was always hanging back, waiting for that...that... feeling. But it never came. Except with music. Sometimes I get lost in music." His smile was bitter. "It's a hell of a feeling."

"Someday you'll have that same feeling for God."

He slowly shook his head. "I don't know. Music can't betray me."

"Neither will God, Michael. Neither will God."

Inside Anthony Stonz' rented limousine, Selene related how Michael's wounds had miraculously healed. "They think it was psychosomatic."

Stonz shook his head. "No. They were real enough."

" Could this have been a sign?"

"Oh, it was a sign all right. But not for Michael."

Selene's face paled. "For me. For singing in the church."

"No. Not you. For me."

"You? But why?"

"I think I'm being warned."

"Warned? Of what?"

"Not to try to harm this man Michael." He smiled. "In a way, I'm glad this happened. It fits with my plan."

"How could it? You can't harm him. You can't bring him down."

"True. So, I'll have to help him bring himself down."

Selene relaxed against the soft leather of the car's cushioned rear seat. "Then we don't have to worry."

Stonz's eyes narrowed and his hands tightened their grip on the head of his cane. "We shall see. Yes. We shall see."

Chapter 25

On Wednesday morning Reverend Gregory called Michael, asking if they could meet at some address on Fair Oaks Avenue in Glendale. He had an offer on a building that might be suitable as a church and he wanted Michael to take a look at it.

Michael had again been on the edge of despair. Reporters had made his life so miserable he had to slip out at two o'clock in the morning to shop for food at an all night market. He had been searching for a topic for Sunday's sermon, and Gregory's call gave him a welcome excuse to procrastinate, even though he knew the threat of a Sunday's failure would take the joy out of his escape.

The address led Michael to an area of tree-lined, well-maintained streets in an upscale Glendale neighborhood where the homes, although old, were large and handsome. Their lawns were emerald green; their plants and shrubs looked as though they were cared for by conscientious gardeners. The several churches he passed were constructed for large congregations.

The building at the address Gregory had given Michael turned out to be a large domed structure flanked by parking areas. It did not look like a church. There were four cars in one of the lots, and Michael felt a jolt of pleasure when he recognized one of them as Mary's. He should have known that she would be involved in the selection of a new site. She was as much a part of the church as the reverend. Maybe more. Without Mary's help his church would never have survived.

Inside the building, Michael saw that it had been an amphitheater with a half-round stage and tiered seats. He estimated the theatre would seat more than five hundred. Huge chandeliers hung from the domed ceiling on long cables. The room was quiet with no sounds of outside traffic. The walls were decorated with Grecian murals depicting theatrical laughing and crying masks. Hardly conducive to an ecclesiastic milieu. But, Michael realized with amusement, the masks would be perfect for any auditorium where he would be speaking since half of him would be laughing at the irony and half would be crying because he did not really believe anything he was saying.

On the stage Mary and Reverend Gregory were talking to two men who wore suits and neckties. One of the men was tall, distinguished, with flowing white hair. He looked vaguely familiar, but Michael could not place him. The other man was younger, a little heavy like an athlete who no longer had time to exercise. Mary looked cool and delicious in a pale-pink, pants suit. Her hair was plaited into two braids that she had fastened to circle her head like a golden diadem.

The acoustics in the room were excellent, and as Michael descended one of the side aisles toward the stage, he could hear the conversation clearly. The young man was pointing out the features of the building and indicating changes that could be made to convert the theater into a chapel.

Mary saw Michael and said, "Oh, Michael. You've got to see this."

She came to meet him when he crossed the stage. "I think this could be perfect," she said. "It used to be a theater. Almost six hundred seats."

"Six hundred? That's a pretty optimistic jump."

"John doesn't think it's going to be enough the way we're growing. Isn't that right, John."

Reverend Gregory smiled and nodded. "I wouldn't be surprised." He indicated the young man. "Michael, this is Ward Medford. Ward is the realtor for the building. This is the Michael Modesto I was telling you about."

Michael shook Medford's hand. "I hope it was good."

Medford chuckled. "Actually, he didn't have to tell me. Your name is all over the place."

Gregory turned to the other man who had been watching the exchange with a tiny smile. "Michael, I'm sure you've heard of Anthony Stonz. Anthony is our ambassador to the U.N."

Michael held out his hand. "Of course. Now I place you."

The man appeared to hesitate for a second before he grasped Michael's hand. The instant their hands touched Michael grunted. It was like an electric shock. A second. No, a millisecond of shock, cut off so quickly that Michael was not certain he had felt anything. The shock was probably his surprise at the powerful squeeze of the Ambassador's grip. Like many older men, the Ambassador probably felt compelled to prove that he might be past his prime, but his grip could still crush rocks.

Mary said, "Ambassador Stonz saw you on T.V. He wants to contribute."

"I was impressed," Anthony Stonz said. "I'd heard about you before, but...the stigmata. I've never seen anything like it. I had to come."

"Well, we can use all the help we can get."

Stonz shook his head. "After Sunday? You'll have more help than you can use."

Reverend Gregory said, "That's true, Michael. My phone has been ringing at all hours. I'm lucky to get an hour's sleep."

"We're still grateful," Michael said. But he had an uneasy feeling that there was more to the Ambassador's offer than a desire to spread the word of God, and he decided to get as much as he could from the man. "I'm sure, sir, that you would be interested in a program the church is sponsoring to help health-disadvantaged children. Now there's a place we could use some help. Right, Mary?"

Mary quickly nodded. "Oh, yes. Any help would really be appreciated."

"It sounds like something for UNICEF. I'll make a suggestion to their chairperson." Anthony Stonz glanced around the theater. "Meanwhile, do you think this structure will be suitable as a temple?"

Reverend Gregory's eyes widened. "Temple?"

Stonz smiled. "A slip of the tongue. I meant chapel. The temple will come later."

Gregory laughed. "A temple. That would really be something."

"But not beyond the realm of possibility."

"Let's not get ahead of ourselves," Michael reminded. "I'm not sure we can even afford this."

Stonz made a slight gesture of dismissal with his hand. "It will be taken care of, if it's suitable."

"Oh, it's suitable," Reverend Gregory said. "Very suitable."

Stonz turned to Medford. "Can you have this ready for services by this Sunday?"

Medford looked skeptical. "Well, I'm sure we can, depending on how elaborate you want to get."

Stonz looked at the Reverend. "What will you need?"

Gregory blinked and cleared his throat. "Well, uh, it isn't that easy. We have a lease on the building—"

Stonz waved that objection aside. "I'll have my attorneys take care of that. What will you need for Sunday?"

"Oh, uh, I, uh, I think we could get by with a lectern and the organ. And the crucifix, of course."

"I'll have a moving van pick them up—when? Tomorrow morning?"

"Well, yes..."

"Good. Tomorrow afternoon I'll have a printer pick up your bulletin. You might also prepare the text for a press release."

"A press release? I can't do that in one afternoon."

"Just the text. You're church—what's it's name...?"

"Uh, Community Church of Christ."

"Community?" Stonz shook his head. "We have to change that. What about: World Wide Church of Christ?"

"Sounds kind of, uh, pretentious," Gregory said.

"You're right. Perhaps: Church of the Word"

Gregory looked skeptical. "I think that's been taken."

Mary said, "What about: Church of the Message?"

Stonz' head jerked as though he had been struck. Then he quickly nodded. "Perfect. What do you think, Mr. Modesto?"

Michael had been listening with a sinking feeling in the pit of his stomach. It felt as though every suggestion was another shackle anchoring him to the message. "Yeah," he said. "Why not?"

Stonz stared at Michael for a second before he said, "Very well." He turned to Gregory. "Make it 'Church of the Message.' No. Make that: 'Church of the Divine Message,' Reverend John Gregory, is moving to this address. Guest speaker: Michael Modesto. Choir under direction of Mary Shaeffer, featuring the voice of Selene...whatever else you think should go in. Can you do that?"

"Well, yes..."

Anthony Stonz slapped his gloved hands together, the explosion loud in the room. "Good."

Medford had been holding his breath, probably afraid that the bubble would burst. Stonz took hold of his arm. "Get together with the Reverend, if you will. Prepare the papers you'll need for a six months lease and send them to my attorneys." Stonz fished a business card from his vest pocket and handed it to the realtor. "Here's the address. They will provide the lease funds. If the papers aren't ready by Sunday, will it prevent the service?"

Medford hastily shook his head. "No, no. We can work something out."

"Six months?" Mary said. "Will that be long enough?"

Stonz' brusque manner changed abruptly, and he smiled. "Maybe too long, my dear. If Michael can keep on performing miracles, we'll have to move into something larger right away."

Michael had been listening to the proceedings with a touch of awe. It was easy to see why Anthony Stonz had become a world leader. When he took charge of a project, things moved. Only why was he doing it? This was not only going to cost him money—which he could probably write off as a tax deduction—but it was also going to cost him time. Just coming here must have been a strain on his appointment book. The ambassador had a reputation for philanthropic contributions, but Michael wondered whether he had ever done anything like this for any other church.

It had to be because of the miracles. Maybe Stonz had some personal problem that only a miracle would help. Or maybe it was his health. That would explain the shock when he touched the man's hand. Stonz might be looking for a miracle in return. Sort of a quid pro quo. Stonz would probably spring it on him when he thought they were all securely in his debt.

But even at the risk of ruining the whole deal, he should call the man's hand: "I can't guarantee the miracles. I have no control over them."

Anthony Stonz nodded. "Don't worry about it. That's in the hands of God."

"I just wanted you to know."

"Oh, I do know." He smiled again, his lips thin and hard. "What is it they say: 'The Lord giveth and the Lord taketh away'?"

Medford said, "Amen."

Reverend Gregory looked at Michael with a trace of alarm. "Could that happen, do you suppose?"

Anthony Stonz shook his head. "It doesn't really matter, Reverend. Truth is subjective. The pattern has been cast. Now all we have to do is give the people what they want so desperately to believe."

"Sort of 'deconstruct' the truth."

Stonz either did not hear the irony in Michael's voice or chose to ignore it. "Not at all. If a miracle happens, it happens. As you said, you can't will it to happen. But while we're waiting, we can be spreading the world of God. Isn't that right Reverend?"

Holding Gregory's arm Stonz began walking toward the aisle. His laugh sounded genuine when he said, "Deconstruct the truth. I like that. I'll have to use it in one of my speeches."

Melford hurried to follow and as Mary took a step, Michael said, "Wait, Mary. Do you have a minute?"

"Yes." She glanced at her watch. "I don't go on duty until four."

Half way up the aisle, Anthony Stonz stopped and turned back. "Oh, Michael." His voice carried clearly in the theater. "Why don't you continue warning about the Antichrist. It'll go over well on TV."

Without waiting for an answer, he turned and continued walking up the aisle with Gregory and Medford.

Michael stifled a sudden irritation. Was Stonz' 'suggestion' about what he was to say the first payment on his debt? If so, it was not going to work. Stonz was sure as hell not going to tell him what to say or not to say.

"I think that's a good idea, Michael," Mary said. "It's a subject that needs to be addressed. And most ecclesiastics steer clear of it for some reason."

Michael checked to be sure that Stonz and the others had left the building before he said, "Maybe. But I don't like to be told what to say."

"Oh, I'm sure he wasn't 'telling' you. It was just a suggestion."

"Yeah, well. That's isn't what I had in mind for next Sunday."

"Oh? What do you have in mind?"

"The beach. I thought we could play hooky and hit Venice Beach."

She grinned at him and for the first time he noticed that one of her teeth was slightly crooked. So she wasn't perfect after all. Now why should that give him so much pleasure? "How about after church?" she said. "Sort of from heaven to Gomorrah."

He laughed with a delight he could not explain. "I'm sure you could turn even Gomorrah into heaven."

"Of course. I can make miracles too." She took hold of his arm with both hands. "But right now I just have time for a nice lunch before I have to report for work."

Walking up the aisle with Mary at his side should have made him very happy, but somehow, Mary's mention of miracles had yanked his mind back to reality. And with reality, his thoughts turned to Anthony Stonz. There was something about the man that bothered him. It was hard to believe that a man of his caliber could be so interested in their little church, even though he had been able to produce a couple of so called 'miracles.'

Even so, as he and Mary walked toward the door, he looked around the room and thought he would be a fool to make any enemy of the man. "Don't look a gift horse in the mouth," he muttered.

Mary looked at him. "What?"

"Nothing. I was just thinking about Venice and you in a bikini."

She laughed. "That wasn't part of the deal."

"Yes, it was. You just didn't hear it."

"But I don't have a bikini."

"Good. Shopping for one will be even more fun."

She laughed again and clutched his arm tighter, and Michael stopped thinking about Anthony Stonz.

Chapter 26

Stonz had been right. Speaking about the Antichrist produced the desired effect on the audience. Michael had had several days for research, and this time when he stood up in front of more than five hundred people in the church's new venue, he was prepared.

He began by talking about the current breakdown in social order throughout the nation and the world. This gave him a dynamic segue into his subject. "Why?" he said quietly. Then stronger: "Why? Why do we have war after war? Why do we have more crime than ever? Hard crime and soft crime. Our prisons are full. Why has the world lost its sense of reason, its sense of morality? You know the reason: The world is losing its religious commitment. Or—and this is important—religious commitments are being subverted to the side of evil. Why is it we hate those who confront evil, not those who do evil? Is it possible to have a strong religious commitment and still be evil? You bet!"

The theater had excellent acoustics, and as Michael moved up and down the long sloping aisles, his voice rang clear and strong to the farthest reaches of the big room, and the audience sat in spellbound silence. Michael was keenly aware of the effect of his words. He had experienced the same sense of power when he stood in front of his band and let his music impact the audience with a frenzy of sound.

Now, his voice both mesmerized his audience and uplifted him. Again he was in the zone.

"And why is this?!" His words rang against the walls of the theater like stokes against a huge bell. "This moral breakdown is not just happening. It's not a natural act of nature, the swing of a pendulum. It is planned! It is planned! By whom? Who would—who could do such a thing? Who could turn so many people against God? Who could subvert some of the oldest and strongest religions to do evil? Not just in this nation, but throughout the world? You know! You know who is getting his hands around your throat, tighter and tighter, squeezing out reason, squeezing out your moral convictions, squeezing out love. The Son of Perdition; the Man of Sin, the right hand of Satan, the Antichrist!"

He went on to quote Biblical passages—John, Daniel, Matthew, Thessalonians, and Revelations—and the words of prophets who speculated about the identity of the Antichrist. Some said he was not a man; he was a nation, some said he was a city, some a consortium of men, some even said he was the Papacy.

"But," he continued, "according to the modern interpretation of scripture, the Antichrist is a man, not Satan himself, but a man doing the bidding of Satan. Because only a man can work from the inside. Inside our government, inside our churches, inside our hearts, inside our souls!"

He had no idea whether the words he spoke were true. Actually, he did not much care. He was an actor, saying his lines, but also an actor who had the power to make up his lines as he went along. So he selected his words carefully, measuring their effectiveness by the expressions on the faces of his audience, choosing the word, timber, volume that produced the effect he wanted.

His message? Was calling for an awareness of the Antichrist the message? A part of him watched for some sign that it was. Another part of him hoped it was not. Because, he realized with a dull astonishment, that he did not want this to end.

It was immensely exhilarating to realize that he had such control of his audience. In a way he was a conductor, leading a five hundred piece orchestra, an orchestra that responded to his direction like trained musicians. And the music was his creation, the music of glory.

To his surprise, he spoke for more than thirty minutes. Perhaps it was because he wanted to postpone the next part of the service.

It had been Anthony Stonz' idea. When Michael had said he wanted no part of any more 'miracles,' the ambassador had suggested that he use the tried and true technique of pseudo faith healers, that of calling those with infirmities to the stage where he could heal them. That way he could select only those he wished to deal with.

So after he ended his speech with the usual "And may the grace of our Lord Jesus Christ be with you all. Amen," Mary led the chorus into "Lead Kindly Light." Selene's incredible voice, sounding like the song of an angel, increased the mood of reverence so that when the last notes faded away, everyone, even Michael, held his breath, fearing that any movement, any sound would dispel the feeling that they were in the presence of glory.

Finally, Reverend Gregory rose and moved to the makeshift lectern, and Michael, sitting in the front row, sucked in his breath. Here it comes

A dozen chairs had been set up in the stage arena facing the audience, and at the Reverend's invitation, they were quickly filled. The TV cameraman with the mobile camera took up a kneeling position near the front of the stage.

Looking at the people, Michael wanted to run. Two or three of them seemed to have minor injuries, which he was sure he could handle, but the others appeared perfectly normal; there was no way to tell their afflictions

Would he be able to maintain control? Or would some person draw him into a wrenching world of fear and pain? He would have to watch for those whose ailment was of such a nature that their transmigration would not cause him more harm than he could handle. Control. That was the answer.

Sitting beside him, Mary squeezed his hand. "You can do it, Michael. I know you can."

"Yeah, that's the trouble. So do I."

Ignoring her puzzled look, he got up, and as he moved to stand before the people seated in the chairs, there was not a sound in the room, not a cough, not a whisper

"You must understand," he said. He stopped and cleared his throat. "You must understand, I am but an instrument of God. I do not heal. God does. And,"—here, here was his salvation, his 'out'—"God only heals those who are ready in their hearts to be healed. I will leave it to God as to whom he wants to heal today and who is not yet ready."

Feeling that he had laid the groundwork for his rejections, he moved to stand behind an elderly man seated in the first chair. He was sitting with his hands clasped, but Michael could see that they were trembling. But not badly. It looked like something he could deal with.

"How can I help you?"

The man held up his hands. Now that they were no longer clasp, the tremors were more pronounced and Michael wondered if he was making a mistake.

"Hodgkins," the man said. "Can you help me?"

"If it is God's will. Do you have faith in God?"

"I do. Oh yes, I do."

"We shall see."

Michael breathed a silent prayer, not for God to heal the man, but for God to make sure he hadn't made a bad mistake.

Poising his hands above the man's head, Michael was acutely conscious that everyone in the audience was leaning forward in their chairs, holding their breaths. He drew in his own breath, held it, and lowered his hands to the man's head.

Ohhh! A gasp exploded from his lungs as in his head a flash of intense light and a burst of pain drove him back a step. He stood, clutching the back of the chair, his eyes glazed, his legs and hands trembling.

Slowly, strength flowed back into his body, and he straightened. He expelled his breath in a surge of relief. That hadn't been too bad. He could handle that.

"How do you feel?"

The man turned his head to look at Michael, his mouth open with surprise. "I feel..." He held up his hands. They no longer trembled. "I feel wonderful."

"Good. Just remain seated, please."

Michael heard the entire congregation release their breathes in a long sigh, followed by the murmur of voices.

Michael left the man staring at his hands as he moved to stand behind a young boy seated in the next chair. The boy had a thick bandage on his right hand but Michael could not tell why. Was it simply because of a cut or a broken finger? Michael thought he could handle that. But if the boy had lost one or more of his fingers, he wanted no part of it.

"How can God help you, young man."

The boy held up his bandaged hand. "A dog bite me."

Michael smiled. A dog bite would be painful but certainly within his capabilities. "Do you have faith in God?"

The boy nodded vigorously. "Yes, I do."

"We shall see. Give me your hand."

The boy lifted his hand. "Don't squeeze hard. It hurts."

"I won't."

Michael, conscious that the TV cameraman had moved in close, steeled himself against the pain and took the boy's bandaged hand in both of his own, The slash of pain was sharp, but he managed to keep hold of the boy's hand. On the back of his right hand he saw a ragged tear that quickly faded. When the pain subsided, he released his grip.

"You can take the bandage off now."

The boy quickly unwound the bandage, then stared at his hand. There was no sign of a wound. "It's gone." He looked up at Michael. "Thanks."

"Don't thank me. Thank God."

A woman sat in the next chair. Michael judged her to be in her sixties. Her clothes were plain, her face deeply lined as though she had endured great hardship. Michael tried to stand close behind her, but something caused him to move back a step. He did not want to touch this woman. Whatever her illness was, he knew it would be more than he wanted to bear.

"I'm sorry," he said. "You are not yet ready for God."

"I am. I am ready."

He was glad he stood behind her so that he did not have to see the despair that was reflected in her voice. "I'm sorry," he repeated.

Her shoulders began to shake and she put her hands over her face. Michael started to lift his hand. Oh God. How could he allow this woman to suffer?

Then he remembered how the dying baby had almost cost his own life, and he let his hand drop. From the corner of his eye he saw Mary looking at him, her brows drawn in disbelief. She did not understand. Like everyone else, she had no concept of the horror he would experience. He would not go through that again, not for her, not for anyone.

A younger woman occupied the next chair. As he moved to stand behind her, she twisted her head to stare at him. One side of her face was misshapen, her mouth pulled into an ugly grimace, her eyelid drooping, her eye red, swollen. Michael had seen such a face before. A woman who had lived next door to their house in Texas. What had his dad said it was? Some kind of palsy. He remembered that the woman's face had gradually straightened over time until she once again looked normal.

Should he ignore this woman, allow nature to take its course? But suppose he was wrong and her disfigurement would not go away. Could he stand to have his face contorted so grotesquely even for a short time?

He looked at the nearby TV camera. Its cold glass eye stared at him, urging him to perform a miracle it could see. Well, if he was right, this should satisfy all its grisly desires.

"Do you have faith in God?"

"Yes," she almost shouted. "Yes, I have faith."

"We shall see."

Looking directly at the camera, Michael stiffened his body and placed his hands on her head. Uggghh. He felt his face twist, pull, his flesh ripped by the hands of a giant, his eyes gouged from his head. The cameras. Let the cameras see. But he could not stand; he could not think. He sagged to his knees, his hands covering his twisted, pain-wracked face, a groan forced from his grotesque mouth.

The woman rose to her feet, feeling her face with her hands. "Oh God," she shouted. "Thank you, God. Thank you." She ran, ran back to her place in the audience where she threw her arms around a young man who had stood up. He kissed her face over and over.

But Michael hardly saw them from his tearing eyes. Slowly, oh, God, so slowly, the pain, the horrible twisted sensation began to subside and he felt his face gradually relax.

He moved his jaw, afraid that some part of the transformation had been left. But everything felt normal, even the searing pain in his eye had abated to a dull ache.

He used the back of the woman's vacant chair to pull himself to his feet. He tried to move to the next chair, but suddenly felt so weak that he had to stop and cling to the back of the chair.

Mary was quickly by his side. "Michael. Are you all right?"

He straightened, releasing his grip on the chair. "I think so. That one was...bad."

Reverend Gregory had come to stand beside Mary. "We can stop," he said. "This might be too much for you."

"No. I'm okay." He looked at the remaining people in the chairs. They stared at him with eyes filled with hope and—something else—fear, fear that he could not go on. He could not ignore them. He would just have to be more selective.

"All right," Mary said. "But if it's too much, you stop."

"Believe it."

Mary and Reverend Gregory slowly moved away, hardly taking their eyes from him long enough to find their seats.

Michael looked up at the audience. "I'm all right," he reassured them. "I'm all right."

He moved to the next chair where a middle-aged man sat. When he stopped behind the man's chair, the man tensed, his fingers clutching his thighs. He did not turn his head, but Michael could see enough of the man's face to recognize the signs of heavy drinking. If he had any doubts, the man's breath quickly dispelled them. He had not been able to control his drinking enough to come to church sober. Was he here because of his drinking, or was his drinking only a symptom of something far worse?

Once again Michael cursed his blessing: God had given him the ability to perform miracles, but had neglected giving him the ability to determine who should be cured and who he should not touch.

If it were only the drinking, he was sure he could handle the man's problem. After all, being drunk would not be a new sensation to him. But how would it look to the cameras? There wouldn't be much to see except a drunken evangelist.

Visualizing being intoxicated on camera made him smile and he decided to take the chance. "Do you have faith in God?"

The man nodded vigorously. "I do. I have faith." Then he surprised Michael by adding, "Dear God, I pray you can help me."

Michael had been about to put his hands on the man's head, but something in the words made him hesitate. The man's plea seemed to go beyond his drinking.

Too late. Too late to back out now with the cameras and five hundred people watching. Flicking his tongue across his dry lips, he forced his hands to descend to the man's head.

Nothing. No explosion of light. No pain. Nothing but a warm glow that started with his fingers and diffused throughout his body. He had been right. It was the drinking. He could tell he was smiling, a silly, twisted smile of drunken relief.

He was about to take his hands from the man's head when: bam! A fist of pain slammed into his groin, driving an explosion of anguish from his lips, driving him to his knees, driving his hands down to clutch between his legs. Cancer! Prostate cancer! That was why the man drank! God! The thick, viscous pain coursed through his stomach, his thighs, his lower spine. He felt his eyes roll back in his head, and he fought the dreaded blackness.

He felt cool hands on his forehead and heard Mary's voice saying, "Michael. Fight it, Michael. Fight it."

She was kneeling beside him, and with her cooling touch, the pain began to subside and he was able to force his chin up. "Easy...easy for you...to say."

To his surprise, tears appeared in her eyes. "Oh, Michael," she said. "I love you."

He rocked back on his heels, blinking at her. "Uh? What was that?"

She put her lips close to his ear. "I love you."

When Reverend Gregory came to help, Michael wanted to push him away. He want to hear Mary say the words once more, words that he desperately wanted to be true.

But the reverend and Mary lifted him to his feet and held him as he clung to the back of the chair.

"Thank you." He focused on the man standing in front of him, tears streaming down his spider-veined cheeks "Thank you," the man gasped. "Thank you, thank you."

Michael lifted one hand and placed it on the man's shoulder. "Amen, brother. Amen."

As Reverend Gregory urged the man back into his seat, Mary peered at Michael's face. "That's enough, Michael."

He could not bring himself to look at the other waiting people, but he knew he had to stop. He had no strength in his legs; he could not stand without holding to the chair. And unlike the previous times when he had felt weak, this time the feeling did not pass, and he knew that without Mary's support he would fall.

"I think you're right."

Mary looked at the waiting people. "I'm sorry. That's all Michael can do today. Leave your names with Reverend Gregory and he'll will put you at the head of the list for next..."

Michael's knees sagged. Next week? She was going to tell them to come back next week. He had to go through this again? He was not sure he could do that. But he was sure he did not want to do it. Who in their right mind would?

As though she read his mind, Mary whispered, "Can you do it, Michael?"

He wanted to shout 'No!' He wanted to tell her that he would never do this again. He looked up at the building's high, domed ceiling, hoping that he would see a growing light and an angel descending, bringing him word that his mission was over, that he had endured enough.

But there was no light, no angel. He was on his own.

He looked into the eyes of the waiting people and this time when he sagged, it was the weakness of defeat. "Yes," he murmured. "Tell them to come back."

Walking back to his seat with Mary's help, the thought that ran through his mind was, 'The hell with miracles.' From now on if he wasn't sure a person's ailment was something minor, he would skip them. He would never go through that again.

Anthony Stonz, watching from inside a TV control van, kept his face impassive as he suppressed a glow of pleasure. It was beginning to happen. Next time Michael Modesto would not be so eager to perform his miracles. It was only a small victory, but it was a beginning. Only a beginning.

Chapter 27

Slipping away from reporters and TV news cameras had been relatively easy. Before the service, Michael had explored the new building for possible exits and had located a door in the rear of the building that had probably been used for delivering stage props and scenery for the theater. So Reverend Gregory would not worry about his disappearance, he told him he was going to leave as soon as possible after the service. Gregory had seen his weariness and said he understood. He would talk to Michael during the week.

Now, with Mary sitting beside him, he drove north on Pacific Coast Highway as slowly as traffic would allow. It was a gorgeous day. On their left, sunlight sparkling off the ocean; on their right, palms topped the bluffs of Pacific Palisades. The highway buzzed with traffic in both directions as people jostled for access to Southern California beaches.

Michael breathed deeply of the salt-tanged air. "I love this place," he said. "I've been in practically the whole world, and I wouldn't trade Southern California for any of them."

Mary nodded. "We're really lucky. Think how many people would give their soul to be where we are."

"Yeah. I've often thought that if we ever have another war instead of dropping bombs we should drop leaflets saying that if you stop fighting we'll give you a ticket to California. I'll bet the fighting'd be over before it got started."

"Make that a ticket to Hollywood. Tell them they could be movie stars."

They grinned at each other, and Michael drove for several minutes in contented silence.

Mary broke the long silence. "Did you ever want to be a movie star?"

"Me? No, not really. I did want to be a rock star."

"You were. You are."

"Not any more." Mary said nothing, and Michael added, "I don't regret it."

"Are you sure?" Her voice was small, guilt ridden.

"I did. At first. But after today... No, I don't regret it."

"After you saw the faces of those people?"

"No." He glanced at her. "After you said 'I love you.'"

Her face changed color and she caught her breath. "Oh."

He wanted to question her about it, desperately wanted to know whether she had really meant it or whether it was simply the passion of the moment, an expression created by the wonder of miracles. But he hesitated. Did he really want to know.? If she said it was true, he would be ecstatically happy. But it would also demand a response from him. And what should that be? That he loved her too? Was he ready for that? It meant he would be committing to a new life that went far beyond his commitment to God's message. Suppose that next week, next Sunday, it all came together and God's message suddenly poured out of him. He would be finished, done, able to go back to his music, his old life. Could Mary be a part of that life? He didn't think so.

So he drove silently, ignoring her unvoiced waiting for his response. After a moment, when she realized he was not going to answer, she said, "Where are we going?" Her voice was firm, controlled.

"I have no idea."

She smiled and settled back in the seat. "Good. It'll take a long time to get there."

She half turned in the seat, her back against the door so she could look at him without turning her head. To Michael, it was disconcerting to feel her eyes on him as he drove, but it also gave him a curious sense of pleasure, the kind he sometimes felt when he was into a song so deeply it took over his body and mind. It was a heady sensation of fulfillment, the kind that stayed with him even after the last notes had died. He was sure the same lingering euphoria would let him bask in the pleasure of her gaze long after she turned away.

They had been driving for almost an hour, and he noticed they were on the outskirts of Malibu with its collection of restaurants, apartments and beachfront homes sandwiched between the ocean and the foothills of the Santa Monica mountains "You hungry? How about some lunch?"

"I've got a better idea. How about a walk on the pier?"

"Okay. If we can find a place to park."

They found a parking lot that, miraculously, still had space for one or two cars and was only a couple of blocks from the pier. Walking on the wooden planks of Malibu pier in brilliant sunshine and breathing the cool sea air, Michael remembered when he was a kid in Texas and had seen movies about Malibu surfers with scenes of the pier stretching out into an unbelievably blue sea. At the time it had seemed unreal, unattainable. Now, here he was. On the very same pier, holding hands with a beautiful girl, watching surfers riding the waves, hearing the roar of those same waves sweeping under the pier and breaking on the shore. Talk about California dreaming

He chuckled at the thought and Mary asked, "What's so funny?"

"I was just thinking we should have some Beach Boys music."

"Or DeBussy's 'Le Mer.'"

"Well, we've finally found a subject where we're not compatible."

"Oh, I like all kinds of music. I even like your band."

"Ouch. Do you have to say 'even'?"

She gave him a mischievous smile. "I was being kind."

They had reached the end of the pier where they leaned against the rail and looked out over the water where scores of young people sat astride surfboards, waiting for an acceptable wave to roll in from China. The shoreline, washed clean by spin drifting water, formed a miles long crescent stretching to Santa Monica and, far in the distance, Manhattan Beach and the Palos Verde peninsula.

An unusually large wave broke beneath the pier and churning water battered the supporting posts sending spray high in the air where the light breeze brought it to Michael's face.

"Thanks," he said. "I needed that."

Standing beside him Mary giggled. "The seventh wave. They're always bigger. At least that's the theory."

Michael pointed at a group of surfers who had ridden the wave to the shore and were now paddling back out to wait for the next monster. "So why are they in such a rush? They've got six more to go."

"Eternal optimists. Maybe this time it'll be the fourth wave, or the fifth."

"Or the tenth."

"Or never."

"No. There's always another big wave. It's probably out there now, out by Hawaii or Guam, barreling in as inexorably as the tide."

"If you don't mind waiting a week or so."

"Yeah. I guess in the meantime you settle for the little ones."

"Like love."

Startled, he turned to look at her. "Love?"

She was staring out across the sea as though she could see the waves of her life stretching to infinity. "I mean we find someone we like, we might even think we're in love, but it's not really the big one, and we know it. But the big one might never arrive. When we get tired of waiting, we take the next wave we can catch."

She seemed so dejected, as though she had given up on ever finding the perfect wave, that he put his arm around her waist. "I guess the trick is to be happy with one of the small waves and hope that the big one doesn't come along and drown you."

"There's something that would be worse than that."

"Oh, what?"

She turned her face away when she said, "For the perfect one to arrive, and you find you can't catch it."

Michael felt a tightness in his chest, a sudden longing that was so intense he had to lean against the rail. "Or be so damn dumb you don't recognize it's the one you've been waiting for."

She looked at him then, and he saw moisture on her face that he didn't think had been caused by mist from the breaking wave. "That would be just awful, like finding the one you've been waiting for and he doesn't want you."

He pulled her toward him. and she came into his arms, her face tilted for his kiss.

Her lips were as soft and sweet as her tears.

When it was time to end the kiss, she turned so he could stand behind her with his arms around her waist, and she could tilt her head back against his shoulder.

"We should be married in the church," he said.

She gave no indication that she was surprised by his words. It was as though the kiss had told her everything. "Yes," she said. "That would be right."

The enormity of what he was planning was so overwhelming that his voice was hoarse when he said, "When?"

"As soon as possible."

He nodded, unable to speak. In one brief afternoon—no. In one brief moment the course of his whole life had changed. He had always known that he would marry someday, had even visualized what married life would be like. But none of his dreams had prepared him for such an abrupt decision, nor for the life he saw stretching out ahead of him like a golden path. He would remain an evangelist until his conscience told him that he had done his best to deliver the message. Then he would go back to his music.

But what if Mary did not have the same dream?

"Look," he said, and something in his voice made her stiffen in his arms. "Just so we don't start off on the wrong foot, you know I'm only in this evangelist thing until I get this message off my chest."

She turned to face him, her eyes shining. "I know. But it isn't what you do that I love, it's you, yourself. You can be a minister, a musician, a bricklayer if you want. I don't care. I'll be there."

He looked over her shoulder at the surfers sitting patiently waiting for the next good wave, and he felt a surge of pity mingled with a deep satisfaction. They might wait forever for their perfect wave, but not him—he had found his.

Chapter 28

They found Reverend Gregory in the old church talking to Anthony Stonz. A group of moving men were already clearing Gregory's office and carrying everything to a huge moving van in the church parking lot.

When Mary told them that she and Michael were going to be married, Gregory's face sagged, but Anthony Stonz rubbed his hands together with delight.

"Excellent," he said. "If you don't mind waiting a little while, you can be married in the new church."

"Waiting?" Mary said. "The church is ready now."

"Oh, not that new church." Anthony turned to Gregory. "Tell them, Reverend."

Gregory turned his ashen face toward them, and Michael realized that he was in love with Mary. The news of their engagement must have shattered all his dreams. Well, that was sad but too bad. Gregory'd had his chance and she wasn't interested.

As though he read Michael's mind, Gregory took a deep breath before he said, "Mr. Stonz thinks that we should build a chapel of our own."

"Not a chapel. A cathedral. I visualize neoclassic."

"And he's going to set up a regular TV program to help pay for it."

Anthony Stonz held up one hand. "Partially pay for it. With the collections we'll be making at the church and from the sale of artifacts, we'll have money enough to insure that you all have good salaries."

Reverend Gregory winced. "Artifacts? I don't know—"

Stonz interrupted. "All the churches have them. Even the Catholics. They have religious shops right on the church grounds. Memorabilia brings in big money. Right, Michael?"

Michael could not answer. They were sealing him into this life as surely as Egyptian kings were sealed into the pyramids.

It was Mary who came to his rescue. "How long will it take to build this cathedral? We don't want to wait years."

Stonz shook his head. "Not years. I can pull some strings. I'd say less than a year." He smiled at Mary. "I assure you, my dear, it will be worth the wait. "

"But a year...? That might not be wise. Michael never promised to help forever."

"I told that to Mr. Stonz," Reverend Gregory said. "He—"

"That's right." Anthony Stonz looked at Michael. "This message from God you're supposed to deliver, once you've done that, you feel that your, should we say, calling is complete."

"Exactly," Michael said. "So maybe going into debt for a new cathedral isn't such a good idea."

"Let me worry about that." Anthony reached to put his hand on Michael's shoulder, but instead pulled his hand back. He quickly said, "I have contacts who, I'm sure, will be happy to underwrite the entire project."

"They may be wasting their money."

Stonz' eyes appeared to harden but his voice remained unctuous. "Nonsense. I'm sure that you have many messages. And your healing powers are phenomenal. You'll be packing them in for years."

"That's another thing. Those powers could disappear any time. I have no control over them. You saw what happened this morning."

Anthony Stonz' voice became as hard as his eyes. "Yes, I saw." Then his gaze softened. "I may be able to help you there. We've got to conserve your strength. As for television... There are ways to provide the drama without the personal trauma." He saw the skepticism in Michael's expression and laughed. "Don't worry, Michael. I'll be with you in this all the way. You won't be the first man of God I've helped. Trust me. You put yourself in my hands and you'll have more power, more wealth than you can imagine." He turned to Mary. "So let's start planning that wedding. Can you wait a few months? I promise, you'll have the world waiting for the event."

Mary frowned. "A few months?" She glanced at Michael. "Well, it's up to Michael."

Michael sucked in his breath. His world seemed to be spinning out of control. Maybe it would be better to wait, to see what God had in mind for him. For all he knew, the end of the message could be the end of him. "I guess we could wait a while. But if I suddenly...well, if anything, uh, happens to me, we won't wait."

"Fine." Anthony Stonz took hold of Reverend Gregory's arm. "Reverend, I think the movers are ready for you. I'm going to get on the phone and start making calls."

Michael watched Anthony Stonz and the reverend move up the aisle, and his stomach knotted with dismay. What had begun as a simple project to raise money for sick children was turning into a circus. He should have stopped Stonz, but the man was a buzz saw. No wonder he had been able to push programs through Washington.

"A year," Mary said. "Michael, do we want to wait that long?"

Michael shook his head. This was one area where he could not allow the Ambassador to dictate. "No. We'll set our own date. There's no reason we have to wait for some glass cathedral."

She let her breath out with a sigh. "Oh, I'm glad you said that. I'd die if I had to wait too long."

"Me too," Michael said with a grin. "I don't want to give you time to change your mind."

"No chance of that, Mister. You're stuck with me."

As they walked out of the building, Michael wondered whether his decision not to wait might be because he had doubts about Mary's love. When he had been nothing but a rock musician, her only interest in him had been to obtain money for her charity. But when he had begun performing miracles, when he seemed headed for fame as an evangelist, she had decided she was in love. Would that love vanish if his powers vanished?

Feeling her warm hand on his arm as they walked, thinking back over the brief time that he had known her, he did not think she could marry any man she did not truly love. And her love would be forever. Wouldn't it?

He lifted his face toward the sky when they walked out into the late afternoon sunlight and the thought that came to him was that even if God should abandon him, Mary never would.

Anthony Stonz sat in his hotel suite having dinner with Selene. The speed in which the church's TV program was gaining audience amazed even him. Much of the credit was due to the church choir, specifically to Selene. Her remarkable voice had already achieved cult status and she was receiving offers from record companies for her own albums of gospel music.

Selene, of course, had refused all offers. Her instructions were to keep close to Michael Modesto not to become a recording star.

Another thing that had surprised him was Michael Modesto's thaumaturgic power. The man had no idea of his strength. If he could ever learn to control it's debilitating side effects, there would be no limits to the heights he could attain. He was already making progress in that direction. He was getting better at judging the severity of people's maladies and steering clear of those that would have painful repercussions.

Not that it mattered. The audience, both in person and on TV, were just as happy to see someone cured of a sore foot as they were to see someone cured of a ruptured heart valve. More so, in fact. Not much visibly happened when a heart was made whole, but seeing a person throw away crutches was exciting.

"I think," he said to Selene, "Michael should heal more badly afflicted people. That's what the audience wants."

Selene's lips curved into a frown. "But he can't. They drain the energy out of him. After two or three, he doesn't have the strength."

"But suppose he only seemed to cure them."

Selene's eyes narrowed. "You mean fake it? He would never do that. He's too honest."

"He seeks out the easiest, even the psychosomatics. That's hardly honest."

"But it's not dishonest either." She shook her head. "No, I don't think he would knowingly do that."

"Ahhh, of course. Knowingly." Anthony smiled at Selene and reached over to pat her hand. "I always knew you were brilliant."

Selene stared at him, her dark eyes level, accusing. "You're going to set it up and not tell him."

Stonz put his hand on his chin and tapped his lips with a forefinger. "I'll have to make sure the patient has some minor ailment. If he feels nothing at all, he'll be suspicious."

"But..." Selene lifted her hands. "Where will it end? You can't just get bigger and bigger miracles."

"Where will it end?" Anthony Stonz stopped smiling and stared into Selene's eyes. "Don't get emotionally involved with these people, especially with Michael Modesto. It is not your concern. Is that clear?"

Selene's ivory skin turned pale. She turned her head but her eyes remained locked on those of Anthony Stonz. "Yes. I...I understand."

"I'm sure you do."

Stonz looked away, releasing her. Perhaps it had been a mistake to divulge even this one little aspect of his plan. After all, Selene was becoming very close to these people, and she was only human. In the future, he would have to be more careful.

Chapter 29

Michael sat in a booth of the small restaurant waiting for Mary to join him. He stared out the window at traffic on San Fernando Road, his mind refusing to focus on the stream of Sunday morning traffic. To his eyes the passing cars, the nearby San Gabriel Mountains, the trees and structures were only a blur, their images obscured by a darkness of worry. Something was wrong and he was not sure what it could be.

He growled with disgust, not disgust at the problem, but disgust with himself for not being able to dismiss it from his mind. Because he knew that if the problem were really important, the cause would be obvious. But no. This was nothing more than a disquieting suspicion that was driving him crazy, too insignificant to even come into focus.

For the past two weeks, instead of the Bible serendipitously providing him with a lecture subject, he had been forced to formulate a subject then laboriously dredge up supporting data .

However, his sermons apparently had not suffered from their lack of spontaneity. If anything, they were even better. The hours spent in research and making notes, tended to expand his range of affirming material. Fortunately, he had a good memory and often could recall some supporting quotation or story that if someone had ask where it could be found, he would have no answer.

Still, he missed the excitement of his early sermons. They had been fun, just as in the old days he had found fun in his music when he could improvise around an extemporaneous theme. But now with each topic thoroughly checked and rehearsed, he was beginning to feel like a jazz artist playing in a symphony orchestra. If it weren't for the miracles...

Ah.

A jolt of guilt caused him to thump the table lightly with his fist. The healings! Without the power to heal, he would be just another preacher. But lately, they, too, had begun to feel as though they were cut and dried. He had become so expert at selecting subjects that he rarely experienced more than a trace of the debilitating trauma he so dreaded.

The problem was that he was becoming so calculating in his selections, deliberately avoiding anyone with a major disability, that reporters were beginning to question his divine powers.

The solution, of course, was to take on one of the more advanced cases and suffer the consequences.

He grimaced, suppressing a shudder. Anything but that. There had to be some other way to prove that he was a messenger of God. That is, if he truly was a messenger.

That, he suddenly realized, was the source of the nagging worry: doubt.

Well, he was not about to put it to the test.

Just the memory of the horrible blackness dragging him to some dreadful form of oblivion gave him a cold chill. No. The hell with television and the reporters. He would rather lose everything than go through that again.

He shifted to get a better view of the restaurant's interior. He had selected the booth so that he could keep an eye on the door and his attention was caught by two people who entered. One of them was Mary. With her was Anthony Stonz.

Watching Mary walk toward him, he again had the pleasant feeling of wonder that anyone so lovely could have chosen him as the one with whom she would like to share her life. She was wearing a pink blouse and a pale gray skirt with a matching jacket. She was one of those few women who could take long strides in high heels and still maintain perfect posture. Her hair, as usual when she was going to church, was braided and, this time, secured in a neat coil at the nape of her neck. She wore no makeup, but her face reminded him of a flower fresh in the morning sun. God, how could he be so lucky.

He stood and gave Mary a hug and a kiss on the cheek. He would have liked to feel the soft warmth of her lips, but he knew that she would be uncomfortable at such a show of affection in public. One more thing to get used to.

He turned toward Stonz, ready to shake his hand, but, as usual, Stonz only nodded in greeting, saying, "Michael, you're looking well."

Mary sat down and made room so that Michael could slide in beside her while Anthony Stonz took a place on the opposite side of the booth. Stonz wore a dark double-breasted suit with a pale blue silk tie, and Michael wondered if this was the day the Ambassador was finally going to attend church services.

Stonz gazed around at the small restaurant as though he had never been in one before, which he probably hadn't. "Charming," he said. "I imagine it's difficult to find a restaurant where one won't be accosted by fans or people looking for a miraculous cure."

"That's true. I guess people who come in here don't watch TV."

"It's the food," Mary said. "There's nothing like greasy cheeseburgers and fat-saturated French fries to keep you healthy."

Stonz chuckled. "Well, the way things are progressing you can soon hire your own chef."

"Oh, How are things going?" During the three weeks they had been using the new church, Michael knew that the collection baskets had always been filled, but Reverend Gregory never mentioned exact figures.

"Very well. Very well indeed. I've already discussed salaries for the two of you, and—"

Mary interrupted. "Me? I don't do anything."

"Of course you do. You rehearse and conduct the choir; you assist Reverend Gregory in organizing and running the services. You're a valued member and should be compensated."

"I'll accept on the condition that the money goes to the Children's Fund."

"That can be arranged. And speaking of arrangements, have either of you had much experience in running a corporation?"

"Well, the Fund is a charitable non-profit corporation," Mary said. "We had an attorney set it up, but it's always been small and there wasn't much to running it."

Stonz turned his attention to Michael. "How about you, Michael?"

Michael shrugged. "Our band was incorporated, but we left running it to Benny."

"Benny?"

"Benny Bond. Our C.P.A. and manager."

"I see. Is he still associated with the band?"

Michael grimaced with sudden guilt. "There's nothing to run. Since I left, the band has pretty well disintegrated."

"Then Mr. Bond might be available."

"Available? To do what?"

Anthony Stonz smiled and lifted his hand apologetically. "I'm sorry. Communication has always been one of my many problems. I tend to believe everyone can read my mind." He leaned forward slightly. "The Church is growing exponentially, and it's going to continue growing. That means organization. Up to now Reverend Gregory has been able to handle the finances and other organizational affairs, but it's rapidly getting away from him. Then there are going to be a wide range of contracts that will need administering: TV contracts, the charitable contributions to the Children's Fund, construction contracts for the new cathedral. In addition..."

Seeing Michael's look of dismay, Anthony Stonz paused and smiled. "Sorry. I get carried away. What I'm getting at are two things: First, we're going to need someone like your Mr. Bond. And second, Michael, I believe you should be a partner in the company."

"Company?"

"If the church isn't incorporated already as a non-profit company, Mr. Bond can make the arrangements." Stonz held up his hand to forestall any objections. "I know it seems premature, but the way things are moving, it simply has to be done."

Michael realized that Stonz was right. Things were moving too fast for Gregory to keep up. And with contracts for the new church, radio and TV contracts, and merchandising there would soon be thousands, perhaps millions of dollars involved as well as attorneys, contractors, permits. Benny himself might be in over his head. "You're right," he said. "But I'm not sure I want to be a partner."

"Of course you do. Your church is well on its way to becoming an international entity with millions of dollars involved. And all because of you. You should share in its success."

Michael looked at Mary. "What do you think, Mary?"

She put her hand on his arm. "Money tends to attract unsavory people. You should be in a position where you would have control."

Anthony Stonz lifted both hands. "She's right, Michael. I've seen it happen time and time again: an enterprise taken over by dishonest people who used it for their own gain. You wouldn't want that to happen."

Michael nodded. "I guess not. But what about you? We wouldn't be going anywhere without you."

Anthony Stonz frowned regretfully and shook his head. "In my position that wouldn't be ethical, probably wouldn't even be legal. I'll help all I can, of course. I believe in you. But I'd better remain in the background."

Mary said, "But you should get credit for all you've done."

Stonz shook his head. "My reward will be seeing the word of God spread around the globe." He smiled. "I guess I am a little selfish. An international raise in morality will certainly make my task easier."

Michael wondered whether that might have been Stonz' agenda from the beginning. It was hard for him to believe that someone of Anthony Stonz' stature would devote so much time and money to God no matter how strong his faith. Maybe he was right; a strong surge of Christian morality could help offset some of the religious fanaticism that was causing trouble throughout the world.

"I'll call Benny," he said. "I'm pretty sure I can bring him on board."

"Excellent. The sooner the better. The way the church is growing he's going to have his hands full." He paused and locked his finger together, resting them on the edge of the table. "And that brings me to a favor I'd like to ask."

"Anything," Mary answer. "If we can help..."

Michael nodded in concurrence. "Of course. What is it?"

"First: call me Anthony."

Mary laughed. "We can do that."

"Second:" Stonz' expression grew serious. "Michael, is it my imagination or are you avoiding some of the people who come to you for help."

Michael stiffened and felt his face freeze in a defensive mask. He had been right; his selective approach was becoming transparent, "Well," he said, "I can't deal with every one. There are just too many."

"It takes a lot out of him," Mary interjected. "A lot of energy."

"I understand. You've got to be selective. You don't want to end up in a hospital yourself. But for the sake of the TV audience—and I'm speaking world wide here—if you could close with something spectacular, it would do more than all the small miracles combined."

"Spectacular?" Michael swallowed. He could visualize what Stonz would consider 'spectacular.' It would be something major, something that would pull him into that world of pain and darkness, a netherworld just waiting to suck him in and never let him go. "I don't know..."

"I understand," Stonz said hastily. "But just this once... I have a friend—a very good friend—I'm sure you could help."

Michael's mouth was dry with fear. "What's wrong with him."

Stonz sighed. "He was injured in an accident. His spinal column. He's paralyzed."

Paralyzed! Oh God. Michael felt his heart spasm in anticipation of the horror. His head began a slow shaking. "No. I can't do that. No."

"As a favor to me. It's the only thing I'll ever ask. I promise."

Michael wanted to say 'yes,' but he could not make his lips form the word.

Mary stared at him, her face betraying her lack of understanding. "Michael, you can do it. I know you can."

"It's not a question of doing it." He paused, searching for words that would, somehow, explain the awful fear.

But there were no words, and the best he could say was, "I just can't do it. Paralysis. It's too much. I can't."

Mary's eyes betrayed her disappointment, but she did not press the subject. After a second she looked at Anthony Stonz. "It really does take a lot out of him."

"It wouldn't be just a favor to me. But I'm sure you're aware that of late the—what shall we call them—miracle cures have been unspectacular. We're beginning to lose our TV audience. This would be your chance to get them back."

Michael shook his head. "No. I can't do it."

"I could have a doctor in attendance—

Michael's head snapped up. "No, God damn it. I won't do it!"

Stonz stared at Michael for a moment. Then he smiled. But the chill in his voice revealed the lie as he said, "It's not important." He slid out of the booth and stood looking down at Michael. "Just think about it."

The razor edge on Stonz' words told Michael that he was supposed to think about what he stood to lose if he refused Stonz' request.

Without another word, Stonz walked out of the restaurant. Michael did not watch him leave. He stared down at the table top, trying to close his mind to the accusation he knew he would find in Mary's eyes.

He expected her to begin imploring him to change his mind. Instead, she glanced at her watch. "I'm not sure we'll have time for breakfast. Not if you want to get there before the reporters."

Michael made no move to get up. He wanted desperately to explain why he had refused Stonz' request. It was important that she knew. The cool, matter-of-fact tone of her voice told him that if he did not explain, some kind of a wedge would have been driven between them.

"You saw what happened with the baby," he said without looking up.

She had started to pick up her purse in preparation of leaving. Now she put it back on the seat beside her. "Yes. I saw that."

"There was more. A lot more...that you couldn't see."

"More? I know you experience the same, uh, malady as the people do. I can understand—"

"It isn't that!" Michael pressed both fingers to his temples. "That's bad enough, but I can handle that: the pain. It's what happens beyond the pain. There's a...a darkness. Like something—I don't know what—but something waiting for me. And I get the feeling that if it wins, if it can pull me in, I'll never get back. Never."

He knew Mary was staring at him. "Is it like that...every time?"

"No. Not with the small things. That's only pain. And it goes pretty fast. But when it's something that...pulls me close to death... I get the feeling there's a presence there... something evil, something...horrible... waiting. With the babies, and with the women in the wheel chair, I didn't think I was going to...get away."

Mary's shoulder's quivered in a small shutter. "Why didn't you tell me?"

"How could I? I can't even explain it to myself."

"That's why you've only been taking the easy ones."

He lifted his head, nodding. "Yeah. I'm too damn much of a coward to go after the really bad ones."

Mary put her hand on his shoulder and gently turned him to face her. "You're not a coward. I saw how you looked. I thought it was just the pain. I'm glad you told me."

"The cathedral. We might lose Stonz' support."

"It doesn't matter. We were doing all right before we ever heard of Anthony Stonz."

"I can still do the minor ones. I can handle that."

Mary took hold of his hand. "All right. But if you ever have the feeling you're losing control, we can walk away."

"We?"

"Of course. I would love a church wedding, but it doesn't have to be in a cathedral."

"Yes, but could you marry a poor musician?"

She touched his cheek. "Only if his name was Michael Modesto."

He kissed her before sliding out of the booth. "Okay, tiger. Let's put the devil back in hell."

She took his hand and they walked out together.

Chapter 30

Michael was beginning to have doubts about his resolve even before he entered the church. He growled in exasperation when he noticed an ambulance parked near the entrance. Two white-coated orderlies were wheeling a man lying flat on a gurney into the church as a portly gray-haired man wearing a suit and necktie gave them directions. The man on the gurney had to be Anthony Stonz' paralyzed friend and the other was his doctor. Well, he was not about to be blackmailed by having the man shoved in his face. When it came time to pick his clients, this was the one person he would pass by as surely as though he had the mark of Passover painted on his forehead.

Michael also noticed that instead of the usual three TV vans parked near the side of the building, there was only one. And the crowd standing outside the church was considerably smaller than it had been the week before.

The dwindling congregation was, he knew, because he had given up performing spectacular miracles. Healing the paralyzed man could change that.

Except that this time the show could result in his death—or near death. He wondered how many of those traumas he could endure before they either killed him or he went stark raving mad. Perhaps their effects were cumulative, and like the brain of a boxer, each hard punch edged him closer and closer to dementia.

The memory shored up his resolve not to give in to Anthony Stonz' request.

When it was time for him to speak, he gave it his best shot. Unfortunately, the topic he had picked for his sermon 'Where Have Our Values Gone?' did not help matters. He had selected the topic because he'd thought it would lead the congregation into thinking about something other than faith and miracles, but as he spoke he felt more and more like a hypocrite, asking himself whether he himself was not shirking his responsibility.

"—we shy away from being judgmental because we do not want to be judged. But that way lies chaos. With no judgment, it is evil that benefits, not good. We cannot escape judgment. The ultimate judge is

God. And even if we abdicate our responsibility, if we fail to condemn what we know is evil, He will not. And it will not be only the evil-doer who receives His judgment, it will also be the one who does not condemn that evil. It will be you, and you and you and—as God is my judge—me!"

Throwing the ending back on himself had a dramatic punch he knew was good. It lumped him—a sinner—in with the rest of the sinners. He was one of them. It sounded great.

Except that after he finished speaking and sat down next to Mary, the words continued to pound through his head. Was he really a sinner for abdicating his responsibility? Was refusing to heal when he had the power to do so the work of the devil? If it was, what would be his defense when he stood before the highest judge of all?

He was still wrestling with the question when it was time to make his selection. Each week he had become more adept at spotting people who would cause him the least discomfort, and as he moved up the aisle while the choir filled in the silence with background music, he pointed to a few people with their hands raised in silent supplication. Inexorably he found himself being drawn closer and closer to the man lying on the gurney at the back of the room. And the closer he came the greater his consternation. What was happening to him? Why was he unable to simply ignore the man, to turn his back and walk away?

He began to sweat and his hands developed a tremble that had to be obvious. He should have held on to his Bible so he would have something to conceal the tremor.

He had almost reached the man when with a gasp of rage and self deprecation, he turned and started back down the aisle.

"Mr. Modesto!"

He recognized the voice: Naomi Morton, the TV director. He would have continued walking, but she already had her hand on his shoulder.

He turned to face her, knowing already what she was going to say. "No," he said. "I'm not taking him."

"I was talking to his doctor—"

"I said I'm not taking him."

She moved closer, so she could drop her voice to a whispered growl. "Look. We're losing audience. He's just what we need. What you need."

He jerked his shoulder free of her grasp. "I don't need him."

He had taken a step when she said, "What about God? Or have you been talking crap all this time?"

A flash of anger made him turn, ready to lash out a reply. Then her words registered and he jerked to a halt. The people nearby were staring, not at him, but at her as though she had committed some form of blasphemy. It was the shock in their expressions that almost drove him to his knees. Which would be worse—the pain he would endure or the pain in their eyes? His voice was hoarse with defeat when he pointed at the man.

"All right! Bring him."

When he walked by Mary on his way to the dais, she stood up. "Michael," she said, "are you sure?"

"I don't know," he answered. "God, I don't know why I did that."

She clasped his hand. "Don't be afraid. I'll be here. I won't let anything happen to you. I just won't."

He tried to cling to her promise as he gave his usual disclaimer and began working with the people he had selected, saving the paralyzed man for last. Only one of the others drew him toward the forbidden threshold. A middle-aged man wearing worn clothing with grease under his fingernails, said that he had a minor hernia, but when Michael placed his hands on the man's head a sharp pain in his chest caused his knees to buckle. He stood swaying, clutching the back of the man's chair with one hand, fighting the pain and a sense of nausea so strong he thought he was going to throw up.

But the feeling passed quickly and by the time Mary had hurried to his side, he was already recovered enough to straighten. Mary reached to help him and he raised his hand. "I'm okay."

"Do you want to stop?"

The irony of her question almost made him start to laugh, but he caught himself. He wanted to tell her that he had not even wanted to start, but he knew that such an admission would only upset her, so he said nothing.

He glanced toward the TV cameras. Their staring lenses reminded him of alien eyes, unblinking, accusing, waiting for something spectacular that they could suck in and spew out to a world of people waiting like hogs at a trough. All he had to do was risk eternal madness.

"Stay with me," he told Mary. "I may need you." He took a deep breath and moved to the man on the gurney.

Above an oxygen mask, the man's wide, unblinking eyes swiveled to watch Michael's approach. From beneath the gurney, the rhythmic sigh of a respirator reminded Michael that soon this might be his world.

A man, who Michael assumed was the patient's doctor, stepped forward with his hand out. "Mister Modesto. I'm Doctor Helmland."

The doctor's eyes were dark blue, the upper part of their irises obscured by drooping lids. His hair, as white as his teeth, was thick, worn heavy above his ears, and like his teeth, had the look of expensive care. With his bearing, tailored suit and perfect hair, he probably projected an excellent image on TV.

"Thank you for being here," Michael said. The doctor's hand felt cold, his grip firm but lacking conviction.

"Perhaps it would help—sort of set the stage—if I explained Mr.

Janik's trauma before you, uh, begin." Without waiting for Michael's reply, the doctor turned to face the TV cameras which, sensing a coup, had moved in closer. "Mr. Janik's *medulla spinalis*—his spinal cord—was severed between the fourth and fifth cervical in a boating accident. He is a quadriplegic with—in layman terms—with no feeling from the neck down." Dr. Helmland swiveled his eyes to look at Michael. "If you can produce even a semblance of sensation in any of this man's extremities, it will truly be a miracle."

Dr. Helmhim took up a position on the far side of the gurney and folded his arms, his face impassive, as though daring Michael to dispute his diagnosis.

Michael nodded. "I'll take your word for it, Doctor."

He moved to the end of the gurney and stood for a moment, gathering his resolve. He turned his hands up and stared at them, wondering why they were not shaking violently. In a few brief seconds he would have to place them on the man's head, an act that would suck him into a hell so filled with pain and fear that he could not even describe it. Paralysis! God! Suppose that this time..., this time he could not recover? It would be worse than death, the end of music, sex, everything, everything except awareness of all that he would have lost, alive but buried in a dead body.

He looked around, desperately searching for a way out. But they were all there, staring at him: hundreds of eyes, television lenses, Reverend Gregory, Selene-—Mary. Short of death, there was no escape.

So get it over with! Do it!

He stiffened, steeled his brain and forced his hands to press on each side of the man's temples.

There! A jolt of pain in his neck.

His head snapped back but he was able to keep his hands in place.

Darkness. The terrible searing pain. The burst of light and the horror of darkness.

When?

Where was the darkness?

He opened his eyes. Straightened his back. There was no pain, no darkness. The malady had no more effect on him than a sore throat.

Why?

He had failed. There could be no other explanation.

His hands dropped to his sides, his eyes closed. It was over. He was free.

Then—he sensed, he heard movement.

He opened his eyes and his gasp was echoed by every person in the room. The man was attempting to sit up. The doctor lurched forward to help him. "Easy. Easy,"

The man reached up and pulled the oxygen mask from his face

and sucked in air. He turned his head toward Michael. "Thank you." He voice was hoarse, tortured. Tears coursed his cheeks.

He began to cough, and Dr. Helmland put the oxygen mask back in place. "You'd better keep this on until we sort this out." Keeping his arm around Janik's shoulders to support him, the doctor reached out with his other hand and touched the man's toes. "Can you feel this?"

Janik nodded. "Yes. I feel it."

Dr. Helmland stared at Michael. "I don't believe this. I don't believe this." He turned to the television cameras that had moved in until they were only inches away. "I don't know what to say."

The two orderlies hurried to help the doctor hold Janik. They had to fight their way past TV reporters and several audience members to reach their patient.

Michael stumbled as he moved away, and Mary took hold of his arm. "Michael, what happened?"

"I don't know." He put his hand over his eyes and allowed her to steer him down the aisle that was crowded with people straining to see what was happening.

The front of the room was relatively clear. Even members of the choir had joined the crowds in the aisles. Reverend Gregory stood in front of the pulpit with Selene beside him,

"Michael," Gregory said. "That was incredible."

"Incredible is right," Michael said. "You have no idea."

A reporter was trying to maneuver through the crowded aisle toward them and Mary said, "John. Talk to that reporter. We'll slip out through your office."

Gregory turned toward the reporter. "What should I tell him?"

"Tell him it's a miracle," Michael said. "Tell him I have no more idea how it happens that he does."

He moved toward the office, and Selene hurried to open the door. When the three of them were inside, he closed and locked the door. Mary pulled a chair forward for Michael, but he shook his head. He needed to be on his feet.

"I don't understand it, Mary. With that kind of trauma, I should be half dead. But all I felt was a kind of shock, then it was gone. I'd say the guy was psychosomatic, but you heard the doctor: he was quadriplegic."

"Could the doctor have been wrong?"

"You saw him. I don't think so."

Selene had been standing quietly. Now she said, "Maybe you're gaining control."

Michael swung to face her as hope surged through him. "Control? God, I hope that's it."

"I'm sure it is." She gave him a small smile. "But it might not be wise to overdo it."

"She's right," Mary agreed. "Even if you have developed some control, you shouldn't try to do too much, not right away."

"Don't worry. I have no intention of replacing all the doctors."

There was a sharp knock on the door, and the voice of Naomi Morton called, "Mr. Modesto."

"Let's go." Michael headed for the rear door. "I don't want to talk to anybody until I can sort this out."

But he knew there would be no sorting it out. He had no idea why he had escaped the horror that should have taken him. Perhaps Selene was right and, somehow, he was gaining control of his power. If so, there were no limits to what he could accomplish. If the people wanted miracles, he would give them miracles just like Jesus Christ had given the people miracles. But unlike Christ, he would not end up suspended on a cross.

Chapter 31

That afternoon Ambassador Anthony Stonz was at the airport waiting in a VIP lounge to board a plane for his return to Washington when he received a phone call from Selene. Her report on what had happened at the church was not really necessary. The entire matter had been on television.

"Make sure," he said, "that Doctor Helmland keeps Janik away from the press. Let him handle the interviews alone."

"He won't be able to keep the reporters away for long. Even the other doctors will be curious. And that man, Janik—

"Mr. Janik is not your concern."

He heard Selene suck in her breath before she said, "Yes, I understand"

His voice had regained its usual charm when he said, "About next week: I think a follow-up miracle would be beneficial. Talk to Dr. Helmland. Something highly visible, of course. But tell the good doctor not to be so dramatic this time. We don't want to arouse Michael's suspicions."

"It might be better if the doctor wasn't there."

"Good point. Make sure the patient understands his role. He must not become involved in interviews with the press. Not yet."

"I'll stress that with the doctor."

"Good. You might also remind Michael about this C.P.A. Benny Bond. I think it's time for him to become involved."

"I'll tell him."

Anthony hung up without saying goodbye. Selene was right about Janik. Dr. Helmland was in his control, but Mr. Janik could be a loose cannon. There was no point in taking chances.

On Wednesday afternoon Michael was driving to meet with Benny Bond and Reverend Gregory when he heard the news on his car radio: Mr. Maxwell Janik had been killed in an automobile accident as he was on his way to a TV interview only three days after he had been miraculously cured of paralysis.

Michael could scarily believe the news. It seemed so incredibly unfair that God had released the man from a horrible fate only to allow him to die in such a short time. But he had given up trying to understand God's decisions. If God's actions were based upon logic, Michael Modesto would never have been picked to be His messenger. One thing was certain, however, the reporters who had been waiting to interview Janik would have to rewrite their stories.

When Michael walked into the church office, Reverend Gregory was showing Benny Bond the many newspaper articles about the Janik miracle. The story had even made the front page of papers as far away as England and Japan.

When Benny saw Michael he backed a step, his eyes wary. "Michael," he said. Instead of offering his hand, he tapped one of the stories in a newspaper. "This guy. Is this really you?"

Michael grinned and spread his arms wide. "I always told you I was a god."

Benny did not return his smile. "Yeah, yeah. But this isn't stuff to fool around with. This is serious shit."

Michael lost his smile. "Yeah, I know, Benny. Don't ask me to explain it. I don't know what the hell is going on. One minute I'm a second rate guitar player, and the next minute I'm pulling off miracles."

"God moves in mysterious ways," Reverend Gregory said.

"So what happens now?" Benny asked. "Where is this thing going?"

Michael sighed and moved away. "I have no idea. It might go away as quick as it came. All I know is that I'm supposed to deliver a message."

"What message is that?"

"That's just it. I don't know. But I get the feeling that when it happens, this will all come to a screeching halt. It could be tomorrow...or never."

Benny slowly nodded. "But there's big money involved."

"It's getting bigger. TV, radio, memorabilia."

Mary added, "It's all set up for the Children's Fund."

Benny pursed his lips, thinking. "Who's handling the account now?"

"Well," Reverend Gregory said, "I was until Ambassador Stonz engaged the accounting firm of West, Stoddard and ..."

"Stonz? The U.N. Ambassador?"

"Yes, but—"

"What's he got to do with this?"

"He has given us his support."

"Well, if you've got an accounting firm, why do you need me?"

Michael had been hoping that the question would not come up. Now that it had, he found it difficult to answer. Benny wanted facts, not just some vague instinct that he would feel better having Benny involved. He avoided a direct answer by saying, "What we need is someone to look out for the church's interests."

"The point is," Reverend Gregory said, "I'm no accountant. And dealing with this accounting firm—it's way over my head."

Michael said, "We need help here, Benny. I told Reverend Gregory you could do the job."

"Yeah, well." Benny rubbed the back of his neck. "I've got so many clients now—"

"Don't bullshit me, Benny. Beside, there's more money involved here that you'll see from a hundred clients."

Benny's eyebrows went up. "Yeah? What kind of money?"

"If this goes on for a few more months: millions. Maybe more."

Benny blew out his breath. "Is that right, Reverend?"

Gregory nodded. "I've already had TV contracts offered in the millions."

Benny said, "I see." He walked in a circle like a dog preparing to lie down. Then he stopped, looking at Michael. "Millions?"

"At least."

"But this could end,"—Benny snapped his fingers—"like that."

"True."

"Okay, okay." Benny put his hands in his pockets. He made another circle before he stopped. "One thing bothers me..."

Michael smiled. "Only one?"

Benny's voice was grim, his eyes boring into Michael's as he said, "How do you know this message is from God? It could be the work of Satan. He can work miracles, too, when it suits his purpose."

Benny's question sent a shiver down Michael's spine. It was the same question he had asked himself a thousand times. Would God pick such a sinner as himself to be his messenger? Probably not. But Satan might. He thought of the personage he had seen and the voice he had heard. Could they be the work of the devil? His voice was a whisper when he said, "I just know."

"But you have no proof."

Michael sank onto a chair, shaking his head. "No, no. I saw the hand of God. I'm sure of it."

Reverend Gregory took a step toward them. "I know it's not evil. I have prayed so many times. If it were evil, I would know."

"All right," Benny said. "I'm going to do some praying myself. I'll get back to you."

Michael nodded without looking up. "Okay, Benny. Thanks."

"Yeah, okay." Benny started to leave, then paused and turned to Michael. "If this thing doesn't work out, are you going back with the band?"

Michael looked at Reverend Gregory. He was staring at Michael, waiting for his answer. "I don't know. I really don't know."

Benny said, "Yeah, okay." He walked out and pulled the door

closed.

Michael sat with his head down, one hand over his eyes. A single thought filled his mind, leaving no room for sight or sound: What if it were the devil? It would explain the horror of the darkness. But it did not explain the heavenly light, and the personage must have been an angel of God. It also did not explain the miracles. Or did it?

He had to talk to Mary. She would know.

He stood up, feeling better.

Sensing his mood, Reverend Gregory put his hand on Michael's shoulder. "Don't be afraid, Michael. The devil is an evil, negative force. Everything you have done has been positive: the word of God. The devil could never allow that to happen."

"Yeah. I think you're right." Michael moved toward the office's back door, then changed his mind and went out the church door. He had to find Mary, talk to her as soon as possible. There would be no rest for him until she told him again that what he was doing was right. "I'll talk to you tomorrow."

As he went out, he heard Gregory said, "I'll pray, Michael. I'll pray."

Sitting in his car, in the fading warmth of the afternoon, he used his cell phone to call Mary at the hospital. When he said he had to see her as soon as possible, she did not question why. She simply told him to go to her apartment; she would be off work soon and would meet him there.

He was sitting on the steps leading to the building's security door when he saw her drive into the apartment garage. She had seen him waiting and came around to the front of the building to meet him. He stood up and watched her walk toward him, She wore her white nurse's uniform and the image was so ethereal that Michael would not have been surprised to see that she was floating toward him instead of walking.

She smiled, and he thought his heart would burst. He went to meet her and she held her arms out, and when he kissed her, he knew she was the answer he was seeking. It would be impossible for anything evil to survive in the circle of her arms, in the wonder of her kiss.

"Thank you," he said.

She tilted her head to look at him, her hands still locked around him. "Oh? For what?"

"For making me know the truth."

Her eyes widened. "The truth. About what?"

He stepped back, the spell broken. "Let's go in. I'll explain."

Inside her apartment he sat at the table in her small kitchen, watching her make tea in a ceramic pot decorated with yellow flowers. He could not believe the pleasure he felt just watching her. She had taken off her nurse's cap and tied a colorful apron around her waist, but she still retained an ethereal aura.

He was almost disappointed when she finished brewing the tea and poured them each a cup. "I hope tea is all right," she said. "I ran out of coffee."

The very idea of anyone so efficient ever running short of anything struck him as so odd that he laughed. "Tea is fine. I probably drink too much coffee anyway."

"So do I. But I think I'll give it up. Tea is supposed to be good for the heart."

"In that case, I'd better drink a gallon. My heart is having a tough time."

She paused. Her hand lifting her cup, trembled. "Oh, God, no Michael. Maybe you're under too much tension."

"True." he said. "And there's only one cure."

She put the cup down, her eyes clouded with worry. "An operation?"

He pressed his hand to his chest. "Marriage."

"Marriage?" She stared at him, then smiled and shook her head. "You idiot. You almost caused me to have an infarction."

The relief in her voice was so overpowering that Michael leaned across the small table and took hold of her hand. "Let's not wait for the new church? Let's elope."

Mary studied him for a moment before she said, "I can't remember how long I've dreamed of a church wedding with my mother there and walking down the aisle with my father and all my friends wishing they were me. But if that's what you want, I'll give it up for you."

Looking at her, wanting her more than anything in his life, Michael had to close his eyes before he could shake his head. "No. Believe it or not, I've had the same dream. It's just that it's so hard to wait."

"We don't have to wait. Getting married in the new cathedral was Anthony Stonz' idea. I think our church would be perfect."

"Me too. When?"

Mary thought a moment. "There are so many things... What about—three months?"

Michael winced. "Three months." But he knew she was right. There were a million preparations that would have to be made. "Okay. But it's going to be a long three months."

"I know." She startled him by lifting his hand and kissing his finger tips. "But it'll be worth it."

They sat for a moment in silence, holding hands, drinking in the wonder of each other.

Finally, Mary sighed and took a sip of her tea. "It's cold."

She poured their untouched tea back in the pot and put it back on the stove to heat. Without turning, she said, "What was the urgent thing you wanted to see me about?"

Michael did not reply immediately. Here in the cozy confines of Mary's kitchen and with her spirituality filling the room like an ethereal effulgence, his concerns about evil forces seemed incongruous. But he was also aware that when he left this sanctuary, doubt would come flooding back with all the irresistible horror of a plague.

He got up and put his arms around her. "Three months," he said. "That's forever."

"I know."

He pulled her closer and, to his surprise, she made no move to escape. He either had to push her away or carry her into the bedroom and he wondered: Would she allow him to make love to her? The smoldering depths of her eyes told him that she wanted him to take her, but he knew that if he did, they would have lost something.

With a muffled groan he stepped back, wondering if he were making the right decision.

She stood looking at him. Her face was flushed, her breathing irregular, but he couldn't tell by her expression whether she was glad or disappointed. One thing he did know: he had to put some distance between them while he had his hormones under control.

He sat down at the table and hoped she would not notice that his hand trembled as he poured tea into their cups. "I've got an idea for the church. I think it would improve our image."

Mary smoothed her skirt as she walked around the table and sat down. "What's wrong with our image?"

"Too old fashioned. Have you noticed the ages of most of our congregation? I'd like to reach out to some of the younger people."

Her hand was steady as she sipped her tea. "Oh?" It amazed him how quickly her face had returned to its usual pale ivory and her breathing back to normal. He was sure that his own face was dripping perspiration.

"What do you think about bringing in my band?"

Her eyebrows lifted. "Your band? Your rock band?"

"We don't have to play rock. I mean, we could play gospel rock."

"Gospel rock? That's an oxymoron."

"Not necessarily. There are some great bands doing gospel music."

"But we've got a choir. Which, by the way, is getting a reputation."

"I know. But we could augment it with the band. It'd really go over big on TV."

"I don't think I'd like to hear a rock version of Amazing Grace."

"I heard it played by about three hundred bagpipes. If it could survive that it could survive anything."

She stirred her tea slowly before she said, "I suppose it could work if you wrote some new music."

"Damn right. Er, darn right. I'll talk to Benny about it."

"What about your guys? Maybe they won't go for playing in church."

"From what I hear, they'll be glad for the work."

"Can we afford them?"

"Hey, if we can afford a cathedral we can afford a band."

"Anthony Stonz is building the cathedral. Do you think he'll go for the band?"

Michael nodded. "Most people have to be bribed to go to church."

Mary's eyebrows lifted. "Bribed?"

"Sure. They're bribed by promises of heaven or they're bribed by fear of hell. They're bribed by the music, the camaraderie. I don't know what motivates Anthony Stonz, but as long as I can bribe him with miracles, he'll do whatever I say. They all will."

Mary studied him as he gulped the remainder of his tea. Was he mistaken or did he see worry in her eyes.

Chapter 32

The date they had set for the wedding, although three months away, seemed to be charging toward Michael with the speed of light, probably because he was so occupied with church activities. The invitation list he had given Mary was embarrassingly small, consisting almost entirely of people from his music career. He had few relatives. His parents were both dead and he had lost track of his one uncle and a couple of cousins. It seemed pointless to invite them even if he could run down their addresses. Mary, on the other hand, expected hoards of relatives, most from Iowa. Her mother and father would be flying in from Des Moines along with a couple of uncles and a multitude of cousins.

He would not have to worry about meeting them. Mary had assured him that they regularly watched his church services on TV, so they knew him quite well.

It even looked as though they might be able to hold the wedding in the new cathedral. Under the leadership of Anthony Stonz, the building was going ahead at an astounding rate. There would be a great deal of detail work to be done, but it would be finished enough to be inaugurated with a wedding that in terms of global press coverage, promised to rival the weddings of English royalty.

It was all due to the church, which was expanding beyond Michael's wildest expectations. A single Sunday service could not accommodate the huge audience, and they had begun a morning and an evening service.

A large part of the success was due to Mary's choir, featuring Selene. And the introduction of Michael Modesto's band had also been a huge hit, especially with the TV audience.

But although Michael knew he was improving as a speaker, he was not so naive as to believe the congregation came to hear what he had to say or to hear the music. They came to witness a miracle.

Hundreds of people with ailments came every week. Michael found it increasingly difficult to select the pitifully few he knew he could help without destroying himself. And they came with increasingly complex illnesses: cancer, missing limbs, paralysis, heart disease, mental illness. They came on crutches and on gurneys; they arrived in trucks and ambulances. One man brought the body of his wife in a hearse.

Michael had been forced to be more and more selective at picking those he knew he could cure without major repercussions. But he did have the help of Anthony Stonz' friend, Dr. Helmland. Almost every service Dr. Helmland brought a patient suffering with some major illness that dismayed Michael when he saw them. And each time he steeled himself for the laying on of hands, the shock was less than he expected. The cured patients of Dr. Helmland, however, made for spectacular TV.

Michael attributed the unexpected results to experience; he was getting better at preparing himself for the mental and physical anguish that accompanied every cure. Sometimes he made a mistake in his selection and the person's disability brought the horror surging back, but it was never as bad as in the past, before he had learned to select the least debilitating cases.

The one thing that continued to dig at Michael's conscience was the realization that all this had been created so he could deliver some nebulous message. But as time passed and there were no more manifestations, no more reminders of his task, the apprehension began to fade. Sometimes in preparing his sermon, he actually forgot that this might be the one, the true message of God.

His commitment had been reinforced the day Anthony Stonz had taken Mary and him to the site where the new cathedral was to be constructed.

Stonz' limousine driver drove them up a rugged and dusty firebreak road to a field of dry chaparral on a rocky ridge backed by the towering San Gabriel Mountains with the huge San Fernando Valley spread at their feet. Except for the muted roar of cars, trucks and industry that welled up from the valley like a mist so nebulous that the sound was felt more than heard, they might have been thrust back to a time when saber-tooth tigers roamed among the chaparral and oaks.

Anthony Stonz spread his arms to encompass the panorama. "You can see the entire valley from here. More than a million people. More important, the people will be able to see the cathedral."

Mary looked back along the steep firebreak road. "How are they going to get up here?"

"Not a problem." Stonz pointed to a shallow arroyo behind the ridge. "That will be filled when they grade the top off this ridge. It will provide parking for at least five hundred cars. The road we used to get here will be graded and paved."

Mary stared down at the valley that appeared to doze in the brilliant sunlight. "Are you sure this is a good place? It seems so...so remote."

Stonz smiled. "The design is traditional, so it needs a traditional setting."

"Traditional? You mean a white building with a steeple?"

"Not that kind of traditional. Here, let me show you."

Stonz motioned to the driver of his limousine and the man took a large portfolio from the car's trunk and brought it to them. Stonz extracted an artist's sketch from the portfolio and smoothed it flat on the hood of the car. When Michael saw the full-color drawing of the cathedral and its grounds, he blinked with surprise, and beside him he heard Mary draw in her breath. He had expected a New England-style church or even a modernistic cathedral, but what he saw was a Gothic Cathedral with a huge bell tower between spires that reached for the sky like supplicating fingers. Wide marble steps led to two massive bronze front doors that were topped by a large stained glass rose window. The Gothic walls were festooned with stained glass windows while the cornices were protected by protruding gargoyles. Magnificent trees set in verdant lawns and beds of flowers amid glistening fountains transformed the surrounding hillside into an Eden.

"Beautiful, isn't it? I never did like those modern all-glass and chrome monstrosities," Anthony Stonz explained. "In Europe they knew how to make cathedrals: Palma, Milano, Paris, Barcelona, the Vatican... Now those are places of worship."

"The Vatican? Holy hell," Michael breathed. "This won't be that big."

"No, no. I'm speaking of architecture. The best of Romanesque and Gothic. I had in mind something akin to the Cologne cathedral. Only smaller, of course."

Mary had been standing with her hand over her mouth, her eyes wide. "It's beautiful but..."

"I know what you're going to say," Stonz interrupted. "What about the inside? Now there I think we have really achieved the impossible." He flipped aside the drawing to reveal a full-color sketch of the cathedral's interior. Michael's felt his mouth gape as he stared at the heavily baroqued structure. The floor was constructed of various types of polished marble inlaid to form complex patterns. Twisted marble pillars supported a high vaulted ceiling where diagonal buttresses interlinked with delicate tiercerons. Like the ceiling in the Sistine Chapel, a fresco of clouds, cherubs and angelic figures adorned the interior of the dome over the apse. Stained glass abounded both in clerestory windows and in large rose windows over the front entrance and behind the high alter.

"The interior maintains the Romanesque-Gothic architecture but the motif is baroque, akin to the chapel in the so-called prince-bishop 'palace-of all palaces' of Wurzburg. Not as ostentatious, of course."

"Of course," Michael echoed.

"Notice the twisted marble pillars and the Gothic ceiling. You can't see it in this drawing, but they've even included a dove entrance in the ceiling."

"A what?" Mary said.

Stonz chuckled. "Congregations were not always as sophisticated as they are now. One of the monks would hide in the attic with a white dove. When the bishop or priest had the congregation in the proper state of passion, the monk would open the trap door and release the dove, representing the holy spirit. He would close the trap quickly so the dove appeared to materialize. It was very effective."

"Well, I don't think we'll need any doves," Michael said.

"Of course not. Merely a concession to tradition. The centerpiece, of course, is the eight-foot gold crucifix. I think it's a trifle small, but it should not overpower the magnificent triptych behind the high alter, although I wish the architect had not borrowed quite so obviously from Malorca's La Palma cathedral."

Mary pointed to banks of bronze pipes set into the walls on either side of the choir. "What are those? An organ?"

"The largest in the world. The cathedral in Passau, Germany claims to have the biggest church organ with approximately seventeen thousand pipes. Ours will have more than twenty-thousand."

Mary put her hand to her forehead. "Twenty thousand? You'll drown out the choir."

"No, no. The acoustics have been designed around the choir and the alter. And you'll find this interesting: the whole thing has been engineered as a TV studio without interfering with the overall Romanesque-Gothic design. Believe me,"—Stonz looked up from the drawing and swept his arm to indicate the horizon—"up here on this hill, it'll be a sensation."

Michael let his breath out in a gust of admiration. "Jesus. That is really going to be something. Can we afford it?"

"My boy, one does not consider money when one is building a monument to God, a monument that will live for eternity."

"Eternity." The word had a ring that appealed to Michael. It had not occurred to him that the foundations he was laying would survive long after he was gone. Generations would look back and know that it had all begun with him.

"That's right." Stonz turned his head to look at Michael, his eyes bright with an inner fire. "What takes place on this very spot in the next few months will affect the world for hundreds of years, perhaps forever. That I promise you."

Mary put her hand in Michael's and he clutched it, glad for its warm reality. "How long will it take?" she asked. "To build, I mean."

"Less than a year, according to the architect. But if we expedite, I believe it could be done in six months."

Michael stared out over the sun-bleached rocks and wild chaparral. "Can you picture Selene standing in the middle of the choir with that gold crucifix behind her, belting out 'We All Have The Power?'"

"I'm afraid I can," Mary answered.

The derision in her voice did not escape Michael, and he thrust aside a trace of irritation. She just did not understand the value of showmanship.

But Anthony Stonz did. "I've ordered special clothes for the choir," he said. "I think we should put Selene all in silver."

"Why not gold?" Mary said. "She would match the crucifix."

"Good idea," Michael agreed. "Wait'll that hits the TVs."

"Right." From his shirt pocket, Anthony Stonz took a flat package containing six cigars. He selected one and offered the package to Michael. "Try one of these. Cohibas. Made for Castro. I think you'll like it."

Michael started to reach for one, and Mary said, "Michael has given up smoking."

A quick irritation made Michael jerk his chin up. He took the cigar, saying, "Cigars aren't considered smoking. Besides, it's a celebration."

From the corner of his eye he saw Mary's face change color. She turned her head away and he felt a stab of remorse that was almost as sharp as had been the stab of resentment. He justified his actions by telling himself that she had put him in a position where he could not refuse even if he wanted to.

To mask his contrition, Michael looked at the brand name on the cigar band. "Cuba? I thought there was a ban on Cuban cigars."

"They're not Cuban. Brazillian. Menendez Amerino." If Stonz had noticed the tension between Michael and Mary, he gave no indication. He merely selected one of the cigars for himself.

As Michael clipped the end of the cigar with a gold guillotine cutter supplied by Stonz, Mary turned away, saying, "I'll wait for you in the car."

Michael stifled an impulse to catch her arm. He knew that she had not intended to embarrass him. He wondered if she even realized that she had. Probably not. She would be thinking about how he had embarrassed her in front of Stonz.

But Anthony Stonz gave no indication that he had noticed. He was going through the ritual of lighting his cigar when he asked casually, "This message of yours. Have you made any decision?"

Michael took the cigar from his mouth. "No. Nothing. It would seen that God is in no hurry."

Anthony Stonz took a calculated risk by pressing the matter. "If there even is a message."

The implication pulled a crease between Michael's eyebrows. "What does that mean?"

"Nothing probably. But it occurred to me that you may have mistaken what was told to you."

"Mistaken?"

"For example, perhaps the message is in the miracles."

Michael stared at him, seizing on the possibilities. "If that's true, this doesn't have to end."

"It also means you can stop searching. You've already found the message."

Michael nodded. "That'll be a relief."

Anthony Stonz took a long pull on his cigar and blew out the smoke. "Just continue the miracles, Michael, and"—he indicated the drawings of the cathedral—"this will be just the beginning."

When he snuffed out the cigar and climbed into the limousine, Michael's thoughts were not on the cathedral. He was wondering why he had lost his cool with Mary. He knew he had a quick temper. But in the past his bursts of anger had more justification. He would have to watch himself. Especially with Mary. There had been no reason for his resentment. She had only been thinking of him.

She had slumped back in the seat, staring out the window as the limousine bumped down the road. "I'm sorry, Mary," he said. "I shouldn't be so touchy." When she did not respond immediately, he added, "I guess I'm just tired."

She turned her head to look at him, then smiled and put out her hand. "I guess we both are. I'm sorry too."

Michael moved close to her and folded her hand in his. Now the one thing that nibbled at his euphoria was Anthony Stonz' idea that the message might not be a message at all.

But by the time the limousine reached the paved road he was sitting back in the seat beside Mary and smiling as he remembered how Stonz had said that his church would last for eternity. Eternity. His words might not live very long. But the church... That could be his legacy.

Chapter 33

Anthony Stonz had an uneasy sense that events were proceeding too well. Perhaps it was because the rate of the church's growth was disquieting. It appeared that religion throughout the world—especially in the United States—was far from dying.

He was also deeply disturbed over Michael's relationship with Mary. Instead of being debilitating as he had expected, Mary's influence added to Michael's strength and resolve. Their marriage—especially when they had children—could only make her influence stronger.

It meant that if he simply waited for events to unfold, Michael's influence might grow to the point where it would be impossible to counter. It meant that he had work to do—and soon.

His first move was to meet with Selene in her Glendale apartment which was located in the fifteenth floor penthouse of an apartment complex that was so new the room still held a faint odor of concrete and paint. From huge picture windows in her small but comfortable living room, one could look almost straight down at the swiftly flowing traffic on the Ventura Freeway or out at the estates sprinkling the nearby foothills of the San Gabriel Mountains. She had furnished the apartment with fluffy sofas, armchairs and caftans over a thick, textured carpet of pale blue. A huge TV was part of an entertainment center that occupied the wall opposite the picture windows. The other walls held a variety of colorful paintings. Many were original oils that she had ferreted from local galleries.

Selene had piled her hair on top of her head so that her exotic features were in perfect display. Her long, sleeveless dress of dark-green crushed velvet was supported by thin shoulder straps that highlighted the pale bronze skin of her arms and shoulders

"Very good," Anthony Stonz said when Selene took his Homburg and placed it on a shelf in a small closet near the door.

"I'm glad you approve."

Anthony did not have to tell Selene that she could have a larger, more elaborate apartment if she wished. But she had used good judgment. In the unlikely event that someone from the church should pay a visit, it would not be appropriate for Selene to be living in abject luxury.

He walked to the windows and stood silently watching a fiery sunset fade. As darkness enveloped the surrounding hills, lights of streets and homes began to appear like sparkling signposts of civilization. He took a cigar from his pocket case and Selene automatically prepared it, clipping off the end and applying the flame of a match.

"How are you getting along with Michael Modesto?"

"Well."

"Has he given any indication that he's attracted to you?"

Except for a slight lift of her eyebrows, Selene gave no indication that his question had startled her. "I'm sure that both he and Mary like me."

"I mean sexually."

She hesitated before answering, considering his question. "No. He has given no indication."

"Could you change that?"

This time there was a reaction. Her lips came apart, her eyes widened and her placid features tightened. "I don't know. He's very much in love with Mary."

Anthony Stonz turned from the window to examine a bronze head of an African gazelle with real horns. "Nice. Who is the sculpture?"

"Lawrence Rivera. He likes to mix sculpture with authentic elements."

"Get me something of his."

"Very well." She waited for Anthony. When he remained silent she said, "Do you want me to seduce Michael?"

He began walking around the room, pausing to look at the paintings. "Michael is stronger than I thought. I believe that Mary has something to do with that. But if a wedge could be driven between them, it would certainly have an adverse influence."

Selene did not answer. She knew better than to question his intentions.

"Take your time," he said while continuing to study a colorful Chagall print. "I think it would have more impact, if the seduction were brought to—-shall we say-—fruition on the eve of their wedding.".

"But that won't be for several weeks."

He turned his head slightly so she could see the irritation in his expression. "I'm aware of that." He turned back, drawing on the cigar as an excuse to delay his answer while he considered her reply. She had been right about the time. He had convinced Michael and Mary that they should be married in the cathedral, but even at an accelerated pace, construction could not be completed in less than three or four months. The trick to bringing Michael down was going to be in the timing. All the elements of his plan had to come together at the same moment, like a cook preparing a gourmet dinner, timing each dish so that each of its diverse elements was ready for serving at the same instant.

Except that in this case, there was a power that could easily destroy his masterpiece if he was not extremely careful.

"Be subtle," he said. "Prepare the field. I will tell you when to make the kill."

It amused him to see her shoulders stiffen at his deliberately crass choice of words. It also gave him a strange sense of wonder that she could have a conscience after all this time.

Ordinarily, that would be no problem. This time, however, there were forces at play that could draw her in, could pull her asunder. Suppose her love of music made her reluctant to do anything that would destroy the church choir. Then there was the danger that she would began to believe in Michael's sanctity. Suppose she actually fell in love. That would make the denouement even more delicious.

He was almost chuckling when the door closed behind him.

Chapter 34

In just four months the Church Of The Divine Message had grown so large and powerful that, like a juggernaut, it seemed nothing could stand in its path. Television and the internet had opened windows around the world and each time Michael spoke and performed his miracles, thousands of people rushed to become converts.

While waiting for completion of the cathedral, he took his show on the road, performing in U.S. and foreign cities. And it was a show, a carefully choreographed show with the choir providing gospel music and his band lifting emotions into a religious frenzy.

The money that poured into the Charity Fund went to fund hospitals, modern equipment and educational programs.

Michael and his band members were used to hotel living, but at first, living away from home had been difficult for Mary, Selene and Reverend Gregory. Then, as Michael's fame spread, they began receiving invitations to stay at the homes of wealthy converts.

To Michael's relief, even the miracles were becoming easier. After he began healing Dr. Helmland's most severely ill patients without unduly traumatic consequences, he had begun to believe that he had passed through some sort of portal that now allowed him to heal while controlling the catastrophic transmigration that he so feared.

Michael loved it. It seemed that his entire life had been directed toward the precious moments when he could stalk the huge stages with a microphone in one hand and a Bible in the other, working the audience like a conductor leading a huge symphonic orchestra, pulling emotions from its members like passages from a mighty requiem.

And when he lead his band through hard driving arrangements of old hymns and gospel songs, he felt as though God was truly transporting him to heaven.

There was one major difference from the times in the past when he had been on the road with his band. Instead of wild parties, there were splendid affairs in sumptuous mansions with men in tuxedos and women in beaded and sequined gowns. Instead of whisky and beer, there was champagne and expensive wine. And instead of teenaged groupies, there were mature women with hunger in their eyes who slipped notes or keys into his hand.

But Michael was more amused by them than excited. He knew they didn't really care about him. Like groupies, they wanted to go to bed with fame. With the groupies, he had not cared. He got what he wanted and they got what they wanted. But with the righteous women, he had no desire for their bodies.

The few times he allowed himself to wonder why, he attributed his lack of desire either to his love for Mary or to fear of betraying his mission, a fear that was growing weaker with time. This weakness manifested itself in his decreasing apprehension about experiencing another manifestation. Apparently, God did not believe he required constant reinforcement.

The one fear that he kept hidden in the back of his mind was that without the manifestations, his ability to heal would be taken from him. He was not so naive as to believe that his congregation would stick with him if he lost his miraculous powers. As he told Mary, "It's not difficult to be a prophet; all you have to do is say things that can't be proved but people want to hear."

The first crack in his euphoria happened the night he received a call from Benny Bond. At the time, he was attending a black-tie reception with Mary and Selene in the Santa Barbara home of Lawrence Borgstrum, CEO of a micro technology company. He was ready to refuse the call until he realized that Benny would not have called unless it was urgent. Still, he was anxious to get back to the party.

"Benny," he said, "could we talk another time? I'll call you tomorrow."

Benny whispered harshly, "No, dammit. This is serious. You've got to get back to L.A."

"Why are you whispering? I can't hear you."

"I'm in the office. I don't want anybody to know about this."

Michael felt a knot grow in his stomach. It was not like Benny to be upset over nothing. "What? About what?"

Benny hesitated before answering, and Michael knew that Benny's next words would be bad news. He was right. "I don't have any proof yet,"—-Benny was so agitated he forgot to whisper-—"but I think somebody's been skimming the Children's Fund."

"Skimming? How is that possible? We've got more damn accountants than City Bank."

"I don't know. But I've got my suspicions."

Michael thought for a moment before answering. "Could it be a mistake, some kind of accounting error?"

"I don't think so. I'm working on it."

Michael grasped at the slender straw. "But you're not sure."

"I'm about seventy-five percent sure. I think the money's being funneled to the Cayman Islands."

"Well, when you've got that much money and that many people, I guess the odds are that you could get a bad apple."

"Yeah, well, this is a hell of an apple. We're talking big money here."

Michael had to hold back an impulse to say that there was plenty more where that came from. Even though the money could be replaced, a bad apple could damage their reputation and that was much more important than money. "Who else knows this?"

"I have no idea. If I caught it, somebody else could, too."

Michael pulled loose his black tuxedo tie. A scandal. That was all he needed. "Okay. See what you can find out and let me know. We've got to get this weasel out of the hen house before he eats all the chickens."

"You can say that again."

"And keep it quiet. But you know that."

"I can't. Not for long. You've got to get over here.

"All right. I'll be by first thing in the morning.

"No. Tonight. This can't wait."

"Tonight! I'm in Santa Barbara."

"What's that, two hours. I'll wait for you."

Michael considered refusing. Whatever the anomaly was, it couldn't be so bad that it couldn't wait until morning. But Benny was not given to panic, and right now there was panic in his voice.

"Okay. I'll leave as soon as I can break loose here."

"Don't kill yourself, but get here as soon as you can."

"Yeah, Okay."

Michael slowly returned the phone to its cradle. Benny had given him a headache. Suppose it was true that someone in their accounting firm was stealing church money. They could quietly fire the bastard, but getting the money back would be difficult to keep secret. It might be cheaper in the long run to just write it off.

He found Mary with Selene. As usual, Selene was surrounded by men and it was easy to pull Mary aside. When he told her about the phone call from Benny she shook her head in disgust.

"There are so many evil people. They don't care who they hurt."

"The money isn't important. It can be replaced. But if people get the impression that we're a bunch of con artists, it could be a disaster."

Mary glanced around the crowded room as though expecting a group of people to put down their cocktail glasses and descend upon them like irate vigilantes. "How are we going to get away without a lot of questions?"

"I can be sick. Nobody questions a migraine."

"Better make it me. It wouldn't look right if a healer suffers from migraines."

"A good point" He took her hand and moved toward the group surrounding Selene. "Try to look like you're in pain."

"That'll be easy. I've felt like crying all evening."

He stopped, staring at her. "Crying? Why?"

"Six more weeks. It's like forever."

"I know. But May'll be here before we know it."

"Not before I do."

Returning to the group, Michael had trouble even making conversation. Benny's phone call had made him realize he was building a house of cards that even a breath of scandal could topple in an instant. But right now he could only hope that Benny could ferret out the miscreant before any real damage was done.

In Los Angeles, the party where Ambassador Anthony Stonz was the guest of honor was quieter. There were only eight people and they were seated at a dinner table in the home of State Senator Hector Rebozo when Stonz grimaced and stopped in the middle of a sentence and took the napkin from his lap. "Oh, dear," he said with a smile. "I just remembered something. I wonder if I might use your phone."

Senator Rebozo said, "Of course. In the study. I'll show you."

Rebozo started to get up, but Stonz motioned for him to remain seated. "Thanks. I know where it is."

As Stonz walked out someone chuckled, "Anthony, I thought you only forget golf scores."

"Selective memory," he admitted. "Great asset for a politician."

In the study he stood near a large walnut desk and stared at the phone. Selene's call would have to be important. She knew better than to call him with anything trivial. When the phone rang a moment later he picked it up quickly. "What is it?"

"Michael got a phone call from that accountant, Benny Bond. A little while later Mary said she had a migraine headache and they left. I think they're going back to Los Angeles."

Stonz grunted in surprise. Too soon. This was too soon. "You didn't find out why he called?"

"Only that it had something to do with the Children's Fund."

"Ah..."

He hung up the phone absently. Bond was smarter than he had anticipated. He was not supposed to discover the accounting irregularities for another month. It could ruin everything if Michael Modesto was discredited before the rest of his plan was in place. The house-of-cards he'd carefully built around the man could not be sustained forever.

But he wanted Modesto's destruction to take place when he was ready, not before. So this man Benny Bond would have to be silenced. And quickly. If it was not already too late.

Twenty minutes later in the lobby of a new high-rise office building, Anthony Stonz walked past an unseeing security guard. An elevator door opened as he approached, and he punched the button for the twenty-eighth floor where he walked into the deserted office suite of the accounting firm of West, Stoddard and Marx.

Benny Bond was in his office staring at a computer's monitor and his head jerked around when Anthony opened his door. Bond's look of annoyance changed to surprise when he recognized his visitor.

"Mister Stonz." He sat staring at Stonz, waiting for an explanation.

Stonz closed the door behind him. "Aren't you working rather late?"

"Not really. Sometimes I'm here all night."

"Very commendable."

"And you?" Benny Bond moved his chair so that he had a better view of Stonz. "I've never seen you here."

Stonz smiled. "I was passing by and I saw your light."

"I doubt that. We're on the twenty-eighth floor of the Oceana Bank building. Most of the lights are left on all night."

"I know. I'm going to have to talk to them about that. You wouldn't believe the utility bill."

Benny's forehead developed a crease between his eyes. "You own the building?"

Stonz made a slight nod.

"And this accounting firm: West, Stoddard and Marx?"

Stonz did not bother to answer. "I've heard rumors about the Children's Fund. I thought it would be prudent to discuss it with you when we wouldn't be disturbed."

Benny glanced at the computer monitor that was displaying rows of figures. "What kind of rumors?"

"Misappropriation of funds. Have you encountered any indications of fraud?"

Benny rubbed his face with his hand. "Maybe..."

Stonz put his cane on the seat of a chair and moved around the desk. "I think I can clear this up if you'll let me use your computer for a moment."

"Can't do that right now. I've got a program running."

Stonz stopped beside Bond. "Oh. It seems that you already have the fund's account. Let me show you."

Benny thought Stonz was reaching for the computer's mouse and he reached to block Stonz' move. "I'm sorry, but I—" His words died abruptly as Stonz put his hand on Benny's shoulder. Benny stiffened and his face knotted in a flash of agony. His hands came up to clutch at the front of his shirt. His breath came out in a gust and his head fell forward, banging hard on the computer keyboard, his eyes open, already staring at nothing. The figures on the computer's monitor raced crazily before they stopped in a variegated mixture.

Stonz carefully lifted Benny's head from the keyboard, and using the tips of his fingers, positioned the insertion marker at the end of the numbers on the monitor. Then he lifted Bond's right hand and placed it on the keyboard in such a way that it pressed down the 'backspace' key. He watched the figures begin to disappear as though being eaten by a real mouse. They were still being gobbled up as he picked up his cane and left the office. It would, of course, be possible to retrieve the deleted figures from the computer's hard drive, but now it would make no difference. The only person who would find anything strange about them had just died from a heart attack.

Chapter 35

It was nearing midnight when Michael and Mary entered the suite of West, Stoddard and Marx. The only sound was an almost subliminal buzz from banks of fluorescent lights that wasted their illumination on a deserted field of work stations separated by waist-high partitions.

Michael and Mary walked side by side down a wide, carpeted hallway toward the end of the room where individual offices could be seen through wide, glass doors.

"Nobody goofs off here," Michael said

"Not unless you can sleep with your eyes open."

Michael chuckled. "I used to do that. In church. The trick is to keep you head from nodding. That's a dead giveaway."

"You slept in church? Michael!"

"I know. Look where I'd be today." He slowed to look at the office doors. "I wonder which of these is Benny's."

Mary pointed to the door on their right. "That one has his name on it."

"That's a clue." They moved toward the door. "The corner office. I might have known."

Michael was reaching to pull the door open when he stopped with a sound of surprise. Through the glass door he could see Benny Bond slumped forward over a chrome-steel desk. His head, resting near a computer keyboard, was turned away from them. "I take it back. Looks like Benny's taking a nap." He pulled the door open. "Hey, Benny! Rise and shine."

He held the door for Mary to enter. She had only taken a step into the room when she stopped, staring at Benny. "Oh, my God."

Michael, gripped by a sudden, horrible fear, grunted as though he'd been kicked in the stomach. "Benny!"

He took two quick steps and was reaching for Benny's shoulder when Mary grabbed his arm. "Don't touch him."

He allowed her to pull him back where he watched in dreaded fascination as she expertly checked Benny's carotid artery for a pulse. She turned her head to say again, "Call nine-one-one. Now!"

Her sharp command jarred Michael and he jerked Benny's telephone from its cradle on the desk. One of six lights in the telephone base illuminated and he was about to punch the buttons when a voice on the phone said, "Front desk."

"This is Michael Modesto," he said. "Emergency. Call nine-one-one. Benny Bond's office. Looks like a heart attack."

"Yes, sir," the guard said instantly. "They're on the way."

Mary said, "C.P.R. Help me put him on the floor."

Michael jammed the phone back in its cradle. He hooked his hands under Benny's armpits and lifted him from the chair, startled at Benny's weight. No wonder he had a heart attack; he had to be fifty pounds overweight.

He placed Benny on his back on the carpet and was frantically pulling at Benny's necktie when he became aware of Mary kneeling beside him, saying, "Michael. It's too late. He's already cold. It's too late."

"No. No, it can't be. How do I do this? Push on his chest. That's it!" He straddled Benny and used the heels of his palms to push on Benny chest. "Breathe, dammit! Come on, Benny. Breathe!"

Mary put her hands on each side of Michael's face. "Michael. Listen to me. It's too late. He's gone. He's gone."

Michael froze, focusing on her face so close to his. "Gone?"

"At least an hour. Probably more. It's too late for C.P.R. For anything."

Energy drained out of Michael and he almost toppled to the floor. He got to his knees and stared at Benny's face, noticing for the first time that's Benny's eyes were open, cold, set, as though life had gone while he was staring at some distant horror. "Oh, Benny," he whispered. "Oh, God, Benny. I'm sorry. I'm sorry."

Mary reached across Benny's still form to touch Michael's arm. "Michael," she said. "Listen to me, Michael."

He turned his head to stare at her, tears blurring her image.

"You can save him," she said. "You can save him."

Michael stared at her, unable to comprehend her words. "Save him?"

"Bring him back. Like you did with the baby. Remember."

He did remember. Oh, my God, he did remember. He remembered the horror, the horror in the blackness, reaching for him. He stood up and backed away, shaking his head. "I can't do that. Not again. Not like that."

"You've got to try, Michael. You've got to."

He closed his eyes. She was right. For Benny. He had to. But, oh God, he didn't want to. The beast waiting in the blackness had almost destroyed him when he had pulled the baby back to the light. But the baby had not been dead. With Benny... To bring Benny back from the depths of blackness, he would have to enter the blackness himself, allow the blackness to pull him into it's unknown horror.

"It might..." He stopped. "It might take me."

"What? What might take you?"

"I don't know. Something...in the dark. Waiting. Waiting for me."

Mary came to stand in front of him, taking his hands in hers. "Whatever it is, Michael, you can beat it. God is with you. He will make you strong."

"He didn't before. It was there. It almost...I didn't feel the hand of God."

"You are the messenger. You will live!"

"Will I? I'm not so sure."

For the first time, doubt appeared in Mary's eyes. "Michael, I don't know where or what it is. I don't know what happens to you. I know it must be terrible. But I do know God. He won't let it take you. He will not!"

Michael's head bowed and he took a long, sighing breath. He had been led to this moment by something outside himself. There had been no free will, no possibility of refusal in his mission any more than there was free will now. He could not refuse. His whole life, his mind, his body, had been programmed so that now it was impossible to turn away. He moved toward the body. There was no feeling in his legs, no feeling in his entire body, only a numb resignation.

He sank to his knees beside Benny, conscious that Mary was kneeling beside him.

He reached out, steeling himself. He would not allow the darkness to frighten him. It was the fear that was so unbearable. He had to conquer the fear. If it took him, if the darkness pulled him into its horror, he must not be afraid. He would embrace it, because in the darkness was salvation for Benny.

He placed his hands on Benny's forehead! Now. Now it would begin.

He waited.

Waited.

Beside him, Mary intoned the words of a prayer.

His fingers on Benny's forehead were cold. That was all. Just...cold.

He let his breath out in a sigh. Safe! He was safe.

He put his hands on his knees and sank back on his heels. "It isn't working. Mary, it isn't working."

She stopped her prayer. "Michael." Her voice was a whisper. "What is it?"

Michael tilted his had back, his eyes closed. A strange mixture of joy and sorrow gripped him. "It's gone. The power. It's gone."

She was staring at him with a look of terrible anguish when the door opened and two paramedics hurried in.

Chapter 36

Ambassador Anthony Stonz attended the funeral of the late Benny Bond. There were too many people aware of his support for The Church of the Divine Message and the Children's Fund for him to stay away. Besides, the funeral had given him an opportunity to investigate a situation that needed answers: Had Michael Modesto attempted to bring Bond back from the dead? He was quite sure that it would have been beyond his power. But it was best to be certain.

Apparently, it was a question that also puzzled the reporters because it was put to Michael several times. With mounting irritation, he would answer, "I can't bring anyone back from the dead. Only Jesus Christ could do that."

The reporters were not satisfied with the answer, but Stonz was. Michael's power might have its limits, but it was still dangerous. If those powers were not curbed, they could seriously disrupt his far-reaching plan. People the world over were slowly turning away from God and redemption so that, given enough time, the final outcome would be his. Time. That was the key element. He had a disquieting suspicion that the message entrusted to Michael Modesto had something to do with time. But time of what? The Apocalypse? The return of the Messiah? The Redemption? The Millennium?

To Anthony Stonz, uncertainty was an alien feeling, one that he detested, one that had to be resolved.

He could not afford to simply wait for God's prophesy. It was important that he prepare for the event, whatever it was. Unfortunately, there was no way he could prevent the revelation, but there might be a way that he could cause it's delay. Michael Modesto, the messenger—there was its weakness.

With Modesto neutralized, it would be necessary for God to find another messenger. And that would take time. Decades. Centuries. Perhaps ions.

Anthony Stonz smiled as he murmured, "If one can't kill the message, one has to subvert the word of the messenger."

But he had better act soon.

Using his cell phone, he began dialing the number for Dr.

Helmland.

⁂

The following Sunday, seated in the front row of the church, as the time grew closer to the moment he would be forced to stand in front of the Sabbath congregation, Michael seriously considered walking out. He had slept little since Benny Bond's death. His mind churned with possible explanations, but all his rationalizing had led to but one conclusion: when the chips were down, when he desperately wanted to save someone, he had failed. Had God deserted him?

Would he fail today? If he did, he could walk away, his conscience clear. Outside there would be sunlight, freedom, a return to a life of his own. It would be the end of doubt, the end of responsibility. But it would also be the end of his relationship with Mary. Surely, she would not, could not, respect someone who would walk out on God. And without respect, there could be no love.

So he sat quietly with a bitter taste in his mouth, listening to Selene's voice draw beauty from the music, watching Mary lead the choir, her face radiating the glory of absolute faith. His failure to revive Benny Bond had not shaken her faith. How wonderful it must be to have such certitude.

The choir finished its song and Reverend Gregory began his introduction. Michael clutched his Bible with sweaty palms. He had planned to talk about the Ten Commandments—a nice, safe subject. But when he got up and begin to speak, the words that came from his mouth matched the gall in his stomach: "I'm a hypocrite," he said. "A damned hypocrite. I stand up here in front of you good people and I tell you to believe in God when I don't believe in Him myself!"

It was as though a mutual gasp swept the room. Some expressions registered the shock of disbelief, others a puzzled expectation, assuming that he was using blasphemy to get their attention.

"I can't prove there's a God. You can't prove it. We can't see Him, or touch him, or, yes, we can't even hear him. And anyone who says they can is a liar!"

Now there was a gasp and even the skeptics shifted uneasily.

"We worship on faith. Pure faith. Christ said: Blessed are those who seeth and believe, but more blessed are those who do not seeth and still believe. Well, I have seen, but I don't believe. Not any more."

He held up the Bible. "What is this? A Bible. The word of God. I don't believe it!" He threw the Bible to the floor so hard that the sound of its impact echoed throughout the room. Some voices cried out. A few people rose to their feet where they stood staring at him, now ready to believe that he was not acting.

"You think I'm a prophet. I can't even tell you whether the sun will rise. You think I'm a healer. I couldn't even save the life of a friend."

He stood for a moment, his hands at his side, his head down, and everyone waited, scarcely breathing. Then he raised his head. "I have no faith. I don't belong here."

He started walking up the long middle aisle and someone shouted, "We believe in you, Michael. We believe."

"Yes," someone else echoed. "We believe in you."

Other voices joined in, imploring him to stay. Still, he continued to walk. And would have walked out the door except that Mary was suddenly beside him, taking his hand. She said nothing, but walked beside him with her chin lifted as though in defiance, her eyes straight ahead.

Michael stopped. Turned. "Mary. You shouldn't be here. This is not for you."

"Where you go," she said, "I go."

He shook his head. "You still believe. I don't. I wonder if I ever did."

"Because of Benny? That had nothing to do with you."

"Didn't it? I brought him in to this. If it wasn't for me, he'd still be alive."

"How do you know? You're not a prophet. You said so yourself."

Michael lifted his face toward the ceiling, standing for a second. No one moved, no one coughed nor drew breath as Michael said, "I'm not worthy. I never was. I can't be the messenger. I just can't be."

"Then how do you explain the light? How do you explain what happened in the elevator? How do you explain the people you healed?"

"I don't know. I'm not sure any of it happened."

"There's a way. There's a way to prove it." The words came from Dr. Helmland who led a middle-aged woman with scraggly gray hair down the aisle. She was blind, clutching the doctor's arm, her eyes concealed behind dark glasses.

Michael backed away from them, his hands up defensively. "No. I can't."

"Please," the woman cried. "Please."

"Michael," Mary said, "You've got to. You've got to know."

Michael shook his head. "I already know:

"You can't be sure. If you fail...If you fail we'll walk out together."

Michael stared at the woman. She was heavy, bulky in a shapeless, long dress, her shoes worn, scuffed, looking as old as the woman. Was Mary right? Had his failure with Benny been an omen or had Benny simply been beyond recall? Maybe he was simply a conduit, and it did not matter whether or not he believed.

"All right," he said. "All right.

But if he was wrong, if the power was still there, he would be stricken blind. For how long? Forever?

It really did not matter. Better to be blind than to struggle with doubt.

He put his hands on the woman's head, closed his eyes and waited for the pain, the agony, the darkness.

A tingling. Only a strange tingling. Nothing more. No shock. No darkness.

He opened his eye and sighed deeply. Thank God. Failure. Blessed failure. He could still see.

He took his hands from the woman's head. "I'm sorry, I'm so sorry." He said the words, but he did not mean them. Because it was over. He had lost the power, and with it, the responsibility.

Then, to his surprise, the woman tore off her dark glasses and raised her hands above her head. "I can see!" she cried. "I can see."

Michael stared at her, unable to comprehend. How was it possible? There had been no pain. No healing. Was it possible that he had moved beyond the pain?

"Michael," Mary said, her voice singing with joy, "you did it. I knew you could."

"I don't understand—"

That was as far as he got before the woman straightened and pulled a wig from her head. Shaking out a main of dark hair. Michael stared at her, stunned. Naomi Morton, the TV reporter.

She shouted, "Listen, everyone! It's a fraud!. A fake!"

The murmur of voices died as her accusing words penetrated minds that did not want to hear.

"I'm a reporter. I'm not blind. I never was. Tell them Doctor."

Dr. Helmland stepped forward and raised his hand. It was not necessary to call for quiet; the entire congregation seemed to be holding their breath. "I'm Dr. Helmland. Mr. Modesto has been paying me to provide fake patients for some time. There has been no healing." He turned to face the TV cameras. "I decided to prove it with the help of Miss Morton, here. As you can see, Mr. Modesto was ready to take credit for her miraculous recovery." He paused for effect. "Just as he did with the others."

By now members of the congregation had recovered their voices and several shouted, "No! No! I don't believe it!"

But a few who, somehow, had the loudest voices, shouted, "Fake! Fraud! God will punish you!" Other voices joined them until the voices swirled in an explosive mixture of faith and doubt.

Michael stood dumbly in the center of the maelstrom, his face like a sculpture carved in ice, staring at the woman who shook her finger at him while she shouted condemnations. His mind was numbed by the sounds, by the sight of the wild faces, and by the stunning realization that he had been deserted by God.

"No," Mary shouted at the woman. "He could not heal an illness that doesn't exist."

Her voice was lost in the rising cacophony, a torrent of angry voices led by the reporter and Dr. Helmland. Reverend Gregory rushed up the aisle and tugged at Michael's arm. "Come on, Michael. You'd better get out of here."

It was Mary who answered. "No. They've got to know the truth."

Gregory had to shout to be heard. "Later. If he doesn't leave this could be ugly."

Mary turned to Michael. "Michael. They'll listen to you. Michael! Do something!"

Michael turned his head to look at her and, with wrenching resolve, brought his eyes into focus. "Yes, you're right. It's me they want." He raised his arms and shouted, "Quiet. In the name of the Almighty! Quiet."

Those nearby who could see and hear him slowly quieted and the silence grew. Even the woman reporter and Dr. Helmland fell silent under the imploration of Michael's eyes.

When he could be heard, Michael spoke, his voice cutting through a residual murmur, "This is a house of God. But I am not God. I am only a man. A man with doubts. A man who is weak. You wanted a miracle, and I failed to give you that miracle. I am not God. These hands are the hands of a man. If they failed, it is because God wanted them to fail. And why is that? Why did God take away the miracle? Because I am not worthy? I have never been worthy. These people say there have never been miracles, that it's all a fraud. I can only tell you that *I do not know*. Only those who have been touched by God can tell you the truth. Ask them. Ask God. Go home and ask God."

In total silence he walked up the aisle and out into the sunlight.

Chapter 37

Within minutes of becoming aware of the debacle in the church, Ambassador Stonz was on a plane to California. The newspapers and television reporters, smelling blood, were digging into Michael's past like badgers going after a rodent. They were already talking to some of the Dr. Helmland's 'patients' who had benefited from Michael's miracle cures. And they would soon learn about the skimming of funds from the Children's Fund. Of more importance, Michael Modesto was beginning to crack. He had already lost his confidence in his link with God. "The trick now," Stonz said to Selene, "is to keep him from learning that nothing has changed."

"He still has the power?"

"I'm afraid so." He had ordered champagne and Beluga caviar from room service as soon as he had checked into the Los Angeles downtown Hilton. Now he dipped another cracker into the dark concoction that he adored. "I've got to stop being so successful," he explained. "These celebrations are ruining my figure." He raised his champagne glass. "Cheers."

Seated on a huge couch, Selene's impassive expression did not change, and she made no move to touch her glass of champagne. "You might be a little premature. If he discovers he still has the power, he could change everything."

"So we must make sure he does not discover. Or, if he does, that he is so mentally debilitated that he won't care."

To his surprise, Selene's smooth forehead wrinkled with concern. "Insane? You want to make him insane?"

Anthony Stonz gazed at her for a moment. It appeared that she had developed some feelings toward Michael Modesto. Perhaps even some affection. So much the better. It would made her role more—he searched for the word he wanted—authentic.

"I wouldn't think of it," he said, "even if I could, which I doubt. No. We must keep his mind occupied with other things." Regretfully, he turned away from the chilled bowl of caviar. "The wedding is soon, I believe."

"Next week."

"Ah, yes. In the cathedral. I understand it's construction won't be entirely complete, but enough for the wedding. Excellent. It will make the loss greater."

"After what happened yesterday, I don't think he'll want the wedding in the cathedral."

"It doesn't matter. I doubt there'll be a wedding."

She stood up, and as usual, he was struck by her sleek beauty. She wore a long, sequined gown, gold colored, slit to the hip on the left side. "You plan to stop the wedding."

"No, my dear." Stonz moved to stand in front of her, and he cupped her chin in his hand. "You will."

She stood unmoving, staring at his face.

He dropped his hand and turned away. She did not have to be convinced of his decision. "Tonight. The gown you're wearing will be perfect. I suggest you arrive at his apartment a few minutes after eight. That will give you almost an hour before Mary Schaeffer returns."

"Returns."

"She's on her way to see him now. After she leaves, I'll 'arrange' for her to return. You just make sure the stage is set, as it were."

"Suppose Michael does not cooperate?"

"You have the recording?"

"Yes. In my purse."

Stonz nodded. "Good. He may be a messenger of God, but he's still a man."

For the first time her voice came alive. "True. He is a messenger of God. He may not respond."

The smile that Stonz turned on her was as dead as his eyes. "I expect you to see that he does."

"And if I fail...?"

Stonz lifted his arm as though to strike her, but she did not move nor blink. Instead of striking her, Stonz pulled back the French cuff of his shirt and looked at his watch. "It's almost eight. You should get started. There'll be a taxi waiting."

Without a word she slipped on a jacket and picked up her purse and went out the door. Anthony Stonz started to dip another cracker into the caviar, then hesitated. "I really shouldn't." He shrugged. "But how often does one destroy a messenger of God." He dipped the cracker into the caviar.

It had not taken long for the story of Michael's defection to appear on TV and in print. Sunday night, hiding in his darkened apartment, the words that echoed in his mind were: 'I'm a hypocrite. Why should God listen to me?'

In his heart, he had never believed that he was the chosen one. Not really. He had simply done what the voice told him to do. Even when he had performed miracles, he had always believed that God's choosing him was a mistake, a macabre mistake.

The one truth that he could cling to was that the reporters were wrong about the miracles. They had happened. Hadn't they? Could the trauma he experienced each time have only been in his head? If so, then he was not a messenger of God, he was a madman.

Given a choice, he would chose to be mad.

He found an unopened bottle of beer in the refrigerator and an old cigar in one of the kitchen drawers. He sat on his couch and used the remote to turn on the TV, leaving the room lights off. Putting his feet up on the coffee table, he ran his hand across his stubble of beard. This was like old times. This was the real Michael Modesto: swilling beer, kicking back. The life he thought he could never know again. So maybe what had happened today was really a good thing.

Except for Mary. She would never understand. She was not in love with this Michael Modesto. She was in love with the evangelist, the Michael Modesto who did not swill beer nor have a day-old beard. The Michael Modesto who could perform miracles.

Well, those days were gone. He would have to get the band back to playing the good music. That would be the final test. If Mary really did love him, she would stick with him through the miracle of heavy metal.

The image on the TV settled on the face of Naomi Morton who all day long had been harping on what had happened at the Church of the Divine Message. Michael's despair quickly returned as he listened to her accusations of fraud. Before she closed, she dropped a bombshell: "There is evidence that the accountant for Michael Modesto's Church of the Divine Message, Mr. Benny Bond, who recently died of a heart attack, allegedly was involved in misappropriation of funds from the church-sponsored Children's Fund.—"

Michael quickly changed to another channel before he settled back on the couch, his head in his hands. He knew that Benny Bond was innocent. But who would believe him now? Every one knew Benny was his man, so he would probably be painted with the same brush.

A knock at the door jerked him out of his speculation. He cursed under his breath. That's all he needed now—some reporter looking for a story.

The knock was repeated, this time accompanied by a muffled voice, "Michael. Michael, open the door."

Mary.

He had no more desire to see her than he had for seeing a reporter. She would have a million questions he had no desire to confront, even if he had the answers.

"Michael!" She called again. "Please. Open the door."

The few seconds it took to reach the door seemed like the longest of his life. The thought that kept running through his mind was that if you loved someone, you should want to share your misery. So why did he dread facing Mary? Was it because he did not love her, really love her?

He realized the thought was absurd when she came into his arms and said, "Oh, Michael. I've been so worried. I've been calling you all afternoon."

"I'm sorry. I didn't feel much like talking."

"I know. But I wanted to be with you."

Ah, there it was. She loved him and wanted to be with him. He tilted her face up and kissed her. "I'm glad you're here. But...How did you get in?"

"I called the manager. He let me in the back."

A stab of anger made Michael grimace. He had told the manager not to let anyone in.

Just as quickly the anger was replaced by the realization that it was not the man's fault; he knew that Mary was his fiancée. "If you're looking for an explanation, I'm sorry. I just don't have one. I guess I just lost...whatever it was." He snapped on a lamp and clicked off the TV.

"Because of Benny Bond? We both know he was beyond help. There was nothing you could do."

"It's not about him. Oh, yeah, I guess it was when I shot off my mouth about being a hypocrite. But after I found out the healings had been fixed—"

"No," she interrupted. "Only one. That woman reporter."

He could meet her eyes when he said, "I think there were others."

"Others? What do you mean?"

"Look. When I...When I heal someone, really heal them, I feel it. It's like a...a transfer of what they have to me, to my body." He moved around the room, unable to stand still. "So, okay, I picked the people with minor problems. You know, like a headache, or a split finger. And I felt those, but not bad enough or long enough to hurt me. When that Dr. Helmland brought in those really bad ones. God, I didn't want to touch them. I knew what would happen. But it didn't." He turned to look at Mary. "I didn't know why, but when I touched them, I didn't feel a thing. They were healed, but I felt nothing. Nothing. Now I know why: they were fakes."

"But why? Why would Helmland do that?"

"Anthony Stonz. I told him I didn't want to do the healings, not the bad ones. You remember. He said—-insisted, really-—I give it one last shot."

"That was the paralyzed man. I remember."

"Yeah. I couldn't believe it. He was healed, and I felt nothing—not a thing."

"Weren't you suspicious?"

Michael waved the thought aside. "I was just damned glad. I thought maybe I'd moved past the...the trauma. When it happened the second time, I stopped questioning it. I guess I should have smelled a rat when I still felt it with the others. But I didn't want to. I wanted to believe. Things were going great-—the TV and the papers were eating it up—-and the people loved it." He sank down on the couch, his palms pressed against his eyes. "I shouldn't have listened to Stonz."

Mary twisted to face him, "That doesn't explain what happened to the Children's Fund."

"I don't understand that. Why didn't Benny catch the—."

He stopped and turned his head to stare at Mary. Her eyes were wide, staring at him. "You don't think I had anything to do with that?"

She gave a little shake of her head. "No. But if it's true and the money is gone...Well, what happened to it?"

Michael felt heat building in his head. "I brought in Benny Bond. If they think he was cooking the books, they'll think I had a hand in it."

Mary reached out to touch his shoulder. "No, Michael, no. You would never do that. I'm sure it will turn out to be a mistake."

"And if it isn't a mistake? If the money really is gone?"

"That doesn't mean you had anything to do with it."

"So who did?"

Mary stood up, moved away, twining her fingers together. "There were a lot of people involved. That accounting firm where Benny had his office..."

She hesitated and Michael finished the thought for her: "It was Stonz's idea to use them."

"Well, yes. But that doesn't mean-—"

"What about Reverend Gregory? He handled the collections."

Mary turned, startled. "Gregory? You can't mean that."

"I'm just looking at who could have had their fingers in the till."

She stood facing him, her body stiff with anger. "Don't forget me. My name was also on that account."

But some reason he could not name, Mary became the target for all the anger, all the frustration that had been building in him for hours. "Yeah, well, you sure as hell wanted it bad enough."

He couldn't believe that the words had come from him, and he stared at her stricken face, his shock almost as profound as her own. He should go to her instantly. He should put his arms around her and tell her he was an idiot. But he could not. The fires of resentment that had been smoldering throughout the day had burst into flames of irrational rage-—rage at himself-—rage at circumstance—rage at God himself.

So when Mary picked up her purse and walked stiffly to the door, he did not move. He hated himself, but he did not move. She opened the door and stood for a second, looking at him, and, God help him, he turned his back. He heard the door close. And still he stood.

Minutes later, he turned off the lamp and sat on the couch in the dark.

His mind refused to focus, refused to think at all. He clicked on the TV and turned the sound off, staring at the screen with no understanding of what he saw.

He growled with disgust. Why was he feeling so damned guilty? It was her fault. She had as much as accused him of taking the money, even of going along with the deception on the healings. If anything, she should be apologizing to him.

He got up, unable to stay seated, and walked into the bedroom where he had left his jacket. What he needed right now was a drink in a nice quiet bar where nobody knew Michael Modesto from Adam.

As though his thoughts had been transported to Mary, he heard the door open and a surge of joy shook him. She had come back—to apologize. He dropped his jacket and strode to the living room, He stopped. "Selene."

He stared at the open door as though it had betrayed him. "How did you get in the building?"

She smiled. "Does it matter?" She closed the door, and he heard the lock snap into place.

"I guess not." He moved toward the door. "Uh, Selene. I really don't feel much like talking to anybody right now—-"

She interrupted. "I know. I'm so sorry about what happened this morning." She walked across the room and put her purse on the desk. "It wasn't your fault. But...you know that."

Her long, clinging gown, slit to the hip on the left side, revealed black hose and sandals with high heels that made her legs look incredibly long. She had let her hair loose from its usual braids and it tumbled across her shoulders. Flickering light from the TV played across her face so that her eyes seemed to smolder through flames of a cold fire.

"Yeah, thanks," Michael answered. "I guess this'll be the end of the choir."

"I don't see why. You still have the church."

"I don't think so. It was the miracles that brought people in. Now they're gone...and with the problem with the Children's Fund...well, they'll find somebody who can talk better than I can."

"So..." She made a small shrug. "What will you do?"

Michael relaxed. She was not going to try to talk about what had happened. "Go back to my band I guess. What about...?" He was going to ask what she would do, but it occurred to him that he had no idea what she had done for a living.

"Me? Oh, I've had offers to record."

"If you need a band, we'll be looking for work." He started toward the kitchen. "Would you like something to drink? I've got anything you want as long as it's in a can and cold, except beer."

She shook her head. "No, no, nothing."

Michael stopped, looking at her. The ball was in her court.

She ran her tongue across her lips. "I, uh, actually I came for some advice."

"From me?" Now that was a surprise. He went back to the couch and picked up his cigar."My advice is to ask somebody else."

Her marvelous voice made her laugh sound like crystal bells. "It's about music. I'd like your opinion about a song I've written."

"If it isn't rock or rap, forget it."

"It's kind of Middle East." She opened her purse and took out a gold CD disc. "I brought a demo."

"Yeah, well, the Middle East is a little out of my style."

"I know." She crossed to his player and slipped the CD in place and pushed the play button. Michael was going to turn on the lamp, but decided that the less he saw of Selene, the better. The dim light from the TV was more than enough.

The music began with the tinkle of a balalaika that was quickly joined by other instruments. The music became a driving beat that evoked images of smoky rooms in the shadow of ancient pyramids.

Selene turned from the CD player and stood for a moment facing Michael with her head lowered so that she watched him from beneath her dark brows. Then her hands sinuated above her head, and she began clapping her hands in time with the beat of the music, softly at first, gradually louder. Almost imperceptibly her hips began to move and the muscles of her stomach began to flex in the sensual moves of the belly dance.

She glided to the center of the room, her hips and stomach beneath the clinging gown, roiling in time with the primordial beat of the music.

Michael sank to the couch, unable to take his eyes from Selene. Some part of his mind sounded a warning, but he was unable to respond. He sat, dazed, as Selene moved closer so that she stood in front of him, the image of her legs, her hips, her stomach, her eyes turning him to stone.

Her hands paused in their beat and went behind her back. In a moment, with a shrug of her shoulders the gown slid gracefully to the floor. Below her black brasserie the muscles of her flat stomach rippled like golden waves.

She moved closer and placed her hands on his temples, and held him motionless while the warm, golden curves of her stomach undulated in front of his eyes.

Her hands moved down to his arms, lifting him, pulling him close against those Delilah hips. She directed his hands to her waist and he shivered as her warm, bare skin rippled beneath his touch as though it had a life of its own. She leaned back, her eyes locked on his, her shoulders shaking, her hips pressed against his, watching him, her lips parted, her eyes hot, smoldering, heated by an internal volcano.

Michael had no memory of when the music ended, nor of when he lifted Selene, and she lay atop him on the couch, and he was seared by her burning lips. He only returned to conscious when he heard the door open and saw Mary looking down at him, her eyes wide with disbelief. And standing beside her was Anthony Stonz.

Chapter 38

It seemed appropriate that after a night of aimless driving, Michael should watch the faint glow of dawn from the site of the new cathedral. He sat on cold Siena marble steps leading to the huge bronze doors that, like the marble, had been imported from Europe, and watched the lights in San Fernando valley slowly drown as the light of dawn washed over them in a rose-colored tide.

The death of the lights seemed appropriate. They were like the life of The Church of the Divine Messenger, a pitiful struggle in a world of darkness, suffocated by a tide of lies. It was gone. All of it: the church, the Children's Fund, the power and the glory. Mary. All that he held so confidently only yesterday, was now gone. Forever.

Only yesterday. A lifetime ago. Yet only hours since Mary had walked out and he had run after her and she had driven away, her face streaked with tears. When he had found his way back to his apartment, Selene and Anthony Stonz were gone.

It did not matter. Mary was the only one who mattered. And she was lost forever. Like a fool, he had quarreled with her, knowing all the time that she was right. He had let his fame go to his head but was too damned proud to admit it. Instead, he had hidden the truth behind a curtain of self-righteous anger, an anger that was even more intense because he refused to face the truth.

Now, even the anger was gone, leaving him empty, empty even of hope. And that was the worst of all.

In the still air of dawn, he heard the sound of an a powerful engine and saw the lights of an approaching car. Mary? He stood up, buoyed by a happiness that was just as quickly dismissed. It was not her car. And, besides, why would she search for him here? Or anywhere, for that matter. It was probably a truck belonging to one of the workmen arriving to put finishing touches on the cathedral.

It was not a truck. It was black sedan, and when it stopped, Anthony Stonz got out. Through the open door Michael saw Selene sitting in the passenger seat. That seemed odd. Why was Selene with Stonz? And what were they doing here?

He watched Stonz ignore the cement walk to stalk across the newly installed lawn, swinging his cane as he walked. He had changed into a black suit with a black shirt and white necktie. His head was bare, his thick mane of hair unstirred by a morning breeze. He walked directly toward Michael, although in the dim light of dawn, Michael was not sure the man could see him standing in front of the dark cathedral doors.

"Ah, there you are," Stonz said when he was a few feet away. He stepped onto the walkway, his cane pinging against the concrete that was still dark gray from having recently been poured. "I thought you might be here."

"What gave you that idea?"

Stonz stopped in front of the steps and turned to look at the vanishing lights of the city. "Because it's all here: the cathedral, the multitudes. Everything you've lost. Everything you could have had."

"Except the one thing I really wanted."

"Ah, yes. Mary." Stonz put one foot on the bottom step. "I'm sure you can patch that up."

"I doubt it. When trust goes, everything goes."

Stonz was silent for a moment, studying Michael. "Would you like to have it all back?"

Michael had been watching the buildings and trees of the valley slowly come into view. Now he looked at Stonz, uncomprehending. "All what?"

"Everything." He pointed to the cathedral with his cane. "This." He swept the cane to take in the cities below. "The people. Miracles. Everything you had before." He slowly turned his head to look at Michael. "Even Mary."

Michael stared at him, dazed with unbelieving hope. "You can do that?"

"And more. So much more. You thought that you had power before. I can give you power beyond your dreams. Wealth. Your name will echo around the world for ages to come."

"I don't understand. How—-"

An image burst upon Michael's brain, an image of words burned into wood: 'Beware the Antichrist. Beware.' He looked toward the car where Selene was waiting. Selene and Stonz. Suddenly, it all made sense.

"My God. You. The Antichrist."

Stonz's face seemed to lengthen and his eyes burned. "The name does not matter. The point is that I have the power to give you everything you ever wanted, everything you ever dreamed of."

"And what do you want in return?"

Stonz came up the steps. "Only one thing: the message. What is the message?"

Stonz was so close, his eyes so filled with rage, that Michael backed a step. "I can't tell you."

Stonz reached out as though to grab Michael by the throat, then pulled his hand back, formed into a tight fist. "Tell me!" His voice had changed to a deep growl that lifted the hair at the back of Michael's neck. "Tell me!"

Michael wanted to tell him. It was as though Stonz' fist was locked on his brain, trying to wrest the words from him. "I don't know. I'd tell you if I knew. But I don't know."

Stonz' fist slowly relaxed. He backed away, his eyes shrewd. "All right. It can still be yours. I'll make a bargain with you. One thing. Just give me one thing. The one thing you cherish most in the world."

"What? My soul?" Michael barked a laugh. "It would be a poor bargain."

"Not yours."

Michael's brows creased. "Not mine. Then who...Mary! You want Mary?"

Stonz lifted his hand. "Why not? She doesn't want you."

"You want me to give you Mary. For what? For power? Your power. For money? Your money. For a church you'd control. No, thank you."

"Are you any better than Abraham? He gave his wife, Sarah, to the Pharaoh."

"I'll not bargain with you. You've got nothing I want. Nothing. Go back to hell where you belong."

Stonz bared his teeth, startlingly white in the dawn. "I'll take her. I can't take you, but I can take her. And I will."

"No," Michael took a step toward Stonz. "No. You will not."

"The message" Stonz eyes burned into Michael's. "The message or her."

"No. You get nothing! Nothing!"

"And who will stop me? God?" Stonz sneered. "Go ahead. Call him. You've tried it before."

Michael's rage was swallowed by despair. Stonz was right. He had called upon God. So many times. And God had not answered. And now, after his selfish arrogance, God had surely deserted him.

Stonz laughed ."You're a fool. You could have anything, anything in the world. Now, you'll have nothing—not even your God—and I'll have her."

Stonz started down the steps and a blaze of anger wrenched a word from Michael. "No!

He threw himself at Stonz, knowing even then that it was a useless gesture. No mortal could harm this creature who called himself Anthony Stonz.

As though expecting the attack, Stonz whirled, his teeth bared, his cane swinging. Michael never felt the blow. The instant his hands fastened on Stonz' neck, a shock struck him like a bolt of lightning, lifting him from his feet. He held on desperately as a powerful force savaging him like a mad dog. And yet he knew that if he relaxed his grip for an instant, if the creature threw him off, Mary would be lost forever.

Rage gave him strength, rage and fear, fear for Mary. He clenched his fingers tighter, his mouth open in a howl of insane rage. "You can't have her. You'll never have her!"

Stonz dropped his cane and grabbed Michael's wrists, attempting to pry Michael's fingers from his throat. They staggered back, struggling across the lawn, locked in a raging dance. Around them the air crackled with lightening, and the smell of burning ozone fouled the morning air.

Stonz' mouth opened in a guttural howl and the cathedral's two massive entrance pillars split with a thunderous crack, and the huge bronze doors ripped from their frames, crashing to the marble steps.

Michael's hands were on fire!. Sulfuric flame crackled over his clutching fingers, flames engulfed his arms as though to strip the flesh from his bones. Still he held on!

Then it came! The darkness! Advancing upon him, spreading from beneath his feet, creeping, growing, reaching for him. Get away! He had to get away from the darkness before it swallowed him.

And, suddenly, he knew. He knew! Stonz! The darkness belonged to the Antichrist. It was the darkness of a abyss! A bottomless pit! It always had been. And each time, with each miracle, it had tried to suck him into its demonic hell.

Desperately, Stonz fought to drag him into the horror.

He had to let go! He had to escape, to flee.

But if he did, the hell would be for Mary!

And so he held.

Stonz' hands tore at his arms with the strength of hell's demons, his nails driving into Michael's flesh, dragging him, forcing him over the edge!

With a keening scream of pure terror, with the throat of the Antichrist locked in a grip of steel, Michael plunged into the horror of the pit.

Down.

Down.

Fear tightened Michael's grip, fear for Mary, fear that the darkness would tear Stonz away.

Down.

Down.

Stonz wrapped his arms around Michael and held him so he could not escape the awful, demonic darkness. And Michael screamed with fear as they fell, tumbling, twisting down, down.

And still Michael's fingers remained locked with the desperation of consuming fear.

Blackness! Stygian blackness. The only sense was falling, falling. And the feel of the creature's neck crushed in his grip and the creature struggling, fighting, clawing, thundering with rage, determined to break free!

Down.

Down.

Bursting into light, horrible light. Red! Ghastly red light, light generated by flames exploding from a bubbling, roiling lake of lava, a lake of fire, a sea of fire, a mighty caldron with heads, limbs, bodies churning, writhing, in perpetual agony, their screams drowned in rivers of liquid fire.

Down they tumbled, closer and closer to the roiling sea of fire, and awful heat seared Michael's flesh, burning with incredible agony.

And still he refused to release his terrible grip on the throat of the snarling, flailing creature. If he were to die in the fires of hell, so, too, would the demon.

Down.

Down.

Falling.

Falling.

Faster and faster.

Michael breathed a last prayer as they plunged into the molten sea. He screamed as the boiling lava cooked his flesh and his scream was drowned in a red horror.

Still, he held. And was taken by darkness,

But even in the dark, still falling, falling, his terrible grip remained clenched on the awful throat of the Lawless One. And from the creatures gaping maw, the screams of rage became a terrible roar, and Michael was conscious that the throat beneath his clutching hands had changed and the nails raking his flesh had turned to rending claws.

Then, suddenly, light. Out of smothering darkness, blinding brilliance reflecting from crystalline facets of ice and snow. Falling, falling into cold. Bone-chilling, mind-numbing cold. And in the light Michael saw that the creature beneath his hands was a lion, roaring and rending with mighty claws.

Down they plunged, and Michael's harsh cries of rage and fear mingled with the snarls of the beast, and his fingers were frozen in a grip of death even as a frigid wind drove needles of pain into his scalded flesh.

Down.

Down.

Plummeting toward the frozen world of ice.

And Michael beheld naked human forms writhing in the stultifying cold, struggling to find some small place of respite from icy blasts, trapped forever in the pain of freezing, yet, unable to find surcease in the warmth of death.

Down.

Down.

Crashing through the field of ice, locked in savage combat, clawing, biting., roaring, down into the dark abyss.

And in the drowning, choking darkness, the creature changed, grew, the foul breath from its gaping maw magnified its roars of rage, its coarse hair thickening, its ripping claws elongating, sharpening, driven by awful power as they tried to rip Michael from his fanatical hold, and Michael screamed in fury, screamed over and over as they plunged deeper and deeper into the yawning abyss.

Then they were spewed into a Persephonian horror of twisted, entwining bodies in perpetual torment, unspeakable torment inflicted by winged demons.

Into the writhing mass they plunged, engulfed by putrefying flesh, into air so fetid as to score the very lungs, and the lion was now a great bear that raged and clawed in a vain attempt to rip free of the grip of Michael.

Falling.

Falling.

Down.

Down.

Ever deeper into the horror of the abyss. deeper into the bowels of Hades.

And again, the beast changed, became scaly, slippery with slime, its thick body crushing Michael in coils of awful power, its mighty roars a keening hiss, its eyes glowing in yellow slits, its great jaws gaping wide, its forked tongue lashing like a whip.

And Michael held the great, blunt head at bay, refusing to allow the beast to return to the living world to claim its demanded prize.

And, now, he was on a barren plain, his fingers locked around the scaly neck of a great dragon, a dragon of blinding red, its head threshing, attempting to reach him with horrific fire from its flaring nostrils or to batter him with its lashing tail.

And on the back of the dragon was a woman who called to him. "Michael. Help me, Michael. Come help me!"

Selene.

Astride the back of the great red dragon, she stretched her arms out to Michael, her face twisted in anguish. "Come to me, Michael. Help me. Please help me."

He wanted to go to her. He wanted to release his grip of death on the red dragon, to help. Too late! Searing flames from the dragon's mouth washed over her. Blazing, burning flames, white with the heat of Hades. But she was not seared. She sat erect in the flames, laughing. And he knew! Selene. She was Selene, handmaiden of the Lawless One, the Antichrist, the Beast of Hades.

And he screamed in defiance as once more he tightened his grip on the scaly neck, and the beast threw its head back with a roar of rage.

And then Selene was gone and the great beast had six more heads and ten horns and on its horns were ten crowns, and the six heads turned on Michael, and their fetid jaws ripped him from the seventh head and hurled him to the ground.

The great beast came for him, its seven heads weaving, its eyes glaring, its jaws open, reeking of death.

Michael rose to his feet to meet the dragon, knowing that there could be no victory, not over the great beast, not over the terrible claws, not over the seven gapping jaws with their razor teeth and fiery breath.

And he fell to his knees in prayer, not prayer for himself, but prayer for Mary, prayer that the Antichrist would not enslave her soul the way he had enslaved the soul of Selene.

And the beast came closer and its mighty roars of rage changed and the beast laughed, laughed at Michael, laughed at this messenger of God, this angel of heaven, this mortal who dared to challenge him, and frogs came from its mouths, mocking the words of prayer from the mouth of Michael.

The laughter stopped. The beast's heads reared to strike. And the heavens opened and a Man appeared riding a great white horse. And the Man's eyes blazed with fire and on his head were many crowns. He rode to Michael and from his mouth he drew the golden sword, and He gave the sword to Michael.

Michael took the sword, and it felt familiar in his hand, and he ran to meet the great beast.

They fought a mighty battle. The great beast ripped and tore at Michael with its fangs and claws and seared him with its flaming breath. And Michael raged against the beast. He fought with the strength of anger, anger at the creature of hell, anger at himself, anger his God; he fought with the desperation of fear, fear for the soul of Mary, fear of being dragged deeper into the pit, so deep there would be no escape. But in the end he fought with a berserk rage against the Antichrist.

And on the earth above, lightening split the sky and thunder howled like the voice of doom, and mighty earthquakes savaged the mountains and the valleys and the seas.

And Michael fought on and on, fought with desperate strength, fought with the fury of despair and the power of hope. And as his body weakened, a great light came down and entered into him, and one by one the sword of heaven severed each of the seven heads of the great beast, and each time a head was severed, a part of the great cathedral, the cathedral built by the Antichrist, shuddered, split asunder and collapsed with the sound of a mighty fall.

Long the battle raged, but when night began to darken the heavens, Michael stood over the quivering body of the Great Beast and he knew. He knew the message!

He took a great breath and with a mighty cry of "Hallelujah!" threw the sword up, up into the heavens and the heavens opened and took the sword, and Michael fell to the ground, and the brilliant light bathed him and lifted him, up, up beyond the darkness of the pit.

Chapter 39

Michael lay face down on rocky rubble that gouged his body. He opened his eyes, focused on what had once been steps of Siena marble, marble shattered into shards of rock.

He tried to move, to turn over, and winced with pain. Every muscle, every ligament in his body felt as though it had been ripped from his bones. Had he been in an accident? What kind of an accident?

He had a vague memory of falling from a great height. If so, and he had landed on stone, he probably had broken bones. Still, it couldn't be too serious; he could move his arms and legs, even turn his head. And in turning his head, he saw that he was lying amid piles of rubble that still emitted tendrils of smoke and dust. A collapsed building. That was it. He must have been in an earthquake.

He pushed to his knees, fighting pain. His clothes hung in tatters, looking as though they had been singed by fire and shredded by powerful claws. And yet, there wasn't a mark on him, not a scratch, not a broken bone. Except for sore and painful muscles, he was not harmed.

So why did he have a memory of falling? Falling where?

He found he was kneeling in the glow of a setting sun on the crest of a hill that overlooked cities sprawled across a vast valley. He knew this place. The cathedral! He was on the site of the new cathedral. But where was it?

He turned his head. My God! There was no cathedral, only piles of rubble. An earthquake. It must have been a mighty earthquake. And the cathedral was gone, reduced to seven wind-blown heaps of stone and glass. Seven? Why did that seen significant?

His shoulders sagged and he put his hands over his face. Everything gone. All that he had worked for. There would be no wedding in his cathedral. There would be no—

Mary! Oh God. Where was Mary? Had she been with him when the building collapsed?

Fear brought him to his feet. And with the fear, came the memory of a greater fear. Anthony Stonz! He had tried to take Mary? Oh, Mother of Jesus. The pit. The Antichrist! He had fought the Antichrist to keep him from taking Mary. But had he succeeded?

From what seemed like a great distance, he heard someone call his name, and a great joy drove away the fear. Mary. She was here.

He turned and saw her running toward him from her car, her hair a golden cloud, her face white with anxiety. And behind her was Selene, walking, with her face as radiant as the rising sun.

Then Mary was in his arms. "Oh, my God, Michael. I was so scared. I saw it! I saw it fall."

"You saw it? You were here?"

"Selene called me. She told me to come here."

An awful coldness swept over Michael. "Stonz. He wants you here."

"Anthony Stonz? But why?"

Selene was beside them, her eyes alive with happiness for the first time that Michael could remember. "Because he was the Antichrist. He had to stop you, Michael. And he could only do it by taking Mary."

"Stop me? From what?"

"From destroying him."

Mary stared at Selene. "You brought me here—for him?"

"I had to."

The image of a great beast with severed heads flashed in Michael's head like a picture of horror and he looked at Selene. "You don't have to fear him any more."

"I know. I felt it when...it happened."

Michael looked down at his ripped and torn clothing. "It was more than that."

"The Antichrist. He had to find the message."

"He found it. And it destroyed him."

Selene stared at him. "The message? How is that possible?"

Michael shook his head at the irony. "The message was not in words; it was a task: to destroy the Antichrist. That's all it ever was. It's over."

"No." Mary took hold of Michael's arm. "There's still a message. A new message." She smiled at him, her eyes bright with tears. "Michael, we have the church. We can start over."

Michael looked at the piles of rubble. "Yes. But it won't be easy. There'll be no miracles."

"We don't need miracles. We have the word of God."

Michael took her in his arms and realized that all his pain had disappeared. "We'll have our miracle," he whispered. "The greatest of all: the miracle of love."

The End

About the Author

Robert L. Hecker was born in Provo, Utah but grew up in Long Beach, CA. Graduating from high school just as the US entered WWII. Enlisting in the Army Air Corps, he flew B-17s in thirty missions over Europe, earning five Air Medals and the Distinguished Flying Cross.

After the war he began writing radio and TV dramas, then moved on to writing and producing more than 500 documentary, educational and marketing films on subjects ranging from military and astronaut training, nuclear physics, aeronautics, the education of Eskimos and Native Americans, psychology, lasers, radars, satellites and submarines. His short stories and articles have been published in numerous magazines, and he is currently working on several movie screenplays as well as other novels.

A graduate of the Pasadena Playhouse School of Theater and the Westlake College of Music, recently Robert has begun song writing and has songs in country, gospel and big-band albums. His wife, the former Frances Kavanaugh, a legendary screenwriter of westerns, has a permanent exhibit in the Autry Museum of Western Heritage. They have two children and four grandchildren. And he still is a pretty fair tennis player.

The ChroMagic Series

by Piers Anthony

1,000 years ago Earth colonized the planet Charm. But the population of Charm is now far removed from their ancient ancestors. Technology has been lost over the years but the people have something better—Magic!

Key to Havoc

ChroMagic Series, Book One

Once again, Mr Anthony creates a complex world unlike anything we might imagine.

—Amanda Killgore, Scribes World

Oh my lord, this was a fantastic book!!

—Chris Roeszler, Amazon Reviewer

Trade Paperback • ISBN 0-9723670-6-3
Hardcover • ISBN 0-9723670-7-1
eBook • ISBN 1-59426-000-1

Key To Chroma

ChroMagic Series, Book Two

Chroma continues to fascinate, making readers anxious for the final book in the trilogy.

—Amanda Killgore, Scribes World

Trade Paperback • ISBN 1-59426-018-4
Hardcover • ISBN 1-59426-017-6
eBook • ISBN 1-59426-019-2

Key to Destiny

ChroMagic Series, Book Three

Piers Anthony is one of those authors who can perform magic with the ordinary.

—A Reader's Guide to Science Fiction

Trade Paperback • ISBN 1-59426-044-3
Hardcover • ISBN 1-59426-043-5
eBook • ISBN 1-59426-045-1

Printed in the United States
51584LVS00005B/1-24

9 781594 262562